THE
HINT
OF
LIGHT

THE
HINT
OF
LIGHT

a novel

KRISTIN KISSKA

LAKE UNION
PUBLISHING

Text copyright © 2023 by Kristin Kisska
All rights reserved.

No part of this book may be reproduced, or stored in a retrieval system, or transmitted in any form or by any means, electronic, mechanical, photocopying, recording, or otherwise, without express written permission of the publisher.

Published by Lake Union Publishing, Seattle

www.apub.com

Amazon, the Amazon logo, and Lake Union Publishing are trademarks of Amazon.com, Inc., or its affiliates.

ISBN-13: 9781662512513 (paperback)
ISBN-13: 9781662512506 (digital)

Cover design by: Shasti O'Leary Soudant
Cover image: © Yori Hirokawa / Shutterstock; © EyeEm / Alamy

Printed in the United States of America

To my mom and dad.
I love you forever.

CONTENT WARNING

While potentially triggering content is mostly referenced and not depicted explicitly, this novel contains references to sexual and physical assault. Suicide, addiction, and alcoholism are also mentioned within this novel.

Prologue

Motherhood is not for the weak.

In my opinion, it should have a warning label attached to it—only dedicated individuals with boundless energy, unconditional love, and a high tolerance for pain need apply.

She didn't arrive in the normal way. My water broke while I was waiting tables, so my manager drove me to the nearest hospital. I waited on a gurney in the emergency room because there were no available beds in Labor and Delivery. The nurse had teased me, blaming the full moon. Straps across my belly were hooked to monitors showing my contractions and the baby's heartbeat. I was dilated enough and in such intense pain the anesthesiologist was called to administer my epidural. But as the bands of fire slicing across my swollen belly faded, the monitors pinged, summoning the nurses to hover over me, scanning my printouts.

They called it *fetal distress*.

Within minutes, an orderly rushed me to the operating room. Though drapes hid my view, the surgeon's clipped orders to the scrub nurses put me on high alert. Reflections off the metal light fixture overhead afforded me a blurry view of the movement, but I couldn't discern what was happening. Dread seeped through my numbed body. I had no one there to help advocate for me, not the baby's father or my parents.

I begged for updates, but my oxygen mask absorbed my shouts, making them inaudible to others, though amplifying them in my head. The surgeon's tangible silence confirmed my worst fears. I was losing her.

Suddenly a team of neonatal doctors and nurses swooped by me, taking my baby with them to the far corner, again shielded from my view. Controlled panic infected every air molecule in the room. Still, no one would answer my ever-escalating pleas. My only consolation was that my baby must still be clinging to life if everyone was so focused on her. *Fight, my precious love. Be strong!*

A tugging sensation below my ribs indicated that my doctor was suturing my splayed-open belly. So I counted. To ten. To fifty. To a hundred and beyond. With each ragged breath I drew, I whispered a prayer that God would not take my baby from me. Not after everything I'd been through. He couldn't do that, could He?

As I reached five hundred, a nurse wandered around my drape and showed me the most beautiful purple-faced burrito swaddled in a white blanket and a doll-size knit cap embellished with pale-blue and light-pink ducks.

"Meet your daughter."

Relief rushed through my veins. No one warned me that the nano-second I clapped my eyes on her, I'd be a goner. This perfect little creature chose me to be her mother out of all the other women in the universe. *Me.* In that instant, I vowed to never let her suffer one single moment of pain. I'd risk my life to protect her.

Over the years, I've devoted every waking moment, every cent I've ever earned, and every prayer I've uttered to support her care and well-being. To lift her higher. No repayment expected. She has no idea the countless nights I've stayed awake in awe, watching her sleep. Don't get me wrong. I'm no martyr. I'd do it all over again and twice as hard.

She was—is—my everything.

But I have two regrets . . . no, that's a lie. The truth is I only have one. The first instance brought me her. In a million years, I'd never regret that. Had I been young, reckless, and overtrusting? Guilty. But being a single mom has been my badge of honor. I'm proud of how far we've come together.

My true regret was my mistake. A momentary lapse of judgment that I've paid for ever since.

She is my everything. Throughout her lifetime. My lifetime. No, time is meaningless here.

A mother's love is infinite.

Chapter 1

MARGARET

AFTER

The first time my son, Kyle, flatlined, I wasn't with him. Nor his second.

"You'll freeze to death out here." Martin steps onto our deck and then covers my shoulders with my winter coat. I cringe at my husband's choice of words.

A blast of warmth and lamplight from our kitchen follows him, but I prefer Chicago's bleak January dawn. Each exhalation crystallizes in the frigid air, muting my view. Honking from rush-hour traffic in the distance echoes against the barren trees. The wind bites my skin, an ironic reminder that I'm alive.

"We always joked that Kyle had nine lives, like cats." I shake my head, still incredulous at the hell we endured last night. A brittle shell freezes my lungs, keeping them from expanding freely. My sweater still smells of antiseptic from the hospital, a scent I've loved my entire adult life. Until now. "We were wrong."

My husband grunts, wrapping me in a bear hug. What is there to say? Yesterday we had two children. Today we have one. So we cling to each other. Our family started here with us. Together we'll weather this blow. I hope.

Thirty-seven years, eleven months, and seventeen days. Not nearly enough time on earth.

My feet are rooted to this iced-over deck. My brain is numb. There's so much I need to do. People I need to call. Kyle has already been gone for twelve hours, and I haven't told a soul yet. Not even our daughter, Kimber. But if I tell someone—anyone—then it'll be real.

"You know, about a year ago, Kyle mentioned—" Martin's face is devoid of the emotion I know must be roiling within. He is in shock as well.

"Tell me later, honey." Shaking my head, I press my finger over his lips. For just this moment, I need to be alone with my thoughts. We'll have the rest of our lives to dissect every complicated layer that was our son. What we did right. What we did wrong. What we should've done differently.

Martin nods and retreats inside our home, leaving me awash in gratitude, the last emotion I'd ever have expected to experience under the circumstances. I revel in our son's pure essence.

At this very moment, some medical examiner is conducting Kyle's autopsy. But it doesn't matter what tests they run or what the report will reveal. As I stare off above the rooftops into the cloudy gray horizon, my pulse beats a slow cadence. I may not have been present when Kyle died, but I know his underlying cause of death.

Me.

◆ ◆ ◆

Zero hours of sleep and meals eaten.

One urn purchased.

Three readings and four songs selected for his funeral mass.

Twelve flower arrangements displayed.

Thirty-three mass cards received to pray for my son's eternal soul.

Five hundred prayer cards printed with my son's portrait, birth date, and date of passing.

Funeral by the numbers. What sort of fresh hell is this? But I'll take all that over what's coming my way in the next forty-eight hours. Because by the end of this marathon, Kyle's remains will be buried.

My mind chants the four words I wish I'd last said to him five nights ago while he was still alive—*I love you, Kyle.*

Instead, my last words to my son were *Get out.* I don't even know where he went that night. Less than twenty-four hours later, we found him dead in our house. What a twisted sense of humor God has.

"I'm back." Our front door creaks open, and winter air whooshes in. Kimber stomps snow from her boots before stepping inside. She stopped by the funeral home to confirm last-minute details for tomorrow's wake.

These past few days, having our daughter, Kimber, here with us as the face of the Dobrescu family has been a blessing. She's a competent adult with a graduate degree, a career, a spouse, and three beautiful children. We successfully launched one of our brood of two from our nest. Why Kyle never took flight will be a mystery I'll ponder to my grave.

"Mom, you'll need this document for Kyle's estate." After shedding her coat and scarf, Kimber hands me a manila envelope, then guides me to the couch.

One glance at the header on the form inside is yet another layer of finality. Kyle's certificate of death. Date. Time. Location. Doctor. Funeral director. Every fact is there—every typed letter and number solidifying the end of his life.

After locating the box confirming an autopsy had been performed, I read the section entitled "Cause of Death." The immediate cause is no surprise—blunt force trauma to the head. That the manner of his death had been an accident. A gash to his head when he slipped in the bathroom and hit his head on the side of the tub. That horrible night, the emergency room doctors confirmed that his head injury had been too traumatic to survive. His scan showed brain swelling. I try to imagine what Kyle must've experienced while still conscious, blood pouring down his face. Did he panic? Was he aware this was the end? Or did God take pity on him, letting him slip mercifully into unconsciousness before he could figure out what was happening?

"Oh, my God, no . . ." Had I been standing while reading the form, when I got to the underlying cause of death, I would have crumpled to my knees. Yet again, I'd failed him. The proof is displayed right here on this vile piece of paper, the irony slapping me in the face like a sledgehammer. After his years of struggling to stay sober. And my tough love parenting. And countless arguments that nearly destroyed my marriage. And continuous prayers. I believed he'd overcome the worst of it. That he'd been sober for months. Many months. "This can't be right."

Kyle's immediate cause of death may have been a head injury, but according to the medical examiner, that wasn't the whole story.

Kimber snatches the paper from my grip as Martin joins us in the room. "As a consequence of a drug overdose?"

◆　◆　◆

While searching the top drawer of my nightstand, I rifle through a lifetime of collected trinkets, orphaned hardware, and knickknacks. Somewhere in here must be at least one of the Alcoholics Anonymous tokens Kyle gave me over the years. I'm sure I saved all of them somewhere.

After combing through a few other drawers in my home, I finally find the royal-blue six-month sobriety chip he gave me a couple of years ago. It commemorated one of the longest stretches he'd been alcohol-free in his adult life. I was so proud of him, though what good did that do him the next time he relapsed?

How could Kyle have died of a drug overdose? I've mulled this question over in my mind ever since reading his certificate of death. I wasn't with him for the last hours of his life, so perhaps he had been high on a drug trip.

But the evidence didn't add up.

Kyle never used drugs—not the illicit, hard kind. I'm certain. For one thing, he couldn't have afforded it. Plus, I never found any paraphernalia at home, and I've hunted for needles, razor blades, scuffed mirrors, little packets lined with powder residue, and unmarked pills. I checked every nook and crevice of our house, every backpack and coat pocket. Nothing turned up. Though I did find several hidden stashes of vodka, his forever drug of choice.

My beautiful, broken son. It took me decades to accept the fact that Kyle's alcohol addiction was more a disease than a choice. My side of the family tree is Irish Catholic, with our fair share of branches laden with alcohol dependencies. But Kyle wasn't merely dependent. He abused it. Most people couldn't have survived for long with his liter-of-vodka-per-day habit.

But overdose? What drug was in his system at the time of death? The logistics behind how and why Kyle died are blurry. Not that it matters anymore—dead is dead. Even so, my mind can't let the question go.

While I walk downstairs clutching the sobriety token, a ringtone sounds from the console table next to the front door. Martin, Kimber, and I freeze, glancing at each other with widened eyes, dread filling our veins. Kyle's cell phone.

Kimber, no longer wasting her breath to ask if either of us wants to answer it, slips from her chair and dashes to take the call. "Local number. Does anyone know who 'A. O.' is?"

Martin and I shrug, shaking our heads. It could be anyone. A patient from Carrefour Residential Center. A participant of AA. A classmate. A band member.

Kimber answers the phone, and from her end of the conversation, I know we're on the exact repeat of similar phone calls she's fielded these past few days. "No, this is Kyle's sister . . . no, he can't come to the phone . . . I'm sorry to share this news with you, but he passed away last Saturday . . ." Then there's always a long pause while the caller processes the tragedy. Kimber squeezes her eyes shut, then composes herself before continuing. "No, he died of medical complications . . . Kyle's visitation will be tomorrow evening, his funeral mass Friday morning . . ."

God bless my daughter for being able to articulate the unspeakable. After answering a few more questions, she asks, "How did you know my brother?"

The pause becomes endless. Kimber's face remains unreadable. Every few seconds or so, she nods, then finally ends the conversation with "Again, I'm so sorry to break this news."

"Who called?"

"Some woman named Ally. She sounded young. They were taking a psychology class together. She must've known him from the community college. Apparently she was supposed to meet up with him to study the night he died, but he never showed."

◆ ◆ ◆

"Mom, I think we should also bring these tonight." Kimber runs downstairs from Kyle's bedroom, holding his black wool winter overcoat and a pair of loafers. He had excellent taste in fashion. But since he spent every spare dollar on vodka, God only knew how he afforded his wardrobe. Martin probably paid for it all. Throughout Kyle's years of addiction, Martin played the role of good cop to my bad cop. He could never say no to his son.

"That's fine, sweetheart. Put them by the door with the other things we need to bring." The funeral home encouraged us to display a few of Kyle's personal belongings at the visitation tonight. One of his guitars, a small stuffed animal he'd used to tease his nieces and nephew when they were little, the one-month AA token I found in his wallet because I'm carrying his six-month chip next to my heart.

Martin clears his throat, drawing both Kimber's and my attention.

"Can we talk for a minute?" Martin, who spent the past few days speaking even fewer words than normal, pulls up an extra chair in the living room. "There's something I need to tell you."

Kimber and I exchange confused glances before joining him. Hugging my sweater tighter around my now constantly shivering body, I wait. Martin's face remains neutral as he rests his forearms on his knees, his hands clasped together as if in prayer. But his shoulder twitches, a nervous tic he's had since before we met. Alarm bells sound off in my head. He could deny it as much as he wants, but whatever he's about to say is causing him intense anxiety.

"Kyle once told me . . ." Martin's voice is barely audible over the heat blasting through the vents. ". . . one of his ex-girlfriends had a baby. A girl. She claimed the child was his."

"What?" My breath catches; then I shake my head, convinced I couldn't possibly have heard him correctly. Shocks zing through my body as I lean forward on the sofa, trying to grasp the scope of what Martin revealed.

"Are you saying Kyle had a daughter?" Kimber's eyes narrowed as she crossed her arms. She'd teased him time and again about his perma-bachelor status, wondering aloud if he should celebrate Father's Day. Kyle never dignified her gibes with any comment—denying or affirming. But not for one minute did any of us ever give the idea of his fatherhood any credence. "No way."

"What's her name?" I inch forward on the edge of my seat, not entirely processing this news.

"I don't know." Martin stays hunchbacked while staring at his folded hands.

Kimber follows suit with rapid-fire questions. "How old is she? Five? Fifteen?"

"I don't know."

"What's her mother's name?"

"Kyle never mentioned it." Martin holds up his hands as if surrendering to the attack.

"When did he tell you about her?"

"Last year."

"Let me get this straight, Martin." My pulse throbs, vibrating my chest through my bulky sweater, but I force my voice to be as clear as possible to avoid confusion. "You've known for a full year that we have another grandchild, yet you kept that information from me?"

Martin exhales, still avoiding eye contact. His voice drops deeper, making his baritone a full bass. His shoulder tic kicks into a higher gear. "Margaret, it was complicated. Once his legal problems calmed down, I wanted him to get a paternity test to make sure she was his daughter before we told anyone."

"You've had a year since then." My voice counters Martin's by going up an octave. A wave of heat radiates through my core as my mind scrolls through countless times I'd been with Kyle and had talked about nothing more serious than the weather. So many lost opportunities. "You should've brought it up so we could've helped him. We would've had time with her, gotten to know her. But you kept this detail to yourself? Why would you do that?"

"I thought we'd have time. To contact the girl's mother. To come up with a solution. Kyle agreed with me."

"A solution?" Then they must have deemed this child some sort of problem to be fixed. In what universe was a grandchild a problem? I flex my fists to keep my hands from shaking, but what I'd really like to do is slap him. And Kyle. "Is that all you have to say?"

No response from Martin. No defense, and no new relevant details. My husband and son conspired to keep my granddaughter a secret from me. This news would've brought such joy—not just to me but to all of us. And after everything I sacrificed for the sake of my family. Everything we'd been through together. Unbelievable.

After swallowing a sour taste, I stomp away because I can't tolerate the presence of my spouse and his flexing shoulder for one more minute.

Before leaving the living room, I turn an about-face. Martin is still staring at the floor, his back hunched over. Kimber looks at me with widened eyes as if she's seen a zombie rise from the tilled dirt in a field. "I swear on my son's grave, I will find her."

Chapter 2

KYLE

BEFORE

Sunlight sliced around the edges of my bedroom curtains, searing my eyes. I rolled over, but the damage had been done. I was conscious—the last thing on the planet I wanted to be.

What time was it anyway? My clock blared 7:48. Was that a.m. or p.m.? Oh, right. It was late February, I think, so it would be dark if it were evening. When was the last time I'd awakened this early in the morning?

Prying my eyes open resulted in a seismic shift deep within my skull, so I gave up. That my mouth could double as the Sahara desert setting in some Hollywood B movie was nothing new.

Crap.

I'd kill to slip back into sleep. A deep sleep. The kind devoid of dreams, bypassing nightmares straight into a blissful state of nothingness. The kind that erased all traces of memories. Especially the ones from my younger self.

While patting around my nightstand, I tipped over the lamp and several liquor bottles. I held one open over my mouth, but only a lingering droplet hit my tongue, teasing me like a lifeline dangling out of reach.

Shit. All were empty.

Note to self: hide the empties before Mom returns home from work. Not that it'd stop her nagging. Her threatening to throw me out of the house. But it might stall her from another witch hunt, searching for and purging my stashes of vodka. Even worse than watching Mom pour my contraband liquor down the drain was the look of disappointment that would wash over her face. The slump of her shoulders. The welling in her eyes. The hitch in her voice. I'd had to get pretty damned creative hiding them around the house these days.

Now, where did I store my latest purchase? Back of the closet? Behind the towels? Under the stairs? I hoped not, as I was in no condition to tackle the steps with this vertigo—bruises from my last fall still hurt.

Slithering from my sheets, I lowered myself to the floor, then reached under my bed. Nothing but dust bunnies and more empties. I braced myself on all fours before inching my way up to standing, as if my floor were a surfboard and the room around me one of those epic funnel waves in California.

Whoa, too fast.

My heartbeat thumped in my chest. My head was about to explode. My hands shook. The realization hit me. I was going through some combination of a hangover and early-stage alcohol withdrawal. After surviving a detox program, you never forget the symptoms. And I was a regular by now.

I stumbled to the bathroom and then lunged for the medicine cabinet, yanking it open. It should've offered a buffet of options. But Mom must've swept through recently because even my container of prescription antianxiety pills was empty.

Shit. Tubes of ointment, orange bottles, and Q-tips clattered to the sink as I scrounged for something, anything that might work. After gulping water straight from the faucet, I slid down the side of the wall until my bare skin flinched on the chilly floor tiles. Raking my hands through my hair, I rocked back and forth to the beat of my throbbing temples.

The landline rang in the distance, but I let it roll to voice mail. No one nice ever called here for me. Only robocalls, doctors' offices, and credit collection agencies.

The knob to the cabinet under the sink taunted me. Was this where I'd stowed my stash? I peeked inside. Goddammit. No vodka. Nothing but cleaning sprays, extra rolls of toilet paper, and . . .

Mouthwash.

Bingo.

◆　◆　◆

This morning, my dad assessed the icy roads as if he were at the top of a ski slope picking the optimum run. I used to ski with him as a kid, but I hated winter weather, so I gave up once I was old enough to stay home alone. It wasn't the only way I'd disappointed him.

If March roared in like a lion, then today, there was a whole fucking pride roaming around Chicago. Dad had built in extra time to get to the courthouse in case the frigid driving conditions proved hazardous. I hoped so. It could be a reasonable cause for another continuance. Or, in my case, a stay of execution.

"Drink your coffee, Kyle."

As if that could diminish the bags under my eyes. As if the judge would be lenient if I appeared more alert. As if I had a prayer of walking out of the courtroom without a guilty verdict.

Instead of arguing, I took a swig from the steaming travel mug. Gross. When would Dad ever figure out that instant coffee tasted like dirt? I choked it down anyway, hoping the caffeine would take the edge off my splitting headache.

As we merged onto the highway, I hardly noticed the barren trees, the grass, the road, and the sky, all gray. All as bitter as Mom had been before she left for work about an hour ago, which tolled the end of her preaching at me for the time being. Yes, I should never have driven on a suspended license for my original DUI. No, I shouldn't have run the red light, especially with a cop behind me. Yes, thank God I didn't cause an accident and hurt anyone. Yes, if I hadn't been hungover, I wouldn't have overslept and missed my first court date.

Mom would be proud that I'd heard every word. Of course, I'd ignored her and didn't give her any indications I spoke or understood English. So instead, my deadpan reaction as I knotted my tie fueled her anger until her simmering grew to a rapid boil. Because otherwise, I'd have to admit—out loud—that I'd fucked up. A lot. And right now, before heading to court, I couldn't bring myself to incinerate my last remaining fiber of self-esteem.

Mr. Davenport, my lawyer, was practiced at crafting me to appear like a reasonable, down-on-his-luck guy trying to get his two feet back on the ground. The classic underdog. He'd recommended I register for a course at the local community college. I attended a couple of lectures already, but I didn't remember much of what the professor taught. Was it a marketing class? He also advised me to update my résumé and submit a few for job postings, ridiculous as the suggestion seemed. What company would hire an adult with a DUI on his record, no college degree, and a restricted license, who lived at his parents' home?

It'd been years since I collected a steady paycheck, even for part-time work. But I wouldn't mind becoming a graphic artist. I used to design great T-shirts for my band. Hell, could I even freelance with my record?

Red brake lights stretched for as far as I could see up the road. I slipped my hand into my wool coat pocket and rubbed my thumb over my twenty-four-hour chip. Judges needed to see proof of effort, so I attended three AA meetings this week for good measure. Staying sober was akin to giving up breathing. I coped for the first thirty seconds; then the pain kicked in. I couldn't think about anything else except that I'd give up living for one more drink.

As we idled, Dad called his supervisor to remind her that he was taking a personal day from work this morning. My gut churned in a wave of nausea. Or guilt? I'd already pushed Mom past her breaking point, but not Dad. He'd never once given up on me, though I repaid him by turning every hair on his head gray. All he ever wanted was to keep me alive and out of jail. Not exactly a fair deal. Now he was taking time off from work to drive me to court instead of hitting the ski slopes one last time before the spring thaw. He was a saint—if an agnostic could be sainted, Dad should be canonized.

"Thanks for driving me today." Too little gratitude, too late. I appreciated Dad's tenacity, despite my burning temptation to slip out of the car and jog back home. What if the judge locked me up? I'd spent time behind bars before, but never longer than a night or two to sober up or until I could post bail. No wonder Mom didn't even consider witnessing today's bloodletting.

With his eyes on the traffic inching forward, Dad nodded his acknowledgment. Dammit, with every minute of bumper-to-bumper traffic, my real-coffee window was closing on me. I pretended to thaw my hands over the heater to cover up my tremors in case Dad noticed. We sat in silence, with only the hum of the engine to soothe my anxiety.

"Any surprises I should know about before we meet with Mr. Davenport?" Dad's Eastern European accent, normally so subtle, was now more pronounced. Probably from nerves. I could relate.

At least Dad didn't rant on and on like Mom did with her exasperated *What else have you done that we don't know about?* She tended to tack that on whenever she'd run out of steam from dissecting the fertile material I'd already given her. In my defense, I've never denied any of her accusations, because they were pretty much all true.

"If the judge sentences me, I'll kill myself." Okay, that came out a little too harsh. After Dad winces, I soften my statement. "Sorry, but I can't go to prison."

With his lips pressed together in a tight line, he remained silent. I'm not sure if he assumed I was waxing dramatic or if he believed me. Either way, my message was delivered. I'd already put my parents through hell and experienced it firsthand. Why follow it up with the pain of living behind bars? It wasn't as if my life was worth much anyway. Who would miss me?

Blue lights flashing in the distance proved my earlier theory correct—a traffic accident blocked the road. Under the guise of rubbernecking to see the carnage, I considered my next words with more care than I tended to use.

"Also, I got a phone call a couple days ago." I was still trying to wrap my head around the whole conversation. The local number that had flashed across my cell phone's screen hadn't been one of my contacts. Though I avoided ever picking up my parents' landline, I usually answered my cell phone in case it was a possible band gig, ever hopeful I could get the old gang together onstage again, even though we hadn't played together in years.

While I didn't recognize the woman's voice, she didn't leave me guessing for long. *This is Hannah O'Leary. We met each other at Spring Mountain University.* Weird. Of course, I remembered Hannah. But I never expected to hear from her again. I'm still not sure how she got my phone number.

"And?" God bless Dad, who'd waited for two more car-length moves forward before prompting me to continue.

I drew a deep, steadying breath. "And it was from an ex-girlfriend." Hadn't ended well, and that was being generous. I'd forgotten about it all decades ago.

From the soft whistle Dad exhaled, I had enough confirmation to know that he'd already figured out the whole worst-case scenario. He raked a gloved hand through his scant, graying hair, then rubbed his chin. But I gave him the spoiler anyway.

"It turns out I have a daughter." And by default, that meant that Dad learned that he had a fourth grandchild. But given the clenching of his jaw at hearing the news, I gathered he didn't embrace the silver lining. Dad knew all about surprise pregnancies. It happened to the best of us. That's why I was ten years younger than Kimber.

Still, my news shocked his system, so I should give him as much time as he needed to process my situation. By now, Dad had maneuvered into the single lane creeping by the accident. Several ambulances, police cruisers, and a fire truck had responded to the three-car collision. Airbags had deployed. Vehicles so bashed up, the makes and models were unrecognizable.

Kind of like my life.

Once we'd safely passed by, Dad accelerated to five miles over the speed limit, his personal maximum, then cruised toward the courthouse. A quick glance back at Dad proved he was still digesting my news, but he was logical and rational to a fault. He hadn't survived escaping Communist Romania without being able to change plans and adapt on the fly.

"Did you know about . . ." His brain must be whirling, searching for some reasonable explanation among the chaos and, if not finding it, then defaulting to a conspiracy theory. He needed a logical answer for everything. ". . . the pregnancy?"

"Yeah." I shrugged because it was true. Almost twenty years ago, I faced what scared the hell out of every young single man on the planet—a positive line on a pregnancy test. Hannah and I had hooked up for a few weeks. I didn't offer her solutions. I certainly hadn't proposed. Regret emptied out into every cell of my body. "She told me she was going back to her hometown to have an abortion. I never saw or heard from her again."

Problem solved—end of story.

Except now I knew the story hadn't ended then.

She must've changed her mind and had the baby after all. Or she'd lied. Why? To get me out of the picture? Did her family intervene? But she'd waited decades to track me down and let me know.

"Did she ask for money . . . for the child?" Dad's words were clipped. Efficient. Devoid of emotion.

"Um, no. I offered, but she declined." Not as if I had much money to spare, so I was relieved I didn't have to make any promises to Hannah I couldn't keep. The last thing I'd want to do was add *deadbeat father* to my list of transgressions, but I'm sure raising a kid hadn't been cheap.

"Then why would she tell you now?" Dad's shoulder twitched, a dead giveaway that his anxiety level was spiking.

Fair question. The truth was, I wasn't sure why now, except that my daughter—Ally—would turn eighteen soon and had been asking about me. I guess Hannah didn't want me freaking out if she ever knocked on my front door.

"Maybe to warn me?"

Dad turned into the courthouse parking lot. Near the main door, Mr. Davenport stomped his feet and blew into his gloved hands. He must've been waiting outside for a while. God, I could use that coffee now.

We parked. As I reached to open the car door, Dad grabbed my arm to stop me from exiting.

"Don't tell your mother. Not yet. Let's get you through your court situation first. Then we'll figure out a plan."

Yep. Maggie May would shit a brick.

Chapter 3

ALLY

After several wrong turns, I found the funeral home. I'm late, but then again, no one is expecting me. The parking lot is already packed, so I keep driving laps until one of the early attendees of the visitation gives up his space to me.

When Kyle's sister answered the phone the other day, I didn't believe her. He'd ghosted me before, several times. So I hung out at our usual coffee shop, hoping he'd show up with some reasonable explanation. That he was sick. Or his phone died. But this time, he never came.

Then I saw his obituary in the paper. Actually, Mom showed it to me. One small paragraph, no picture. All his surviving family members were listed, even his two nieces and a nephew—all except me. No one knows about me.

My world turned unrecognizable, as if someone had flipped a switch. No more coffee dates or attending AA meetings as his guest. No more letters. No more study partner. No more Kyle.

I tried to convince Mom to attend his visitation service with me. She didn't think it would be appropriate, especially since she'd never met any of his family members. Instead, she said she'd stay home tonight and try to remember nice things about my biological father—way to go out on that limb, Mom.

He's really dead. A week ago, we were plotting how to introduce me to his family. How could I have finally met my father to then lose him forever? Screw fate.

What can I possibly say to them tonight? *I'm sorry Kyle passed away. By the way, I'm a member of your family. Surprise! Oh, he never mentioned me before?* Not quite a subtle approach.

The last thing the Dobrescu family needs right now is drama, so I won't make myself known. Not tonight. But I need to say goodbye to Kyle.

After stepping out of my car into the frigid February night air, I tighten my ponytail. In my pocket is the six-month AA sobriety chip he gave me last week. I keep squeezing it in my sweating palm, drawing strength from it as I force myself to walk toward the front entrance of the funeral parlor. This is only the second time I've ever been inside one. The other time was for Jenna's grandmother. Mom thought it essential to support my best friend.

Jeez, Mom can go to a stranger's wake but not my father's? She liked him enough at some point to have sex with him. That their relationship tanked soon after is ancient history. Her history. The guy can't hurt her now that he's dead. You'd think she'd at least want to support her only child.

But no. Mom is at home, and I'm here, about to walk inside a funeral home and tread water through a choppy sea of strangers. I squeeze the token harder. Bitter wind whips around my legs, puffing my black dress Marilyn Monroe–style despite me wearing my winter coat. Bracing myself to face the unknown, I trudge toward the illuminated glass-door entrance.

Here I go, crashing my dad's funeral. Is that even legal?

Once I'm inside, a young woman dressed in a modest navy skirt suit points out the coat closet.

"Welcome. Are you here for Kyle Dobrescu's memorial?" She pauses until I nod. "His family is receiving visitors in the Hancock Suite. Water bottles and tissues are in the far corner. Please be sure to sign the guest book before you leave."

After she resumes her post by the door, I'm left drifting through the crowd of mourners by myself. Awkward. Butterflies circle my stomach like a tornado. I should've taken up Jenna's offer to come with me tonight.

Wow, Kyle sure knew a lot of people. While waiting in line to sign the guest book, I try to keep from bouncing too much on my heels. I peek over those mingling nearby to glimpse what awaits me inside the Hancock Suite, but it's too crowded to see beyond the open double doors. Hundreds of voices conversing in muted, respectful tones echo around the cavernous ballroom.

After making it to the front of the line, I sign the guest book, then hand the pen to the man behind me. In a small basket are a stack of holy cards, so I take one. A photo of Kyle dressed in a dark-blue business suit stares back at me, and my heart turns a cartwheel with a twist. My eyes sting, and I can barely read the rest of his card. Struggling to inhale, I absorb the shock of his death—again—as if it's new news. It's not like my brain has forgotten he died. But for some reason, the realization knocks me over like a fresh tidal wave every time I stand back up.

Clasping his memorial card to my chest, I slip through the opening of a large gathering room. After swiping a couple of tissues from a nearby box, I join the chorus of eye-dabbers.

Oh, Kyle, why did you have to leave me so soon? I lived for eighteen years without you. I was hoping for at least that many with you. But all we had was ten months together.

Slipping around small clusters of people, I wander toward the far corner of the massive ballroom; then every cell in my body freezes.

A polished silver urn etched with scrolls sits on a pillar. Flower arrangements surround the vase. A huge black-and-white portrait of him—a younger and healthier Kyle in his twenties and smoking a cigar—rests on an easel to the side. For a split second, I could see why Mom had been attracted to him in college. There was a challenge in his eyes, a rebellious take-it-or-leave-it vibe. The decades had already taken their toll by the time I met him.

The green velvet church kneeler positioned in front of Kyle's urn is unused, so I take my turn. Collapsing to my knees, I stare at the urn—his remains. No.

This is so unfair.

My stomach twists and turns. No words come to me. I can't even remember any prayers. I'm supposed to say goodbye, but I'm having trouble breathing. How can I pay my respects to my dad when I feel so cheated by the universe?

As I'm about to stand up, my old bedtime prayer pops into my mind, however silly or irrelevant it may be for this moment. Kyle and I talked about it once or twice, so I pray the Angel of God prayer now, in front of his urn. Hopefully it counts.

Mom always told me I'd never needed a guardian angel since I had her to watch over and protect me, but right now, I could use one.

"Kyle, I'm sorry our time together was so short, but I'm glad we finally met after all those years of wishing for you. Please watch over me from heaven. Would you be my guardian angel?" Once I notice a line of people growing behind me, I whisper, "I miss you. Goodbye."

After letting the next person have a turn on the kneeler, I drift around the edge of the room. What made me think I could pull off crashing his funeral? I don't belong here. I keep waiting for some bouncer to stop me and insist I leave. Kyle's family members have formed a receiving line, but I haven't worked up the courage to shake their hands. What would I even say?

As I'm about to exit, Kyle's father clears his throat before walking across the room to stand in front of the urn. The guests cluster in a semicircle around him. My grandfather—who probably has no memory that we once met—offers his hand, inviting my grandmother to stand next to him. Though dark sunglasses hide her eyes, her swollen nose and the tissue scrunched in her fist betray her weeping.

"Margaret and I thank each of you for joining us tonight to remember Kyle. We'd especially like to recognize those family members and friends who traveled great distances to help us say goodbye. We've met friends from his school days, his band days, and those who battled addiction with him. It means a lot to us to know that he was so loved and cherished. We invite anyone so inclined to share your favorite memory of Kyle."

A few coughs, a little rustling; then a tall brunette woman, a few years older than my mom and dressed in a tailored black skirt suit, moves to the front and turns to address the guests.

"For those who don't know me, I'm Kyle's big sister, Kimber." She dabs her eyes, then takes a deep, calming breath. "Kyle could always make me laugh, no matter how stressed I was. When I was visiting home from college, he asked me to drive him to the store. It was breezy and warm, so we had the car's windows rolled down. As I backed out of our driveway, a big cicada flew inside his window. The next thing I knew, the passenger side door was open, and Kyle was no longer sitting next to me. He'd jumped out of a rolling car because of a bug."

Polite laughter follows my aunt's memory. When she shuts her eyes, nods, and mutters "I'm gonna miss my little brother," the levity is doused. A man I assume to be her husband squeezes her to his side.

Different people stand in front to share fun memories, each quirkier than the last, as friends and family try to outdo one another. One was about when Kyle was a kid at the beach, and some lady asked if he was sitting while buried in the sand, and Kyle replied, "Yes. On a horse." Another memory was about him announcing to his aunt that he thought he knew how to say *stop* in Romanian—*Kyle!* Ripples of appreciative laughter circulated the room. As humorous as each story was, they made me want to run to the ladies' room, sobbing. Why hadn't he shared any of these memories with me?

Then again, we both believed we had more time together.

After a few more stories, the crowd breaks out into smaller groups, allowing me to find a bottle of water. As I take my first swig, the woman who spoke first steps toward me.

"Hi. I don't think we've met. I'm Kimber." Her eyes are swollen and pink, but her smile is warm.

"Nice to meet you. I'm Ally." My mouth suddenly turns as dry as a desert. Kimber is my aunt, but she has no idea we're related. God, this was the worst timing ever. It would all have been so different if Kyle had only lived a few more weeks. He'd have introduced us. I'd have been part of his family—his known family—not some huge secret. I unscrew the cap and take a long sip, scrambling to figure out how to gracefully escape from this conversation without saying something totally embarrassing. "I think we spoke the other day. I called Kyle's cell phone, and you answered. Told me about . . . what happened."

"Right. He was in your class at the community college?"

"Not exactly. Different colleges. I heard him speak at a couple AA meetings. We sometimes met to study together since we were both taking psychology classes this semester."

Kimber kinks her head to the side, and her brow furrows, probably trying to link my disconnected statements. Berating myself to shut up, I try to end this conversation before it gets any more uncomfortable. "I still can't believe he's gone."

"Me too. I keep expecting him to walk through the door as if he were pulling a prank. It's still so surreal." She squeezes her eyes shut, her chin quivering. Someone reaches for her arm, but before she turns away, she leans toward me. "Thank you for coming tonight, Ally. I hope Kyle knows how much he's missed."

Since the crowd has thinned, the receiving line is no longer assembled. I drift back to the slideshow to watch pictures of my biological father scroll by for a few more minutes, all the while wishing I knew the story behind each of these captured fragments of time. Nearby is a table with a photo album open. I flip through a few pages, but my curiosity loses out to my grief.

Plopping onto the couch, I bury my face in my hands, my shoulders shuddering.

"Here's a tissue."

Through blurry eyes, I see a white sheet of fluff dancing in the air close to my head.

"Thanks." After dabbing my eyes, I look up and see a woman I've seen once before tonight's visitation. My grandmother. I can't see her eyes because of the dark sunglasses she's wearing. To her, I'm a random stranger here to pay my respects to her son.

"How do you know Kyle?"

I stand back up to be polite. "We met last year. But hearing he passed away was such a shock."

"You didn't, by chance, happen to date him at some point, did you?"

Date Kyle? Gross. I wave my hands in adamant denial. "No. No, nothing like that. We studied together. Psychology."

"I see." Her shoulders slump, but then she clears her throat and brightens. "Thank you for coming to celebrate Kyle's life. I hope you'll join us at his funeral mass tomorrow morning."

Inching away to end this conversation before I say something stupid, I shake my head. I'd give anything to introduce myself to her as her granddaughter. To hug her. But I can't drop that bomb. Not tonight. Not in public. "I wish I could, but I have to go to my class. Sorry."

Then I escape, beelining for the coat closet. Why the hell would she think I dated him? That would've been my mom, not me. What a freaking awkward mess.

Dammit, Kyle was supposed to be the one to introduce me to them. Now he's gone, and it's all up to me. Inside, among the racks of winter jackets, I lean against the coat closet's doorjamb, hugging my stomach, letting my tears spill unchecked.

I miss you, Kyle.

Chapter 4

ALLY

"Happy birthday to you . . . ," Mom, still dressed in her navy scrubs from last night's shift at the hospital, sang as she entered my bedroom carrying a cupcake with a single lit candle. Her ponytail sprouted flyaways along her hairline, and she looked exhausted. But when she noticed I was already awake and scrolling on my computer, she stopped cold.

"Oh! Hey, Mom." I snapped my laptop cover down and plastered an exaggerated grin on my face. I prayed she hadn't glimpsed what was on my screen. "Thanks!"

"Allison Marie O'Leary. Not again. Stop all that nonsense now."

"Sorry." Ugh. Busted. Mom never called me by my full name unless she was ticked off. It killed her that I'd been combing ancestry websites. But food might help distract both of us from our forever argument. "How about I make us both some breakfast?"

"Make a wish and blow out your candle first." Mom didn't miss a beat. She leaned in to kiss my forehead. "Your gift is sitting on the coffee table in the living room. It was a little too heavy to carry in here with your cupcake."

My stomach twisted at the word *heavy*. If my birthday gift was heavy, then it wasn't even close to what I'd asked for—what I'd been pestering her for these last few weeks. Months. Years. Practically my entire life. I leaned my head on my hand, steeling myself for a renewed burst of faux birthday energy, but my heart had already checked out of the conversation.

She lifted my chin, then stared into my eyes until I returned her gaze. "I want you to have an extraspecial birthday, Ally-cat. A girl only turns eighteen once."

Once. Exactly. Today was the day I'd hoped to unlock the door to my past. Today I was legally allowed to investigate my birth father. Mom could've made it so much easier by revealing his name. But she didn't. Instead, she was giving me a *heavy* gift. Maybe I could mail a swab of my DNA off to a genealogy site to see if there's a match. "Give me fifteen minutes to get ready for school."

Mom beamed, which made the dimple on her right cheek appear. This was the face I loved—the one she sported whenever she surprised me with a summer day trip to a beach on Lake Michigan. The one she flashed when she closed her eyes while inhaling the steam from her first cup of coffee in the morning.

My dimple matched hers, but that was where our similarities stopped. She was petite with hazel eyes and baby-fine ginger hair, which she dyed blonde. I'd inherited big bones, a square jaw, and brown hair that matched my deep-set eyes. I must've taken after my birth father.

After she left my room, I dressed, taking extra care to look photo-worthy for a few selfies with friends. No zits and a good hair day, so that was a plus. My phone buzzed with happy-birthday text messages and Snaps.

It had always been the two of us, with our cat, Lulu, turning our duo into a threesome. In some ways, I could understand why she didn't want to introduce another human into our clique. Shoot, I'd turned ten before she even let me meet her parents—my grandparents. What was she so worried about? I wasn't trying to leave her, let alone reunite her with my biological father. I just wanted to meet him.

What was so wrong with that?

By the time I emerged from my bedroom, morning sunlight had flooded our living room, creating a glow around Mom and making her look angelic. How could I not give her a break? Today was her day too. Eighteen years ago, and not much older than I am now, she'd given up everything—her home, her college classes, her parents—to raise me. Had the tables been turned, would I have had the courage to do the same? Probably not.

Over the years, I'd begged her to retell the story about the day I was born. When the nurse held me up for Mom to meet me, she decided to go into medicine to help others in need. I was four years old by the time she'd trained and certified as a med tech. She'd beaten all the odds by juggling work, attending school, and being a single mother.

Mom was my hero.

Every milestone I achieved was a testament to her hard work. I dropped my backpack on the sofa and wrapped her small, fierce body in a bear hug. "I love you, Mom. Thank you for everything."

"Ally-cat, you are my world." She tightened her arms briefly before releasing me. "I'd do anything for you."

"Any chance you'd let me play hooky today?" I side-eyed my calculus textbook. Twenty more hours of studying wouldn't prepare me for this test. My senior year in high school couldn't end soon enough for me. Plus, I just started a new charcoal sketch of Lulu I'd love to finish. "Pretty please, for my birthday?"

"Not a chance, honey." Mom's yawn was so giant I could've given her a dental checkup. Wrapping the throw blanket around her shoulders, I pointed her toward her bedroom. "Wait, you haven't opened your birthday gift yet."

Right. The *heavy* gift. But Mom's face was so bright I perked up. For her. Why not? It was still a gift. As Mom said, a girl only turned eighteen once. I removed the yellow bow and stuck it on Lulu's head before unwrapping the lump.

"Two cans of paint? Gee. Mom. You shouldn't have." I didn't bother masking my sarcasm.

"Oh, stop pouting. It's that shade of dove gray you've been mooning over for ages." From behind the couch, she resurrected a color swatch card, tape, a paint roller brush, a tray, and a plastic tarp. "I even took Sunday off work. It'll be fun, like one of those home DIY makeovers."

My bedroom isn't the only part of my life that could use a makeover.

Eight hours, seven classes, and a calculus test later, I trudged up the three flights of stairs to our apartment door. At least my friends spoiled me today. Taryn and Marie decorated my locker, while Jenna met me as my school bus arrived, holding my favorite coffee and a new sketchbook with a bow. At lunch, they'd surprised me with a giant chocolate chip cookie and even got the whole table to sing "Happy Birthday"—so embarrassing. I might never forgive them for that stunt.

Lulu met me at the door, but otherwise, the apartment was still. After dumping my backpack and jacket at the kitchen table, I approached the paint cans with my arms crossed and a lump in my throat. Mom was right. I loved this color. And my bedroom would look a thousand times better once we'd finished.

Now that I'd had a chance to process my disappointment this morning, I see Mom's gift in a different—less tantrumy—light. She shouldn't have splurged on something so frivolous. With any luck, I'll be moving into a college dorm in a few months. Mom had been working extra shifts. The other day, I'd caught her supergluing the sole of her tennis shoe to eke a little more life out of it before she had to buy a new pair. Her used economy car had over two hundred thousand miles on it, and her ponytail was two-toned blonde with grown-out ginger roots. Her idea of a night on the town was binge-watching sitcoms while sipping a glass of boxed wine. All because of me.

And still, I wanted more from her. Something that, from the way she reacts whenever I bring it up, would cost her greatly. His name. An address. Maybe a phone number. That would've made me happy.

Mom's legal name was typed on my birth certificate, but the line for *Father* had been left blank. As blank as half my family tree. As blank as the answers to all my questions over the years.

She must have had some good reason why she wouldn't reveal my birth father's name, but she wouldn't even share that much.

How had they met? At a party?

Or perhaps she hadn't known him at all. I swallowed bile at the thought that I could've been the product of a violent sexual attack but instantly dismissed the possibility. Mom taught me to be smart, to not be vulnerable. But she'd never panicked or hinted at any trauma besides admitting that her parents had kicked her out when she returned home to Ohio pregnant after a college summer session. Her dad—my grandfather—had given her a check to cover the cost of an abortion. Instead, she'd ripped it up in front of him, moved to Chicago to live with a high-school friend, had me, and refused to speak to her parents again for over a decade.

Yeah, Mom could hold a grudge with the best of them.

Grandma Vicki thawed first, though I didn't piece any of this together until a couple of years ago. I had two cousins on Mom's side, but I was the oldest of the O'Leary grandkids by a half-dozen years. Still, I loved that I had a real family.

What if my biological father was married with children?

Then I'd have half brothers or half sisters.

Or cousins.

And grandparents, if they were still alive.

There could be a whole group of people belonging to me I'd love to meet.

Mom was the most important person in my life. But now, I craved to know the other half of my family tree. Who freaking shared my DNA?

It was time. I'd waited long enough.

Despite my rapid blinking, I couldn't stop the stinging in my eyes as my birthday cans of paint started to swim in and out of focus.

"Ally, honey? What's wrong?" Mom's voice hitched. I didn't even realize she'd returned home and was standing behind me.

"Nothing." After drying my cheeks on my sweater sleeve, I ran a finger under my lashes to wipe away any renegade mascara streaks before turning to face her. Mom's arms were loaded with take-out food containers. She dumped everything on the counter before rushing to me.

"I don't believe you. Talk to me, sweetheart. Did you bomb your test today?" Her brows were scrunched together, forming elevens in the creases between her eyes. I'd hate to see how worried she'd look if I really needed help. Her navy scrubs looked freshly ironed, and she sported a white turtleneck underneath. If I didn't know better, she could've passed for twenty-five. But in a couple of years, she'd turn forty. Half of those years had been pretty tough.

"Hmm, dinner smells amazing. Thanks for picking it up." As I reached for the containers, she blocked my access with her body, her hands on my shoulders.

"No way, young lady. Don't change the subject."

"It's nothing, really. Just having a life-goal moment, that's all."

She jutted her chin and crossed her arms, assessing me. "This is about your biological father, isn't it? You've been so obsessed with finding him."

Yep. She could read me like a billboard. I bit the inside of my cheek to keep from blurting yes or even lying. Honestly, no answer was needed, because my quivering chin delivered the truth. Mom wrapped me in her arms. I blubbered into her shoulder, craving her trust. Her support. Her understanding.

"I thought we went over this, sweetheart. I thought you'd give me some time."

"I did, Mom. You've had eighteen years to come to terms with it." Hot, ugly tears broke through the last barrier of my dam. My shoulders shuddered after we plopped down on the couch together.

She rocked me side to side, one arm around my shoulder. After a few minutes, she hummed a song I didn't recognize. "Remember when you were little? Every night, you'd sit in my lap, I'd read you a story. Then we'd say your bedtime prayers."

"God, it's been, what . . . a dozen years? More?" I wiped my cheeks with my sweatshirt sleeve, giving in to my old little-girl memories. "My favorite was always that angel prayer."

"Which one?"

"Angel of God, my guardian dear . . ." It was a singsongy, rhyming prayer we used to say together. "When I was little, I believed that an angel would be waiting to save me, but only if I said this prayer every night."

"It worked." Mom laughed as she stroked my hair. "You survived this long, and I never had to use the Heimlich maneuver or perform CPR on you."

Me and my mom. Forever and ever. Amen.

"I want to know my dad's name." Sniffling, I broke away from her embrace to compose myself. She had to leave for her hospital shift soon. After kissing her on the cheek, I wandered toward the kitchen to set the table for my birthday dinner. I called back to her. "Just so you know, I'm not trying to replace you."

"Thank you, sweetheart. You don't know how much that means to me." Mom followed, setting out our take-out containers. From the corner of my eye, I caught her pausing for several heartbeats before dishing food onto our plates. "And I hope you know that I only want what's best for you."

Turning to face her, I searched her eyes, telepathing as much love and respect as I possibly could. But the subtext to my message was *Trust me, Mom. Believe in me.* "More than anything else, I want to know who I am. Where I came from."

"Look, Ally-cat, I know you've been chafing—especially lately—to know about your biological father. But every cell in my body is screaming to keep you from him. He is not the best influence."

"I can take care of myself, Mom. I'm an adult now."

The hour we shared before Mom had to leave for her work shift drifted by with laughter and memories of birthdays past. She'd even baked a cake for me that afternoon. A birthday party, just for two.

After she left for the hospital, I lugged my backpack into my bedroom to tackle my homework. Lulu claimed her favorite spot at the foot of my bed. As I flipped on the light and pulled out my desk chair, something caught my eye.

A folded piece of notepaper rested on my pillow. On it, in Mom's handwriting, was a name—Kyle Dobrescu.

Chapter 5
MARGARET

AFTER

Too many people. Strangers. Friends. Family.

Last night, I screened every female I met at the funeral visitation to be a potential mother for Kyle's daughter. I asked each how she knew Kyle. Sometimes, I'd even asked if they'd dated. Or if they had children.

No attendees fit the bill. Those with husbands were immediately eliminated from contending. As were his female friends I'd known for so long; it would've been too awkward to suggest. I even cornered one of his band members to ask if he could point out anyone in the room Kyle had dated.

Every time someone shook my hand or hugged me, I looked over their shoulder to scan the room. At one point, Kimber must've noticed me sleuthing because she shook her head, admonishing me. God, had I sunk so low that my hospitality and manners were replaced by such rudeness?

But who would've suspected we have a secret granddaughter somewhere out there? How could Martin have possibly known of her existence for an entire year and never even bothered to ask Kyle anything about her? All he'd considered was a goddamned paternity test. Men can be so short sighted. How could Martin have been so focused on protecting Kyle that he didn't think about the bigger ramifications? She's our family member. Our granddaughter.

I've known about Kyle's daughter for a single day, and I'm ready to canvass every neighborhood in Northern Illinois to find her. I can't yet, not with family and friends still in town to celebrate Kyle's life, so instead, I've been combing through the guests at his visitation. If they'd been on civil terms, the mother might have shown up to pay respects to her daughter's father, assuming she'd been made aware of his passing. Chances are, though, they hadn't parted on good terms.

Oh, I wish the universe would grant me a few more minutes with Kyle. Is that too much to ask? First, I'd clear the air and tell him I love him so my last words to him wouldn't have been *Get out*. Then I'd ask him his daughter's name. How did he never let slip that he was a father? My heart is crushed that he told Martin a year ago.

Why not me?

After all, Kyle and I survived so much together. Such horrors. Why wouldn't he also share the good news? Was he worried about my reaction? My judging him?

This past year was different from the decades before. Sure, Kyle had lost some big battles against his addiction, but he was happy and productive his last few months. He seemed—at least from my perspective—to be winning the war. I'd never seen him happier or more energetic than he was these past few months. I suspected he'd reconnected with his former fiancée, Becca, or met someone new. Kyle invited Martin and me to celebrate his birthday with him two weeks from now. I couldn't remember the last time he wanted to celebrate anything with us, birthdays included. Even the court summons for next week hadn't seemed to faze him. Could his positivity have been because of his daughter?

If only he'd shared one more piece of information with Martin. One more clue. Her age. Her name. The mother's name. Anything.

Then I might be able to figure out who she is. At least it would help me eliminate those who aren't contenders.

As we left the funeral home after the wake last night, the director handed Martin the guest book. Instead of letting him keep it, I'd snatched it, then protected it as if it held the key to heaven's pearly gates. I may not have identified my phantom granddaughter or her mother last night, but that doesn't mean one of them didn't attend Kyle's visitation.

◆ ◆ ◆

This morning, Kimber, Martin, and I collected Kyle's urn from the funeral home to transport him to the church. His remains were waiting for us at the reception desk, already stowed in a specially designed kelly-green tote bag with the funeral home's logo splashed across the front in white ink. Sick, twisted advertising. As if someone would ever dare to reuse this bag in public.

Now, I sit in the back seat of the car on the way to the church with Kyle's remains resting on my lap, carrying him one last time. My body supports his. When did he last sit on my lap? He must've been five or six years old. We used to read stories together. Or to cuddle when he'd had a rough day or was not feeling well. I miss those innocent days.

Little did either of us know his last moments existing aboveground would be spent riding in our family car on my lap one last time. I press his cold urn to my heart, wishing I could hug his body, not ashes. Wishing I could hear his voice. Ask him my questions.

Dread clenches my stomach. Every cell in my body rejects the prospect of referring to Kyle in the past tense. No. His presence is here in the car with us. I know it. I can sense it. He's shaking his head and teasing me right now. *Hey, Maggie, lighten up. If you don't smile soon, I'm gonna have to sing your song . . .*

Who will ever call me Maggie again?

Despite his constant struggles, he carved a space in my heart that can't be occupied by another being in the universe. It belongs to Kyle and to him alone.

My consolation in this madness is that he's no longer battling his addiction. The demons he continuously fought can no longer hurt him.

"I love you, Kyle." My whispers don't mean very much on this gray, frigid February day. Frost blankets the ground, and I wonder if the cemetery's caretaker will be able to dig deep enough today for Kyle to be interred. Will they need to wait until after the spring thaw?

Every few blocks, Martin jams on the breaks. The congestion of Friday-morning rush-hour traffic reminds me that most of the world continues to function. Running late for work. Dropping kids off at school and day care. Deliveries and coffee errands along the way. Couldn't God have at least sent us a blizzard to slow everyone down? To throw a cog in the wheel of life, so everyone else can, at the very least, experience the interruption, the loss we've been dealt.

But outside this car, life is carrying on as usual.

Martin pulls up in front of the church, and Kimber takes the urn from me as I scoot out from the open car door. Once outside, with the bitter wind whipping around me, I grab the hateful urn tote, yet cling to it as if it were the last life vest on the *Titanic*.

The priest welcomes us into the vestibule.

"Mrs. Dobrescu, please accept our condolences. May I please take Kyle's urn to place it on the altar?"

My son is cradled in my arms. I will never let go.

◆ ◆ ◆

My mind has tried to protect me. Voids exist where memories should. How did they pry his urn from my arms? At first, he was there; then, he wasn't. Now he's resting on a stand on the altar in his silver vase surrounded by an artful arrangement of white lilies and greenery, a gift from Becca.

My mind keeps tripping over how to grab his urn and run. Would anyone notice if I walked up to the altar while the psalms and the Gospel were being read? God, if Martin weren't holding my hand, if I didn't have to crawl over Kimber and her family to exit the goddamned pew, I would sneak up there. Right now.

This is why no parent should have their child cremated. Logistics. The urn is too portable. At least with a casket, their baby can't take his final ride in a car on his mother's lap. Wooden boxes need their own hearse to travel from the funeral home to the church and then on to the cemetery. No one warned me that at almost seventy years old, it would take all my discipline and a lifetime of training not to steal my son from a church. An urn makes it much too easy. Too possible. Too tempting.

For some reason, my brain twists his funeral mass into a court trial. The priest, a judge. Kyle, the plaintiff. The readers are witnesses. Their readings, the testimony. The mourners, his jury. His crime, living. Judgment is passed. The gavel struck. Kyle is condemned to be buried for all eternity. Can we appeal?

Kyle's mass passes by like a tornado through a sleeping town. The priest's incense stings my nose. I can't focus on the service. Even the order of worship program Kimber prepared for the dozens of mourners couldn't help me keep track of what was going on. It's all a blur. Just bits and pieces, words and people, colors and shapes that all haphazardly fit together to give an impression of this god-awful day.

Somehow, we've already heard the homily and received communion, and now my nephew is delivering Kyle's eulogy. The clock ticks faster, but I can't make it slow down. In minutes we'll be singing the closing hymn, then driving to the cemetery.

How had I never realized before that time was the real enemy?

My son ran out of time.

And yet this horrid day continued. Blissfully my brain blanked out most of it. The numbness was as close as I've come to actually sleeping in about a week. Fragments sync clearly in my mind, but every element surrounding each memory is hazy.

Parallel parking alongside the cemetery and walking through the wrought iron gates.

Seeing the tree branches wrenching from the bitter gusts but not feeling the chill.

Martin tugging my arm to escort me away from the grave since the undertaker was waiting until all the mourners departed to start digging. So I did the last thing I ever dreamed of doing. I turned my back on Kyle's final resting place while he was still aboveground and stumbled, shuffling away from him.

Pushing food around my luncheon plate at the funeral reception because if I risked a bite, I'd spew it and the contents of my stomach like a possessed person from a horror movie.

Scanning the guests at the funeral and reception in case there was someone—anyone—who might fit the bill for Kyle's unknown daughter or her mother. But every face present in the crowd was as familiar to me as my own reflection.

Nodding politely as Dr. Lee, the doctor I work for at the clinic, generously advised me to take all the time I needed to collect myself before coming back to work. Little does she know that day may never come. Then again, she was probably protecting her practice's patients as well as limiting her malpractice insurance claims with this offer of unpaid leave. Smart lady.

And finally, at the end of my marathon, kissing Kimber, my three precious grandchildren, and her husband goodbye before they hopped in their car to return home. She'd offered—begged, even—to stay a few days longer to help us, but instead, I asked her to come back next week. I could use the break to start processing all this madness, and she needed to pick up the pieces of their normal lives again.

What will normal be for me?

Martin drove us back home in the dark. With Kyle buried and Kimber away at her own home, our house feels foreign. Quiet. Uninhabited. Though each corner and nook are eerily familiar, it belongs to someone else—my former self, who had two living children. That woman died with her son. And yet, I'm still here.

After trudging upstairs to our bedroom, I change into my flannel pajamas. I vow to never wear either my visitation or funeral outfits again, so I stuff them into a plastic garbage bag. Might as well donate them to someone who can use them, though burning them might be more fitting. Hopefully the curse will stop with me.

Then I brave entering Kyle's room. After crawling under his covers, I wrap myself in his sheets, absorbing his being. A benediction to my son's thirty-seven-year life. I'm not sure how many hours I lay there. Or if I dozed, hoping I could somehow pass on to the afterworld.

But Kyle is with me. Even my weary bones sense it. I can't see him or hear him, but his presence is real. His laughter. His being. He is with me in my heart.

In the darkness before dawn, the night sky shifts from inky black to gray. Somewhere on the horizon, a person will see the sunrise through Kyle's donated retinas. A burn victim will heal with a graft of his skin. Parts of him live on, as does his spirit, right here within me. He shores me up with energy I haven't felt since before he passed away. Kyle may not be able to verbally answer my questions, but he can guide me.

He must.

Take me to your daughter, Kyle.

Chapter 6

KYLE

BEFORE

Ahh, so this was what it was like to be coherent at nine in the morning. I saw nine at night all the time, though not always vertically.

I couldn't remember the last time I was voluntarily awake on a Saturday morning. A few weeks ago, my mom compiled a list of every substance abuse rehabilitation center within a hundred-mile radius. It's up to me to find a free—and by free, I mean available, though it would also help if my medical insurance policy would cover it—intake bed somewhere.

My coffee may or may not be spiked while I dialed for dollars. Okay, my first mug had been the virgin variety. My second was spiked. Its sequel was a double. As I glanced down my list of phone numbers I still have yet to call, I knew I would need more liquid courage—my fourth mug of joe would get triple spiked. All the caffeine, all the happy juice. I leaned back and stretched, nearly toppling the kitchen chair. The sofa in the living room beckoned me like a siren's call. Normally I'd listen, charmed by the promise of oblivion, but I didn't think I'd look good in an orange jumpsuit.

The judge had given me a choice: I could either check into court-ordered rehab for a year or go to prison. Easy decision, except the only reason that I wasn't in rehab already was that I hadn't found any vacant intake beds yet. My lawyer advised that as long as I called daily, I kept my grace period alive. Placating a judge was a worthy objective.

I knew what I was in for. I'd been a resident at a rehab center several times before. It was actually not that bad once you survived detox—well, except for the whole no-drinking part. The routine took some getting used to, but then I could coast along on autopilot. Patients attended group therapy sessions, met with counselors, wrote in journals, and participated in AA meetings every evening. We usually had some sort of in-house job assigned as well. I assumed rehab was similar to one of those hippie communes out West. A very dry and sober commune.

Once I got in the groove, I didn't mind it. Much. The only real objection I had with rehab was my lack of freedom to do whatever I wanted when I wanted to do it.

What choice did I have?

Thus, the phone and checklist in my hand, and every response I'd gotten so far this morning of "No, Mr. Dobrescu. I'm sorry, but we don't have any available beds at this time. Please call back in another day or so." Each response I received buoyed me. One more day of freedom.

So far today, I'd batted zero. Or a thousand, depending on your perspective.

God only knew where my parents were at this moment. It was Saturday, so neither would be at work. Probably off grocery shopping or going to doctor's appointments. As far as I could tell, they ran their errands together. Or, more specifically, Dad chauffeured Mom around to all her errands. They'd probably be gone until after lunch. Again, typically by the time they returned, I'd still be asleep.

This being-alert-in-the-morning thing was new for me—court-ordered morning.

With a renewed burst of energy reminiscent of my I'm-getting-the-hell-out-of-here high-school days when the bus would drop me off at school and I'd walk out the back door and play hooky, I polished off the last of the phone numbers on Mom's list of facilities. Done.

The court could check up on me if they wanted, but there wasn't a single open rehab bed in Chicagoland.

Freedom bought for another twenty-four more hours.

The feeling was delicious, and I mused what I could possibly do with this temporary reprieve. It would be a shame to waste it by sleeping all day. Soon enough, I won't have the luxury of deciding what to do next. Well, a shower was definitely in order. Maybe even a shave and some breakfast.

Welcome to adulting.

Blue skies peeked in through the window. I rested my knuckle against the pane. For the first time in months, the glass didn't feel frozen, as if I'd touched ice cubes. March rarely delivered a mild day to Chicago. Today's warmth was intoxicating, and to my surprise, my feet guided me to the front door.

I don't think I've been outside my parents' house in over a week, but today I wanted to breathe the fresh air.

After pouring another spiked mug of coffee and grabbing my cigarettes, I ventured toward my parents' front door and opened it. Sunlight surrounded me, flooding me with optimism. Inhaling the earthy warmth, I took a seat on the front steps and basked in the golden hues.

The fresh air was too damned healthy. I momentarily wondered if I should've transitioned outside slower. Talk about a shock to my system after breathing the recycled HVAC air inside for a couple of thousand hours in a row. Instead, I lit up my cigarette to cut the benefits. Didn't want to get too crazy on this wellness stuff.

Five minutes grew to fifteen, then morphed into half an hour. My butt was chilled from sitting on the still-cold front steps, but I soaked in all the vitamin D I hadn't gotten in months. My thoughts turned to Mom and Dad. There was some reason she'd hauled me out of bed extra early to make the calls. Why was that?

Oh, yeah. They were heading out of town for the day to visit my sister in Wisconsin. I used to be invited on these trips, but once my nieces and nephew grew up into school age, my sister didn't want to risk them seeing me—how did she put it? "Compromised." She might as well have called me *possessed*. Or *drunk*. Or admit she was sick of explaining why Uncle Kyle was always falling down and puking in the toilet?

Fine by me. I wouldn't want her kids to see me that way either. I still got to visit with them, but now that I was living with Mom and Dad, Kimber's family would stay at a nearby hotel, and they would drop by the house once they knew whether I was sober. She never told me this directly, but it didn't take a rocket scientist to figure out what was going on. A piece of me regretted I'd let our relationship slip into our impasse, but it was easier to drink away my guilt. I was good at it.

My coffee was too cold to finish, but I'd rather sit outside than warm it up again. Cars cruised by, as did neighbors strolling the sidewalks with kids or a pet. Some even waved and asked about Mom and Dad as they passed the house. Others ignored me, which was my preference.

A few minutes later, a teenager dressed in jeans with a backpack slung over one shoulder ambled up the street. She scanned the mailboxes for house numbers, then backtracked my direction.

"Hey, need help finding someone?" Not that I knew any of the neighbors or their names, but I could offer. I stubbed out the cigarette so I wouldn't blow smoke in her direction.

"Yeah, thanks. Do you know which townhome is where the Dobrescu family lives?"

No shit.

"That's us. How can I help you?" I scanned her winter coat to see if it was sporting an embroidered logo. She looked awfully young to be selling something, though.

"I'm looking for Kyle Dobrescu."

Me?

"Um . . ." My stomach twists, threatening to spew my coffee back the way it came. As I stood, I glanced up and down the sidewalk to see if anyone was nearby. If she was some undercover cop trying to bust me for not being in rehab, I wanted witnesses. No one was in the near vicinity. And I'd left my phone inside the house, so I couldn't even record it. Crap. "How, um, can I help you?"

"Are you Kyle?" The teen—or youthful-looking woman—tucked a lock of dark hair behind her ear and twisted the toe of her sneaker against the sidewalk.

"In the flesh." Something about her nervousness quashed my suspicions of a sting operation, so I descended the remaining few steps with my hand extended. She shook it, her eyes growing wider by the second. The shade of her eyes reminded me of my grandfather's polished mahogany desk.

And as deeply set as my own.

My unexpected warning phone call from Hannah a month or so ago nagged at the fringes of my brain. This couldn't possibly be . . . then again, her age would seem about right.

"And you are?" Softening my voice, I inched away while hiding my hands behind my back, so she wouldn't see them trembling. I couldn't tell if it was from the cigarettes, the alcohol, or the significance of this moment. Maybe a mix of all three.

I'd scare her away soon enough, I was sure. But I hoped to spend a little time with her before then. I was her father. At least I thought I was. So I'd give her space, all the space and time she needed to get comfortable.

"Ally. Well, Allison O'Leary. I think you once knew my mom, Hannah?"

Bingo.

"She told me you might try to contact me someday soon. But she didn't tell me when. Nice to meet you, Ally."

"Yeah, sorry I didn't call first. I found out your name a couple days ago."

"Hannah is pretty good at keeping secrets. I only learned I had a daughter a few weeks ago. You grew up fast." Bad joke. Nervous habit. My humor fell flat. I didn't get any reaction from Ally at all. Awkward, yes. But not horrible.

"I wanted to meet you. I've always wanted to know who . . . who my biological father was." She motioned toward me with her hand. "Is."

"I'm glad you found me." After mentally scanning the interior of our home and rating it a minus-four on the cleanliness scale of one to ten, I decided against offering for her to come inside. "You know, it's so mild out today. Do you mind if we sit out here for a few minutes?"

"Sure." Ally followed my lead and sat next to me on the front step. Now I was relieved Mom and Dad had left town. Dad knew, but I had no idea how Mom would've reacted to meeting her latest grandchild. Surprise! That might require some finessing once I was back in her good graces.

After plopping her backpack at her feet, Ally unzipped it, then handed me a foil-covered blob.

"May I?" Once I peeled back the crinkled foil, I found a triangle slice of chocolate cake and frosting. I licked the bit that smudged my finger.

"It's my birthday cake. I figure you've missed my other birthdays. At least you can celebrate with me now." She handed me a plastic fork and watched expectantly as I scooped a small bite. She did the same, and we clinked forks before shoveling the bites into our mouths.

"Cheers. Happy birthday, Ally." Food didn't agree with me most days. Not much of an appetite. I couldn't taste much, either, after my coffee-and-cigarette breakfast. I was prone to getting pancreatitis, which I'd rather not experience again. Ever. So was selective about what I ate. No oils or fried foods, no butter, low sugar, low sodium. Even gluten could be tough to digest. My digestive issues haven't stunted my weakness for vodka, though, because I was guaranteed to get so wasted I wouldn't remember my stomach-pain attacks and projectile vomiting.

But I choked down this bite of chocolate cake because my daughter gave it to me and we were celebrating her birthday together. Just us. I'd calculated the years after Hannah's phone call. "Eighteen?"

She nodded, a smile brightening her face. I caught a glimpse of a dimple on her cheek. None on my side of the family. She must've inherited it from her mom. I'd hardly be able to recognize Hannah after all these years. Still, I remembered her as having shockingly red hair, a small size, and more combustible energy than a firecracker when we'd dated those couple of months during my SMU days. But that had been a long time ago. So far, her—our—daughter was behaving quite tamely by comparison.

"When was your birthday?"

"A couple days ago. March nineteenth. School day, so not much of a chance to celebrate." She scooped another bite; then I handed her the plate to finish. After a hesitation that hinted at being more insecure than uncomfortable, she looked over at me. "When is yours?"

"February fourteenth."

"Valentine's Day?" My nod and shrug made her laugh. I never knew why people found my birthday funny, but most did. Everyone had to have one. I guess having hearts, red roses, and chocolates plastered over every retail surface for weeks ahead of time added a sense of surrealism to something as ordinary as a birthday. Like those kids who shared their birthdays with Christmas. Or Halloween.

What I didn't tell Ally was that I once had someone I considered my valentine to celebrate with me. To me, Becca still was. I had even proposed. I'd propose again if I thought we had even a small chance together as a couple.

But it was never Hannah.

"So what should I call you?" Her giggle betrayed that we were both suffering from the same level of awkwardness. Yep. I'd drunkenly donated a sperm nineteen years ago, and here we were today, meeting each other for the first time. We were a modern family. "Dad?"

I nudged her shoulder with mine. "Why don't you call me Kyle, and we can get to know each other from there."

Chapter 7

MARGARET

AFTER

Our townhome's basement always intimidated me. Though technically a finished, livable space, it's a huge mess. The couch that abuts the back wall is buried under storage boxes and decades of accumulated junk. This was the family's dumping ground. If Kyle left behind any clues about a daughter somewhere, maybe I'll find them here.

Since Kyle's cell phone is password protected and we can't access his text messages or contacts, Martin wanted to cancel his service. But I argued that we needed to keep his line open—at least for a little while longer—to let those who try to contact him know of his passing. He reluctantly agreed. So I keep it charged and near me at all times to monitor incoming calls, hoping Boo or her mother will attempt to contact him directly.

Boo.

That's what I've nicknamed my mystery granddaughter. I talk to her as I search through boxes, coaxing her to help me find Kyle's clues. He had to have left something behind somewhere.

The basement's work desk took me a full day to rifle through. Each sticky note, doodle, and cubby offered fertile ground. What derailed me was his desk calendar. His birthday—Valentine's Day—was highlighted, and he'd prewritten "Happy birthday to me. Project Valentine." I knew he'd been excited. He even made sure we didn't make any plans for that night so we could celebrate together.

His birthday is still a few days away. We won't be with him.

When his desk didn't offer any new leads, I moved on to tackle his storage boxes—acres of them. Jeez, you don't realize how much your family member hoards until it's your responsibility to wrap up their affairs. Boxes of amplifiers and electronics. An all-you-can-eat spaghetti buffet of power cords. Remote-controlled helicopter? Good Lord, he bought some weird stuff. When I found Kyle's box of old rehab journals, I knew I'd struck gold.

After hauling them upstairs to the main level of the house, I plop down on the couch, pull out a dog-eared, spiral-bound steno notebook, and flip it open. Each painful word chicken-scratched on these pages is a portal to my son's broken world. Endless lists affirming goals he wanted to accomplish. Burned bridges he felt worthy of mending. People he'd let down, and those he respected.

More than once, he'd written *My mom deserves to be thanked. Apologized to. Protected. Loved.* Each time I saw that note, my heart warmed a degree or two.

His soul was poured out in these journals. He'd crafted decision trees and flow charts. Plotted job-hunting strategies and even suggested steps to overcoming his alcohol addiction. I found drafts of his résumés and questions for some peer support groups. Notes and homework from a class he took at the community college last semester. Even a draft of a speech for his public speaking class.

He'd written at length about patching things up with Becca, his former fiancée. In fact, reconciling with her often hit his list of top five goals. We would've loved to have called her our daughter-in-law. He never shared why they didn't get married, but I suspect it was because Becca couldn't compete with his obsession with vodka.

But nothing inside any of these notebooks revealed any hint about Boo. Not a single clue. How could a child exist without any trace of her whereabouts or evidence that she's even around?

A wave of dizziness overcomes me, so I rest my head against the back of the couch. Had Martin misheard him? His hearing isn't quite what it used to be. Maybe he'd somehow misunderstood their entire conversation. Am I searching for someone who doesn't exist?

Why tease me about having a granddaughter and then not send me any clues? One thing is for damned sure, I'm not giving up my search until I've unearthed every possible lead.

After the funeral, Kimber encouraged me to give up my search, to move on with our lives. That it should be the child's mother's decision whether or not to reveal her daughter. With Kyle now gone, this ex-girlfriend has no obligation—ethical, legal, or otherwise—to reach out to us. It's her choice. It's her right to privacy.

That may be true, but this child is a member of my family and a living extension of Kyle. I want to help. While Kyle has no inheritance to bequeath, if Boo's mother needs financial assistance, I'd be happy to contribute to my granddaughter's college fund or upbringing. If she's young, we could also help out by babysitting, assuming they are local. Introduce her to her cousins. We would welcome her—and her mother—into the Dobrescu family.

Four days ago, when I buried my son, I buried his secret. But not all secrets are meant to go to the grave. The only secret he needed to keep was mine.

◆ ◆ ◆

"Mom, are you here?" The following day, Kimber cracks the front door open and yells out for me. She used the spare key to unlock the door.

"Yes. C'mon in, sweetheart." I shuffle upstairs from the basement with yet another armload of notebooks to greet her. She offered to help me wrap up some loose ends from the funeral last week.

"I rang the doorbell several times, but I guess you didn't hear . . . oh, my God, Mom." After dropping her bucket of cleaning supplies, Kimber turns in a circle, inspecting the living room with her arms crossed. A mountain of boxes with their contents half-unpacked covers every horizontal surface. "Did an earthquake hit that I didn't hear about?"

"Don't mind the mess, honey. I've been searching through Kyle's stuff."

"Is anything even left in the basement?" Kimber lifts a couple of boxes from the couch and stacks them against the wall so we both have a space to sit. "I think I prefer your living room's before-the-makeover look to the after."

As she settles down, though, she spies the kelly-green bag the funeral home had given us to transport Kyle's urn. Her cringe makes the hair on the back of my neck prickle. "Are you saving this?"

"Oh, um . . . I haven't given any thought about what to do with it yet." Seeing my cluttered living room through my daughter's lens makes me shudder. Is she judging me? Yes, my home isn't as tidy as it usually is, but what does she expect? "It's going to take a while to get through all of Kyle's stuff. Your father will be home later this afternoon, and he can help me carry some of these boxes back downstairs. What should we do today?"

"Well, for starters, let's return the urn's port-a-bag to the funeral home. I'm sure you have a monster to-do list. We can start tackling that together."

To-do list? It took me a minute to realize what she was referring to. Kyle was already laid to rest. What could possibly still need to be done? But Kimber was right. Casserole dishes needed to be returned. Stacks of mail and packages had accumulated by the front door. Not to mention all the thank-you notes we needed to write. How in God's name had I overlooked all this?

But in my heart, I know why. Every waking breath has been dedicated to hunting for hints of Boo's existence. Yesterday, I spent hours combing through Kyle's Facebook photos. That turned up nothing. But I can't tell Kimber that.

After jotting down a checklist—which took up several pages of the legal pad—for us to tackle, Kimber paused. "Aunt Judy called and asked how you were holding up. Did she call you?"

"Yes, honey."

"She told me she invited you to visit them in Florida." Kimber's words were delivered gently, but there was an underlying current of . . . what? Concern? Worry? "Dr. Lee is giving you leave, so there's no rush for you to go back to work. You hate winter. And you could use a little break to process Kyle's passing. I mean, he died upstairs—in this house. You should get away from here."

"Thanks, honey. I declined Judy's offer."

"What? Why'd you do that?"

As if there couldn't be reasons for me to say no. "I'm not ready."

"Dad and I both think it would be a good idea." Kimber pulls out a piece of paper from her pocket. "Look, I found you a good flight, and I'll pay for it—"

Now my husband, sister, and daughter are conspiring behind my back. A family intervention is the last thing I want or need. "Please don't push me."

"Dad says you're not sleeping or eating. You won't answer the phone. You didn't attend church last Sunday. Did you even step outside the front door this week?"

"Listen, darling. Don't tell me how to grieve. That's my call." Instead of admitting that she may have a point, I stand and slip on my jacket and dark sunglasses—the first time since the funeral. "Let's return Kyle's bag to the funeral home."

From the way Kimber exhaled, I knew the subject was far from abandoned, but at least I'd derailed her efforts to ship me out of town for the moment.

I wish they'd give me some time and space to process this. My son died. I'm allowed to be depressed. To be sad. To avoid the outside world. To grieve however I damn well please.

◆　◆　◆

Several hours into Kimber's and my funeral-wrap-up boot camp, we'd visited Kyle's grave site to brush away all the stray windblown leaves, donated the flower arrangements to our local nursing home, and made a dent in the thank-you-note list. The food was disposed of. We cleared a path from the front door down the hallway to each of the rooms. Kimber even cleaned the bathrooms while I ran the vacuum cleaner.

She and I make a good team.

We were nearly finished cleaning the house when Martin barrels inside, home from work, with a frozen pizza and a bag of iceberg salad in tow. Not that I'm eating much these days, but I really miss Kyle's cooking. As if I need any more reasons to miss my son.

Whenever he offered to cook, I always knew he was sober. He would blast classic rock on the radio and kick everyone out of the kitchen, then whip up some culinary masterpiece from leftovers.

And that one time when Rod Stewart's "Maggie May" came on . . .

My body shudders as yet another tsunami of grief drags me out to sea. I struggle for breath. Happy memories are somehow worse than dark ones. At least when I recall all he suffered, I'm comforted by the promise that Kyle's no longer fighting his demons. That he can rest in peace. But the good ones make me miss him so hard I ache.

Kimber stays and joins us for dinner and pulls together enough fresh ingredients to add to our meal that I manage to swallow a few bites. I doubt it's enough to convince Kimber that I'm coping, but I give myself points for solid acting.

"Any word back from the coroner about Kyle's cause of death?" She hands me a glass of wine, which I decline. A few days ago, I realized the irony of drinking alcohol when my son may have died from it.

"Dead end." My phone call to the medical examiner's office to ask for more information about his drug overdose was a waste of time. "They never ran the toxicology labs after the autopsy."

Kimber nearly drops her glass. "What? Why not?"

"They conducted a partial autopsy because his death was consistent with that of a known long-term abusive alcoholic. His cause of death was obvious: head trauma. No indication of anything suspicious. No need to proceed further. Only the physical evidence was needed to determine the immediate and underlying causes of death."

"So they don't know what kind of drug was in his system when he died?"

"Nope. Nor if it was prescription, legal, or illegal. Perhaps it could've been alcohol."

"What can we do now?"

"Not much. With Kyle's remains cremated, they can't run any more lab tests, even if we offered to pay for it privately. We're too late."

"Wasn't he discharged from the emergency room the night before he died?"

I nod, but my brain time-warps back to that night when he returned, just minutes before I kicked him out to the curb. Kyle claimed the ER doctor had checked him out and said he was fine. His lungs sounded normal. Twenty-four hours later, he was dead.

I should never have let down my guard and should've monitored him once he came back home. How often had I come home from work to find him unconscious, writhing on the floor? Several times, at least. Alcoholics are prone to grand mal seizures. At least if I'd been nearby and he went into respiratory distress, I'd have hauled him right back to the hospital. And he might still be alive.

"We can request his records from the ER visit." Kimber perks up as if knowing answers will bring Kyle back to us. "That should list what medicines the doctor prescribed."

"Yes. That's worthwhile." As I consider my daughter's logical suggestion, another thought comes into focus. "If memory serves me correctly, Kyle was wearing a transdermal patch when he died. I don't know what the medication was, but it was probably applied during his ER—"

"You're both wasting your time." Martin walks into the kitchen, carrying our dinner dishes from the dining room. "Kyle told me very clearly what he would do."

Kimber and I glance at each other, then stare at him while waiting. Since he isn't inclined to continue, I prod. "And that was . . . ?"

"The last time I drove him to court, he told me he'd kill himself before going to prison. Well, this week, he would've had his new court date. When we talked to his lawyer a few days before Kyle died, he was pessimistic about Kyle's new sentencing since he'd violated his court-ordered rehab terms."

A wave of dread crashes through my body, threatening to bring up the dinner I so dutifully swallowed moments ago.

"His overdose wasn't accidental." Martin's shoulders slump.

"Dad, what exactly are you saying?" Kimber articulates the very question I'd have traded my soul to avoid asking. But now that it was out in the open and in play, no deals with the devil were possible.

"Kyle committed suicide."

Chapter 8

KYLE

BEFORE

Heel-clicking echoed along the long hallway's tiled floor. I stopped writing in my journal at my desk and listened to see if their destination was my room or elsewhere. After the noise built to a crescendo, whoever they were passed by my assigned dorm room—a glorified closet outfitted with a firm twin bed, a small nightstand, a generic wooden desk and chair, and a chest of drawers—then their footsteps grew softer as they receded.

I could come and go from my assigned room, but I couldn't walk off the facility's property without permission. My cell phone was locked away. I wasn't allowed to receive care packages. They could search my room and belongings. I could only have visitors who had been officially approved and vetted. Visitation occurred during designated hours on Sunday afternoons. It was all about structure, routine, and saving me from myself.

Ahh, rehab. Together again.

At least it wasn't a jail cell. Technically speaking.

Glancing at my watch, I calculated that I had forty-five minutes until my next group therapy session.

This morning, I'd crossed off day number eight on my pocket calendar. Since the Carrefour Residential Center required all patients to be admitted after detox, I'd completed my five-day visit to Dante's inferno before coming here. In that brutal circle of hell, I shook and slobbered and twisted in agony as my body rebelled against functioning without a drop of alcohol. The worst part was that I remembered every goddamned second of the torture. It hadn't been pretty.

My near-blank journal page taunted me. I was tasked with itemizing my life goals before my next group session.

Life Goal #1 – Get to know Ally better.

Well, it was hard to do that while I was trapped in rehab.

Life Goal #2 – Get a job.

Life Goal #3 – Move out of my parents' house.

Life Goal #4 – Finish college.

Hell, if I could achieve any of these, I'd have finished the marathon. It also meant, in reality, I'd sucked at life. But it wasn't lost on me that each of my goals depended on me staying sober, which had a higher chance of success the longer I stayed in rehab.

But while I consciously recognized the benefits of therapy, every hour of every day I'd spent inside this joint, something reminded me that I wasn't free to go. I wasn't in control of my time or decisions. The counselors were. I might as well be brain dead. Too bad they won't issue a dose of Valium every morning with breakfast. That would help make time slip by faster. I should never have risked getting caught for driving on a suspended license with a DUI on my record.

I needed to keep my sights on the horizon. To reach my goal of getting to know Ally better, I first had to pay my dues here in rehab. Only 357 more court-ordered days to go.

◆　◆　◆

"Kyle, could you please refile these cases?" The receptionist motioned toward a teetering pile at the corner of her desk while holding the phone receiver to her ear.

"On it." I nodded before lifting a ten-pound stack of manila folders, then schlepped them to the wall of metal filing cabinets and opened what could be mistaken for a morgue's refrigerator—minus the body. You'd think in the twenty-first century, everything would be digital by now, but Carrefour was most definitely stuck in the analog era. It was all paper, paper, paper here. They even had a fax machine. Soon they might need a bigger office to house all the file folders.

When I first arrived, I'd been assigned busing lunch tables as my job. We all had one. But one of the counselors noticed that I had a few administrative skills up my sleeve—thanks to helping Dad out with his real estate business—so they reassigned me to work in the Center's office. The hours were longer than most other jobs here, but it helped to pass the time and the days.

Ideas swirled in my head for how to make myself useful enough that I could get permanently assigned to help out in the front office. Jeez, I could upgrade their website. I could even start digitizing their case folders. Maybe help them integrate good medical software to coordinate with doctors, counselors, insurance billing, and legal advisers. You'd think someone would've done this already, but if I could spend the next year—correction, the next 344 days—tinkering on a computer, then I wouldn't complain. Much.

In two days, I should be allowed to receive my first visitors. Mom and Dad would be coming. So far they were my only approved visitors. I gave Kimber the Center's director's information to apply to become a qualified visitor so I could see her if she were ever visiting Chicago. But according to the greeting card Kimber mailed me, she couldn't even get a return phone call from the Center.

If I could get these guys digital, they'd have time to vet my visitor requests. Perhaps I could even get Ally approved.

◆ ◆ ◆

I must've done something right around here, because a week later, the director asked me to work on updating the Center's online presence. Score.

Now, even though none of the entire fifty-bed residential population of Carrefour were allowed cell phones and email addresses, I'd been handed the golden ticket.

Access to the internet.

So far I hadn't done anything crazy, such as search for the nearest adult-beverage watering hole or liquor retail establishment—though trust me, I was tempted. Instead, I stealth-searched for Ally's snail mail address, or more specifically, Hannah's. She'd kept a pretty low profile over the years. I've found three *H. O'Leary*s in the area, and Ally's name wasn't listed as living in any of the addresses. So I kept combing. I limited my googling to five minutes or less whenever the other person in the front office was on a phone call.

For as structured and as routine oriented as this place was, I'd had way too much free time on my hands to allow my mind to drift. I replayed every word of my surprise visit from Ally, which hadn't lasted even twenty minutes, including the birthday cake part. We'd connected one other time for coffee the following Saturday. We met at a café halfway between us, and she said she'd ridden the bus, then was leaving to go study at the library for the afternoon. Her calculus class was stressing her out. Not as if I could help her.

Best of all, I'd made my daughter laugh. Her laugh had this little bubbly quality to it, as if she still hadn't outgrown all her preteen habits. Though she'd also studied the coffee menu to order the least expensive item, even though I'd offered to buy her anything she wanted. She'd refused my offer to splurge on a larger-size cup for her. Or a pump of syrup. But she'd opted for whipped cream with a drizzle of chocolate.

My daughter had a sweet tooth.

God, I couldn't get enough of saying *my daughter*. Two months ago, when Hannah had first called, I'd been angry that she'd lied to me and had the baby on the sly. It didn't take long before my anger twisted into hurt. In all eighteen years of Ally's life, Hannah had never bothered to inform me I was a father. Then again, could I blame her? Had our roles been reversed, would I have voluntarily introduced my child to their unemployed alcoholic parent? Maybe not.

But apparently Ally had been asking about me all along. And Hannah never told her a single detail about me. One of Ally's first questions was whether I had any other children. I guess she'd been dreaming up half siblings in her early years. Hated to burst her bubble on that one, but I came as a solo unit. No spouse. No other kids—to my knowledge. A whole cargo train's worth of emotional baggage, though.

If my stint in Carrefour could help me clean my act up and become worthy of being a dad to Ally, then, by God, I had something to live for. Finally. I wished I'd gotten her address the last time we met, so I could write to her. Figured I'd have more time to fill her in on my plans as she got to know me. I didn't want to scare her off, so in the cumulative forty-five minutes we'd ever spent together, I didn't share with her about my immediate court-ordered future that would be instantly triggered by one of my phone calls to residential facilities.

But three days after our coffee date, my rehab phone calls hit the jackpot. A bed had become available. Two hours later, my dad drove me to check into detox. Just like flipping a switch, I no longer lived in the real world.

It also meant I'd stood up my daughter on our third date. We'd planned to meet for coffee again that following Saturday.

I hoped Ally would forgive me. Eventually.

"Kyle, honey, how do you feel? You've dropped more weight." After hugging me and updating me on Kimber, her husband, and all the grandkids, Mom finally took an appraising look at me. She'd always assessed my health by my coloring and the scale. If I happened to be a little pale to her liking, she'd push the iron and vitamin D. If I was losing weight, she was all about my caloric intake.

"The food's fine. I'm fine. No problems." Okay, I was lying. The food here sucked in the same way that institutional food sucked anywhere. How many limp iceberg lettuce salads topped with shredded mild cheddar cheese and ranch dressing could a person tolerate? Would it kill them to offer grilled salmon or a fresh avocado once in a while?

My finicky eating habits didn't even hit Carrefour's radar. The folks at the Center only cared about me not drinking or taking any pain meds—even over-the-counter ibuprofen was banned here. As long as I stayed clean and attended my meetings, they stayed off my back. Win-win. So every meal, I pushed my sad, limp lettuce around my plate. The apples were fresh, though. And the coffee was strong.

Mom glanced around the room, then slipped a small container across our visitors' table toward me with a conspiratorial smile. I was surprised she was able to get it past the counselors, but when I popped the lid, I closed my eyes and inhaled the scent of sweet butter, brown sugar, and dark chocolate. I could see why she'd made it in . . . a half-dozen superthin chocolate chunk cookies rested on the floor of this translucent container. Nothing hidden. Nothing covertly delivered. The counselors inspected everything and everyone as they entered. TSA could learn a thing or two about security here.

"These are amazing, Maggie May! Did you actually bake?" I doubted it. She hadn't baked anything since I was little. But it was worth the suggestion to see her beam. The stomachache my digestive system promised was almost worth the indulgence. I picked up one of the cookies like a priest venerating the consecrated host at mass. It had been weeks since I last tasted anything with flavor. Period.

But there was something about Mom's calmness that I hadn't noticed while I lived at home. She appeared downright serene. Then it dawned on me. While a resident at the Center, I was no longer her responsibility. She could live the empty nester lifestyle she should have been enjoying all along. She could visit her grandkids. She could come home from work without worrying whether I was on the floor, passed out or midseizure.

"No, honey. Mrs. Roman made them." Ahh, that explained it. Mom's best friend had always reinforced good behavior by doling out homemade treats. She apparently approved of my being in rehab.

"Thank her for me." Snapping the lid back on the container broke the momentary spell it had cast on me. No nibbles. I'd share them with the folks at the front office, buying myself a few extra minutes on the internet. "You know, I'm really sorry for all the trouble I've caused over the years."

Dad's gaze locked on me with his jaw clenched, searching. Assessing.

I belatedly realized I should've thought first before treading into this minefield. My apology could've been misinterpreted as end-of-life-ish. My gut twisted at the thought of causing him more stress. No doubt he was wondering if I would make good on my warning a month ago to commit suicide. I'd been honest at the time, and from the looks of him now, Dad had taken me seriously.

"Easy, Dad. You don't need to worry. I'm fine." Looking from one to the other, I could finally relate to a parent's intense need to know their child was thriving.

On a practical note, how could I kill myself? With a plastic spork? Carrefour certainly didn't leave potential weapons lying around here. Plus, with Ally in my life, I now had a viable reason to make it out of here alive.

"Before we drove over, a young lady stopped by asking for you." Mom raised her eyebrow as if I should know what she was talking about. "She didn't share her name, though."

"Huh. That's weird. What did she look like?" I ran my finger along the cookie-container lid, not making eye contact with Mom while faking a bored demeanor. Could it be . . .

"Tall. Dark hair. A teenager. She had a navy backpack over her shoulder. Nice and polite, though."

Ally.

Holy crap. Mom and Dad had been within feet of my daughter—their granddaughter—and didn't even know it.

"Um, doesn't ring a bell. Probably a political canvasser or high-school booster's fundraiser." My palms grew sweaty. Why had I lied? After all these years, why was my gut reaction with my mom to spin the truth? She'd seen my ugly, and Jesus Christ, we'd survived a nightmare. Plus I'd caused her enough pain over the years. Admitting that I had sex outside of marriage shouldn't pop her Roman Catholic bubble of purity.

Because I sinned. I was sinning. I was a sinner.

I was an idiot. In the grand scheme of things, having had unprotected sex was the least of my vices. Mom would get over my role in this, then embrace the prospect of a new family member. In fact, she could get a little too exuberant and scare Ally away.

Should I tell them?

My heartbeat picked up. Yes. Though it felt like looking over the edge of a cliff, I needed to. I wanted to.

"My group therapy counselor has us working on our life list. You know, goals . . ." Both Mom and Dad leaned in closer, absorbing each positive word I said like parched desert plants in a sun-shower. Neither dared to derail anything I said with hints of skepticism, though I was hardly a safe bet. "Graduating from college and getting a job and . . ."

They both waited, holding their breaths. I paused, trying to select my words carefully. But then the counselor announced to the room that visiting time would end in five minutes. How could I possibly drop the bomb that they had an extra grandchild, then leave them to flounder for another week before I could explain myself? It wouldn't be fair. And maybe I should warn Ally first.

". . . and do you mind bringing me some stamps next time? I need to reply to Kimber's letters."

What I didn't add was that I wanted to mail a letter to Ally once I found her address.

Chapter 9

ALLY

AFTER

Lulu pays me more attention this afternoon than I think she's collectively done in the three years she's lived with us. She curls up on my open Psych 101 textbook, staring me down. When I don't rub the fur under her ears, she nudges my wrist every few minutes with her nose. Her purring stopped about an hour ago, but I still haven't given her a fraction of the adoration she craves. Instead, I lay sprawled on my bed, swaddled inside my Hemingway University extra-large, extra-comfy sweatshirt and wrapped in blankets. I have yet to read a single word of my notes for the midterm exam I have tomorrow on campus.

Instead, I roll over and flip through my sketchbook, looking at drawing after drawing of Kyle. Oh, but he'd been so patient with me, never once complaining or asking me not to draw him. Then I grab his letters to reread for the hundredth time. The ones he snail-mailed me last year when he was in rehab at Carrefour. It's been over two weeks, and I still can't believe he's dead. In these pages, he feels so alive.

If he only knew that meeting him had been my dream come true. He wasn't perfect. I figured from Mom's obstinance and the fortress of privacy she'd built around us that I should never expect him to be dependable.

But Kyle hadn't known about my existence either.

This past year, we duct-taped together our father-daughter relationship as organically as possible for two adult relatives who'd never met before. He wasn't perfect, but I loved him. I still do, even with him gone. And I think he loved me back. At least, he told me so once. I'm grateful that I got the chance to meet him and get to know him before he died, even for such a short amount of time.

Three hundred thirteen days, according to my calendar. And the bulk of it, either he was trapped behind the walls of Carrefour or I was too upset or busy to meet him. But he never gave up on me. He waited days and days until I eventually visited our café and found him there, hoping I'd show up.

I shove my textbook onto the floor, and it slams shut with a satisfying thud. Lulu hisses but then hops back on my bed and circles my head before tucking herself inside the cavity beneath my chin. Her tail stretches across my throat like a noose, but her purring acts as an agitator, bringing forth all my frustrations to the surface of my heart.

How could I have missed my opportunity?

How could the door have closed so fast, even before we could launch Project Valentine?

How could I have fallen for the universe's bait and switch?

◆ ◆ ◆

"Napping again?" Mom switches on the light, causing me to jackknife upright in bed. Lulu ninja-lunges off my body, then bounds out the bedroom door to our family room.

"What time is it?" I shield my eyes from the blinding lamp and yawn. I must've fallen asleep when I got home from campus, as it's well after dark, and I haven't begun studying for my midterm exam yet.

"It's after seven. I thought you'd have eaten dinner and already left for the grocery store." Still in her scrubs from her shift today, she kneels next to my bed while gathering the college textbooks and notes scattered on my rug.

"Oh, no. I'm late for work." After whipping back my blankets, I scramble toward my closet, searching for my uniform. I never used to forget important things such as my work shift. When my essays were due. Study meetings at the library. These past two weeks have been more of a hazy suspension of time for me than living. Except the real world continues charging forward, while I'm adrift, missing Kyle. God, I'm going to lose my job and flunk out of college if I don't snap out of my zombie mode soon. But a big part of me doesn't care.

"Look, sweetheart. You can't keep sleeping by day and studying by night. If vampire hours don't kill you, they'll drive you crazy." She follows me into our shared microbathroom while I splash cold water on my face and power brush my teeth. Then she hands me a towel. "Trust me, it's not a successful wellness strategy."

"Then why do you work the graveyard shift at the hospital so often?"

"Who says I'm not crazy?"

Okay, Mom's got a point there. Crazy protective? Crazy perfectionist? Crazy helicopter mom? All of the above. She's the prototype momzilla. But at least she never sleeps through her work shift's start time, because she's also crazy punctual.

"Honey, you're still growing, but I'm not, at least not vertically. I know how to find balance. Plus, we need the extra money, which is why I try to pick up the shifts no one wants. When you graduate from college and start a career, we'll both be in a better place."

A pang of something—guilt?—rushes through me. Nothing in Mom's tone, now or before, ever indicated that she blamed me for the austerity in our lives. Now that I'm older and have a sense of the basic things she sacrificed for us by being a single mother, I have a parallel vision of how easy and relaxed her life could've been without the burden of me.

I kiss her cheek, then rush back into my bedroom to search under my bed for my sneakers. I'm so damned late, so I resort to yelling as I slip them on. "Did you happen to bring dinner home with you?"

"No. Sorry, sweetheart. Buy something at the grocery store during your break." But she seems downright chipper. Why can't I borrow some of her levity and energy? And punctuality while I'm at it.

Mom wanders through my bedroom, making my bed and tidying while I run a comb through my hair. "What are these?"

Her exaggerated sigh pierces my running-late anxiety, making me cringe. Glancing in her direction, I recognize the papers she's holding. In a split second, I knew what they were and why her question was laced with notes of irritation.

"Nothing, Mom. I just miss him."

"Oh, Ally-cat, I thought you got rid of Kyle's letters last year. He's not worth it. He never was. He contributed a sperm. That's all."

"Mom, I don't have time to argue about this." What I refrain from adding is *for the fourteenth time in the past two weeks*. Every night, she dishes ad nauseam the same mantra: *No man is worth tears. Ever.* No matter that the man in question was my father. No matter that he died before I even had a chance to really get to know him. No matter that I was supposed to finally meet my grandparents the night he died.

Mom marches out of the room with Kyle's letters in hand.

"Wait. Those are mine!" I chase her in case she plans to do something dramatic, like setting them on fire in the sink. I have so few tangible memories of him that I don't want to lose the things I have.

"Look, it's not healthy to keep dwelling on your biological father. I'm starting to worry about you. I wish I hadn't shared his name with you last year. You need to move on, Allison."

Ugh. I cringe whenever she calls me Allison. If she uses my middle name, I'd better run for cover.

"Okay. No more Kyle, Mom. I promise. Please, let me have those letters back." Bobbing in front of her while trying to slip on my tennis shoes sends me toppling onto the couch, but at least I stopped her from trashing them.

She hesitates. "He wasn't good enough for me. He certainly didn't deserve you, sweetie. A struggling alcoholic without a job."

"He was trying to be better. Staying sober, taking classes, and doing some freelance graphic design work. I respected him for that. Even if you were right about him, he can't harm anyone anymore. He's gone now. Dead."

I don't know what changes her mind—maybe it's my quivering chin or my desperate tone—but after a few heartbeats, she relents and hands the letters back to me. Knowing she's liable to regret her decision and dispose of them while I'm at work, I stuff them between the pages of my psych textbook, promising myself to find a new secret hiding place tonight after I get off work.

But this conversation was a wake-up call. Mom will never stop treating me like a child she needs to protect. She'll always be a mama bear, even though I'm legally an adult.

◆　◆　◆

The February winds cut at my exposed cheeks as I huddle in front of Kyle's raw dirt mound of a grave site. No memorial stone has been put in place yet, but I expect it probably takes a little while. After all, no one knew he was going to die two weeks ago. You usually can't plan for that kind of thing unless someone is terminally ill.

This morning's cemetery visit is the first time I've been with Kyle since his wake. I almost decided to attend his funeral mass two weeks ago, but Mom convinced me not to skip my college classes. Her argument made sense. After all, I'll have to pay back my student loans whether or not I attend. And I won't be able to get a good-paying job if I don't pass. Kyle wouldn't have wanted me to fail. So instead of kneeling in a church pew, I sat through my lecture in memory of him. And blinked away stray tears so they wouldn't drip on my laptop. I couldn't concentrate on any notes as my professor droned on, so I might as well have skipped and said one final prayer over his urn.

Later that afternoon, I sneaked into the empty church and found a discarded program from Kyle's funeral mass under a pew. On the back page, it stated the cemetery's address. I didn't find the nerve to come to visit him until now.

Even without his name marking it, I know exactly where he is located due to the clusters of bright new silk flowers sprouting from the small snowdrifts. Someone had even planted a metallic pinwheel that zips along at high velocity in the gusting wind. Most of the other grave sites are adorned with sun-faded and withered flowers and Christmas decorations or stubs of candles.

"Happy birthday, Kyle. You would've turned thirty-eight today." Tonight was our original night. Our plan A, Project Valentine. I was supposed to meet his family. My family. He was going to introduce me as his birthday surprise to my grandparents. Then Kyle moved our introduction up by a few weeks because of his impending court date. But even with plan B, our surprise party never happened.

Today, on his birthday, I'm standing among ghosts and headstones in a cemetery. Kyle's mound of dirt sits right in front of a marble headstone that memorializes two people. A couple. Their family name is different from his, but given the dates chiseled from the stone, I suspect they are his grandparents—my great-grandparents. She lived into her eighties, and he almost made it to a hundred. With such extreme longevity in this bloodline, why didn't Kyle even make it to forty?

The slice of birthday cake I unwrap without taking my mittens off shivers as much as I do. The candle refuses to catch fire in the gusts scattering dried pine needles over the frozen ground. So I sing "Happy Birthday" to Kyle, wishing he were with me to blow out his own candle.

Has he been blowing out my few attempts to light it? The thought warms me despite the frigid morning air. My breath mere puffs of steam crystallizing in front of me.

"I'm sorry I missed your funeral mass. Wish I'd skipped class to attend. I shouldn't have listened to Mom." My nose drips in the wind, and my eyes blur. I nibble the slice of cake that I bought last night from the grocery store's bakery section after my shift ended, but it has zero taste and is about as easy to swallow as sand. He never ate sweets anyway. So much for Project Valentine. We never got around to ordering his real birthday cake.

"When I called your cell phone, your sister told me you died of medical complications. What happened, Kyle? Heart attack? Stroke? Aneurysm?" I should've asked more questions when she answered his phone, but I was too shocked. I could hardly process what she was saying, let alone delve deeper. I'm surprised I even remembered those details. His obituary didn't state anything about the cause of death. I didn't overhear anyone mentioning it at the wake. He behaved normally when we met earlier that day. Excited even. Maybe a little breathless? "I hope dying didn't hurt much."

How can he be gone?

God, I miss him. Especially the little things. Waiting with me whenever I had to catch the bus. Chatting with me as I sketched his profile. Never complaining if I had to cancel one of our meetups. He always seemed so grateful for any time we spent together. As if we were making up for the lost years.

As if I were a gift to him instead of the other way around.

The ache in my chest grows with each passing moment. After placing the cake next to Kyle's mound, I step back into a frigid spot of sunlight, wondering what else to say to his grave, if anything at all. A red bird swoops in to peck at the crumbs. Suddenly a larger black bird dive-bombs the food, but the little one chases it away before returning to continue snacking.

The kerfuffle reminds me of one of the first times Kyle and I met for coffee at our café. A guy at a nearby table had started arguing with his date, a young woman. When his yelling grew belligerent, Kyle stepped in to intervene, but the guy refused to back off and turned his aggression on Kyle. For a hot minute, I worried that the guy—who was easily twice Kyle's size when he stood up—would throw punches.

Instead of countering, Kyle calmly pointed out the security camera and warned him that the police might find the video evidence helpful in the future. Then he escorted the young woman outside, ordered her a car, and stayed by her side until it arrived. She left alone. Safe. When Kyle returned to me, he shrugged off the incident. "Don't ever let anyone bully you, Ally."

He never brought it up again. But the lengths he would go to protect a stranger endeared him to me even more. It wasn't until months later that I appreciated the full force of what he'd done. And why.

My pilgrimage to visit Kyle's grave site ends prematurely with my fingers growing numb and shivers overtaking my body. It doesn't help that I have another midterm exam this afternoon, so I could use a little more study time to prepare.

"I'll come back soon, Kyle. I'll bring you a coffee next time."

But before I leave, I brush away windblown debris and snow from the foot of the silk flower stems jabbed into the dirt. With my car key, I scrape a little groove and bury upright one of my most cherished gifts from Kyle. He earned it fair and square while he was alive, so he should display it proudly, even in death.

His one-month sobriety chip. I'm keeping his six-month chip for myself. And hiding it somewhere Mom will never find it.

Chapter 10

ALLY

BEFORE

A couple of weeks after first meeting Kyle, I met him for coffee at a nearby café, and we agreed to meet the following week at the same place. That date came and went without Kyle joining me. I showed up for two Saturdays in a row, figuring I'd mixed up our rendezvous time. He didn't show up then either.

What the heck? Did he stand me up on purpose? Did I do something to offend him? Or had Mom intervened? He let me believe he was interested in continuing to get to know me. I didn't normally forget details, so I couldn't have gotten the location wrong.

Maybe he didn't want to deal with having a daughter after all these years of not knowing about me.

Since the weather had been mild, I'd trekked over to the house where I'd met him the first time. I didn't knock, but while I waited nearby on the sidewalk, an older couple exited the front door. I'm pretty sure they must have been Kyle's parents—my grandparents. Actually, they appeared quite a bit younger than I'd expected. My grandparents on Mom's side sported silver hair and withered postures. These two seemed downright sprightly in comparison.

"Excuse me, please." On impulse, I jogged toward them, stopping a polite distance away. I hoped my smile would come off as friendly. "I'm sorry to interrupt, but are you the Dobrescus?"

"Yes, we are." The woman's face revealed her surprise, but her eyes softened, and her demeanor turned welcoming. "Can I help you with something, dear?"

"I was wondering . . ." Butterflies spiraled in my stomach, and heat radiated from my T-shirt collar, betraying the blush that I knew was washing over my face. "Is Kyle around?"

"No, dear. He's not." She glanced at the man—my grandfather? He nodded, then opened the car door on the driver's side. She bit her lip, pausing for a moment, then answered slowly as if choosing her words carefully. "We're going to visit him now. May we tell him who dropped by?"

Oh, crap. What should I say? Whether or not he told his parents about me had never come up in our conversations. But since he didn't invite me into his house, even when we sat on his front step eating cake, I can't assume he did. And I didn't want to surprise them right now. Somehow, *I'm your long-lost granddaughter you never knew about* might go a little smoother with Kyle leading the charge.

Someday. I hoped.

"No, thanks. I'll catch him another time." Waving, I turned, sprinting away before they could ask any more questions. Dammit. I still didn't know why he'd stood me up.

◆　◆　◆

A little over a week after my brush with Kyle's parents, his first letter arrived. He was pretty smart about it, actually, not including a return address on the envelope. My name and address were typed on a label with a single sheet of paper inside.

When I came home after school one day, the envelope was one of a couple of pieces of mail Mom had left for me on the kitchen counter. Mom must've assumed it was a notice from school or the library or junk mail. I didn't open it right away. My acceptance to Spring Mountain University was the first piece of mail I opened. How could I not? I'd already been notified through my online application, so the news wasn't a surprise, but here was something tangible for me to hold. To see. Physical evidence that an institution of higher learning wanted me to study there. Whether or not I picked this school, I was college bound.

By the time I'd celebrated with Mom, scared Lulu into hiding with my end zone dance, and called her parents, I'd forgotten that I had mail to read. I'd shoved Kyle's envelope in my backpack and didn't notice it again until the next morning at school.

"Hey, Ally, you dropped this." Jenna handed me the envelope. After my teacher had started the class, I stealth-slid my finger through the back to rip it open as quietly as possible. On the page, Kyle had typed:

> *Dear Ally,*
>
> *I'm sorry I didn't meet you at the coffee shop as we had planned. I'm now living in a full-time rehabilitation center for substance abuse. My move was sudden, so I didn't have a chance to let you know. Since I'll be living here for a year or so, I won't be able to meet you for coffee, but I hope you don't mind continuing to get to know each other through snail mail. When I was little, we called it pen pals. No pressure, but I hope you decide to write back.*
>
> *Kyle*

My stomach clenched as I read the words *substance abuse*. That news hit like a brick wall. But as I thought back to both times I met with him, I couldn't remember anything unusual or off about his behavior.

As much as I craved all the details about him instantly, I had to admit that Kyle being a patient in a rehabilitation place solved one logistic headache: trying to leave the apartment on Saturday mornings without piquing Mom's curiosity.

Two more snail mail letters from him later, I learned his answers to my questions. That he never graduated from SMU, either, but still took occasional classes at the local community college. That he used to play bass guitar in a garage band called Silence Deconstructed. That he never married, though he'd proposed to someone once. That he was pretty confident that he never fathered any other kids. He also shared his family's health history (his pancreatitis, a sprinkling of cancer, light on heart disease, heavy on depression, addiction, and Catholic guilt, but my great-grandfather lived to see a hundred years old).

Most importantly, he answered every single question I'd asked about his alcoholism and his court-ordered rehabilitation.

◆ ◆ ◆

A week or two later, I returned home after school, my mind occupied by thoughts of prom, graduation, and college. As I closed our apartment's front door behind me, Lulu rushed to my feet and wouldn't let me enter the apartment before I showered her with adoration. After thirty seconds of allowing me to scratch behind her ears and under her chin, she dismissed me.

When I stood back up, Mom was in the center of our living room, with her arms crossed and tapping her foot. Her right eyebrow arched higher than her left.

"Allison Marie, what are these?"

Squinting, I caught a glimpse of some white envelopes in her hand. Three, to be exact. My stomach plummeted somewhere down toward my ankles. How had she found them? I stared at my shoes, not knowing where to start. I hadn't expected an ambush. Then again, I hadn't expected Mom to go snooping under my mattress while I was at school.

But I knew exactly what she was holding—my letters from Kyle.

"Did you reply?"

Crap. I couldn't lie. Even if I tried, she'd see right through me. In fact, not answering was more of an admission than anything else.

"Yes. You gave me his name." I tucked a piece of hair behind my ear, still standing in front of our apartment door, wondering if I should dash out. You didn't tick off my mom and expect to get away with it. "Did you seriously think I'd say, 'Oh, great, my birth father's name is Kyle Dobrescu; mystery solved. I have everything I need in life now.' Come on, Mom."

"Yes. Or at least let me know you were thinking of contacting him." Her eyes were red, and her nose was swollen. A pang of guilt ran through me. I dug the toe of my shoe into the worn parquet floor. She gave me a side-eye. "Did Jenna put you up to this? The two of you have a knack for getting into trouble together."

"No, Mom. And before you ask, neither did Taryn or Maric." While I'd been giving all my friends at school updates at lunch ever since I learned Kyle's name, Jenna warned me that being alone with him might not be safe. She insisted I text her whenever I met him so she could follow my location on our phones in case I needed help. But seeing Mom's reaction now, I should've planned more carefully.

Why hadn't I included Mom in this process? But the answer was no mystery. I didn't want her to stop me. Besides, I was an adult now. It had taken eighteen years of pestering her to finally relinquish his name. It might've taken another eighteen to get her approval to meet him. I didn't want to wait that long, though I'd dreaded seeing the pain on her face once she discovered I'd done it without her blessing.

The same pain I was seeing on her face right now.

"I'm sorry, Mom."

"He has our address. He knows where you live." She waved the envelopes in the air as if I didn't know that I'd received mail from him. "You could be in danger."

"Kyle's living in a rehab facility and will be staying there for a year." While I thought that would calm her down, she started pacing and using clipped, sharp words.

"Rehab? What kind of rehab?"

"Substance abuse."

"Substance abuse?" She stopped cold to stare at me. "What kind? Alcohol? Drugs? Prescriptions?"

"Vodka."

"Of course, he's an alcoholic. How did I not see this coming? Your father was in a band when I met him. Partying all night, every night." She popped up, pacing again. This time circling me like those old wagon trains did whenever the settlers were under attack. Or sharks. "How in God's name did I allow this to happen?"

"Look, he's a nice guy, Mom. And funny. You dated him, at least for a little while. Something about him appealed to you, right? You even said you weren't interested in his helping us financially or otherwise. This is low risk."

"Convicted prisoners are nice too. When the alcohol doesn't get him high enough, it'll be something stronger. Opioids are a big problem everywhere these days. Then it's 'Can I borrow money?' This isn't low risk, honey. This is catastrophic." She guided me by the arm to sit me down on the couch, then squeezed my hands. "You don't get it. I see these broken people on a constant rotation through the emergency room. Half out of their minds. Possessed. All they can think about is their next fix. They beg me for prescription painkillers as if they would trade a limb for them. I've called child services to protect their children. I'd never have willingly exposed you to him if I'd known he was an alcoholic."

"Okay, don't overreact. It's not like that. I've seen Kyle twice in person. He was calm—normal and sober, even—both times. Alcohol isn't illegal. Plus he's totally up front about it and getting the help he needs. That's positive, right? You've always said you believe in second chances."

"You've *met* him?" Her voice turned icy. She stared me down as if I were an alien. Crap, I shouldn't have revealed that, but I figured she'd already assumed we'd met in person by this conversation. She wasn't saying anything. And she squeezed my wrist so tightly my fingers began tingling.

"Yes." I barely eked out my answer, but I knew she heard me because the vein in her neck started pulsing. "Mom?"

After releasing me, she leaned back against the cushion to rub her eyes, then her temples. I'd never seen her this upset before. Scared. She was a live wire. I knew enough not to add to her distress.

"I'm sorry, Mom. I wish I could go back in time and let you know that I was planning to meet him. You could've even come with me. I thought I was helping you because I figured that might be awkward for you, considering the last time you saw him, you told him you were pregnant. But I should've asked and not assumed."

While she still didn't answer, at least the redness in her face started to dissipate. Her breathing became more controlled. I just wish she'd look me in the eyes so I'd know if I'd been forgiven.

I placed my cheek against her torso and hugged her to me, both of us sprawled on the couch. As soon as she stroked my hair, I knew I'd won a temporary reprieve. "Please don't hate me."

"I could never hate you, Ally. But listen to me. That man is the reason I didn't finish at Spring Mountain University. Your biological father wanted nothing to do with us and told me to get an abortion. You wouldn't have been here today if he'd gotten his way."

But had he really stolen her future, or did she let it slip away? Yes, he got her pregnant, but then again, she could've had the abortion and resumed her life without much of a hiccup. Or given me up for adoption. Thank God she didn't. But she'd had options, and she'd made a choice. She also could've kept in touch with her parents. And Kyle. She didn't have to raise me all by herself. Hell, she could've even gone on a date or two or found her soulmate to share the burden of parenting.

"Sweetheart, you are on the verge of so many exciting opportunities. Within a few weeks, you'll decide which college you want to accept. I don't want your biological father to take that away from you too. He has a way of screwing things up. Trust me."

My borrowed prom dress hung inside my closet, ready to be worn next month. My date was Chase, a cute guy from school I'd been crushing on, and we were going as a group with Jenna, Taryn, Marie, and their dates. Inside my desk were the offers of admission to four different in-state public colleges. I had to decide which one I'd send my deposit to in the next few weeks. Then a few weeks after prom, I'd wear a cap and gown to claim my high-school diploma with honors. Mom was right. My future would be insanely exciting.

But now that I'd met Kyle, I also wanted to get to know him. Somehow, I'd appeased Mom enough that I left our argument before she could stipulate that I never write him again.

But even better, I never promised to not see him again either.

So, technically speaking, I wasn't disobeying her.

Because hidden in my backpack was the fourth letter Kyle had mailed me, with instructions on who to contact at Carrefour to be authorized as an approved visitor.

Chapter 11

MARGARET

AFTER

Turns out I'm not the only person who visited Kyle's grave on his birthday. Had he lived two weeks longer, he'd have turned thirty-eight today, Valentine's Day. Instead, he's a forever thirty-seven-year-old.

Sprigs of mismatched red silk flowers stand jabbed into the frozen ground next to the tasteful bunch I already planted, and even a pinwheel spins at alarming speeds. At least he's being loved by his friends. Remembered. Missed.

And crumbs—from what? chocolate cake?—lay scattered over the still raw dirt. The birds can enjoy a little snack. I'm surprised the gusting wind hasn't already swept everything away from his little mound.

Kyle and I agreed on few things, but one was a shared loathing of cold weather. I hope he can't feel the igloo he's buried inside. Spring can't come soon enough. As if my wish conjured reality, a bright-red cardinal swoops by me, then lands on a nearby pine branch to watch.

What would happen if I brought my gardening shovel when the ground thaws? Would anyone notice if his dirt sank a little lower?

Maybe not if I planted a square of sod over the top. I could exhume his urn and bring his ashes home. Hold him again. Protect him. But from what? Or whom? Silly whim. Who could possibly hurt him now? I suppose I'm just experiencing the aftershock of being his mom, not dissimilar to amputees who complain of phantom sensations from their lost limbs.

Something glints as a sunbeam cuts through the low, heavy clouds and shines nearby. Kneeling beside his grave, I lean closer. At the base of the memorial flower stems, a tiny red aluminum coin peeps upright, half-buried in the frost-covered dirt. I know exactly what it is—an Alcoholics Anonymous sobriety chip. Kyle had several of these stowed among his things throughout the house from the many, many times he attempted and then reattempted to get sober.

One of his rehab friends must've visited the grave and left it for him. A trophy. They all battled together every day. This one made it a whole month sober.

Too bad Kyle lost the war.

When I called the hospital administrator to request a review of his medical records or at least the meds he'd been prescribed while he was in the emergency room, she fell silent.

"I'm a nurse. I understand how complicated medical care can be—especially for my son." I try but fail to keep the begging tone out of my voice. "Look, I'm just trying to find answers."

What I refrained from articulating to this curt woman is that over the past couple of decades, I'd collected thousands of pages of his medical notes, invoices, insurance claims, and records for his doctors' appointments, hospital visits, and pharmacy, all organized chronologically. Every time he saw some new specialist, I'd review his records to stay up to date on his diagnoses and meds.

Had I overlooked something with his last ER visit? How could Kyle have died of a drug overdose, as the autopsy report concluded? On the other hand, maybe I'm just trying to find some kind of proof that my own bad parenting decisions hadn't driven my son to commit suicide.

While the admin agreed to order an internal review of the ER visit from the night before he died, she advised that the audit could take up to two months. In the meantime, they offered to suspend billing pending the outcome. But during our phone conversation, I got the distinct impression she would've said absolutely anything to get me to hang up.

If her enunciation had razor blades, I'd have died by a thousand cuts.

◆　◆　◆

After yet another evening of not eating dinner and another night of not sleeping, I say goodbye as Martin leaves for work, then trudge down the flight of stairs to our basement.

How many days have I been at this? How many boxes have I unpacked, sifted through, repacked, and moved into the checked pile? I'd barely cracked the surface of all things Kyle when Kimber visited last week.

Our basement is a pseudotribute to all our nearly fifty years of Dobrescu family life, including two house moves, one former business now closed, two sets of parents passing away, two kids, and three grandkids' worth of stuff collected. And by *stuff*, I mean meaningless discarded and forgotten junk stowed alongside important documents, photographs, and treasured mementos in stack after dusty stack of boxes. No home-organizing diva would ever willingly tackle our basement on one of those popular reality TV shows.

But more than that, this was Kyle's man cave. He may have slept upstairs in his bedroom, but he lived his life down here. His guitars and band equipment are woven through, under, and in between the banks of boxes. When he moved back in—after his bandmates grew up and embraced adulthood, leaving him in the dust—he relocated all his worldly possessions to this space, including his legal papers, his medical bills, and all his rehab stuff. Somewhere in this altar to hoarding might be a clue about Boo.

It's the first time in years I've had any inclination to do more than throw crap into an empty box for Martin to schlep downstairs. Once, decades ago, in my tackle-the-world, energetic youth, I made a New Year's resolution to label everything, only to get derailed after organizing a dozen boxes.

Back then, both Martin and I rejoiced that we were through the business of birthing children. We were raising our beautiful daughter, finally out of diapers and cribs. We were well on our way through elementary school. Life had relaxed into a comfortable routine. So ten years after Kimber was born, when my home pregnancy test showed positive, a new baby's impending arrival knocked my world off its axis, and I never quite regained my bearings. Kyle was the result of my surprise second pregnancy—not counting the miscarriage I had when Kimber was still a toddler.

Sure, I was as good as any B-rated actress at faking my enthusiasm for restarting the newborn days. Kyle was an easygoing little guy, and with Kimber a tween, I had a built-in extra set of hands to help care for him as a toddler. But I resented being back at the starting gate. When Martin's sole proprietorship business hit rocky times, I went back to work and picked up as many shifts nursing at the hospital as I could to help keep us financially stable. I spent less time with the kids. Soon, Kimber moved away to college. Those years flew by too quickly.

It was just Martin, thirteen-year-old Kyle, and me. That's when the floor collapsed from under us. How can your life go from normal to hell in one trip to the mall? Only Martin didn't know. I never told him. He was so busy scrambling to try to save his business and working around the clock I don't think he even noticed that our lives had imploded.

And I made Kyle promise never to tell him either.

Now, rummaging through my umpteenth box of the day, I open the lid to find half a dozen bottles of vodka, some still full.

Oh, Kyle.

Sitting down, I let the wave of grief wash over me. Sometimes they are tsunamis, and I give up for the rest of the day. Other times, the waves are stormy and make my heart and lungs collapse; but then they move away as quickly as they came. I find it's best if I tread water and breathe through the moment. It's much worse if I fight it. Instead, I mutter a little prayer for my son's eternal soul to rest in the graces of God. Breathe in, two-three-four; breathe out, two-three-four.

I expected to find evidence of his addiction, and this isn't the first stash I've stumbled across in my sleuthing for Boo. However, it reminds me of Kyle's mortality. His brokenness. His limits. At least I haven't found any tourniquets, syringes, or unopened packets of powder.

Yet.

Kyle never gave me the impression he was using hard drugs, but I guess with one abusive addiction, a mom always worries about the worst-case scenario. And the coroner's autopsy report flagged an overdose. What other skeletons did Kyle hide in these boxes?

Maybe Martin was right. Maybe Kyle did commit suicide.

The truth is, he wasn't a functioning alcoholic. It started with binge drinking vodka until he developed a liter-per-day habit. I was either too naive or in denial. He was in his midtwenties before I consciously recognized that he not only had drinking dependency but that he'd reached the point of self-abuse. His hands would shake. His edgy mood swings became as predictable as the lever arm of an oil drill.

Kyle wasn't living with us then. I knew he partied with a fast crowd, playing in a band, but he was an adult. He lived with a bunch of guys. Paid rent. Worked as a waiter while wrangling every band gig they could book. He designed their T-shirts and cut demos. Though he lived locally, we hardly ever saw him unless we invited him for dinner or he needed to use our garage for band practice.

So it wasn't until we got a phone call from one of his roommates that he was behind paying rent that my little bubble of denial burst. Kyle hadn't launched. Not really. He couldn't hold down a job because he kept sleeping through his restaurant shifts. His buddies were fed up living with a drunken slob. They held an intervention, and he shaped up.

Instead of giving him handouts, Martin hired Kyle as his only employee—part time, afternoons. His hours ebbed and flowed—but at least we knew he had a steady source of income. It also gave us a glimpse into the chaos that had become our son's world.

We were his parachute. He moved back in with us, pissed off at the world and his friends in particular for giving up on their rock and roll dreams. One by one, his buddies dropped out of the band, moved out of their group house, started careers, and got married.

Kyle was in his late twenties by the time I noticed a dangerous pattern emerging. His binging would intensify until he had a medical crisis that put him in the ER. The doctors would stabilize him and prescribe antianxiety meds. He'd flirt with sobriety for a few weeks to a month. But he'd swallow those prescription pills at a much faster rate than the label recommended. As soon as he heard the words *no more refills*, he switched to his readily available and legally obtainable drug of choice, vodka. Eventually the alcohol-induced seizures came. Which would land him right back in the ER, and we started all over again.

At first, his binge cycles were long. After one of his experiences with detox and rehab, he even lasted six months sober. I believed he'd kicked his addiction and found his direction into adulthood. He worked extra hard for Martin, attended daily AA meetings, reconnected with Kimber, and brushed the cobwebs off his résumé. Most nights I'd come home from work to him hovering over the stove, preparing dinner worthy of any newspaper restaurant reviewer. He even started interviewing for jobs while composing music in our basement every evening. And every month, he'd hand me his new AA sobriety chip. I held my breath. I danced the end zone dance.

The only one who was fooled was me.

That autumn, he and his girlfriend attended a friend's destination wedding and celebrated a little too hard. Actually, he was so belligerent, I'm surprised the airline allowed him to board the flight home. I'm also amazed Becca continued dating him.

After that, his cycles spun faster and faster until we could hardly document his sober time before he crashed again. I'd find his stash and pour bottles of alcohol down the sink. I even came home from work one day and found him midseizure on the floor. Then we'd start over.

Time and again, I'd reached my limit at helplessly watching him self-destruct, so I'd kick him out. In my exasperation, I'd hoped that if we gave Kyle an ultimatum— drinking or a nice warm bed—he'd choose us. But Martin never agreed with me and refused to let Kyle suffer tough love. In retrospect, I'm not surprised our mixed signals backfired. Somehow, Martin would find Kyle wandering the streets and either put him up in a hotel for a couple of nights or drive him around until he was sober enough to come back home.

We'd get the weirdest calls from the police for disorderly conduct and even trespassing. Once, someone found his wallet in the back of their car—we later deduced that he'd walked down a line of parked cars looking for his. Since he couldn't find his keys, he'd slept in the back seat of an unlocked car and left his wallet behind.

Our silver lining was that at least after his DUI, he lost his license and couldn't drive anymore. We didn't have to worry about him getting hurt or, infinitely worse, hurting someone else. With the credit card Martin gave him, Kyle was one Uber ride away from any destination he wanted.

But that wasn't my real son. He may have lived his life balancing on the edge of a cliff, but at his core, he was a good person. Every once in a blue moon, his true self would shine through and blow my mind.

Like that one afternoon I was driving Kyle to some event in downtown Chicago—I don't even remember why.

"Hey, Mom. Can you pull over?" Kyle unbuckled his seat belt and unlocked the door. "Stop the car!"

"What happened? Why?" I'd already thrown on my signal to change lanes, but given I was navigating gridlocked city traffic during rush hour, I didn't have many options. It took me at least a block to maneuver to a lane closer to the sidewalk. He'd jumped out of the car before I could come to a complete stop, then jogged back to where we'd passed.

By the time I'd driven around the city block to circle back, I'd found Kyle kneeling on the sidewalk and assisting an older gentleman who'd collapsed. Kyle had already called for an ambulance, had helped him phone his daughter to assure her he was fine, and was redirecting pedestrian traffic around them.

Despite all Kyle's problems and complications stemming from our past, I believe my son was a good person at his core. An empath. Vulnerable. At least, I hope he was. He helped those in need. He cared about others but not himself.

Never himself.

When he was sober, Kyle was the son I'd always dreamed about. The one I convinced myself he could be full time if he tried hard enough to avoid temptation. But when he was drunk, he could be the devil incarnate. Or comatose. I was never sure which I would encounter.

As such, the only time I could truly relax was while Kyle lived in a residential rehabilitation facility like he did at Carrefour for a few months last year. Our home was peaceful and quiet. And I could sleep at night knowing Kyle was in a full-care facility with rules I'd never been able to enforce here at home. God love Miss Genevieve, because I owed her for every easy breath I'd inhaled last year.

And now, every new box I unpack in the basement shreds my heart into ribbon curls. Something in each one reveals a new element of Kyle, sometimes good—he used a tattered picture of the two of us as a bookmark in one of his rehab manuals. And sometimes not so much—my missing debit card stuffed inside a tennis shoe.

Did I ever really know my son?

It's been three weeks since Kyle passed away, and already I'm suffering a full-blown existential crisis. I failed at motherhood. Not only did my son die an early death, but I also couldn't help him change his lifestyle choices. One kid launched. One crashed and burned from our nest. And I couldn't stop it.

Nothing, not a single note or knickknack in my search, has revealed any clue proving my mystery granddaughter exists. Nothing but the conversation Martin had with him a year or so ago. Had he heard Kyle correctly?

"Please, Kyle, send me some sign. You had a daughter, right? Help me find her."

I stack my current box on top of my already-searched pile and reach for one of his many backpacks near his desk. Papers. School notebooks. A list of his current class schedule for this semester, and I have a half-baked idea of sneaking into the back of one of his lectures to experience what he would've learned had he survived. Perhaps one or two of his classmates might be able to give me more insight into my son's head.

Sifting through the stack of papers, I'm about to discard the whole untidy batch to rifle through later when an envelope slips onto my lap. In it is a bank receipt for a cashier's check dated last December. Exactly one month before he died, he withdrew several thousand dollars, almost bringing his bank account balance to zero. I didn't even know he had any assets to his name.

Behind the receipt was a purchase contract for a used car.

Chapter 12

KYLE

Carrefour's shiny new website was coming along really well, if I did say so myself. After creating their new logo, I dug up an ancient digital camera. With a little elbow grease and editing, I staged some brochure-worthy glam shots of the interior reception area and exterior. I took a couple of candid photos of our counselors in different group therapy sessions, all patients blurred past recognition, and got some damned good reference quotes to promote the place. My closet-size bedroom looked downright cozy and charming with the filters I'd used. And even the cafeteria food appeared appetizing.

I might as well be marketing upscale dorm living at a university. The kind of college where a judge sent you but you couldn't graduate until your court-ordered time expired.

Lately I'd been building a secure patient portal, which was particularly dicey given privacy regulations. I was no lawyer, but hell, I got the point of privacy. My mom once tried to convince me to give her power of attorney over me should I be incapacitated, but I'd never relinquish that gem of adulthood. No, thank you.

The director, Miss Genevieve, was a tough customer, but I scored points this past month. If Mom kept delivering Mrs. Roman's cookie goodness, and I pulled my weight by making Carrefour look all spiffy on the internet, then I could be promoted to peon rather than subpeon.

Next up, I plan to campaign for better computers and some cool software.

Working in the Center's office was my oasis. Even so, every goddamned minute of every goddamned day, I wanted to sneak out of here to a bar. Couldn't I get a reward for good behavior? For every week I was continuously sober, I should be able to earn one hour of unchaperoned free time.

Crap, who needed an hour? Just fifteen minutes.

Jeez, I'd journaled my ass off every day, bled on the pages listing how I'd wronged my family and those who care about me, why they were worth struggling to override my cravings. Somewhere in all those pages, I realized that my pilot light was still burning. I had hope, especially now that I'd met Ally.

But nothing—no amount of journaling, AA meetings, or talk therapy sessions—ever diminished the allure of vodka. The need. The temptation.

Just one drink.

Sometimes it felt like a tug-of-war between sumo wrestlers, and I was the rope.

And then other times, I was that guy with an angel and a devil on his shoulders, both pitching their own side. But now that I had Ally to stay sober for, the angel's side was stronger.

If our group sessions in rehab taught me anything, it was that I wasn't alone. We are all learning to manage our cravings. How to coach ourselves through the rough spots. To take things minute by minute, if need be. To remember our goals and why we should stay sober.

I could relate.

But what eroded my patience was the therapists' new-age mumbo jumbo helping me dig through layer after protective layer of self-deception to get to the root problem. No fucking way. I'd evaded their efforts so far. If I'd grown scars over my core fault line, why in the hell would I want to rip the scab off to expose what I'd been hiding all these years?

I'd rather get help building a résumé. Or networking contacts. Or practicing interview skills. Or maybe the Center could even officially hire me as their IT guy and pay me for the website development work I'd started. They certainly could use an IT specialist on their staff. Hell, their operating platform was so obsolete new versions of software and search engines weren't even compatible. I could help them.

The clock—the analog clock on the wall—showed that in five more minutes, I was scheduled for my next group therapy session.

Miss Genevieve exited her office, stood in front of my desk, and crossed her arms, assessing me. The exotic muumuu she had draped around her ample girth absorbed all color from planet Earth. The scarf wrapped around her head was so large it could be hiding a beehive hairdo circa the 1960s. But as far as Carrefour was concerned, she was our queen.

"Mm-hmm."

Clearing my throat, I sat a little straighter. Shit, did she catch me surfing the internet without permission? I was only pricing out new computers for Carrefour. Scout's honor.

"I've been watching you, Mr. Dobrescu. You're smart. Maybe too smart." If she was trying to dish compliments, she should edit out the underlying notes of threats. I blinked first, but then I wasn't sure if this was a contest or not. "Don't make me regret helping you out, son."

"Yes, ma'am." I gulped. I couldn't help it. Shit, no nun I'd ever encountered in my Catholic grade school could wield a temper as sharp as this swarthy lady.

After leaning on my desk and lingering there until I was ready to confess all my sins as well as those of every other resident here, Miss Genevieve turned to leave the office.

On my desk, she'd left behind a folded piece of paper. After she was out of sight, I steeled myself to open it up.

> Kyle Dobrescu
> Approved visitor: Allison Marie O'Leary

◆ ◆ ◆

This morning, I mopped the reception floor, wiped the dining area's plexi-topped tables, and even spruced up a vase of flowers to cheer up the place. The second hand took a year to make each minute revolution around the Center's clock. I even hopped on the treadmill, hoping that jogging a mile or two would help bring my anxiety level down a few notches.

No matter. By the time two o'clock arrived, I was pacing out in the hallway, waiting for my name to be called. Somehow, I'd convinced Mom and Dad that I had an extra therapy session this afternoon so they wouldn't bother dropping by today. Miss Genevieve might limit my office time since I wouldn't be providing home-baked cookies this week, but who cares?

"Kyle?" My counselor fist-bumped me before allowing me access through the door.

My pulse jackhammered as I slipped into the dining hall, our designated visitors' area. Ally sat at an empty table by the windows. Good choice. She was wearing a lemon-colored sundress, but with the air-conditioning blasting through nearby vents, she untied the sleeves of the shirt draped over her shoulders, then slipped it on. Though I hadn't seen her since our coffee date over a month ago, I'd thought about her nonstop.

"Hey." Trying to keep my pace casual and my small talk easy, as if any sharp movement might cause Ally to panic and run away, I approached her table and then sat across from her. Her hands remained folded in her lap. No hug. I'd love one, but only when she was ready. "Where's your backpack?"

"Temporarily incapacitated. I think the bomb squad is detonating it out back." Her bubbly laughter brought my pulse down to a healthier pace. On the table in front of her rested a thick spiral notebook and a couple of pencils.

"Hope you don't leave thirty pounds lighter than when you arrived."

"You mean like you? Don't they feed you here?"

"C'mon, cut me some slack. Did my mom put you up to this?" My quip didn't distract her from her point, so after a moment's pause, I leaned forward and admitted, "That's the risk when a foodie is restricted to institutional food."

"Sounds a lot like my near future. Campus cafeteria food."

"Oh—did you decide which college to accept?" I tried to wipe any hint of concern off my face, hoping she didn't choose somewhere out of town.

"Yeah. Hemingway University. I paid my deposit this week."

"So you're going to be a Dagger." Could my pride grow any deeper? Nope. And local, thank God. "Congratulations, Ally. Great school."

What was scrolling through my head at warp speed were ideas on how I could find a job somewhere within walking distance from Hemingway U's campus to spend more time near her. We could meet for lunch once or twice per week next year, once I was free from Carrefour. I could treat her to a nice restaurant, far, far away from any-thing that could be described as *institutional food*. After I save a little money, I might even be able to rent an apartment nearby. Who knows? What if the great deans of admissions would allow me to register and transfer my ancient credits from SMU and my community college?

But I got so carried away that I realized I'd missed most of what she was saying. ". . . the economics department is strong. Plus I'll be able to commute from home for a year or two to save money. Mom offered to help me apply for student loans to cover tuition, but I won a small scholarship. I'm going to work two summer jobs, and then if my class load isn't too crazy, I can get a part-time job somewhere near campus."

Wow, my daughter had plans on her plans. She didn't inherit her work ethic from me. Paternal pride was soon replaced with wonder. Hannah must have been one hell of a mother for Ally to become the driven young person she was.

I could take some tips from Ally. Or at least some life coaching. No entitlement issues with my daughter. She was even trying to ease the financial burden on her mother's shoulders.

Once I realized that she was waiting for my response, I cleared my throat. "Impressive. I'd hire you if I could. What does your mom think of all this?"

"I'm not sure. She says she's happy that I'm staying nearby for the next few years, but before I made my final decision, she tried to convince me to leave Chicago. She kept reminding me that SMU in Mount Vernon is four hours south, and I'd be able to create my own independent life."

"I'm sure she only wants what's best for you." And by Hannah's *what's best for you*, I wondered if she meant the farther away from me, her biological father, the better. I dropped my voice to a whisper level. "Does she know we've met?"

Ally nodded timidly at first. But something new graced her youthful, blemish-free forehead. Frown lines. Hannah could get in our way. As much as I wanted to be a part of Ally's life, I had the uncanny super-power to ruin everything I cared about. Just by being me.

And I didn't want to hurt her.

"Your mom's right. You have to do what's best for you. If going out of town to school is it, then you should consider it."

"Well, I think she's on board for Hemingway U now. She gave me the deposit payment. I'm committed."

My exhale was more audible than I'd hoped, but dang, I couldn't fight the smile that threatened to erupt all over my face. So I ran with it. "Congratulations, Ally. That's great news. You're gonna crush college."

"Mind if I sketch while we talk?" She opened the spiral notebook and picked up one of her pencils, which she explained was actually made of charcoal. "I'm not very good, especially drawing people, but I really love trying."

Well, crap. I could compete for the title of the world's worst art model. But her eyes widened and looked so earnest that instead of turning her down, I shrugged. "Sure, why not?"

"Okay, turn your head this way, and relax your shoulders . . ." She motioned me to move my limbs and parts in different directions until, finally, I'd claimed a pose she liked.

As she twisted her head this way and that and scratched big arcs and lines over her sketchbook page, we spent the next half hour talking about her plans for prom tonight. I squeezed my fists together at the thought of my daughter spending hours with some hormone-driven teen—because that was me twenty years ago—but I kept reminding myself that this is technically Hannah's jurisdiction, not mine. I haven't earned an opinion on the subject.

Fuck it. I only had one daughter. "You'll make sure your date behaves like a gentleman?"

"Um, gross." Red blotches invaded her neck as she realized the subtext of my comment. She couldn't have been more adorable if she were toothless, bald, weighing fifteen pounds, and cooing in a stroller—suddenly I craved seeing her baby pictures. "Don't worry, Mom's already read me the riot act. She's making Chase pick me up at the apartment. And we're going with a group of friends."

Changing the subject was welcome to both of us, so we talked about her tabby cat, Lulu. And how she'd spent a whole birthday weekend painting her room light gray. Hannah surprised her with new throw pillows for her bed.

I was a little less forthcoming about my day-to-day routine. I mean, my existence couldn't be more boring. But she seemed interested in my website work for Carrefour and promised to check it out the next time she was online.

"Done." She turned her sketch pad around for me to see my profile image.

She'd nailed me. Especially my eyes. How the hell did she do that?

Damn, my daughter was an artist. A really good one. I sputtered, trying to find words to convey how fucking impressed I was without sounding over-the-top enthusiastic. "That's incredible. Where did you learn to draw so realistically?"

I guess I must've said the right thing because she blushed and flashed me her dimple as she bit back her smile. Then, of course, she tugged on her ponytail, which made her even more endearing. Classic Ally move whenever she gets nervous or self-conscious.

"I've always liked art." She closed her sketchbook. I hoped she'd let me flip through it someday and see what else she's drawn. "It was my favorite elective in school."

As the counselor came in to announce that visiting time was ending in five minutes, inspiration struck.

"Hey. I want to give you something." After digging in my pocket, I slapped a red aluminum token on the table and slid it over to her. I'd intended to give it to Mom the next time I saw her, but at this moment, it meant more to me to give it to my daughter.

Ally picked it up to examine it closer.

"One month?"

"Yes. I go to Alcoholics Anonymous meetings every night with the other residents. Last night, I earned my thirty-day sobriety chip." What it should really have read was *720 hours*, because even without a drop of liquor accessible in the Center, my struggle was hour by hour. No, actually, more like minute by minute. My brain continually looped back to strategizing how I could smuggle in a bottle of vodka until I coached myself away from the ideas.

She held it in her palm, examining it. My eyes stung. I hadn't been this close to crying in . . . well, longer than I could remember. The words on the outer edge of the coin read *To thine own self be true*. That was no longer the case for me. I had someone else who deserved my being true. And she was worthy of my sobriety more than I was.

"I'm not perfect, Ally. Your mom knows that all too well. But I'm working to be a better person for you. Thank you for giving me a chance."

Her eyes welled, then a tear snaked down her cheek, so I slapped my pockets, but they were empty. No tissues to help her. She laughed while wiping her face with her forearm, my token still squeezed inside her fist.

As I escorted Ally to the Center's main entrance, I took a risk. "Occasionally we're allowed to bring guests to our AA meetings. Think you might want to join me sometime?"

Chapter 13
MARGARET

AFTER

My son bought a car.

Kyle didn't even have a valid driver's license, but he bought a used car for five thousand dollars. What on earth was he thinking? He already owned a car, though he hadn't had access to it for the previous year, as we'd taken the keys away as soon as he was charged with the DUI.

After finding the title papers in his name two days ago, I scoured all the old boxes I'd searched, because I knew one of them had his bank statements. Every couple of weeks these past few months, he made small deposits. Five hundred dollars here. Two hundred fifty dollars there. The deposits were chunky at best, and no details of where they'd originated from were on the statement.

I knew he'd been doing some freelance graphic design work, but this much? I don't even want to think about how else he may have gotten the money. Selling drugs? Fencing stolen property? Laundering money? Stealing from us? Chills ran down my spine, making me back away from the papers and forcing me to return upstairs to stare at my computer as if a black hole were forming in front of me.

The cursor blinked double time with my pulse.

Kyle was always my go-to tech helper, so if I ever needed to access my bank account online, he'd help me. He knew all our passwords. In fact, every few months, he would admonish me for not having strong enough security on my phone and desktop computer, and we'd change the passwords. He had us go paperless years ago, so we no longer receive paper statements.

My fingers shake as I type my banking username, making me hit all the wrong keys. It takes me three tries before I've typed the right ones. Now for the password.

Grasping the arms of my swivel chair, I concentrate, breathing deeply to temper my panic. Did Kyle siphon our nest egg? Will my cash balance hover near zero when I open this account? Have I been writing checks that are predestined to bounce? With his cremation and all the funeral arrangements, my credit card spending swelled past flood-zone levels. A wiped-out bank account would be catastrophic. My nursing salary is reasonable but hardly enough to reboot our savings balance, and I haven't collected a paycheck since before he died.

Steeling myself, I watch my computer screen buffer. Any relief I enjoy from successfully logging in is replaced by dread at what the online statement might show.

What seems like hours later, my statement pulls up. All account balances are about the same level as they were last month. A quick scroll through the past few months' worth of transactions proves that we haven't suffered any surprise withdrawals.

Thank you, sweet Jesus. But my relief is wiped out by guilt. How could I have doubted my son?

My head throbs, so I swallow two aspirin, then retreat to my bedroom. I crawl under my covers to lie down, despite it being the middle of the afternoon, hoping the late-winter light will dull my senses long enough to drift into blissful numbness.

Instead, I stare at the ceiling. I failed my son. Again.

Like when I forced him to get out the night before he died.

Like the time I assumed his water bottle had vodka in it when, in fact, it contained water.

Like so long ago, when he wanted to buy those damned shoes.

In a flash, my mind is back in the mall—my pulse races. My breathing turns shallow. I try to scream, but my throat doesn't work. My fists can't punch. I'm as defenseless as a wet noodle. All I can focus on is my terrified, helpless young son.

Squeezing my eyes shut, I repeat the same litany of phrases I've recited so many times over the years like a mantra: *It's over. We're safe. It's over.*

Then, just as suddenly, my memory mercifully washes blank as if my brain triggered a safety switch to override all my thoughts. The monsters haunting my past dissipate, but I'm drenched in sweat. My heartbeat slows, and with it comes a limbo of quasi sleep. I languish in blissful nothingness since it's the closest I've come to rest in weeks.

As dusk deepens, a soft glow from the streetlights illuminates my room. Gently a new realization dawns on me. The one box I never found in the basement was the one containing Kyle's journals from his most recent rehab stay at Carrefour. Since he was evicted from the program before his year was up, he must've moved his journals and personal effects back home. Now where could he have stored those?

◆　◆　◆

"Honey? Are you home?" Martin's voice carries through the house, bringing inside a crisp wintry draft with it.

"I'm in the kitchen." I glance at my watch. How did it already get to be evening without me noticing? These February days blur, with the outside daylight waxing from dark to charcoal to gray, then waning again. I'm not even sure what day of the week it is anymore. Nor do I care.

"Still at the computer? You were here this morning when I left for work." After plopping today's mail on the counter, he picks up the empty coffee cup next to me, a holdover from my breakfast. Or was that yesterday's breakfast? "Tell me that you moved from your chair at least once today."

Ignoring him, I scroll through more Facebook photos. This time, I stalked every female *friend* of Kyle's. Scrutinized their posts. Checked out every photo for some clue suggesting she has a child. Kyle's child. But maybe his daughter's mother is married now, even while raising his child.

How old would Boo be? Five? Twelve?

The overhead light blinds my eyes when Martin switches it on. I squint until they adjust, then continue scrolling with my mouse. Martin tinkers in the kitchen, but over the years I've learned to tune out the background noise and stay on task. It was one of the special skills I honed as a scrub nurse in the operating room. Everyone there has a job. Let them do theirs. Focus on mine. Distractions can be deadly. I lost two patients on the table in my entire nursing career. Both cases were extensively analyzed by the hospital's review board and deemed beyond our control. Still, it was two deaths too many.

The kitchen was quiet for some time before I realized that Martin had already fixed dinner, eaten, and moved into another room to keep working. The dinner plate he prepared for me needs to be warmed in the microwave. I take a bite and a half before scraping the rest down the disposal, then returning to my sleuthing.

In Kyle's former fiancée's feed, I find Becca hugging a young girl— preschool age at the time. That would make her about seven now. But there's something about the little girl—the deep-set chocolate eyes, the chubby cheeks, her lips pursed like a rosebud. She's not looking directly into the camera, but I can tell she's got the beginnings of a square jaw.

So similar to Kyle's.

He proposed to Becca in the hospital while being treated for one of his pancreatitis bouts. They announced the engagement to both families, but then I guess it fizzled. They never shared the details, and I don't believe a ring was involved. To be honest, I was a little worried about what roller-coaster ride Becca was committing herself to by marrying Kyle, but I loved her like the daughter-in-law I always hoped she'd be. Still do, but from afar now.

Come to think of it, that short engagement occurred about six or seven years ago. Now, when was that? I text Kimber asking if she remembers the details.

"Margaret, it's after midnight." Martin appears from nowhere, dressed in pajamas, and his hair looks topsy turvy, as if he's already been asleep for a while. He squeezes my hand to stop me from scrolling my mouse. "What are you still doing up?"

"I think I found her, Martin."

"Found who?"

"Who?" I look at him as if he's started growing horns out of his forehead. Who the hell does he think I'm talking about? There's only one person I'm searching for. And I won't stop until I've found her. "Our granddaughter."

"Come to bed. You haven't had a good night's sleep in over a month. You'll get sick if you keep up this pace." Martin tugs my hand to pull me into a standing position, but I flinch away. He knew Kyle had a daughter and didn't ask about her. Not a single question. And now he's trying to distract me from finding her.

"Go back to bed, honey. I'll be up in a little while." But what I really want to tell him is *Stay out of my way, Martin.*

Hours later, my head throbs, and my eyes sting from spending too much time staring at the computer screen. After reluctantly shutting down my computer, I creak into a standing position while my stiff hips reprimand me for not having taken a break sooner. The stack of unread mail collecting on the counter is easy to ignore, but the return address and logo from the envelope on top send a shock wave down my spine.

The hospital.

After ripping the envelope open, my hands shake so hard I can barely read the enclosed letter.

> *After conducting an exhaustive accountability review of Kyle Dobrescu's emergency room visit, our internal review committee has deemed the medical triage, assessment, treatment, prescribed medication, and the decision to discharge were conducted appropriately. As such, our review committee has closed the case, and we will resume billing.*

I fight the intense urge to burn the letter with a match. Their summation seems too tidy. The hospital denies any liability through malpractice or negligence. Though they gave a summary of his diagnosis, physical exam, and vital statistics during his ER visit, the hospital ignored my request for information about the specific medication dispensed. Could they be covering something up?

So where does that leave us? Accidental overdose? Suicide? We are no closer to knowing exactly how Kyle died. If only I'd accompanied him to the ER, then I wouldn't be searching for the information now.

Still, I think it's worth a consultation with our family's lawyer, Mr. Davenport. We should at least attempt to dig deeper.

◆ ◆ ◆

"Mom?" Kimber sounds surprised to hear from me when she answers my phone call. She shouldn't. We've been texting daily since Kyle died.

Damn, that was four weeks ago. How could a month have zipped by so quickly while each passing minute stretches to an eternity? "What's going on?"

"I think I've found her." The silence that follows on the other end of the line is deafening. If I didn't hear the background noise of my grandchildren giggling, I'd have assumed our connection had dropped.

"Her who?" Kimber pronounces her words slowly, her voice wary as if she's managing her response. Or bored. Either way, her demeanor sets off my alarm bells. She has two modes of reacting to any situation: either being excited about life or venting about problems. I never know which persona I'll greet when I speak with her. But not this. Not careful and tentative.

"You know exactly who. Your niece." Oh, hell. Calling Kimber may have been a mistake. I glance at my watch. Five-thirty in the evening. Not sure what day, though.

"Mom, I thought you agreed to give up your search." I sense a free fall in this conversation, and I don't understand why. Kimber has known my interest. I've been forthright in my search efforts. I have a fourth grandchild—a living extension of Kyle. Why shouldn't I want to find her and get to know her?

"No, sweetheart. You must've misunderstood something I said." Now I'm the one choosing my words carefully, trying to keep the edge out of my voice. "I never agreed to stop, and I think you've known that."

"So tell me . . ." The childlike chattering in the background grows louder and turns from happy to argumentative. Kimber must be approaching her daughters and son to intervene. As much as I adore spoiling and visiting my grandkids, I don't miss those days of playing referee to young siblings. "What did you find?"

Her audible sigh hints at a reluctance I don't normally hear in my daughter's voice. My response catches on my tongue, so I remain silent. Waiting to follow her lead, whatever direction that might be.

"Mom, look. The funeral has been hard on all of us—especially you. I miss Kyle every minute of every day, but he was your son. I can't even imagine how you're coping."

Thoughts collide within my head, but I brace myself for whatever my daughter will say next. I need to stay on my guard. She's placating me. Managing me. I recognize it because I use this technique with distraught patients all the time. And with Kyle. Pain management isn't only delivered in pill and IV form.

"Dad mentioned you're not eating or sleeping. You haven't been to work in weeks. You haven't left the house since I last saw you. It's not healthy, Mom."

"You've been talking to your father about me?" A lump thickens in my throat, choking my words. They discussed me behind my back? After all that I've done to support them. They have no idea the secrets I've kept so they could live their lives oblivious to my pain.

"He called the other day. He's worried about you, Mom."

"I'm fine, sweetheart. Learning to cope. How are the kids doing?"

"Don't change the subject. When was the last time you showered?"

Come on now. Really? My personal hygiene has never been deficient. *Cleanliness is next to godliness.* The nuns at my Catholic nursing school hammered that phrase into us until I could fold hospital corners and sterilize surgical instruments in my sleep.

"I took a shower . . ." Wait, when did I last take one? I glance at my nails and notice the dirt underneath. Goodness, I can't remember precisely the last time I washed my face. Or changed out of my yoga pants and sweatshirt. Or combed my hair. I summon my clipped voice, the one I reserved for reprimands and last-chance-warnings for Kimber and Kyle—I use a gentler one with my grandchildren. ". . . yesterday. Next time your father calls to vent about me, do me a favor. Tell him I'm fine and to give me some grace."

"Don't get all defensive on me, Mom. Dad doesn't know what to do. He asked for advice. I wish I lived closer so I could help out more.

The kids have spring break over Easter. We plan to come down for the week. But in the meantime, I've been researching local grief counselors and support groups near you and—"

"That's nice, dear. Goodbye." Hanging up on my daughter floods me with belated irritation. Suddenly I feel like I could sack the quarterback of a professional football team.

No one gets it. Not Martin, Kimber, or my sister. Yes, I lost my son. A gaping hole exists where my heart used to be. I would give every breathing moment of happiness my future holds to buy his return ticket back to life. But I can't. He's gone.

But Kyle left behind a piece of him that still walks this earth. A gift. Boo is a magnet, pulling me toward her. Once I find her, I will start to heal. She is the answer. For every way I ever failed my son, I can make it up to him through her. She's my salvation.

And if I have to traverse this road alone, so be it. But first, I'll shower.

Chapter 14

KYLE

BEFORE

When I woke up this morning, something was off. I stared at the ceiling, trying to figure out what it was. Why I felt an intense need to sprint. But I hardly ever jogged, let alone ran. Restless energy zinged in my fingers, my palms, and my legs, so I hopped out of bed to pace my rehab dorm room, turning faster and sharper. My room felt like it was contracting, but it took the same number of strides to get from one side to the other. The air was stale.

I needed to get out of here. To breathe real air. To not be trapped.

What day was it? I opened my countdown calendar. It showed that I had 323 days of court-ordered time left to serve in Carrefour.

What the hell.

I must have made a mistake. Did I miss marking off a day in there somewhere? I double-checked the date on my calendar, and sure enough, it was May 22. I'd been in here for forty-two days, but I might as well already be serving an encore sentence.

Shoot me now. How could I possibly still have so much time left? I whipped my journal against the wall, then paced the patch of carpet in my coffin of a room. My zigzagging turned faster and faster. My heartbeat accelerated like a broken metronome, my feet matching its tempo.

I ran my hands through my hair, and they came away damp and sweaty. God, I felt like a fucking caged animal. No freedom. I burst into the hallway. Every square wall tile mocked me.

"Kyle?" Mark, one of my counselors, jogged up toward me, so I slipped back inside my room and slammed the door, hoping he'd leave me alone. Didn't work. Instead, he waited outside in the hallway, knocking. "Hey, what's going on?"

"I can't do this anymore." I searched the crap under my bed until I found my duffel, then started jamming my clothes inside. Every crack as I shoved the drawers closed, splintering the veneer paneling, felt more satisfying than the last. I couldn't stay here another minute longer. I yelled back at the door, "I'm busting out of here, dammit."

"Can you please open up?" Pretty considerate of him. He knew the door wasn't locked. No keys or locks so residents were never too comfortable about breaking the rules. The door offered the illusion of privacy. But Mark respected that boundary, at least for now. Somehow, that realization sank in, and my frustration thawed like fractures around the outer edge of a frozen pond in early spring.

Mark's intermittent knocking continued. I stepped back from my duffel. "Come in."

"Why don't you come out here? We can take a walk together in the courtyard." So goddamn reasonable. I wanted to stay angry. I wanted a fight. Every fiber of my being was ready to combust in front of all these people to show them I was more than some fucking court judgment.

Instead of replying, my soundtrack of slams and punches ebbed as I focused on the disarray caused by my rage. Seconds later, I twisted the knob and stood face to face with a guy who was a foot shorter than me but at least fifty pounds heavier, all muscle. But he'd respected my privacy, and for that, I was grateful.

"Let me guess. You've been here for six weeks. Right?"

"To the day." I shrugged and turned away so he couldn't read the disappointment on my face. Apparently I was a walking cliché.

"Don't worry. Anger is expected right about now." Mark stole a glance in my direction, and I raised my eyebrows in exaggerated shock. He laughed, then held the door open for me as we walked into the warmth that Illinois calls late spring. We were welcomed by blinding sunlight and insects. "I'm serious. It's a good thing. You know, unless you hurt someone. Or yourself."

"For some reason, the walls closed in on me today. Not sure what happened. I went to bed last night totally fine and woke up feeling trapped." I'd been in long-term rehab before, but I don't remember this kind of panic attack. Then again, I can't say I'd ever fully committed to trying to rehabilitate then.

"You're right on track, Kyle. Look, you've been a resident for long enough that the novelty of the routine and people have worn off. You explored every corner of this facility. There's nothing new. I hear you've even been Miss Genevieve's go-to tech guru and have been bringing Carrefour's technology into the twenty-first century. That's no mean feat, but you've checked that box." Mark weeded a dandelion from one of the manicured mulch beds surrounding the walkway. "You're transitioning into what we call the action stage of addiction recovery."

The courtyard—a generous term for this open-air cube of a garden bordered on all sides by glass walls—provided residents with a reminder of what we were missing on the outside. Since the day I'd checked in, I'd only seen the horizon on the occasional van ride to our AA meetings when they were held off site. "If by action, you mean punching the walls, then yes, I have arrived."

"Not quite."

"So what now? I've done everything. Know everyone. Why do I still have to be here if I'm progressing on time?" My question was rhetorical, but I let it hang in the balance anyway as I blinked back hot tears. If rehab has taught me anything, it was that learning to manage my addiction is a marathon, not a sprint. A lifelong marathon. I couldn't stop my training and expect that I'd ever break through my cycles. My cravings.

"Well, your court-ordered sentence, for one thing." Mark was a patient guy. I'd give him that. "But you've explored your outer world, at least as much as the Center has to offer. It's time to explore your inner space."

No thanks. I'd spent a lot of time in my inner space, and it wasn't pretty. I'd rather bust out of here and explore the world outside Carrefour. *That* would be exciting.

"Please consider leading one of our peer-group meetings."

Seriously? Um, didn't this guy just witness me destroying their property? I stopped on the gravel path and waited until Mark turned around to face me. "Do I have a choice? Will I get kicked out and have to go to prison if I say no?"

"Nope. It's entirely your call. Your time here counts whether or not you lead a group. But I've been watching you. You have a lot of life experience to add. You're smart and rational. You have an empathetic streak. I think some of the residents could benefit from working with you."

This guy had a warped, optimistic sense of blind leading the blind. Me driving this bus meant we were all doomed. Together.

"I'm not really much for public speaking."

"That's okay. It's more about group sharing. You'll lead the group, helping and encouraging others to engage." We strolled toward the glass doors to the facility, but before we got there, Mark stopped me by the arm. "I've noticed that the stories you share in our group discussions have been insightful. Respectful. You've never tried to hog the spotlight or one-up anyone else's contribution. I think you'll make a natural mentor."

But what if I turned out to be the hopeful rookie who was called up to the majors only to strike out every damned time? I didn't want to be sent back to the minors embarrassed and whimpering.

"It's also okay to be vulnerable, Kyle. The flip side of exposing who you really are means people get to know the real you." Shit. Were all the counselors Zen mind readers too?

"You're not selling this well." I'd spent a lifetime learning how not to be vulnerable. And for a good reason. Meeting my daughter was the first time since—well, since that afternoon so many years ago that I'd failed my mom—that I tried to dismantle the fortress around my memories. Even Ally hasn't seen the real me. It was too weak and ugly to share with anyone. Especially her. But I was trying to prop myself up so I could be vulnerable again for her.

"Why don't you go clean up your room? Then we can talk specifics later. You don't have to decide right away."

I followed Mark back inside and headed down the hallway toward my room. Lead a group? Hell, I couldn't even lead myself. I was a fucking disaster. Even though it wasn't lunchtime yet, I shoved all the crap off my bed and crawled under my covers, willing sleep to zap me out of this place, at least for a couple of hours.

My last waking thought was something Becca always used to tell me: "Be careful what you wish for."

◆ ◆ ◆

Waiting inside the local Rotary Hall's glass doors, I rocked on my heels and checked my watch. Since Ally didn't have a car, she'd ridden the subway and then transferred to a bus to meet me. It was daylight, but I still got nervous about creepos following her on mass transit. Stalking her. I wished Hannah would buy her a car, but finances were tight for them. As soon as I got out of here, found a job, and saved a little money, I would take her used-car shopping.

Once her dark ponytail was visible, bouncing toward the Center's door, I focused on calming down. Mark had already offered to escort us to her bus stop this evening—both for Ally's safety and to make sure I wasn't a flight risk—before he drove our carpool van back to the Center. Hannah was scheduled to work tonight, so Ally didn't have any problem sneaking away for the evening.

For the next hour, she would join me as my guest—Carrefour approved—at tonight's off-site AA meeting. At first, I thought it was weird to bring along a guest, but a year or two ago, Kimber asked to attend one with me. Then I noticed a lot of AA members bringing an occasional friend or family member. They were building a support network. Worst-case scenario, it could scare Ally off. God, I hoped not.

Last weekend, she'd walked across a stage to "Pomp and Circumstance" in her school's auditorium to get her high-school diploma. I hadn't been there, but she'd shown me a picture on her phone of her all decked out in her cap and gown. So instead she was joining me tonight in this sad multipurpose room—some graduation party.

After procuring our metal folding chairs, we found a spot together by the token table. As people wandered up to collect their sobriety tokens, I leaned over and whispered, "In three more meetings, I'll earn my gold two-month chip." She looked impressed, and I mentally promised to make sure she joined me when I earned my three-month token.

The meeting opened with a moment of silence; then together, the group chanted the Serenity Prayer, which I'd recited so many times I could say it in my sleep. Ally read it from a worn sheet of paper that had been handed out as we entered.

A few people stood up to talk; then I raised my hand. Butterflies dive-bombed in my gut, but I had to do this with Ally present. After getting a nod from the leader, I stepped up to the front.

"Hi. My name is Kyle, and I'm an alcoholic."

"Hi, Kyle." Though the reply from the attendees was standard, I found it bizarre to hear dozens of people say my name in unison. I hadn't prepared my speech, but I needed to share my journey. I wanted to validate myself for my daughter with all these anonymous soldiers bearing witness. Some even more broken than I.

"My problems started when I was thirteen years old. I fell in with a fast crowd. We'd skip school. I no longer respected my parents, their rules, and their restrictions, so I ran away. A bunch of times. The police had a rap sheet on me a mile long, even though I was a minor. Underaged drinking. Trespassing. Fake ID. DUI. Nothing I'm proud of. I graduated high school because my parents never gave up on me. They sent me away to college, hoping I'd meet a new crowd of people. I did. My band. And the partying continued until my bandmates moved on with their lives. But I didn't."

My hands shook as I sipped from my water bottle, spilling a little on my T-shirt. I snuck a look at Ally. She sat forward in her chair. Her face trained on mine. I could guess she was running the math in her head. Yep. That was about when I knew her mom. And yep. That was about when she came into the picture. Maybe my journey would've been different had I been a part of Ally's life when she was little. But probably not. I'd been a self-centered asshole then. One could argue I still was, but at least now I was trying.

"I never really liked myself when I was sober, so I'd start drinking, then binge drinking, which eventually got me fired from every job I've ever had. My liter-of-vodka-per-day habit earned me a raging case of pancreatitis, which flares up every couple of years, each one worse than the last. And back into the hospital I'd go."

I couldn't look at Ally anymore. I might as well be inside a confessional booth asking for penance from a priest. *Bless me, Ally, for I have sinned* . . . But I didn't deserve forgiveness. I was only asking for understanding and patience. I swallowed back saliva that seemed to be in overproduction mode.

"I would go through periods of sobriety. My band members threw an intervention. They all came into town for a weekend to confront me. And then my family did a few years later. That time, I ended up in the ER. Since I'd lied about what meds I'd taken when the nurse started pumping the antianxiety meds through my IV, I went into cardiac arrest and flatlined—so I've been told. My father had the privilege of watching the doctors shock my heart back to life."

The silence in the hall hung heavy over my head like a noose.

"Right now, I'm in my fourth residential rehabilitation program. But this time, I have something new to live for. Someone to stay sober for." My throat constricted, and I wasn't sure if I could continue. But I had to. She had to know. After pausing to sniff a few times, I wiped the snot from my nose with my sleeve. "The universe has seen fit to introduce me to the daughter that I never knew I had. It's given me a new reason to redeem myself. I want to be a better man for her. A father. Her sober father."

I walked toward my chair to a chorus of "Thank you, Kyle." But at the last second, I turned and beelined out the door, finding a trash can just in time to baptize it with my puke.

When I'd finished dry heaving and was still gripping the sides of the can, a soft voice behind me called me back to the present.

"What happened when you were thirteen?" Ally's voice embraced my shredded heart, but her words hit a nerve that had been numb for a long, long time.

"My mom needed . . . help." I slid down to the floor, and she sat next to me, leaning against the wall. Mark peeked his head out the door, nodded, then slipped back inside. I'd opened Pandora's box. I couldn't close it now. "If only I hadn't insisted we go to the mall . . ."

"My mom always says that no one who has a mom needs a guardian angel."

Oh, but Hannah was so very, very wrong.

"We needed one that day."

Chapter 15

ALLY

AFTER

"Kyle—Dad—sorry I haven't visited your grave since your birthday." The March afternoon sun casts a rosy hue on the newly installed marble memorial stone in the ground, inlaid with his name, date of birth, and date of death. "But I wanted to stop by to celebrate my nineteenth birthday with you."

Another birthday—this time, mine—commemorated with a graveside visit. Once again, I take out a piece of birthday cake from my bag and light a candle. This time, though, the wind doesn't extinguish the flame before I can blow it out.

What should I wish for this year?

My wish last year came true almost immediately. Part of me still can't believe Mom actually revealed Kyle's name.

Today, the one wish I'd make is that Kyle could come back from the dead. Or that two months ago, he didn't die at all but had been confused with someone else. I wanted him to be far away in a residential rehab program like Carrefour. In a few weeks, I'll get another letter. We'll have a good laugh over his mistaken death, and we can pick back up where we left off. He could keep the joke going forever: "Remember that time everyone overreacted and thought I died and even buried me?"

When I mentioned my birthday wish to Mom this morning, she plopped her hands on her hips and shook her head, confused, as if I'd sprouted an extra ear on my forehead. "Seriously, Allison?"

Now, I have no more wishes.

Why doesn't she understand? Why can't I grieve my own father's death? Sure, I didn't know him for very long, but she was more supportive when I delivered the I-just-want-to-be-friends relationship death blow to Chase after prom. Or when I vented about my college midterm exams. Or when I had trouble sketching her. I haven't wanted to pick up my charcoal pencils since he died.

After I set the paper plate with the slice of my birthday cake on the ground, a bright-red bird swoops by, narrowly missing my head. After nudging the plate away from me a couple of feet, I sit as still as the statues overlooking their gravestones nearby and wait. Moments later, the cardinal lands on the edge of the plate, pecks at the cake, then flutters off into the pine tree overhead. Not even spooked by the flickering candle flame.

At least someone—something—is celebrating my birthday.

Nineteen years old and back at the starting gate. With no plans other than to meet Mom later for dinner, I settle in on the straw-colored, dormant grass next to his new memorial stone. The polished granite is so shiny I can see my reflection. I wonder if Kyle can see me, like those one-way mirrors the detectives use when interrogating people on TV cop shows.

"Last week was spring break at school. I was able to take a couple days off of work, so I drove to Cleveland to visit my grandparents— my mom's parents, not yours. I needed new scenery and to find out if they knew anything about you." I'm talking to a gravestone as if it can transport messages to angels at the speed of thought. I must be going crazy. "Mom never told them much about you either. Wow, she's an expert at keeping secrets."

Last week, over mugs of hot chocolate, I told Grandma Vicki everything, from the minute Mom relented and gave me my biological father's name to crashing his funeral wake. Grandpa even joined us and built a fire in the fireplace. So I spilled the Kyle beans. Every single last one of them. Mom might not be happy about it, but it felt so good to have someone listen to what happened last year. To understand and support me. It took a long afternoon and evening to share everything, and I still had more tears to cry. The local weather forecaster could've dubbed me Tropical Storm Ally.

Grandma had boxes of tissues at the ready, and she used them too. She squeezed my hand with knuckles swollen with arthritis. But her reddened eyes and voice husky with emotion were as welcome to me as a hug from heaven. "Mercy, child. I would've loved to have met your father too. At least in person."

Somehow I doubted that. Who would've wanted to meet the man that ultimately caused their daughter to sever ties with her entire family for a decade? It wasn't as if I had been the result of a planned pregnancy, but not many of the people involved behaved like rational adults once I was on the way. Especially Kyle.

"Your father sounded so nice and charming on the phone."

Whipped cream from my hot chocolate sloshed onto their oriental rug, but Grandma stopped me when I dropped to my knees to sop up the mess with my napkin. As I slinked back into my chair, I could barely eke out, "You talked to Kyle? When? What did he say?"

"He called us just after Thanksgiving. He introduced himself and wanted to let us know that the two of you were getting to know each other. He apologized for not having reached out sooner."

Well, I couldn't have been more surprised than if she announced that she was packing up and moving in with Mom, Lulu, and me.

Kyle never hinted that he knew anything about them, let alone called them.

"He also suggested that one day we could all meet, including his parents, if Hannah approved. He suggested we all meet this spring." Grandma Vicki bit her lip as she looked away, pausing.

Mom's approval? Fat chance. Even if Kyle hadn't died, the last thing she'd have ever allowed would be a family reunion for both sides of my family. She wasn't even comfortable living in the same time zone as him, let alone the city.

Still, the thought that Kyle had tried to duct tape together a loving, supportive family for me spurred a fresh wave of aching, so I reached for more tissues to hide behind. I didn't realize I still had tears left to cry.

"Of course, I would've loved to have met him. In time, I think your grandfather would've found it within him to move on from . . . the not-so-ideal circumstances surrounding your birth."

"I doubt I could've forgiven him." Grandpa crossed his arms and leaned back into his leather armchair, his cheeks turning a brighter shade of rose. I suppose the unexpected phone call from Kyle ripped a scab off a decades-old wound. His huff was as endearing as it was stubborn. "But for your sake, Ally, I would've considered setting aside my resentment and at least meeting your biological father and his family."

Grandma stared him down until he had the decency to avert his eyes and fidget in his seat. Yeah, I didn't believe him either. If grudge-holding were a collegiate sport, he'd have qualified for a full-ride scholarship. I could see where Mom got her epic skills. Grandpa hadn't kicked her out. She moved out on her own. Still, I loved him for his loyalty to his daughter. He only wanted what was best for her.

And for me.

Now, as I sit next to Kyle's grave, I shiver. A chill sets in with the setting sun. Spring may be right around the corner, according to the calendar, but she had yet to show signs of booting our lingering Chicago winter out the door.

No, I lied. I do have a birthday wish this year—a real one. So I blow out my melting candle.

I want to meet my other grandparents. Officially.

◆ ◆ ◆

After stumbling through my front door with the weight of my school backpack burning my shoulder, still sporting my grocery-store-cashier polo shirt, I collapse onto the sofa. Mom comes out of her bedroom in a fresh pair of scrubs, inserting a stud earring—the only kind she's allowed to wear while on duty at the hospital.

"I thought you weren't working today."

"Oh, Ally-cat. I'm sorry. The flu is going around, and both med techs called in sick tonight, so they called me into sub. I'll be back before you wake up tomorrow."

"But we always try to spend my birthday evening together . . ."

"I know, sweetie. I'm sorry. Your dinner is on the counter: take-out Italian." Mom grabs her work tote bag, then kisses me on the forehead. Before she shuts the door behind her, she turns to me. "We'll do something special tomorrow night to celebrate, okay? Your pick."

As the door shuts behind her with Mom yelling "Happy birthday!" from the hallway, Lulu hops on the couch next to me, settling in for a nap.

Last year I got the one name I'd been begging for years to learn. This year, I'm apparently getting nothing. That's okay. Meeting Kyle took care of all my future birthday gifts from my mom.

But when I wander into the kitchen to prepare my dinner, a birthday card leaning against the take-out containers catches my eye. Written on the pink envelope in Mom's distinctive half-cursive, half-printed handwriting is "To my favorite daughter on her 19th birthday."

The greeting card itself is the kind I'd usually ignore while browsing a card shop's display case, all full of pastel watercolor flowers on the cover. I plop onto the couch next to Lulu to read it. But as soon as I open it up, my eyes fill, blurring my mom's handwritten note.

Happy happy birthday, my precious Ally-cat,

Nineteen years ago this evening, you graced my life with your first sweet, lusty cries. I've spent every second of every day since thanking God that He gave you to me. Somehow, despite my misgivings, He saw fit to allow me to be your mother. You've been the brightest light in my life. I can't imagine my world without you in it. I am truly blessed because of you.

In these years, I've watched you grow from being a little girl in pigtails who loved giving me angel kisses with her eyelashes to a surprisingly serious student who works her tail off at college. You inspire me with your heart, your passion, and your mindfulness in all that you've accomplished.

Everything I've ever done, from moving to Chicago to becoming a med tech, I've done for you. For us. No surprise, I regret some of the decisions I've made, including waiting so long to reconcile with my parents. This past year, I've even wished you'd have moved away to college, not so that we wouldn't have seen each other as much—never that. But because you deserve the time to live among your peers and discover who you are, who you want to be, and what you want to do in the future without your mom living in the next room.

I've cherished being your mother. Sometimes it's hard for me to see the young independent woman you've become. I'm so used to making decisions for both of us— those of great significance and mundane—that it is hard to recognize you for the capable adult that you've become.

You're no longer dependent on me. Probably not a surprise to you, but a big one for me.

Know that I'm consciously giving up my parental control and deferring your life decisions to you. My transition won't be smooth, but that's not your problem. Even so, please be patient with me as I adjust. If you see me being too protective, a gentle reminder should be enough to redirect me from treating you like the little girl you once were.

You will always be my daughter. You will always be my raison d'être. And going forward, you will always be my dearest friend.

But Ally, never ever doubt my love. You have it forever. Happy birthday, sweetheart. I celebrate you and everything you have become. I am so proud of you.

Love you to the moon and back,
Mom

Lulu purrs while snuggling her forehead into my neck, a paw pressing against my jugular. All I can think of is how writing this card must've stripped Mom's soul naked. Even mentioning regrets was new for her. Mom has always been a make-a-decision-and-move-on kind of person. Reflecting on the past is not in her nature.

Shrugging away from my furry, purring noose, I reread the card. I'm no longer hungry for my birthday dinner.

We are a team. And I couldn't love her any more than I do at this moment.

Chapter 16

KYLE

BEFORE

My bandmates and I used to joke around about what it would be like once we reached middle age. The aches. The pains. The thinning hair. The clichéd crisis would manifest itself in affairs, sports cars, or divorces. With my lifestyle, I never assumed I'd survive long enough to join the chorus of complainers. Until I did.

This morning, the suggestion of playing flag football in Carrefour's courtyard had been my not-so-brilliant idea. A little fresh air. A little vitamin D. A little friendly competition between peer groups before the Center's dry July Fourth barbecue picnic. Miss Genevieve had supported the idea, and all the nonplayer residents and staff gathered around the sidelines to cheer us on.

After twenty minutes of *hut, hut, hike,* one of our opponents forgot that this was tag football—not tackle. Turns out, my collarbone was no match for a guy who once played linebacker for his high school's varsity team. Nice guy, but not too smart.

Tonight, instead of watching fireworks, I had x-rays taken at the hospital. I couldn't remember the last time I was in the ER sober, but observing the results of all the Independence Day stupidity was more intense than I'd expected. Burn victims, car accidents, drowning rescues, gunshot wounds, and broken bones. Hope these doctors and nurses were paid extra for suffering through all the holiday idiots. Myself included.

"Kyle! What happened?" As I rested on the gurney dressed in some hospital gown from the 1970s, Mom rushed into my room, purse flying off one elbow. Wincing, I stuck up my good arm to block her from hugging me, because I instinctively knew the shock waves through my body would be seismic if she were successful.

"Mom? How did you know I was in the ER?"

"We were at a pool party when Miss Genevieve called." Mom skirted around the hospital room in her red-white-and-blue sundress, snapping a photo of the whiteboard with the names of all the hospital staff who were assigned to help me. Next up, she scanned my monitors, checked my IV line, then pressed her hand against my forehead. As if I had a fever. "Your father's parking the car. So what's this about a football game?"

Before I could explain myself, a doctor dressed in seafoam scrubs and a white lab coat entered with Dad on his heels.

"Well, Kyle. You did a number on yourself." The doctor pulled up my x-rays on a monitor. With the clicking part of his pen, he pointed to a bone that looked more like a zigzag than a straight line. "You fractured your left clavicle here, here, and here. You're going to need pins to hold the bone together while it heals. We're going to admit you tonight, and I have you scheduled for surgery tomorrow morning."

Mom, slipping into hypernurse mode, stepped away from my bed to speak with the doctor, which got me off the hook from having to pay attention. The fewer medical details I knew, the better. The prospect of surgery didn't bother me. After all my trips to the operating room, I was a pro now.

Dad's shoulder twitched in high gear. Couldn't blame him for being nervous. Usually, whenever I was a patient, I'd been convulsing or flirting with the grim reaper. I tried to smile to prove I wasn't standing on death's threshold, but the effort made me groan. "I'm okay, Dad."

"You were doing so well at the Center. Now you'll have to be on pain meds after surgery. I don't want to see you lose ground."

"No. Carrefour doesn't allow prescription pain meds. Besides, the pain isn't that bad. I'll be fine." But as the words sank through my cognitive reasoning, it occurred to me that the IV line in my arm was probably administering medication right now, boosting my pain tolerance. My palms turned sweaty. Pins in my collarbone? Surgical incision? Resetting my bone into one piece? No way. I wouldn't be able to recover pain-med-free. I'd be living in a court-ordered torture chamber. But my only other option was prison.

Pinging from one of the machines accelerated. Both the doctor and Mom observed the monitor as my pulse reading increased.

"Kyle, honey? Are you feeling okay?" Then over my head, her tone turned demanding. "Martin, what did you say to him?"

But I couldn't answer or defend him. All I could do was concentrate on my breathing. Each lungful didn't seem to keep up with what my body demanded. The oxygen probe on my finger started flashing, reminding me of E.T.'s finger.

A nurse rushed in behind Mom, pushing various buttons. All I could do was watch the walls closing in until I was looking at Dad through the wrong end of a telescope. No, I couldn't do this. Warmth seeped into my arm and up through my body. I embraced the swan dive into a pool of relaxation.

I would never survive the next few weeks of pain.

Seventy-two hours later, I'd moved to a private room in a regular hospital ward. Not only was my shoulder a mess, but my throat was killing me. Apparently I'd earned a bed in the ICU for a couple of days due to a complication after my surgery. At least the clear-liquid diet I was required to follow was staying down. Tomorrow I might get to start eating bland solid foods.

After a soft knock on my door, I looked up to see Kimber standing with her arms crossed and a massive smile lighting up her face. Couldn't remember the last time I'd seen her; definitely before my stint at Carrefour. She must've driven all the way from Madison to see me.

"Rumor has it you ripped your breathing tube right out of your mouth. Not behaving for the nurses, huh?"

"You know me. I'm never happy unless I'm giving someone hell."

"Mission accomplished. Good to see you upright, bro." She laughed as she pulled up a chair next to my bed and gave me a fist bump. "You gave us all a bit of a scare. When Mom called to tell me you were being stepped down from ICU, I figured I had to take advantage and see you. Hope you don't mind me crashing your postsurgery party."

"Mind? Of course not." As my only sibling, she'd tried a bunch of times to be authorized as a visitor at Carrefour, but for some reason, Miss Genevieve never approved her request or returned her phone calls. Ever since then, we'd communicated by snail mail.

"So what's the food like in this joint?"

"I prefer the lime Jell-O over the cherry flavor, but you can't beat the house chicken broth. Want the name of the chef?"

"Thanks, I'll pass. Any chance we can sneak you into the hospital's kitchen and whip together seared tuna for me for lunch? Maybe a little asparagus with roasted pecans and blue cheese on the side? Or grilled root vegetables?"

"Enough . . . uncle!" I couldn't help my groan. That menu sounded so divine I'd even risk a pancreatitis flare-up for a nibble. "It's all liquids for me right now."

As if we'd summoned the demons, my stomach grumbled, which caused both of us to laugh. Didn't realize how much I'd missed seeing Kimber. I was eight years old when we packed her up and dropped her off at college. According to the Dobrescu family's lore, I'd been so distraught after moving her into her dorm that Mom drove me back to her campus the next day to convince me Kimber was fine. Not sure how true that part had been, but I was grateful we had that extra afternoon together.

"Aren't they feeding you? Think you could weigh less than Lauren right now." My tween niece couldn't flirt with a hundred pounds soaking wet. Her weight combined with my six-foot frame and . . . God, I hoped I didn't appear anywhere near that skinny.

Her mention of Lauren summoned thoughts of Ally front and center into my brain. Little did Kimber know that she had a niece. That her kids had a cousin. Someday, I'd introduce them.

"What aren't you telling me?" Kimber scooted her chair up to my bed and stared into my eyes, as if she could see the gears grinding in my head. "You have that same goofy grin Mom gets whenever you call her Maggie."

"Nothing, really." Yikes. Didn't think I'd get busted that easily. But as I dismiss all thoughts of Ally, inspiration hits. All those hours, days, and weeks of helping Miss Genevieve overhaul Carrefour's website had proved to me that I could help other small businesses reboot their online presence. Maybe. Kimber, with all her professional experience, would be the perfect person to help me. "Actually, there is something I'd love to get your take on. I've been tossing around the idea of launching a freelance graphic design business once I'm done with rehab."

I'd always appreciated my big sister for not being too judgy about my addiction. At her core, she cared about me and my struggle with alcohol. Kimber had even joined me as my guest at an AA meeting once.

Leaning back in her chair, she crossed her arms, her lips pursed. After a long pause, she nodded. "Yes. That would suit you well."

If she thought I could pull it off, then it was within my reach. Her validation mattered. I didn't realize until this moment how much. "Cool. So how would I go about starting?"

Two hours and a forgettable hospital tray of beef broth, tea, and Jell-O later, Kimber had helped me pull together a master checklist of what I needed to do to hang my own shingle. After I graduate from Carrefour. Easier said than done.

"Listen, I have to head back to Madison before the kids' bus drops them off, and freeway traffic in Chicagoland is murder this time of day." She scooped up her jacket and purse, then fist-bumped me. "Great seeing you, even for just a couple hours."

"Thanks for coming. Mom and Dad didn't tell me."

"Dude . . ." She stood, pausing as if trying to choose her words. Her brow furrowed.

"Yeah?"

"I love you." Kimber bit her lip, then nodded. "Unconditionally."

Miss Genevieve waived my return requirement until after I got the all clear from my post-op doctor's appointment. But—as we were all aware—from the second I walked through the door, I had to be sober and taking no pain medications. No exceptions.

Two weeks after I'd left on a stretcher in an ambulance, I returned with my left arm immobilized in a navy-blue sling Velcro-strapped to my chest. Dad drove me to the Center and carried my duffel bag for me. Before heading over, Mom supplied me with a new set of T-shirts with the left sleeves cut open, so I wouldn't have to raise my arm to get dressed. I also brought along homemade cookies from Mrs. Roman as a peace offering to the administration for allowing me to stay home to recuperate after surgery.

"Welcome back, Kyle." Mark grabbed the duffel from my dad, then gave us a couple of minutes of privacy. Since no one but residents and staff were permitted in the unauthorized areas, including my dorm room, the reception area was our official goodbye zone.

"How are you coping?" Once again, Dad's shoulder jerked, eliciting phantom pain from mine. I never wanted to move my left arm again, ever. But once my sling came off, my journey to recovery would include a whole lot of physical rehabilitation, a.k.a. a living hell in a sea of sobriety.

"At least I'm not in prison." I should probably be thanking him for driving me. For treating me to good restaurant meals while I was home. For taking me shopping for some new clothes and toiletries. I was even able to meet Ally for coffee at our café.

Life was pretty damned sweet on the outside of this joint.

"Be in touch, Kyle." Dad—the way he pronounced it sounded like *bean touch*—held out his index finger; then I pressed it to mine. It was always his way to say goodbye. *I love you, and there is nothing in this world I wouldn't do for you.* My group counselors had hinted that he was my enabler. But I thought of him as my safety net. Dad's intentions had always been pure.

"Bean touch." I fell in step behind Mark, then turned for one last look as Dad exited the building, taking my small taste of freedom with him. With my lips pressed together, I ignored the stinging behind my eyelids. I refused to cry in front of these people.

This time, I returned with a secret—my liquid courage. Carrefour might not allow me to take pain medications while healing from surgery, but I never claimed to be Superman. I'd brave the pain as much as I could tolerate. If it became too much to endure, I'd smuggled in half a dozen airport bottles of vodka hidden wrapped in socks and T-shirts inside the duffel Mark was carrying over his shoulder. I was lucky they didn't find them when they unzipped my bag.

Hope I wouldn't have to use any of them. But knowing I had access to a lifeline would give me strength.

As I walked down the hallway—a hundred percent sober—residents poured out of their rooms to stand in front of their doors in a pseudoparade. Their clapping and cheers built into a roar that resonated in my chest, causing me to perk up my step. Despite my best efforts to be stoic, I totally couldn't hide the grin that overtook my face. I stopped in front of my door and faced my friends. My people. My trench mates.

Flexing my good arm, I turned a full circle of triumph. Rocky, eat your heart out. "Who's up for a rematch?"

◆ ◆ ◆

"Kyle? Are you in there?" Someone knocked on my dorm-room door. Then pounded harder. "Kyle, are you okay?"

Using my good arm to prop myself up, I squinted around the room as I tried to swallow, but my mouth felt as dry as a wad of cotton balls. Why was I on the floor? Didn't I go to bed . . .

But then memories of last night filtered through the haze, and I looked at the carnage around me. Empty minibottles and stray socks littered the floor.

Oh, shit. What had I done?

More pounding, but I wasn't sure if it was from my throbbing head or from the door.

"Jus' a minute." I wobbled to my knees and tried to sweep the bottles under my bed, but my tripod stance sent me crashing against the bed onto my injured shoulder—a lightning bolt of pain rocketed down my side. The whimpering definitely came from me.

"Kyle, I'm going to give you ten more seconds, then I'm coming in."

"Mark, everything's okay. I overslept. Hang on." Making it fully upright, I swayed. Shit, I only wore boxers. What time was it anyway? I swallowed back a gag; then my stomach heaved. I lunged toward the trash can in case a second heave was in the works. He couldn't see me in this condition. "I'll meet you in a few minutes."

"You missed breakfast and the first group meeting." More banging on the door when I didn't answer.

"I have an upset stomach. I must have eaten something bad at dinner." Yeah, if the empty bottles on the floor were any indication, I'd indulged in quite the pity party last night after returning from the AA meeting. Goddammit. I ruined everything.

The door creaked open on its hinge as my head ducked down inside the trash bin. But I didn't need to watch Mark to know what was happening. First, he saw me puking my guts out. Then he noticed the empties scattered around the floor.

"Mark, please! Wait. Don't call Miss Genevieve." I was already on my knees, so begging wasn't so much of a stretch. If I were kicked out, then I would be violating my court-ordered rehabilitation requirement. And I knew exactly where that would lead me.

I was so close. Why? Why had I opened the bottles last night? My shoulder wasn't hurting that badly. It was an easy excuse. My ego hurt worse. I didn't want to be stuck in this place for the next eight months. No more freedom. No more decisions. No more adulting. Apparently one bottle had led to another, then to all the rest. Now I'd give up every wisp of freedom to finish out my year at Carrefour. I leaned against my bed and hid my face in my one good arm.

"Mr. Kyle Joseph Dobrescu . . ." Shit. Miss Genevieve called me by my full name, which she hadn't done since before I redesigned her website. ". . . I'm disappointed. I had high hopes for you. But as I explained to you the morning you arrived a hundred days ago, Carrefour has a single-sanction policy. By drinking alcohol, you violated our rules."

"Wait. I can explain." My plea was earnest, but my brain couldn't keep up with my dashed hopes, so we both waited on my empty promise like a wind chime without a breeze.

"Pack your bags. You have one hour to say your goodbyes."

Chapter 17

MARGARET

AFTER

Slipping into the house, I bring the bitter chill inside with me. Whoever said March came in like a lion and out like a lamb never lived in Chicagoland. No lambs skipping around here. Very few things could've pried me outside in these still-lion-roaring days.

Were it not for a frosty glimpse of sunshine last week, I'd have waited until the temperatures warmed to spruce up Kyle's new memorial stone with spring decorations. Nothing too Eastery, but a few sprigs of pastel silk flowers to brighten up the straw-colored grass.

But today is the first day of spring—according to the calendar—a new beginning. So I donned my winter parka, gloves, hat, scarf, and boots and even brought along a mug of steaming-hot coffee to visit my son's grave.

"Kyle, you probably hate these decorations." I schlep my craft-store bag of spring-themed goodies and rags through the cemetery gates to polish his marble stone. "If you don't want to be the laughingstock of hereafter, then get your rear end back down to earth and give me some hint of your daughter's whereabouts."

Okay, he hardly acknowledged a word I said while he lived with me, so why should I expect him to comply with my nagging now? It's not as if he depends on me to keep a roof over his head or food in his stomach anymore. Lord, do I miss Kyle's cooking. To him, cooking by microwave was a crime. I lived for those evenings when I arrived home from work to a set dinner table, classic rock blasting from the radio, and platters of food made from fresh ingredients I couldn't pronounce. Not that I can eat anything these days, even when Martin throws together something for dinner. But when Kyle cooked, it signaled that he was in a healthy, balanced place. And my anxiety over him would flitter away for a few hours. Perhaps I was Kyle's version of Pavlov's dogs.

Oh, Kyle's daughter. I'd convinced myself that Boo was the young girl from Becca's photo, but it turns out that it was a mirage. My wishful thinking. A week ago, I finally got the nerve to invite Becca to meet me for lunch at a nearby deli. While waiting for our soup and salads to arrive, I asked her point-blank if she and Kyle had ever had a child together. The shock that registered on her face was so instantaneous and genuine that I knew in a nanosecond I'd drawn the wrong conclusion. It turns out the girl she'd been hugging in the photo was her niece.

A disappointing and awkward dead end.

As I traverse the uneven stone slabs forming a pathway to Kyle's grave, something catches my eye. Caught against my mother's memorial stone, which hovers behind Kyle's, is a paper plate anchored by a partially eaten piece of chocolate cake and a half-melted pink birthday candle standing sentry. I glance around to see if a fork or napkin has blown away, but nothing appears to be littering nearby gravestones.

"Kyle? Is this a sign?"

It must be a clue, because why would he toy with me otherwise? I'm surprised the birds haven't pecked it to crumbs, given all the chirping today.

A pink birthday candle usually indicates a girl. Someone made a wish on this cake and blew out the candle. Or the wind snuffed it out. But either way, it was lit and celebrated. Recently.

It rained three nights ago, but this plate isn't soggy. Whoever left the cake did so sometime in the last two days. March 19 or 20. I have no idea what her year of birth is, but this is more information than I've had before.

"Thank you for the lead, Kyle."

My knees cave as I kneel against his stone and bless myself, hoping against hope that this isn't a random coincidence. That it's not another figment of my wishful thinking. But proof that she exists and is local.

I polish the marble with my rags, then jab the new silk flower stems into the rock-hard ground surrounding his inlaid stone. I snap a few pictures of the cake slice before dumping it and the tattered remains of the Valentine's Day silk flowers into a nearby trash can, then head home to strategize.

◆ ◆ ◆

Reconnaissance missions were never meant for almost-seventy-year-old ladies who wear sensible shoes. Nothing but the possibility of seeing my secret granddaughter would ever compel me to sit by Kyle's grave for hours in the bitter cold, day after day. Even with a blanket wrapped around my legs and ensconced inside a foldable spectator chair, I grow more frustrated and miserable with each passing half hour.

My fingertips are so cold the skin is now blanched and numb.

Kyle is laughing at me. I know this as if it were drawn into my body's blueprints. His birthday cake sign didn't really give me any leads. A birthday? What a tease. In all my hours scouring his boxes, I never found a single note or suggestion corroborating a March birthday. The big desk calendar had a single scribble on his March 19 square—*AO*.

That's it. Could that be Boo's initials? Or could it be someone else's initials, a location, or even one of his graphic design clients?

So here I am, keeping my graveside vigil running for my third frigid day in a row. With nothing else to go on other than the knowledge that *someone* had to have left the cake here, I camp out, clutching my rosary beads and praying she—ideally my granddaughter—returns soon for another visit so I can intercept her.

Not a living soul ventured to the cemetery except once when the caretaker arrived to prepare a new grave site on the opposite side for a funeral. Every now and then, a car rolls by, but that's to be expected. People live nearby. This small fenced-in plot of land may be a Catholic church's property, but it's squatting right smack in the middle of a charming old neighborhood located several miles away from the church. The reason we buried Kyle's cremated remains here was that my parents were already eternal residents.

My optimism from finding the birthday cake a few days ago has waned to a small thread of personal distrust. What if the cake was an accident? Or someone's thoughtless littering while visiting another grave resident near our family's plot?

Once the trees' shadows cover the cemetery, I pack up my folding chair. With legs that move as gracefully as Frankenstein's, I lumber away, promising Kyle that I'll return tomorrow.

Hopefully it'll be warmer.

◆ ◆ ◆

"Mom? Are you home?" My front door slams shut, echoing downstairs to where I am huddled in the basement.

"Kimber, honey? Is that you?" I creak into a standing position, but I don't reach the stairwell before she comes bounding down two steps at a time, still wrapped in her winter layers. "We weren't expecting a visit. What brings you all the way here?"

"Can't I check in on my mom and dad?" She squeezes me in a bear hug that tugs the first smile since . . . well, I can't remember when. I wasn't sure my facial muscles still remembered how. When she holds me at arm's length, her face flashes a frown, which is instantly replaced with bright energy. "You've lost weight, Mom. Are you feeling okay?"

"Yes, sweetheart. I haven't had much of an appetite since . . ." She doesn't need me to remind her. She knows. If the dark circles under her eyes mean anything, she's living in my hellscape too. "How have you been coping?"

As if we don't text every day, sending notes of encouragement or some random heartwarming memory of Kyle. I already know we've all shared fifty-nine sleepless nights, up wide awake at 4:00 a.m. No amount of melatonin can knock either of us out. Her sallow complexion and the telltale dark circles under her eyes confirm that she suffered insomnia again last night.

But when her gaze breaks with mine to search the room behind me, I'm left stranded in a void. What's going through her mind as she sees the mountain range of open boxes shoved haphazardly on top of one another? Our basement must look like a hoarder's nest.

"Mom, what's going on?"

"Oh, honey. You know I have to go through all of Kyle's things. We have to wrap up his estate. Close accounts. Pay bills." I didn't even consider telling my daughter the truth. She'll judge me. She already has.

After turning a full circle in slow motion to get a panoramic view of the chaos, she reaches for my hand while shaking her head. "We should talk."

Kimber leads me upstairs to the family room without saying another word. Martin steps out of the dining room's shadows, staring at the floor while covering his pants fly with his clasped hands. The ultimate position of male supplication.

Judy is here, too, scrutinizing me and my body language to gauge my reaction. I'd hug her, but I know better. I love my sister, but her presence here doesn't bode well, especially since she still has another month to go on her Florida condo rental.

Kimber guides me to the lounge chair. Recognizing what's going on instantly, I accept their hot seat with the grace of a matriarch sitting on her throne, my spine ramrod straight, my head held high.

So here we are.

The intervention.

I figured this day was coming. Hell, I'd even organized one for Kyle to force him to address his alcohol addiction. Didn't work. Everyone defers to Kimber as the leader—no surprise, given her corporate managerial experience. I can't even sneak a peek at my husband. As far as I know, he planted the seeds, expressing concern and getting her all riled up from afar.

"Mom, I'm worried about you." Kimber faces me from the sofa across the room, her voice laced with her signature blend of control and panic. "We all are."

"So I see." My tone, I hope, is compliant, if not welcoming. I can't risk giving them any more ammunition than they already have. One by one, they'll take turns mentioning their concerns until finally they'll give me the prearranged ultimatum. Continue on my merry way without them, or seek professional psychological help. Immediately.

The irony is I haven't consumed a drop of alcohol since the moment I buried Kyle, so I know their concern can't be alcohol dependency. Or prescription medications, because I don't have any. Maybe they're worried about my not sleeping or only eating when I'm force-fed. It's not as if I'm underweight, by anyone's definition. My love handles grew a spare tire once I hit menopause.

Baffled, I clamp my mouth shut and mentally compose myself. Everyone's eyes are trained on me. Each heart beating inside my living room is keeping me here among the living. If they are concerned about me, then I need to know.

"Mom, Kyle's death has been hard on all of us, but we know it's been especially hard on you." Urgency wells in Kimber's eyes, lasering her entire focus on me. Sometimes I think I should've given her the middle name *Empathy*. "I don't even know how any mother could bury her child, adult or young, and still keep on breathing—functioning. You know we all love you. Care about you—"

"But that's not the point." Judy jabs her finger in my direction. "You turned down my offer to visit me in Florida after the funeral. It's been two months, and you haven't gone back to work yet. We're all grieving Kyle's death, but somehow the rest of us have all gotten our lives back on track while you keep living in fantasyland. When was the last time you asked about how *we* are coping? You've abandoned—"

"Please, tone it down a notch, Aunt Judy." Leave it to Kimber to rein in my vivacious but impetuous little sister. Not that Judy would often defer to her niece. But this time, blessedly, she simmers down. "This meeting was a total surprise to Mom."

Surprise? More like an ambush.

"The intervention coach told us we need to go point by point to share our concerns and why they are important to resolve." Judy crosses her arms in a huff. "I'm just being honest with her."

"The coach didn't tell us to bludgeon her, Judy." Martin still can't make eye contact with me, but at least he cares about how I will weather this confrontation. My shoulders relax a hair's width.

"Then how are we supposed to make Margaret understand how she's letting us down? I flew half a day to get here." The vein in Judy's neck protruded, a telltale sign ever since we were young that she was upset. "I'm not leaving until I know she knows—"

Lovely. Infighting among my closest family members. I'm not sure if I should excuse myself or wait, but I refrain from rolling my eyes.

"Look, we're here because we all care about you, Mom." Kimber talks over Judy's rant. Martin stands motionless, a study in statue modeling if there ever was one. "I'm personally worried that you've been in denial. About your grief. Have you ever broken down and cried since the funeral?"

Cried? They have no idea the ocean of tears I've wallowed in for months—no, decades—over Kyle. I've always spared them that burden. What none of them seems to understand is that people grieve in different ways. There's no *How to Bury Your Son* manual to follow. I know I'm usually more expressive than I have been lately. I guess you could say I've been preoccupied. But my search for Boo has given me direction, a reason to keep breathing.

"Seeing you all here together, in this room, and the efforts you made to be here make me realize how much you all care about how I'm faring." I take the opportunity to lock eyes with each one and try to telepathically ask for more time and a bit more patience before they expect me to revert back to my usual self. "What is it you want me to do? I'll do absolutely anything you ask if it'll make all of you more comfortable during this transition."

They exchange glances; then Kimber takes the stage. "You have three living, breathing grandchildren you've forgotten about since Kyle died. We want you to give up searching for this phantom granddaughter. You've been obsessing over her for weeks, but there's been no proof of her existence other than some random conversation between Dad and Kyle over a year ago. Go back to work. Get on with your life. Let her go."

No. Anything but that.

Chapter 18

ALLY

BEFORE

Hurry up. The city bus was taking forever today. The driver must be new, because usually they had no fear of pulling out into traffic and cutting off cars to stay on schedule. This guy hit the brakes so often I might as well be sitting in a broken rocking chair. At this rate, I'd only be able to spend a few minutes with Kyle during his visiting hours before racing back to the restaurant for my hostess shift. Saturday nights were always crazy busy.

It was late July. In a few more weeks, I'd be an official college student. I had my student ID and my class schedule. Mom took me back-to-school shopping at Hemingway University's campus bookstore after my freshman orientation. The sale rack had a few green-and-black T-shirts, and I got one—I was officially a Dagger. I even brought something to give Kyle. Not one of those *HU Dad* mugs, because Mom bought herself the complementing mom version, and that would've been too weird. But I figured a small green-and-black woven keychain would be discreet and something he could use.

All summer long, I'd been working two jobs, as a daytime cashier at our local grocery store and as a hostess at a local restaurant during the dinner rush at night. With my savings, the college fund my grandparents had been investing in since I was born—despite not meeting me until I was ten—and a small scholarship I'd been awarded, I almost had my first two years' tuition covered. I planned to live at home to save on room and board, and my boss was letting me stay on as a part-time cashier after classes started. My goal was to graduate with as few student loans as possible.

In all this, Mom had been working so often at the hospital I barely ever saw her anymore. We were lucky if we could high-five in the morning as she walked in the door wearing scrubs and I headed out sporting my royal-blue golf shirt and black pants, my grocery store uniform. I was collecting more and more work uniforms in my closet.

As soon as the bus screeched to a halt at Carrefour's stop, I jammed the button to open the doors, then dashed outside, nearly whacking some poor old lady with my backpack. After pausing to help her up the bus's stairs—it was the least I could do after scaring her—I jogged the rest of the way to the Center. Visitors trickled out the front door, but according to my watch, we still had half an hour.

Racing up to the front desk, I slammed my driver's license down with a thump. "I'm here to visit with Kyle Dobrescu, please."

The receptionist, a young man who I hadn't seen before, kinked his head to the side and looked at me for a moment longer than necessary. More people milled by us as this guy clicked away at his keyboard. I flirted with the idea of slipping into the crowd and sneaking past, but Mr. Slowest Typist on Planet Earth still had my license. Plus, I wouldn't want to get Kyle in any trouble. Or lose my visiting privileges. So I made do with trying to appear patient.

Come on, dude, the visiting session will end soon.

"Ms. O'Leary, would you mind waiting for a minute?" He ducked through a door as I checked my watch. I was going to have to leave within minutes to make it to work on time. After digging through my backpack, I ripped out a sheet of paper from my sketchbook and started jotting Kyle an apology. Damn. It'd be another couple of weeks before I would be able to see him again. Hope his shoulder felt better.

As I folded the note, the receptionist returned, followed by a large Caribbean woman outfitted in a colorful dress. She motioned for me to follow her to a quiet corner of the lounge. Her face was a study of forced neutrality, stirring all the butterflies in my belly to migrate into my throat. My mind ran to the worst-case scenario, a worrying habit I definitely inherited from Mom. It didn't help that Mom's hospital experience had opened my eyes to a whole host of postsurgical medical complications: blood clots, infections, trauma, and the body rejecting hardware such as surgical steel pins to support a broken collarbone.

Visions of him back in the hospital, unconscious and hooked up to a fleet of machines, flooded my mind. Or worse.

"Is Kyle okay?" I wanted to know, but as soon as I asked, I changed my mind. I glanced away, terrified of the truth.

"I'm Miss Genevieve, the Center's director. Unfortunately Mr. Dobrescu is no longer with us."

My heart belly flopped. I gripped the edge of the counter before articulating the very words I prayed weren't true. Surely the universe hadn't let me meet my dad only to have him zapped away from me so quickly. Please, no. He seemed so healthy last weekend. In pain but coping. He couldn't be gone.

"Did he die?"

◆ ◆ ◆

The next day off work would be a weekday morning. Last Saturday, Miss Genevieve had assured me that Kyle hadn't died, that he'd left in healthy condition. Beyond that, she wouldn't share any details about why Kyle had checked out of the Center, but she didn't give me the warm fuzzies that he'd left because he'd been transferred to another facility or had graduated. She wouldn't even tell me where he'd gone.

I was taking a risk, showing up at his town house unannounced. After all, his parents—my grandparents—could be at home. It was a weekday, though. Kyle once mentioned that both his parents still worked full time, so I didn't think they'd be here.

Standing at the foot of the front steps, I texted Jenna that I was hoping to meet Kyle. I looked up to steel myself. The last time I'd showed up here, he didn't invite me inside. Would he think this was invasive? I chucked the thought to the side as quickly as it surfaced. I was merely making sure he was okay. Then I'd leave. He could contact me when he was ready.

Oh, and now that he was out of Carrefour, I hoped to get his cell number so we could text. This predigital communication sucked. Waiting two days for snail mail to be delivered, then a minimum of another two days to get a reply, was cruel and unusual punishment. How did my mom's generation manage without going insane?

Sunshine beat down on me like a sauna after someone poured water over the coals. Already sweating, I could use another shower, and it wasn't even ten in the morning yet.

First step. Then another. Sooner than I was comfortable with, I paused at the front stoop and said a little prayer that this went well. I could use all the help from the universe I could get.

Biting my lips, I rang the doorbell. And waited.

Nothing.

After a few minutes, I rang it again—this time eliciting scrappy barks from the next-door neighbor's backyard. Okay, so the first ring hadn't worked. But still, no one made their way to the door.

For good measure, I knocked, then pounded on the door. The dog, at this point, was going nuts, probably thinking I was the mailman with a delivery. I hated to give him such a rush, to then leave him hanging.

As I gave up and turned around, the door squeaked open a crack.

"Whatever you're selling, I don't want any." The voice was so hoarse I couldn't tell if it was Kyle's, but it was definitely an adult male. I flinched at the tone. "Go away."

"Is Kyle there?" I backed down a step in case I needed to escape with a head start.

An eyeball peered out the slivered opening. I couldn't see inside, but the place looked dark, as if all the window shades were closed.

"Ally?" When Kyle doubled over coughing, I got a glimpse of his blue arm sling, but he wasn't wearing a shirt. Yikes. I hope he wasn't indecent. I waited for him to finish hacking.

"Um, yeah. It's me." Alarm bells sounded inside my head. I took another step back, not sure what I'd stumbled into. Though a blast of cool air from inside washed over me, tempting me forward.

"What are you doing here?"

"I'm checking up on you. When I went to our last visiting hours, you were already gone. What happened?"

His groan wasn't the answer I'd expected. It was guttural, like a wounded animal. Barking nearby picked up in earnest. Oh, my God. Was he hurt?

"Should I call 911?"

"No! God, that's the last thing I need right now."

"Kyle, please tell me what's going on. Why are you back home?"

The door inched open a little farther. His hair was topsy turvy, and his chin sported several days of stubble. But when the odor of decay and stale urine wafted in my direction, I covered my nose and mouth while moving down another step. My eyes threatened to jump out of their sockets, but even though I told myself to turn away, I couldn't.

"What happened to you? What's going on?" Dread washed over me at the sight of him.

"I'm sorry, Ally. Can I meet you in a couple hours? At our coffee shop?"

"Have you been drinking? Is that why you're back home?"

"It's not what you think. I can explain—"

His whiny tone made me cringe. I didn't want his excuses or justifications.

"You told everyone at that AA meeting that you had something new to live for. That you were going to stay sober for me." I turned and marched down the rest of the steps, then all the way to the sidewalk, before turning around. I yelled up at him, not caring if his parents, his neighbors, or the whole world heard my accusations. I was trying not to cry, but my breathing became more rapid, and I kept flexing my fists. There was a staccato to my voice that wasn't indigenous to me; more like my mom's judgy tone. "I believed you."

"I'm sorry. I screwed up. I admit it." Desperation oozed from every slurred word he uttered. "You're the only thing I have to live for now, Ally. Please give me another chance. I'll do better. I promise."

I couldn't freaking believe this. I legit should've listened to Mom. She'd warned me not to get to know him. She didn't even want me to introduce myself to him. He might be my biological father, but he'd never been my dad.

Deep within me, I knew he struggled. That while his addiction to alcohol would never be cured, he could manage it. That's why he'd been in Carrefour. That's what he'd promised everyone at the AA meeting he would do. Was I the only one gullible enough to have taken him at his word?

Mom always had my best interests at heart, even if I didn't always understand why. She must've seen this coming. He'd failed her back then. He was failing me now.

History repeated itself.

Suddenly it dawned on me that this was what life with him going forward would be like. Lots of promises and one too many setbacks. Did I have the energy for this? The stamina?

"Meet me at our coffee shop. Please, Ally? Two thirty." His pleading brushed past me as I walked away, my back to him. At least he couldn't see my face, because the last thing I wanted him to see was my wet cheeks. I flipped him my middle finger, but I didn't turn around, so I had no idea if he was still standing at the door, watching me.

As I trudged back down the street, I chucked the HU keychain I'd bought for him into a nearby garbage can.

Not a shot in hell, Kyle.

◆ ◆ ◆

By the time I got home after my dinner shift at the restaurant, Mom had already left for work. I stayed up late, camped out on our living room couch with pillows and a blanket with Lulu snuggled on my lap, purring. I flipped through channels on our TV, but all I stumbled across were sitcoms and news with headlines more depressing than my life. Even Shark Week didn't make me feel better.

I tossed and turned all night long. By early dawn, I was already dressed for work. As Mom's key turned the knob, I greeted her with a steaming mug of coffee—black, because she was a no-frills person in all the details of her life. And for some bizarre reason, she could still sleep after caffeinating.

"Whoa, thank you. But you should still be sleeping, honey. You don't have to be at work for a few hours . . . wait, Ally-cat. What's wrong?"

I didn't know if it was the quiver in my chin or the anomaly of me being up before my alarm clock that clued her in, but within seconds, she led me to the couch. I sobbed onto her shoulder.

"You were right, Mom. I should've never tried to get to know . . . my biological father." I couldn't even bring myself to call him by his name, because I needed to emotionally distance myself.

Mom's back stiffened, and her hand squeezed my shoulder a little too hard.

"What did he do? Did he hurt you?"

"Not me directly. I found him wasted." Every admission gave Mom more ammunition to be worried about me, but I was done with his lies. "He promised to stay sober because of me. I trusted him."

"Allison, look at me."

Though I fought it, when I finally met her gaze, her eyes were as round as bull's-eyes. Her face was so close; her pupils flitted back and forth between each of mine, searching. But if she was trying to divine information telepathically, it wasn't working.

"You may share DNA with your birth father, but that's all. He isn't one-tenth the person you are. Don't let him dim one more moment of happiness. You have the entire world at your fingertips. I regretted sharing his name with you, but if this experiment means that you can now forget where you came from, acknowledge the smart, strong woman you already are, and focus on all the exciting opportunities ahead of you, then maybe it was a blessing."

What Mom didn't appreciate was that I'd hoped Kyle would be part of my future. That I didn't know him until a few months ago, but I'd always loved him. For a hot minute, as a kid who grew up in a single-parent, single-child family, my prayers had been answered. I'd known he was flawed. I'd hoped he'd try harder. For me.

"He broke his promise." Even though my sobbing left wet stains on her scrubs, she rocked me and stroked my hair. In all these years, I didn't think I'd shed buckets over a crush, a bad grade, or even high-school girl drama. An hour later, when I was so cried out, I got hiccups. She grabbed me tissues. But before she let me wipe my face, she stopped me.

"No more tears, Ally-cat. Be done crying. He's not worth it."

Chapter 19

ALLY

AFTER

Mom left home an hour ago for her graveyard shift at the hospital. It should give me plenty of time to snoop during my study break. Lulu takes one look at me as I triple-lock the front door—just in case Mom returns—then ninja-lunges, disappearing to wherever cats can't be found. And I thought I knew every little nook in our postage-stamp apartment.

So much for the sleuthing help, Watson.

I'm not sure what I'm looking for, but I sneak into Mom's room to investigate the box tucked in the back of her closet and pull out her old photo albums, pictures I'd seen thousands of times before. No way would I find a photo of Kyle and her in there. She'd have destroyed them eons ago. But she kept a few pictures from her SMU college days; those I'd like to see again. Some hint of Kyle's life could be hidden inside these oxidized pages.

As I sit cross-legged on the floor next to her shoes—mostly flats, sneakers, and work clogs—I flip through photo after photo of women with big permed hair and bangs. Mom's hair wins the prize for the most teased out, but honestly, it's a close call. I don't recognize anyone in these pictures, except for an occasional holiday group family picture with Grandma Vicki and Grandpa. The late eighties were such a strange fashion era—so many bows, flowers, and shoulder pads, and so much neon.

By the time Mom graduated and moved to Mount Vernon for college, her style had turned more . . . comfy. T-shirts were layered with unbuttoned plaid shirts, with sleeves rolled up to the elbows, and hoodies.

A few time-faded pages later, I find what I'm looking for. Mom was captured in a photo inside some dark dive bar wearing a black T-shirt with a band logo printed on the front. She's hugging another friend who's wearing a matching shirt—*Silence Deconstructed*. Behind her, on a slightly elevated platform, were four blurred musicians, barely recognizable, except one looked incredibly familiar, with the square jaw and hunched-over physique.

My heart backflips as an intense wave of missing Kyle washes over me. Jeez, I'm shocked this photo survived Mom's purge. Maybe it was because of her friend.

Kyle had longer hair back then, like an overgrown bowl cut. And dyed jet black. Since the photo was taken midsong, he's looking at his finger positioning on the neck of his bass guitar. A couple of random-ish spotlights above illuminate the band members from the ceiling, but otherwise the stage area is so dark and hazy it's as if the venue were filled with cigarette smoke.

There's not a chance in hell that Mom saved her T-shirt. But even so, I search through dresser drawers and a couple of plastic storage bins of clothes she keeps stowed under her bed. Nope. Not there.

Still, I search because there's no way I'll have any ability to concentrate on my lectures until I get through this closet. Somewhere in one of Mom's boxes I'm sure she saved some old college stuff. As I tilt one box after another, teetering on my tiptoes and straining for her last box, I nearly send the chair I'm standing on toppling over.

How could snooping be so dangerous?

But I drag the box down intact. It's heavier than the others, full of books, CDs, and a collection of unorganized nostalgia. I flip through everything, none of which makes much sense to me. Bands I've never heard of, photo frames of people I haven't met, take-out menus from long ago. Really, Mom? Why did you save all this junk?

Scattered across the bottom of the bin are dozens of plastic cartridges with labels handwritten and crossed out. That's when I see it. *Silence Deconstructed*, written in Mom's handwriting on one of the labels.

I hold this plastic thingy up to inspect it. I've heard of mixed cassette tapes before. It's sort of like a DIY analog playlist from decades ago. But I had no idea Mom still had any.

How do I even listen to this thing?

Suddenly I have a burning desire to hear one of Kyle's songs.

◆　◆　◆

Thanks to Mom's cassette tape, I'm now famous at Hemingway U's library. Turns out not many people nowadays have cassette players. But whenever I asked premillennials if they could help me find one, I got regaled by stories from a strange predigital era with day-to-day props such as pay phones installed on every street corner, people carrying around a yellow box with headphones called a Walkman. And boom boxes. Apparently, creating mixtapes was all the rage back then.

I didn't intend to get trapped in this 1990s rabbit hole. However, it took asking seven older-generation coworkers before I found someone who knew someone who had a friend who might still have a working cassette tape player.

When that lead fell through, I checked with the library's media staff at HU. By the time I finally tracked one down, it looked like some forgotten toolbox with big black buttons for eject, play, rewind, fast-forward, and stop. Since the jack to my cell phone's earbuds didn't fit in the audio port, I'd have to play it in the library. And since I wasn't allowed to check out the equipment—I guess once something is that old, it's irreplaceable—I studied in the lounge until one of the conference rooms became available.

So here I am, exiled in some micromini conference room in the library with Kyle's band's tape inserted into some ancient instrument of torture, ready to hit the play button. I whisper half a prayer that Mom never taped over it, erasing his songs, but instead of *Amen*, I end with *What in the hell?*

The opening progression of a guitar slide screeches notes so high and piercing students within earshot of the room's glass door all turn to look. After five minutes of ear-bending, mind-numbing crashing, banging, and yelling and no otherwise discernible melody, I almost abort mission as the first painful song ends. I might need to take ibuprofen after this experiment. I wasn't sure how much was music versus speaker feedback. Then the lead singer spoke into the mic: "Welcome to Tracks. We are Silence Deconstructed. Troy on guitar, Kyle on bass, Joe on drums, and I'm Chip on vocals." A trickle of applause sounds, then cheering from two female voices near the source of the recording.

Oh, my God. That's Mom's twentysomething voice chanting Kyle's name. I clamp my hand over my own mouth, willing her to shut up and stop making an idiot of herself. She must've been tipsy. God, I hope so. Giggles laced through her words, probably from some groupie friend. Okay, this all happened a couple of decades ago, but I'm witnessing Mom's swan dive into fandom.

Drumsticks tap a beat until the band devolves into more indistinguishable cacophony masquerading as a new and different song. Incredulous thoughts swirl through my mind as I brace myself for the remaining thirty-minute ear-splitting tape recording.

How on earth could my soft-rock-listening mom have been a fan of such hard-core music?

◆　◆　◆

Rain slashes across my windshield, squeaking with each arc of the wiper blades. My morning turned from dove gray to charcoal and back to cement gray. At least my umbrella is a cheerful shade of tangerine. Mom bought it the last time she shopped at the discount fashion store.

These past few weeks, I meant to get back to the cemetery. But ever since spring break, all my professors have been going full steam ahead with lecture content and labs. It doesn't help that my final projects have crept up on me and are due at the end of April. Since my birthday, I seem to be living at the library on campus. Whenever I even start to think about my final exams, my anxiety froths over like a shaken bottle of soda.

I've even had to cut back on my cashier shifts, which has crunched my wallet. I'll make up for it with extra hours and find a second job next summer. Maybe the restaurant I worked at as a hostess last summer will rehire me. Living at Mom's apartment for another year will help my budget too.

But concentrating on schoolwork has been near impossible. Every time I take a study break, a new wave of grief topples my concentration with the reminder that Kyle is gone. For good. Last April, when Kyle ghosted me, I thought I'd made a mistake connecting with my birth father. Turned out to be one of the best decisions I ever made. But now, he really is a ghost.

Two weeks ago, I made my birthday pilgrimage to visit Kyle. This morning I'm making my third-ever trek to his grave site. No specific reason or occasion this time.

God, I miss him.

Before heading over, I stopped by our café and splurged on a barista coffee to celebrate the occasion. Every time I show up, I bring along food or, in this case, a beverage. Hope I'm not breaking graveside-manner protocol, but I could really use a mocha cappuccino with whip to cheer me up. And conversation over coffee was our thing.

While I park the car alongside the cemetery gates, the rain starts falling horizontally. After opening the car door, I'm glad I grabbed rain boots this morning, or I'd be sloshing through the pond-size puddles with saturated shoes. Despite tugging my sweatshirt's hood over my ponytail, I still need an umbrella to keep my face semidry. My legs are already sopping wet, and I wish I'd packed a spare pair of jeans.

A roll of thunder rumbles nearby, making my chest vibrate. For half a heartbeat, I consider leaving pronto and returning another day. But I'm already here. I might as well at least wish Kyle good morning in person. Even a quick visit will count for something. To me, at least.

Moss grows in patches on the brick retaining wall. I climb the few steps to the wrought iron entry gate with its chain padlock open. I tilt my umbrella sideways to enter, raindrops pelting my cheeks in the process.

Angling my umbrella, I block the worst of the driving rain, but it partially obstructs my view. The stone pavers near Kyle's grave sit barely above the surface of a muddy river, tumbling down the sloping ground, giving me the surreal sense of walking on water.

As Kyle's memorial stone moves into view, my umbrella bumps against something, so I flinch back, lifting the rim enough to see what I'd scraped against. Was that a tree branch?

No, another umbrella.

This one is a black vented golfer-size version but hovering low to the ground as if it were being held by a child.

"Oh! I'm so sorry." I take a few more steps back, thinking this entire venture is a ridiculous idea. And in the rain. Someone else is spending time with Kyle, or possibly the other two buried alongside him, his grandparents. "I didn't see you there."

The edge of the black umbrella lifts enough for me to see that it's covering a woman who is sitting in a folding sports chair, facing Kyle's gravestone.

"Please don't apologize. It's not a problem." Her voice is warm and welcoming. And older. In her lap, her fingers grip a necklace of lavender glass beads with a cross hanging lower. A rosary? She was praying. I can't see her full face with the umbrellas between us, but I have an idea—an excellent idea—of who she is.

Oh, Kyle. A surprise encounter wasn't how I planned to meet your mom. Glancing at my watch, I calculate how much time I have to slog through rain-delayed traffic, search endlessly for whatever parking spots may still be available on campus—if any—and park my butt in my classroom seat before my professor begins her lecture. I have max ten minutes before I need to leave. How can I introduce myself and explain all this complicated mess in ten minutes?

I wanted to plan my introduction better. Improv isn't my strong suit. She's my grandmother, yet she has no idea I even exist. The last thing I want to do is give her a heart attack, especially over her son's grave.

Kyle, help me out here. Please.

"Excuse me, I don't want to interrupt your time with your loved one. I can return later." My steps backward slosh in another muddy stream.

"No. Please don't leave on my account. Are you here . . ." She struggles to hoist herself into a standing position, her umbrella teetering, sending a wave of water crashing off to one side. At least now I can see her face. Her eyebrows scrunch together. For a grandmother, she has very little gray hair. In fact, once again, I'm kind of surprised by how young she looks. Grandma Vicki looks frail in comparison. "Are you here to visit Kyle Dobrescu's grave?"

"Yes." I feel like I've leaped from an airplane and am free-falling toward earth. I hope my parachute works. "Hi, my name is Ally."

Chapter 20

KYLE

BEFORE

I was riding the express train to hell.

For the fifth day in a row, I'd spent all afternoon parked in a lounge chair at the café where Ally and I always met. My decaf coffee grew cold because I'd been nursing it for so long, waiting for her to show up, and I didn't want to give up my seat. Or hers.

No sign of her. I glanced at my watch. In another hour, I'd need to leave to attend my AA meeting. But I'd give her another fifty-nine minutes.

If not, maybe tomorrow she'd drop in.

I'd give up anything to relive the morning last week when Ally rang our doorbell to not have answered the door. To keep at least the illusion that I was an upstanding human. To buy me some more time to get back on my feet, at least to have recovered from my hangover, before reaching out to her.

Why the fuck had I answered the goddamned door?

Nothing good could ever have come of that. It could've been a sheriff coming to arrest me for having left Carrefour. Or a process server delivering a subpoena. Or a debt collector. But it was way worse than any of those.

Ally had caught me at rock bottom.

Who was I kidding? My real problem was that I'd started drinking again. And my failures didn't stop there. After begging her to meet me at the coffee shop that afternoon, I went back to bed to sleep off my buzz and didn't wake up until after it was dark. I'd stood her up. I had no idea if she showed up, but I sure as hell hadn't.

Certainly hadn't been the first time I'd fucked up, but hopefully the last.

I could isolate the moment about ten years ago when I lost my day job at Dad's business as one of my addiction-free-fall milestones. Not Dad's fault for shuttering his business in order to become an employee. More like a chicken-and-egg problem. With the economy tanking, his business had suffered, so he opted for a steadier income. My main hurdle was that no one would hire me once they ran a background check. Even when I was hired to wait tables, managers wouldn't tolerate me missing a shift or two. I'd become collateral damage with too much time on my hands.

Not too long after, friends and family had hosted a couple of interventions.

Ally had no reason to believe in me, let alone trust me, anymore. I failed my mom, my family, and my bandmates. Now I'd failed my daughter more times and in more ways than I'd care to admit.

God, she was so young—only eighteen years old.

I guess I'd been thirteen when my floor gave way. Thirteen years, two months, and seven days old. That was all the childhood God saw fit to let me enjoy. But that afternoon. If only I hadn't insisted that I needed those fucking sneakers. What brand were they? I no longer remember. Some trendy style that I'd been determined to wear to the school dance that night.

Dad had been working late that night. Kimber had already graduated from college and was living in New York City. It was just me, Mom, and Dad living at home then. So I guess I'd pestered Mom enough that she caved and agreed to take me shopping at the mall.

Rubbing my temples with my good hand, I switched off my memories. If there was any truth I'd learned from my AA meetings, it was from the Serenity Prayer. *God, grant me the serenity to accept the things I cannot change.* I couldn't change the past.

But if only I could go back in time and change that single day . . .

One more glance at my watch. One more swig of room temperature coffee; then I'd give up my vigil waiting for Ally. She wasn't coming to the café today. I knew where her home was located. She actually lived within a few miles of this coffee shop. I'd snail-mailed her from Carrefour enough to have memorized her address, but I wouldn't go knocking on her door. No need to freak Hannah out, thinking that I could be stalking her daughter. Our daughter.

No, I'd wait for Ally to come here when she was ready. And when she did, I'd be waiting here to apologize. Sober. She could take all the time she needed. Ally was worth every minute.

It was my fault. Then and now. All of it.

Six days. Seven days in a row. Soon the café's staff could ask me to start paying rent if I continued to monopolize that damned lounge chair. Meanwhile, I tried to look as busy as possible while my coffee cooled off. I'd kept up with my Carrefour journaling. I even worked on organizing some peer-group discussion ideas. Not that Miss Genevieve would ever let me back in the building. But I hoped she'd consider being a reference, especially since I'd updated Carrefour's website. I'd borrowed Dad's extra laptop so I could work on starting my freelance design business. And none of this would even matter if the judge found me before I could check into another rehab facility.

Every time the hanging doorbells jingled, my body snapped into high alert, then deflated once I confirmed it wasn't Ally. My pulse would take a few minutes to settle down so I could focus on my work again.

Waiting for Ally to show up at the café could be one of my stupider ideas. I'd researched Hemingway U's academic calendar online and figured out that fall-semester classes would start two weeks from now. If she didn't show up by then, I'd have to figure out a plan B.

I had a panoramic view of the entire café from my perch. I couldn't miss anything. Today's task while waiting was to prepare a bid on a potential graphic design order. Something small, but I had some cool ideas. Didn't share my plans with Mom and Dad yet. They'd heard me wax on before about my goals—usually to buy myself more time with them off my back—then witnessed me tripping over my own feet. Not this time. I'd fill them in once I accomplished something real.

My lawyer figured it might take a while before the courts learned I wasn't in compliance, so I'd been calling around again, trying to find an empty bed. Nothing yet. But this time, I didn't know if my reputation with Carrefour had preceded me or not. Miss Genevieve could've blackballed me across all the local rehab centers. Day after day, I made my morning phone calls to rehab centers to find an opening. Each afternoon, I set up shop at my café "office" to work on launching my new business. Then each evening I attended an AA meeting. After so many days of the same routine, I was no longer sure what day of the week it was.

The bells jingled again, and I popped my head up from the laptop screen, but the couple that entered was older.

As if my situation wasn't bad enough, I'd lost my letters from Ally. In my haste to say goodbye to everyone and leave Carrefour, I'd forgotten to pack the contents of one of my desk drawers. Ally's letters?

Gone. My journals? All that work faded into the ether. My stuff was probably shoved in the dumpster out back within the hour to make my bedroom ready for someone else. I left several panicked messages for Miss Genevieve when I'd realized my goof but never got a return phone call. It had been almost a month.

I was a classic dipshit.

After standing up to stretch, I followed the couple to wait in line. The pastries in the glass display case looked tempting, but I limited myself to one of their protein packs instead. Not as much taste, but it was easier to digest. It would hopefully keep my energy flowing for the next couple of hours before I needed to leave.

Time buffered in this little shop. I'd submerged back into my work when the door opened again. This time a whole group of young teens wandered in. When did all these kids get so hooked on coffee? But as I refocused on my screen, something caught my peripheral vision. The toes of a pair of tennis shoes stood in front of me, pointing in my direction. I followed them up to the knock-kneed legs sporting a pair of black pants, then to a royal-blue polo shirt I recognized as the uniform of the cashiers at a local grocery store chain. Her hands were on her hips. Her dark hair was pulled back in a ponytail.

Then I saw a carbon copy image of my dark eyes glaring back at me. Hard.

Cold.

My breath caught in my throat, making me choke on the cheese cube I'd been munching.

She could've turned on her heel and run away. I wouldn't blame her. But she waited, judging me.

I'd get hell to pay in the next few minutes. Thank you, God, for granting me the courage to change the things I could. I needed to do right by her.

Every hour waiting in this café had been worth it. My daughter had found me.

"Good to see you." I powered down my laptop and moved my notebook away from the other lounge chair I'd been saving for her. "Can I buy you a coffee?"

"No." She crossed her arms, her voice clipped.

"Do you have a few minutes to talk?" My voice catches, so I shut up.

"Depends." Though making no moves toward the chair, she was at least still with me. After glancing outside, she exhaled audibly. "Look, I'm on my way to work, and my shift starts in twenty minutes."

"I'm sorry, Ally. I'm sorry I wasn't at Carrefour when you came by for visiting hours. I'm sorry you saw me in such bad shape last week—"

"Are you sober?" Her words stung me like vinegar on a cut.

Sober? Hell, yeah.

"Yes. One hundred percent." I yelled my reply but checked myself so as not to draw notice from the other patrons. Not because I was frustrated but because every minute of every day this past week had been an exercise in earning her trust back. I'd even been looking into registering for a couple of classes at the local community college for the upcoming fall semester to earn enough credits to transfer into Hemingway U. "I've been sober for the past eight days."

After digging into my pocket, I handed her my token. "In another twenty-one days, I'll have my one-month token. I hope you will be with me when I receive it."

"I start school soon. I'm not sure how heavy my schedule will be with work and studying and all . . ." She was waffling, stepping back. Shit. I was coming on too strong. I needed to give her time to adjust. Hell, I came shrink-wrapped in more baggage than any teen should have to deal with. Maintaining a relationship with my daughter could prove to be trickier than any romantic relationship I've ever been in. And I'd fucked all those up.

"That's okay." Motioning my head toward the counter, I slipped my good hand into my back pocket. My injured one was still strapped in a sling to my torso. My pose was as vulnerable as I could possibly be.

If she wanted to belt me, I'd be easy prey. "Let me buy you a coffee for the road. I don't want to make you late for work."

After pausing for forever, she nodded, her face relaxing, but her arms remained crossed. "Okay. Iced coffee, please."

I followed her to the counter, floating the whole goddamned way because she'd thawed a couple of degrees. Good thing she couldn't see me grinning or she might get angry again. Actually, I was pretty damned proud of my daughter. She had a spine. She sure as hell didn't inherit it from me. I had Hannah to thank for that.

After paying and collecting her drink, I escorted her to the door. She paused, staring at her feet. Every cell in my body screamed to pre-arrange our next rendezvous, but I didn't want to come on too strong again.

"When I came by your house last week, I wanted to make sure you were okay. I also wanted to ask you for your cell phone number so we could communicate a little easier. But I don't think I'm ready for that yet."

"No pressure. I can wait until you are ready." Holding up my good hand, I stepped back to give her a comfortable space. "I'm not going to push you, Ally. You are worth more to me than time."

"Will you be moving back into Carrefour?"

Oh, I wished it were as simple as if I'd been suspended from school for bad behavior. "No. I broke some rules. Big rules. So I was expelled from the program. I'm looking for a new rehab center now."

Her face was challenging to read. The furrowed brows conflicted with the hint of a dimple that showed up whenever she smiled.

"When you find one, please write to me and send me the address. Hopefully I can get on your approved visitors list again."

Who knew how long that might take? My gut sank somewhere near my ankles. I'd hoped she'd agree to meet with me at least once before then. Ideally more. Then again, she was still offering me an unlocked door to the future, and that was everything I'd hoped for when I started showing up at this café a week ago to wait for her. I nodded, hoping I'd wiped any trace of disappointment from my face.

"Do you want me to walk you to work?"

"No thanks." She slipped through the door with the straw of her iced coffee already in her mouth. I hovered by the window for a moment, watching her walk away in case she looked behind.

She didn't. Ouch.

With my heart bruised, I squeezed my eyes shut. Rebuilding a relationship with her would take a lot longer than I'd initially hoped. As it should. Then I returned to my lounge chair to collect my laptop, no easy feat given my one-handedness. If God's plan was to force me to drive the slow lane in life, He couldn't have dished it out any heavier than three pins in my collarbone. Even zipping my bag took patience, something that was draining out of me like water from an unstopped tub.

"Kyle?"

Jerking at the sound of my name, I turned to find Ally standing behind me again.

"Do, um, do you think we could meet and talk again sometime?"

My throat clenched as my eyes stung. "Name the day."

Chapter 21

MARGARET

AFTER

"Did you say your name is Ally?" Oh, this young woman with the tangerine umbrella and black rain boots standing in the cemetery couldn't have surprised me more if she'd slid down a rainbow to land in front of me. Every cell in my body stands at attention.

"Yes, ma'am. It's short for Allison."

"Very nice to meet you. I'm Margaret." My mind turns backflips at having potentially found the elusive A. O. "You look quite familiar. Haven't we met before?"

But my question is rhetorical, and this is no April Fools' joke. I recognize Kyle's deep-set chocolate-brown eyes in hers. His square jaw. His dark hair, though hers barely peeks out from the hood of her sweatshirt—no need for a birth certificate or DNA test to prove her kinship, not for me anyway. Martin might be a different story.

My granddaughter.

My precious Boo found me at her father's grave. And to think I'd considered staying home today because of the rain. Thank you to whichever divine impulse prompted me to override my reluctance.

Thank you, Kyle, for intervening. In my heart, I believed if I'd waited a little longer, my prayers would be answered. You would lead me to your daughter. Who knows why a golden glow hasn't already descended upon this child's beautiful head?

"Yes. We spoke briefly at Kyle's visitation service." The way she digs the toe of her rain boot into the wet stones warms my heart. She's nervous, but she hasn't broken eye contact with me. I get the sense she's gauging my reaction. She's like that cardinal that swooped down on Kyle's gravestone earlier this morning. I held my breath and didn't move for fear of scaring it away. Instead, the bright-red bird paused, pecked at moss invading the edges, then flew back into the nearby trees.

"Ah, yes. I remember now. Didn't you mention something about studying with him?"

"Yeah. During the fall semester, we were both taking Intro to Psychology classes at our different colleges. We'd occasionally meet at a café to study and compare notes." A twinkle flashes in her eyes. Suddenly they close, and her face scrunches. After a moment, she nods. "I miss Kyle. Miss spending time with him."

Words escape me. I'm not sure if it's because my brain seized or the lump forming in my throat is blocking all intelligible sounds. All I can muster is a hoarse "Me too."

"I'm sorry to dash . . . Margaret . . . but I was stopping by on my way to class." She glances at her watch and then splashes her boot through the puddle. "Do you think we could meet again? I'd love to, um, find out more about Kyle."

Warmth spreads through my limbs, causing nerves to zing. It's the first hint of energy, of life, I've felt in months. The pain is as welcome as the shocks during the first tentative rotation of my wrist after the doctor removed my cast years ago and told me to try moving it. I'd stare at my wrist, not trusting that it would respond to my commands after being immobilized for such a long time. Now, after all these months, I feared that my heart had gone dormant or, worse, died. Not so.

"I'd love that, Ally."

It takes every ounce of self-control to contain my emotions, but I wait until my granddaughter leaves the cemetery and drives off in a little red car. After sinking into my folding chair, my heart opens and spills forth, as if the Hoover Dam had burst a seam.

Tears for having lost my precious son, first to alcohol, then to this physical world.

Tears for having doubted that Kyle's daughter existed.

Tears for having almost given in to Kimber's and Martin's attempts to dissuade me from finding her.

My sweet, elusive Ally. My Boo. Kyle's gift to me—to our family—from heaven.

Why didn't he introduce her to us himself? Did he think I'd be livid that he'd had a child out of wedlock? I might have been shocked, but after the endless stream of nightmares Kyle dragged us through, I'd have welcomed this as a blessing. The silver lining to our decades of skimming the surface of hell.

And she is endearingly beautiful, as only a young person who is so shy—she has no inkling of her potential—can be. I trust first impressions as much as I believe that angels walk among us. Three minutes in her presence proved her worth. Her mother, whoever she is and however she and Kyle met and parted ways, did an outstanding job of raising Ally.

How long have I been sitting here mentally digging through layers of dirt to Kyle's urn? Hours? Days? My soul has resided in this graveyard every waking moment since he was interred—two months, one week, three days, and eighteen hours ago.

My knees and hips creak as I haul myself out of the camping chair. While stretching into a sailor's widened stance to keep my balance, my limbs ache and tingle, reminding me that though my son isn't alive, I very much am. The rain tapers off, first to a fine mist, then to drips forming on the brand-new leaves from the maple tree overhead. Each heavy plop on my umbrella awakens my senses.

A bird whistles in a tree branch far above me. When I finally spot the flash of red feathers, it flies away from my sight. Of course. Deep within my broken soul, I knew he'd be here. One way or another.

As I fumble while folding my camping chair, somewhere nearby young schoolchildren's voices shriek, laugh, and giggle in a chorus of pent-up energy, exploding randomly like trick birthday candles. Despite the chill, I'm guessing the teachers are even more relieved for a break in the storm and to venture outside for recess than the kids.

That's what I've missed most from these endless dark days. Life.

◆ ◆ ◆

Storm clouds hover low as I steer through one neighborhood after another, not sure where my destination rests. I don't want to return home to my grief. Not yet. Not while my heart flirts with hope. Instead, I drift along quiet streets, lost in my thoughts. The hint of spring brought toys dredged from the depths of garages and scattered in front yards, waiting to be played with after school.

I suppose I'm looking for Ally's home, as ridiculously impossible as that seems. But now that I've met her, I'm desperate to know how she grew up. How every unaccountable day was spent, hopefully in sepia-toned memories of laughter and joy. That she never went hungry. Or broke a bone. Does she have siblings? A stepfather? Did she get good grades? Did her mother and Kyle keep in touch over the years? Did they meet in college?

Ally told me she missed him, but when she attended his wake, she didn't identify herself as his daughter. Even this morning, she had no idea I knew we were related. Was she overwhelmed? Embarrassed?

Mile after mile, I wind toward the business end of town, an area overburdened with strip malls and traffic lights. When it takes me more than three cycles to get through a single intersection, I pull into a mall parking lot to wait out the rush-hour congestion.

Nowadays, malls are built with an open-air concept, which suits me perfectly. I haven't entered an indoor mall in decades and never will again. Ever. But this one is open, and I've shopped here many times over the years. Before I head inside, I text Martin.

Me: I'm out shopping.

Martin: I need to work late.

Me: What time will you get home? I'll bring dinner.

Martin's mention of work makes my chest pitch. I've gone off grid for far too long, hovering on this not-quite-alive-not-quite-dead plane of existence. Judy was right. The staff at my clinic may have forgotten I'm still alive, let alone functioning. I need to get back in touch with them and on the nursing rotation schedule. At least part time. The paycheck will help, and it'll do my sanity good to think about something other than surviving my son's death. For a few hours anyway. Nursing, for me, has always been about helping and protecting the living. I should wash my scrubs this weekend.

I stumble toward the mall and make it inside a department store's glass door just as the rain comes down in sheets. I could be here for a while, so I drift from rack to rack of ladies' clothes, which are much too smart and trendy for my sensible taste and comfort-driven lifestyle. But as strong as it is surprising, something urges me to wander into the junior section, perhaps dreaming about future shopping excursions with Ally, which I do with each of my grandchildren when I can get them one on one. I've always subscribed to the strict policy that grandmothers have unlimited spoiling rights. Period. That tradition, which I need to resurrect as soon as possible, also died with Kyle.

Lordy, I have a lot of relationships to reengage, starting first with my grandchildren.

As I turn to examine the sales rack, thinking perhaps I can find something small and personal to give to Ally whenever she realizes I know that I'm her grandmother, I stop cold.

My pulse thumps in my ears.

Holy Mary, how had I not noticed the signs overhead? I've spent most of my adult life avoiding public restrooms. I somehow let my guard down. Why now?

Stepping backward, I try to tear my gaze away, but my eyes zero in. I can't even blink. The water fountain telescopes away from me as if I'm looking through the lens on the wrong end. It doesn't matter. Even if I sprinted twenty miles away, I'd still see that stainless steel tub. The knob. The spout. Remember exactly what I was wearing. And Kyle. Bile stings my throat.

Oh, the cruel, cruel irony.

I'm okay. It's over. I'm safe.

But this time, my mantra doesn't work. My heart races to a billion beats per minute, threatening to burst through my ribs and jump out of my body. Even so, my chest constricts, turning my breathing fast and shallow.

How long have I been standing here, staring at the small alcove meant for people to relax? Minutes? Hours? The roar of a wide-body commercial jet takes off in my throbbing head.

"Ma'am? Ma'am, are you okay?" A sales attendant grips my arm, dragging my attention away from my portal to hell to look at her. Her face swims in and out of focus in front of me, and I steady myself on a nearby rack. She looks so young. How old are they hiring staff these days? Twelve? "Your face is pale, ma'am. Do you want to sit down? Can I get you some water?"

Terrified the girl might take me toward the water fountain, I override the choking sensation and force my lungs to expand despite the vice grip constricting my throat. I take a tentative step toward the front of the store. "No, thank you, dear. But I could use some fresh air."

"Are you sure I can't get the manager?" She grips my side as I teeter, keeping me vertical. "Or call an ambulance?"

"No, no, thank you. I just lost my balance for a moment. That's all. I'm better now." I stutter between gulps of air. Finally I draw my first natural breath since before I panicked, relaxing with each shuffling step we take toward the store's glass-door exit. Rain is still pelting down, but the sky is brightening, so it should pass soon, like my panic attack did. It's been years since I've had one of these. "You've been most helpful, dear. I'll wait out here until the rain stops."

◆ ◆ ◆

"Martin, are you here?" It's well after sunset by the time I arrive home. A stream of light shines from somewhere in the back of our town house, but I didn't see his car parked out front. I sat in my car in that mall parking lot until the rain subsided, but at least I'd been able to calm down enough to drive home without being a road hazard.

"Hi, honey. In the kitchen."

Still standing in the doorway, I turn to look at the parking lot out front. Sure enough, his car is parked right next to mine. How hadn't I noticed? Good Lord, I'm walking around with blinders on.

"I'm starving. What did you bring for dinner?"

Dinner. Oh, my God. I promised to bring home dinner not two hours ago. I'm failing at everything. The door creaks as I close it; then I lock the dead bolt. "I, um . . . forgot. Sorry. I'll whip something together now."

He steps out of the kitchen, casting a shadow large enough to be from an ogre. As he approaches to help me remove my soaking wet jacket, my arms fall limp, a puddle collecting under my umbrella. My feet grow roots into the floor. I can't rip my eyes from his gaze.

"You've been forgetful lately. And more emotional with each passing week. Honey, you doing all right?"

"No . . . yes . . . no." Crap. Now I can't even make up my mind. I don't bother reminding him that I buried *my* son less than three months ago. No one hands you a guidebook to grief. It's a journey we must each travel in our own way. Mine is apparently a rocky path.

But Kyle was his son too. How can he remain so unemotional?

Martin's right, though. Today has been stressful—in a both good and bad way. Still, Kyle took our shared secret to his grave, and I intend to as well. I made him promise never to tell anyone. So I certainly can't tell Martin now, after all these years.

And Martin kept from me the information about having a granddaughter until after Kyle died, so I have zero guilt not telling him about meeting Ally until she's comfortable sharing the news with our family at large.

"I've had a long day is all." The worst part is unless I somehow figure out how to hack Kyle's phone, I have no way to reach Ally directly. I have to wait for her to contact me. So I'll go back to Kyle's grave again tomorrow. And the next day. And the next. Until Ally shows up again.

"You rest. I'll fix us something for dinner." Martin guides me to the kitchen and sits me down. But before tinkering around the pantry, he sits in the chair across from mine. "I heard back from Mr. Davenport today."

My body is equal parts curious and nervous, but Martin's deadpan face gives nothing away. "Is it good news or bad?"

"Both." He leans forward on his elbows, masking a shoulder twitch. "Apparently the department had a shift change while Kyle was at the ER. Someone's card didn't swipe properly when logging into his medical records file in the computer system. It wasn't any of the doctors or nurses. He said the review committee thoroughly investigated all medical procedures, diagnoses, and treatments to make sure they were sound."

An emptiness invades the space in my heart that had been holding on to the hope of answers. Some concrete resolution as to what happened to Kyle. An end to the questions. "So, then, what's the good news?"

"Well, apparently the hospital has offered a settlement of waiving all emergency room charges for that night in exchange for closing the matter. It amounts to saving several thousand dollars in expenses. Obviously we can decline and try to sue, but Davenport recommended we take the settlement." Martin reaches for my hand, but I flinch and pull away. "I agree with him. It's time to move on, Margaret."

That's it? That's the value of my son's life.

The hospital.

Martin.

Mr. Davenport.

They all want to settle and move on. A few thousand dollars to walk away and never, ever raise the subject again. How can a mother give up asking questions? I still don't know exactly how and why he died.

"Before we accept the settlement offer, I'd prefer to talk to Mr. Davenport myself."

"Sure. But, honey, I know this has all been really hard on you. Have you given any more thought to what Kimber and Judy suggested? About speaking with someone?" Martin's brows arch so high they blend with his forehead wrinkles. His voice is tentative, as if he's coaching me through a field of land mines with an obsolete map. It's horrible living with someone who is losing touch with reality and feeling helpless to do anything about it. We both experienced it with Kyle's alcoholism. But these days he's reliving it because of me. "A professional?"

"Yes." I nod, though I can already see the relief washing over his face, his shoulders relaxing. He's right. They all are. I need help.

From his pocket, he slips out a business card. One glance makes me shake my head and flinch. No way would I ever talk to that interventionist they all consulted. "No, not a therapist."

"But I thought you said you'd—"

"I'll talk to a priest." God help me. If that doesn't clear my head, then maybe my pastor can recommend an exorcist.

Chapter 22

KYLE

"Are you nervous about starting college tomorrow?" I handed Ally her iced coffee—her standard order in the dog days of summer. Thank God for air-conditioning and ice.

She nodded. Her quasi answer slipped into the ether for the moment. Each of us sipped our coffees, lost in our own thoughts as customers drifted in and out of the café. To be honest, I was a little nervous myself about going back to school. I hadn't finished a college-level class in years. That last time I registered for one, I dropped it because I'd skipped so many lectures I was on track to fail. This time, I might have to quit if I could move into a new residential rehab program, but maybe they'd grant me off-site privileges for education. Or let me continue classes online. And if I didn't find another program, at least I'd have something positive and current to tell the judge.

"When do you think you'll have time to take a study break?" I clinked my coffee cup with hers.

Excitement washed over her face as she flipped through her phone, looking at her calendar. It still might be hotter than Dante's inferno outside, but her real-world obligations would launch when her alarm clock sounded tomorrow morning. As would new opportunities. New friends. "I don't know. With school starting, and work, and studying, I'm not sure when . . ."

Give her space, give her space . . . , I chanted to myself, hoping I didn't come off as desperate.

"Do you mind if we play it by ear? I might need a week or two to adjust to my new schedule. Then I'll have a better idea."

"Sure." The thing was, without preplanning the rendezvous, my ability to connect with her diminished. But I tried to keep my energy level up for her and clamped down on my frustration. I wanted to support her, not be needy.

"It may be easier to plan something if we exchange cell phone numbers." She hesitated as if she wasn't sure I'd be okay with this plan. As if it wasn't what I'd been hoping for with every eroded beat of my heart these past few weeks. Or since I'd met her.

As I blinked to temper my smile, we texted each other for the first time. Ally was now officially a contact on my phone. But instead of calling her *Ally,* I tagged her by her initials: *A. O.* I'd know who she was, but if I ever had to surrender my phone to a residency program or a court, I didn't want someone to figure out our connection. My reputation could drag her down.

"Oh, one more thing, Kyle. Mind if we take a selfie?"

A few weeks later, I texted Ally and invited her to join me at one of my upcoming daily AA meetings. I was already missing the carefree days of her summer break when she could fit in a coffee rendezvous between her job shifts. Now that her classes had started, she was so busy and overwhelmed that it could take a while for her to have even a small window of free time.

A. O.: Class review session tonight, but I'm off work tomorrow. Can I meet you then?

A year ago, if someone had told me I'd get so giddy at the prospect of going to an AA meeting, I'd have asked them to share their drugs. But now, I was planning a father-daughter date for an AA meeting. Go figure.

Then, inspiration struck. Why hadn't I thought of this before? Probably due to my dwindling supply of brain cells. Dad, who was working across the dining room table from where I'd set up a makeshift workstation, sat down with a cup of tea. Before he dove back into his work, I sprung my idea on him.

"Hey, Dad. Do you mind driving a friend home after tomorrow's AA meeting?"

"Friend?" Mom poked her head out of the kitchen long enough to give me her inquisitive raised eyebrow. Granted, I hadn't mentioned much about any sort of friends in the past couple of years. "Who's your friend?"

"Ally. I met her a few months ago." The white lie might come back to haunt me, but this could be a smooth way to transition into the guess-what-I-have-a-daughter conversation we would eventually host. Later. Once they got to know her, it would be way easier to love her.

"A girlfriend?" Her question lingered like I was a middle school kid with zits and sweaty hands thinking about asking a girl to the fall dance. Nope.

"No, Mom. Just a friend who happens to be a girl. She's a student at Hemingway U and needs a lift home after the meeting."

"Isn't college age kind of young to already be attending AA meetings?" Mom turned back behind the wall. Her question was more rhetorical than literal. She must not remember that the genesis of my drinking habit started long before I'd left for college.

Instead of answering, I nudged Dad under the dining room table and asked him again. His nod took a massive weight off my soul.

Me: Perfect. See you there. I'll drop you off at your home afterward.

◆ ◆ ◆

Ally's face, as she scanned the room from the metal chair next to mine, was a blank canvas. I'd love to know her thoughts. Her face remained unreadable. But she was alert, listening to each AA participant who stood up. We'd been in this multipurpose room for nearly an hour, so my time with her this evening was running out. Why did time always slip by at the speed of thought when I was with her?

Tonight, I collected my one-month token, but unlike the first time she'd attended, I didn't stand and talk. After the guy currently speaking sat back down, I expected the meeting's leader to wrap up by passing around the donation bucket and asking everyone to stand and pray the Our Father. I hardly noticed that Ally moved in her seat until she stood and cleared her throat.

"Hi. My name is Ally—Allison—and I'm a guest of an alcoholic. This is my second AA meeting."

Oh, my God. She was talking about me in public. My gut tightened, and for a nanosecond, I wasn't even sure my lungs would expand enough to allow me to breathe. But she reached for my hand and squeezed, her palm ice cold despite the lingering warmth of summer on this September Chicago evening.

"Tonight I'm here to support someone very special to me, my father. I was with him a few months ago when he collected his one-month token and here again tonight as he celebrates another thirty days sober. I want to tell him, in front of all of you struggling daily, that I support him in his journey."

The entire crowd looked from Ally to me, then back again. Her voice hitched as she spoke about an octave higher than I'd ever heard her reach.

"As a little girl, I prayed every night to God to let me meet my birth father. Someday. This past year, my prayers were answered. And I hope to keep him in my life for a long time coming."

Still gripping her hand, I leaned over my knees, cradling my forehead in my other hand. Not bothering to wipe the snot building at my nose. Allowing her words to wash over me, because I wished for every syllable to be true. As her father, I should be supporting her, not the other way around. But I basked in the ray of sunshine she was offering.

"I thank my birth father for inviting me here tonight. And thank him for welcoming me into his life."

My shoulders heaved as she sat down. The applause around us was thunderous. Yet still I clutched her hand like the lifeline it was.

Surrounded by my daughter and a purgatory of anonymous addiction warriors, my heart melted into a puddle of gratitude.

◆ ◆ ◆

Since the evening was balmy and Ally had already finished most of the prep reading for her classes tomorrow, I texted Dad, asking if he could pick us up a little later. After the AA meeting, we scoured the sandstone sidewalks of Oak Park in search of ice cream. My emotions were still flitting in circles within my less than agreeable stomach, but I didn't want to lose this moment to the night. So, cones in hand and licking chocolate-dipped confections before they dribbled down our clothes, we strolled along the quiet streets with other families and people clinging to the last of Chicagoland's summer evenings.

"You never answered my question." Ally stopped walking, so I turned to face her.

"What question?"

"The one I asked you after my first AA meeting. What happened when you were thirteen?"

My gut contracted, but not from rejecting the ice cream. I didn't answer. I couldn't. After such a perfect evening, how could the universe throw me this curveball? Why couldn't it let me enjoy one more carefree hour with my daughter? Was that asking too much? I inhaled and caught my breath, holding it in as if that might stave off the darkness already invading my mind.

"Please, Kyle. I'm old enough to know. I can handle it."

No. How could I share what I've never verbalized before? What Mom had made me promise never to tell. The nightmare I always woke up from a few minutes too late.

The hell that even Dad didn't know about.

"I'm sorry, Ally." I shook my head, but the memories crashed like a tsunami. Mom had sworn to me if we didn't tell anyone, it would go away. As if it never happened. I lived up to my end of the bargain. But still, the memories breached the fortress I'd built. Even vodka couldn't stop them now.

"You were only a kid. What could possibly have happened—"

"They hurt my mom, okay? They hurt her in the worst way, and it was all my fault." Each new breath was deeper than the one before, but my lungs refused to inflate, as if I were suffocating.

"Who?"

"The men. They were big. Two of them. No, three, because one kept a lookout down the hall. I didn't see them coming. Neither of us did. One of them clamped my arms behind my back, pinning me." It had been a time before mall cops. Before cell phones. Before security cameras were installed everywhere.

Ally's eyes grew wide, but I no longer saw her. Instead, my thirteen-year-old self was screaming in terror, trying to fight my way out of his grip. Mom had been walking me to the mall's restrooms down a small white-tiled hallway. I was carrying a bag with my new sneakers. The men appeared from nowhere, trapping us at a dead end. Mom's purse went clattering across the floor as one of them swung her over the water fountain, pinning her facedown.

I screamed. Dear God, I screamed. But the man holding me shoved his meaty palm over my mouth, so all I could do was puff air out my nose. I kicked. I tried to bite him. When that didn't work, I played deadweight, to try to slip away from him. Nothing worked.

And nothing obstructed my view of Mom.

My poor mom.

A fist grabbed the back of her hair, so her chin jutted up, throat kinked. The water fountain's spout jammed into her torso as her body bent over at ninety degrees.

First one, then the next, rammed into her from behind. Her skirt hiked up over her hips, and her underpants lay ripped at her ankles as little dots of blood dripped down her legs, then grew into blossoms over the white fabric. While screaming, she kept trying to elbow him off and kick, but nothing made contact.

How long did it last? Five minutes? Twenty?

Two lifetimes.

After all three had taken their turn with her, trading places to hold me pinned, they threw me against the tiled wall. The last thing I heard as I lay facedown on the floor was Mom's wailing turn hollow.

The next thing I knew, Mom had slapped my face to wake me up. Her hair looked as messy as the nest birds had built in our mailbox every spring. Her blouse was ripped, and her swelling cheek had a purple cast to it. She dragged me by my shoulders into the ladies' room. She chain-locked the door, then barricaded it with the trash can. All I could do was stare at it, thinking there was no way a little piece of metal and the plastic tub would hold off those big men. Her makeup had smeared down her face. After wiping the blood from her legs and combing her fingers through her hair, she came at my face with a wet paper towel and shaking hands. Each wipe revealed more blood, though I couldn't feel any cuts. She stopped after a minute to vomit into the trash can.

"Stop crying, Kyle." Her voice sounded foreign to me. Robotic. "We have to leave."

First, she listened at the door. All I could hear was my heartbeat jackhammering in my ears. Then, with her keys clutched in her fist so that they all pointed out from between her fingers, we slipped through the door. She grabbed my wrist, and together we rushed down the hallway, burst out into the mall, and kept running until we reached our car.

"Are we going to the police station?"

At first, Mom didn't answer. When she did, her voice had an eerie calmness to it. "No. We have a couple bruises but no broken bones. This is my shame, not yours. We'll both be fine. I don't want to upset your father. We won't tell anyone. We'll pretend it never happened and forget about it. Promise me."

"But—"

"Not one word, Kyle. Ever."

My groan brought me into the present. Lights from the streetlamps made Ally's cheeks glisten, her eyes trained on mine. No. Please tell me I hadn't just told her the entire story aloud. I'd never broken my promise to Mom before. Not to any of my therapists. Nor to my counselors. Not even to a priest. Certainly not Dad or Kimber.

Absolution would never be mine. "Oh, Maggie. I'm so sorry . . ."

"Who's Maggie?" Ally squeezed my good hand as if she were tying a tourniquet around it. If I hadn't already been damned to hell, I was on the fast track now.

"Maggie May. Like the song. It's my nickname for my mom. Her real name is Margaret. At first I called her that because she hated the name Maggie, but over the years, it became our thing."

"So why do you think the attack was your fault?"

I leaned my head back in submission, wishing I could pause the vivid memories from replaying in my mind. Like I've done a million times since I try to punch my way out to save my mom. Though I may not have directly caused it, we would never have gone shopping at the mall in the first place if it hadn't been for me. "Because I insisted on buying those goddamned shoes."

Chapter 23

ALLY

AFTER

Class. Work. Study. Repeat.

My brain is as mushy as the meatloaf Mom left for me to bake for tonight's dinner. I keep plodding forward, hoping I don't spontaneously combust under pressure. I missed so much lecture content in my grief haze at the beginning of this semester that I bombed my midterms. I need to ace my finals in order to reclaim my grades. My scholarships require maintaining a minimum GPA—nothing like a little pressure.

But pressure has also given me my excuse to delay seeing Margaret again. It wasn't until I'd driven off after meeting her that I realized she had no way to contact me. She doesn't know my phone number. Or my address. Whenever we meet again, it'll have to be me that reaches out to her.

My grandmother still has no idea we're related. How do I drop that bomb? *Hi, I know we really never met before, but I'm your illegitimate grandchild. Too bad your son died, so he can't vouch for me.* At least my mom had called Kyle, which had given him a little warning before she passed me his contact information.

Plus, it'll crush Mom if she ever finds out. She hated that I connected with Kyle at all, but what if I breached the walls and developed an ongoing relationship with his family?

Even worse, what if Kyle's family doesn't accept me? Or believe me?

Thus, I've taken refuge in the one thing I have to do. Study. Plus, part of me is so nervous I wonder if Hemingway U offers an introductory-level diplomacy class.

It's been two weeks since I met Margaret at Kyle's grave. Spring has officially sprung. I even broke out my ballet flats and spring sweaters. This afternoon, sunshine floods our apartment. I shut my laptop, then stretch. Jeez, I could use a study break. A butterfly flitting around Mom's potted azalea on our tiny balcony catches my attention. Good thing Lulu escaped earlier to explore the great outdoors, or she'd chase it away. Our cat ran an unchallenged racket and only returned if I bribed her with treats.

As I stand by the open deck door basking in the sunshine—vitamin D, as Mom would call it—something bursts inside me. An idea. I tear back inside Mom's closet and rummage to find the perfect calling card to introduce me to my grandmother as Kyle's daughter.

A bang from the front door of our apartment makes me freeze up. "Ally-cat? Are you here?"

Oh, crap. Mom. I jam the cardboard boxes back onto her shelf. "What are you doing in my closet?"

A hell of a lot of backpedaling later, I somehow convinced Mom that I'd been working on her birthday gift. While I'm not quite sure if she bought my white lies—okay, real lies, because there's no way I'd ever remind her about her Kyle memorabilia—she at least stopped asking me questions long enough that we sat down together for dinner. Now I'm on the hook for crafting one hell of a creative birthday gift next week out of her old junk. I don't have time for this. But that's not all that's worrying me.

Who have I become? Before I met Kyle, I don't think I lied to Mom once. Withheld information? Sure. But lie? Never. I even admitted to her the one time I tried smoking cigarettes with my middle school friends. And yes, she grounded me for weeks, but I deserved it.

Now I don't want to hurt her. Everyone she's ever known has let her down. Well, everyone but her work colleagues. Even though she mended her relationship with her parents, she and I are all we have. I had Kyle for a little while, but no longer. Still, I need to come clean with her about meeting Kyle's family, and she'll hate it. The sooner, the better.

"Mom?" After deciding now was my moment, I wandered into our living room. She's bundled in so many blankets on the couch despite the temperature being rather warm and stuffy inside. She looks like a colorful burrito, but her face looks pale and clammy. Lulu is grooming herself nearby, ignoring us both. "Wait, are you feeling okay?"

"I'm fine, honey. Just tired. Headache. I haven't slept well lately."

"Let me make you some tea." But when I wander over to the stove, I catch sight of the clock on the oven. Mom's shift isn't even over. She shouldn't be home yet. Now I'm concerned. The last time she came home early, she grabbed me and we rushed up to Ohio when Grandpa had his heart attack. She must have the plague if she left work. "Mom, are you getting the flu? Do you have chills?"

"No, really, I'm fine. We were overstaffed, so the nurse manager let me come home. I'm going to sleep it off. I'll be fine tomorrow."

I cross my arms, waiting for a more believable answer. Something isn't right here. How did it take me all through dinner to notice?

"Don't worry about me. Who's the parent here?" Her tone rings of parental authority long established, but her glassy eyes betray the truth. All those nights I woke up in the wee hours to hear her tinkering away in her room. She hasn't been sleeping well these past few weeks. Maybe longer. And her immune system must have caught up with her, forcing her to slow down.

"Me, at least until you've recovered. Now let's get you into bed, Mom." I scoop up the trail of blankets she sheds while shuffling to her bedroom. Once I get her tucked comfortably in bed, dole out doses of aspirin, and deliver her herbal tea, I turn off her reading lamp. Her tiny body is buried in covers. A pang of guilt shoots through my chest. She's been working so hard to help me out and contribute to my tuition and books. I shouldn't have been so self-absorbed that I didn't notice her growing ill.

"Thank you, Ally-cat. Was there something you needed to talk about before you became my nurse?"

"Nothing that can't wait until you feel better. Get some sleep." I cover up my dread with a laugh, keeping my eyes from turning toward her closet. "I love you, Mom."

When I crack open Mom's bedroom door the next morning, her shades are still drawn, and Lulu ninja-lunges out as if she were issued a Get Out of Jail Free card. I've already showered, and I'm getting ready to leave to meet with one of my professors before class to discuss our assignment.

"Mom?"

The lump in the middle of her bed groans but doesn't move. An earthy odor clashes with the scent of coffee and oatmeal waiting for her in the kitchen. A brick forms in my stomach.

I tiptoe over to the side of her bed and place the back of my hand on her forehead. She's burning up. Five minutes later, while I'm gathering everything I can scavenge in our apartment to help her symptoms, I hear her vomiting into the trash can I placed by her bed. Can you still get the flu in April? I wash my hands three times as if I were prepping for surgery and spray the apartment with disinfectant. I'm barreling into these last few critical weeks of the spring semester before exam week. Neither one of us has time to be ill.

Then I called to leave a message with her emergency room scheduler that she is ill and won't be able to come in today. Wow, when was the last time she skipped a full shift? Never. But the nurse manager will understand. I hope. The last thing a patient needs is to catch some germs from the hospital staff. Her colleagues don't want to catch this virus either.

"Mom, drink this." After helping her sit up to take her fever medication, I leave her cell phone plus a note by her bedside, instructing her to text me when she wakes up. And I'll bring her chicken soup for lunch after my class.

After a nanosecond's hesitation, I text Grandma Vicki and ask if there's any possible way she can come visit for a few days to help me take care of Mom. I'm torn, though. If this mysterious illness is contagious, I don't want Grandma exposed to germs, but Mom needs more TLC than I can give her. If she comes, I'll sleep on the couch and let Grandma have my room.

My plans both to meet with Margaret again and to bare my soul to Mom and ask for her blessing are temporarily thwarted until she can whip my proverbial butt.

Because she will.

Except for a quick stop home at lunchtime to deliver broth and crackers to Mom, who hadn't moved all morning, I slugged through two classes, three office-hour sessions, one group meeting, and a couple of hours working at the grocery store. But when I return home afterward to find Grandma Vicki sitting on our living room couch with a cup of tea, I nearly collapse with relief.

"Allison Marie, I'm so glad you asked for my help. You look almost as haggard as your mother. What do they put in the water in Chicago?" Having stowed her leather travel bag next to Lulu's cushion, Grandma stands with the grace of a royal, then embraces me with a tight squeeze held longer than necessary. "I'm sorry I couldn't get here sooner, sweetheart."

I can't answer her past the lump in my throat, so I cling to one of the few living family members I have in this world. Despite her white hair and shrinking frame, Grandma Vicki's Chanel perfume, her tailored pantsuit, and her freshly painted lips all hint at a woman who would never let something as temporary as illness get in the way of style. But she dropped everything, even her book club meeting, to race here at my request. I'd spotted her glossy and dent-free sedan parked next to Mom's clunker when I pulled up.

"My, Allison. You've grown even more beautiful since I last saw you." She holds me at arm's length, which makes me roll my eyes. What a liar. I'm less than adorable, cocooned in the HU hoodie that matched the one I'd given to Kyle and my now-wrinkled grocery clerk uniform. "Please stop growing up so fast."

"I'll try. Thank you for coming. You must've hopped in the car five minutes after I texted."

"Nonsense. I'm happy to help. I packed and even prepared a sandwich for your grandfather's lunch before I left. That small delay worked perfectly. No sense driving smack into Chicago's rush-hour traffic."

We're still holding hands when the door to Mom's bedroom creaks open.

"Mother?" Mom's croak is topped by a confused expression as she looks around at both of us, but no clear explanations seem apparent. "What are you doing here?"

"Hannah, dear, Allison asked me to come help while you are ill. You unlocked the door and let me in when I arrived two hours ago. Don't you remember?"

"I guess I thought I was having an intense . . ." Mom shuffles back into her bedroom but leaves her door cracked open. ". . . dream."

Under her breath, Grandma mutters, "At least she didn't call it a nightmare. There's hope." We both bite back laughter. God, I love Grandma Vicki.

While she checks on Mom, I move her travel bag into my bedroom, change the sheets, and start preparing some dinner for us. Lulu struts figure eights around my ankles. Considering we'll be sharing the living room tonight, this little feline had better behave if she wants couch privileges.

"Smells delicious." Grandma pulls up a kitchen chair opposite mine. Over swirled forkfuls of spaghetti marinara, I fill her in all about school and work. But when she asked me about how I was coping with Kyle's death, I lost my appetite. She might as well be a priest for all the honesty that comes spilling out of me. How I met Margaret at his grave site a couple of weeks ago. That I wasn't sure how to make the next move. Or how to reveal that we're related. That I was considering making a copy of Kyle's band cassette tape for her as some sort of peace offering.

Then I have a brilliant idea.

"Do you think . . . I mean, if you don't mind . . . would you come with me to meet Margaret? We can stop by her house some evening while you're in town. She has no idea I'm related to her, so having you there might soften the blow of the surprise. Please?"

"Of course, sweetheart. It might help her to know that everyone was surprised by your meeting your biological father. Meeting you may even help her cope with having lost her son."

"What? No." We both turn and then freeze to find Mom standing at her door again, pale and shivering while still wrapped in several blankets. Her eyes may be glassy from fever, but that couldn't hide the hurt behind them. "He's gone. There's no need to complicate things. End of story."

"But—" I scramble to find a rational rebuttal, but my words get trapped before I can state my defense. I should've known better than to scheme to meet my other grandmother on the sly.

Mom bristles and shuts her eyes. "Allison Marie, I said no."

Chapter 24

KYLE

BEFORE

Decades before working from home became popular, my dad had commandeered the dining room table as a makeshift office desk. He'd never been one to leave work at the office when he clocked out. For years, I'd helped him out in the family business before he shuttered it to become an employee and generate a steady paycheck.

Now I'd officially forced Dad to scoot over and share the dining room table. On my side, surrounding my laptop and pad of paper, I had three piles: my books for my classes, my list of rehab facilities to call, and what occupied most of my time, my new schedule of freelance graphic design projects that I'd been able to drum up.

Miss Genevieve's ire apparently hadn't extended beyond my rule infraction. A couple of weekends ago, Dad had driven me out to Carrefour during their visiting hours, and I was able to meet with her. While I wasn't welcome to return as a resident, when I mentioned my interest in helping other small organizations update their websites, she passed along a few networking leads. Her recommendation for my graphic design skills must've carried weight, because a couple of them hired me as an independent contractor and a few more were considering my project proposals. Between studying for my classes, meeting Ally, attending daily AA meetings, and working with my new business customers as much as possible, I felt like I had three full-time jobs.

As soon as I could bank enough cash, I'd buy Ally a used car—nothing flashy, but reliable, with enough miles on it that we could get a reasonable price. In my spare time, I combed the online listings for used cars.

It killed me that Ally had been riding the bus to and from Hemingway U and walked home after dark from her grocery store job if Hannah was still at work. The days were growing shorter. It wasn't safe with all the sickos running around. A young woman waiting or walking alone from a bus stop after dark was easy prey. Too easy. If I had a valid driver's license, I'd escort her wherever I could. But according to my calculations, after I get paid for four more freelance jobs, I should be able to take her car shopping. Hopefully before the time changes and we lose all evening sunlight.

My lawyer advised me to keep track of my rehab-facility calls. With any luck, I'd be a resident in one of them before we got the summons from the court. If not, I was crossing my fingers that my call list, my AA meeting attendance, and these successful freelance jobs would convince the judge that I was making efforts to be a model citizen. He might be lenient in my sentencing. But my chances of being granted a full pardon were nil. My time bomb was ticking, and I had a shitload to get done before it exploded.

Why did I let myself fuck up at Carrefour? I could've done better. I needed to be stronger for Ally.

I scooted into the chair across from Dad. "Do you mind taking me to an AA meeting tonight?"

Before I could even swallow, Dad lunged out from behind his "desk," grabbed his keys, and then motioned for me to follow. That was the way he'd always been. Not big on verbal affection and praise, but he'd drop everything at a moment's notice to help me out. Kimber once commented that whenever she'd driven home from college, after a quick hello, the first thing he'd always do was check the oil and tire pressure in her car. She never left without him insisting on filling up her gas tank. Keeping us safe was his love language.

Since I couldn't drive right now, he played my chauffeur. So far, all I'd needed to stave off my shoulder pain was a steady stream of ibuprofen and ice packs. Dad would prefer to keep it that way.

Before we walked out the door, I stopped Dad and spoke loud enough for Mom to hear in the next room. "By the way, I registered for two classes at the community college for the fall semester. Lectures start next week."

Dad, who'd always sought the positive in me, slapped my shoulder to congratulate me, forgetting that his encouragement would send seismic waves of pain through my torso until I winced. "Sorry, son. I forgot. What will you be taking?"

"A psychology class and public speaking. I hope these can help me lead peer-group sessions in the future. I think I can make a difference."

Whatever Mom had been holding—silverware?—clattered to the floor.

◆ ◆ ◆

"You look stressed. Everything okay?" With Ally's first semester of college in full swing, I was grateful she could squeeze in a study break. Since early autumn had a strong grip on Chicagoland, today I treated her to a couple of pumps of pumpkin spice in her coffee.

Instead of answering my question, she fiddled with her ring. I could wait. She could take all the time she needed to gather her thoughts. No pressure.

For more than twenty years, I'd kept my promise to my mom. I never told anyone her secret. Not my dad or Kimber. Not my friends or bandmates. Not my teachers, who'd had a better vision for my future than I'd allowed. Not my doctors, who would prescribe me my antianxiety meds.

Not the cops or judges whenever I'd get hauled into court for some charge or another. And certainly never my counselors at the rehab facilities. I'd deflected their probing questions until they gave up in sheer exasperation.

Once, a few years after the attack, I brought it up to my mom. I thought we should at least discuss it. But she'd become so distraught and shaken up that I'd hugged her and never had the guts to mention it to her again. Ever. I hadn't been able to protect her that day, but at least I could honor her request for secrecy afterward.

So instead I'd buried that monster so deep and under so many scars, self-lies, and hangovers that I never even thought about it anymore. It was like I'd somehow convinced myself that it'd happened to someone else. Some other thirteen-year-old kid. Someone else's mom. Never me. That reality would've hurt too much to revisit.

Until two weeks ago, in my rush of unbridled honesty, out it gushed of its own accord.

Mom's secret. Our secret.

In the end—after all these years of sealing it shut in my mind's high-security vault that contained my memories—all it took was a little question from my daughter to open the trapdoor and allow the monster to escape. My own personal Pandora's box. Come what may.

But even more astounding than me not shriveling up on the spot was that my daughter didn't ghost me. Not for a minute. We'd met several times since that brutally honest evening, despite my sharing my eighteen-wheeler-size emotional baggage.

The insane thing was I learned from it. By seeing my past through her simple, youthful lens, I finally accepted that it was okay to relinquish the blame. To be broken. To allow myself to heal. To forgive.

Hope was a raw, beautiful flame.

"Nope. Everything's fine." Ally shimmied in her lounge chair and shook her head, but I'd gotten to the point where I could tell when she was hiding something. Twisting the silver ring on her index finger. Smooshing her mouth to one side while tilting her head. Tightening her already perfect ponytail. I wondered if she'd developed these nervous habits as a child or picked them up later. One thing was for sure, if she ever played poker, she'd lose her money every time.

"Yeah, I'm not buying it. What's bothering you?"

"Okay, okay. Yes, I'm a bit anxious." Her eyes widened; but then the smirk broke out into a full-on grin. She flopped back against her chair and motioned toward her overstuffed school backpack. "My first class on Tuesdays and Thursdays is Biology 101 in a massive lecture hall with five hundred other students. Who wouldn't be nervous, right? My statistics textbook might as well be written in a foreign language. My other three classes have books and course packets that together weigh more than a hybrid car. My brain isn't big enough for college-level—"

"Jeez, I'd be overwhelmed too." I held up my good hand in mock submission, giving in to my laughter. Her schedule intimidates the hell out of me. "Look, you passed calculus in high school. You can do anything. Have you decided on what you want to study yet?"

Again, tightening her ponytail.

"Don't stress about it, Ally. Most college students don't declare a major until their sophomore year. Plus, your academic adviser will help you decide."

"That's what Mom says. She's discouraging me from studying medicine, though." She reached into her backpack, which I now knew always carried her sketch pad and charcoals, just in case she found a subject she was inspired to capture. "Mind if I sketch you?"

Shaking my head, I followed her motions until I'd shifted to a pose she approved of. Over these past months, I'd come to love modeling for her—not that I was a subject worthy of her talent. Sketching was the telltale clue that she felt at ease in her environment. We tended to have more relaxed conversations while she was scratching, shading, smudging, and erasing. Plus, she let me sip my coffee once in a while. "Why not medicine? My mom's a nurse. Apparently you come from medical professionals on both sides of your family tree. It could be in your blood."

"That's the problem. I don't do blood. I've passed out so many times that my doctor has to lay me down to give me a shot. The whole needle thing creeps me out. Mom says that you can buy medical malpractice insurance, but I don't think doctors or nurses get hazard pay for self-induced concussions."

"Hannah probably knows what she's talking about. She's working in the trenches every day." I couldn't remember if she had been majoring in science at SMU when I'd met her. I hadn't exactly been academically driven then. She must have gone back to school after leaving Mount Vernon and earned her certifications. My mom had to keep up her nursing license with required class hours and CPR, so I figured it'd been tough for Hannah to hold down a job and raise a child as a single mom. I was impressed. Hoped I could tell her so someday.

"Yeah, she's working at the hospital right now. But she's taking the whole weekend off to celebrate my starting college. I don't think she's had more than thirty-six hours off in the last two years. I hope she sleeps in, but more than likely she'll be flitting around our apartment, fixing furniture and cleaning all weekend long. I've been saving up to take her out to dinner to celebrate."

"How's she doing?" And by that, I really mean, What did she think of the two of us hanging out and spending time together? Part of me felt a little guilty that I'd never really sought Hannah's permission to get to know her daughter. In fact, we hadn't spoken since her phone call months ago. Ally might be mine biologically, but her mom had raised her without my help—financial or otherwise. I really didn't have any rights here. Still, I'd feel better about my new-to-me father-daughter relationship if it were graced with Hannah's blessing.

"Do you mean what does she think of me spending time with you?"

"Yeah. That." Busted. Okay, so Ally had also gotten to know me well enough to read into the subtext of my thoughts, a fact that scared me infinitely more than it probably did her. Part of my mind was a very dark, very black hole.

"My mom kinda sorta doesn't really know about our spending time together." Twisting her ring again. "I mean, she knows we've met. A couple times. She freaked out when she found your letters from Carrefour. And then last month when I surprised you at your house and found you drunk, I was super upset when I left. I told my mom I was blocking you from my life. She'd seemed so relieved that I didn't exactly give her the update that we've met for coffee a few times since then."

"Don't you think you should tell her?" Every ounce of me wanted to avoid this conversation, but in a few weeks, I'd have known Ally for six months. It was a small fraction of her short life so far but probably the most significant months of mine.

Hannah might not wield the legal power to keep us apart, but she sure as hell had influence over Ally. I didn't want to cause a rift between them. I also wanted to make sure she wouldn't make Ally choose between us. Hannah would win. As she should. If there was one thing I'd learned in all my group therapy sessions, it was that clear and open communication could bridge a whole canyon of problems, especially the embellished ones.

I couldn't change the past. I'd treated her like shit when we broke up, and I never expected her to ever forgive me. Then again, she waited eighteen years to tell me I had a daughter. But if Hannah believed that she had a voice in her daughter's involvement with me, then she might gain some comfort. Eventually I'd try to earn her tolerance, if not her trust. We didn't have to be on good terms going forward, just civil.

"Soon." If her ponytail could talk, it would be screaming to stop tightening it so hard.

Yeah, I wasn't buying that.

"Sooner rather than later. Okay, Ally?" Then again, Hannah had my phone number. She knew how to reach me. Or if worse came to worse and Ally stalled for too long, I could call her. I knew all too well that secrets kept for too long had a tendency to fester.

The news would definitely be better received coming from Ally, though.

Chapter 25

MARGARET

AFTER

This confessional booth is tucked away in the back corner of the same church where we held Kyle's funeral mass. That was the last time I entered any church. I wish the lighting inside this vertical coffin was pitch black instead of a shade of darkness I'll call *muted sinner*. That way the priest wouldn't even see my silhouette on the silk-screened barrier between us. But the mustiness of old incense trapped with me inside cheers my hollow soul.

I make the sign of the cross and begin as the ritual requires. "Bless me, Father, for I have sinned . . ."

This kneeler has held many a parishioner in its day, but I'm confident I'll win the flames-of-damnation jackpot today. Oh, hell. Here goes nothing.

"I killed my son. I've alienated my family. I've been lying by omission to my husband through most of our marriage. I'm sure there's something else I'm forgetting, but those are the high points."

The priest's pause lasts so long that he's either fallen asleep or stepped out of the confessional booth to smoke a cigarette. A moment later, as I'm about to knock on the wooden panel framing the silk screen to ask if he's still there, he clears his throat. "Anything else you'd care to confess?"

Seriously? Because that's not enough? But then dread twists my gut into a pretzel. My dear lifelong friend, guilt, is always ready to reel in yet another personal fault. "Yes, Father. I forgot to mention that I haven't attended Sunday mass since my son died three months ago."

"So let's go back to your first point. How did you kill your son?" His voice was soft, nonconfrontational. I suspect he thinks he's walking through a potential minefield. Not far from the truth, actually.

"Well, I didn't pull the trigger or stab him—nothing like that. I kicked him out of the house because he had plans to meet up with a friend instead of attending his AA meeting. He'd received a court summons. Any partying would've put him in jail. I couldn't stand around and watch him crash. My last words to him were 'Get out.' I wasn't with him when he died the next day. He was pronounced dead at the hospital after the EMTs tried to revive him for over an hour. My husband thinks he overdosed on purpose, but I know it can't be true. I drove him to the edge." A groan escapes from somewhere so deep inside me it releases a volcano of tears. "I poisoned him. Not his body—he did that to himself with alcohol and, according to his autopsy, drugs. But I poisoned his mind. I caused him to find relief in bottles of vodka."

There, I said it. The vise cinching my heart begins to release its grip. Each deep breath turns easier, somehow more rejuvenating. I never expected the pain to go away, but by admitting my fault aloud to God—to myself—I feel empowered. I sense that there might be a place on this planet where I can embrace hope. I've never forgiven myself, but I may be able to live out the remainder of my life in semipeace. Maybe.

In fact, my sense of buoyancy is so mood altering I scoot off my arthritic knees to allow easier circulation in my legs while waiting for my penance, ever in awe of the mysteries of the confessional booth. How do the faithful of other religions shed their guilt without the sacrament of reconciliation?

"How?"

"Excuse me, Father? How what?"

"How did you poison your son's mind?"

My shoulders slump as I slam back onto the warped wooden kneeler, folding my hands in prayer. Images flash in front of my eyes like a slideshow in fast-forward mode. The steel water fountain. Kyle's thirteen-year-old face. His innocent child's eyes were terrified and gawking at me. We were both helpless. The most enormous relief of my life was that my rapists didn't also turn their lust on Kyle.

"I swore my son to secrecy when he was a young boy. He kept it for twenty-five years, then took it to his grave. I thought if he could forget it ever happened, he could move on and live his life normally. I hoped so, anyway. But I couldn't have been more wrong."

"What was your secret?"

"With all due respect, Father, God knows exactly what happened. He let it happen. So I can't share it with you. I've never even told my husband or daughter. Only my son knew because he witnessed my shame."

"I see . . ." His sigh is audible.

Where the hell is the lightning bolt with my name on it? I might be the first practicing Catholic in the history of the church to defiantly tell a priest I wouldn't confess something to him. That I'm sorry but not *that* sorry. Surely I've committed yet another mortal sin.

"My sister, I believe you are experiencing one of life's great ironies. The secrets we bury deepest can hurt us the most."

"I wanted it to disappear forever. Erase it from our history as if it had never happened." I knew I could never forget, but I insisted it didn't happen for Kyle's sake. I hoped that if I didn't make a big deal out of it, he could forget about it so he could move forward with his life. Everything on the outside healed, and we could pretend it never occurred and carry on living normal lives. Now I know how my decision created the unstable fault line within him. What if I'd had Kyle meet with a therapist as a boy once I'd realized he was unstable? But there was so much stigma surrounding shrinks back then I wouldn't have dared. Would that have changed Kyle's lifestyle? I could play the what-if game for the rest of my days, and I'll still never know.

"It sounds like your son suffered much in his life. For better or for worse, his pain is over. But are you feeling any better?"

The proverbial pendulum swings back and strikes my soul, knocking me off balance. Bull's-eye hit. So much for my buoyancy from a minute ago. I count to ten and ask for divine patience. How would any mother react while her son's remains are buried in a graveyard?

"No, I don't feel better. That's why I'm here, Father. Confessing my sins." This wasn't the best idea. Is there another priest I can confess to, one that won't ask such obvious questions?

"God gave us all free will. You can keep your secret—as your son did—to your grave. But every decision we make has consequences, and God will never interfere with the outcomes we create by our actions."

"I may not have murdered my son, but I caused his death, even though that bad decision was twenty-five years ago. If I could go back in time, I would change everything." Like reporting the gang rape to the police and pressing charges.

"They say hindsight is twenty-twenty."

Oh, sweet Jesus, save me. Everything out of this priest's mouth is a fortune cookie saying. I expected wrath. Fire and brimstone. Instead, some new-age, feel-good-about-yourself priest is trying to soothe me. Mercy is so unsatisfying. I deserve to be excommunicated.

At some point—after another antsy parishioner knocks a third time on the booth's wooden door to remind the priest to hurry things up because a long queue was forming outside—he clears his throat.

"My sister, do you love your husband? Your daughter?"

"Absolutely. I'd do anything for them."

"And your son, who passed away?"

"Yes. I always loved him. With every fiber of my being." Truer words have never been uttered from my lips.

"Don't they deserve to know what happened?"

Squeezing my eyes shut, I shake my head harder and harder. He may have good intentions, but the priest is asking the impossible.

"For your penance, I want you to go home and talk to your family. Be honest with them. Trust them. Share with them your hurt. Reveal your secret. If you love them as much as you say you do, then they love and care about you as well. Let them support you in your hour of need."

As the priest absolves me from my sins, somewhere in the universe, a judge's gavel cracks. My soul splits in two.

◆　◆　◆

I take the scenic route home from the church, driving around this gorgeous sunny spring afternoon with the windows rolled down and the warm breeze on my cheeks. Redemption is in the air for everyone but me. Somehow, the car seemed to steer itself over to that mall—the one where I was attacked. Years ago I'd read in the newspaper that a developer had bought the property and converted it into segmented big-box stores rather than the indoor concept it had once been. Though I'd rejoiced in its destruction, I never actually went back to see it. Since that horrible day, I'd driven miles out of my way to avoid it.

My heart thumps so hard that I have to wait in my parked car for half an hour until I pluck up enough courage to step outside. The main entrance—the one I limped out of while holding wet paper towels to Kyle's bleeding temple—no longer exists. Instead some big-chain, members-only warehouse squats in its phantom memory. Deep within its cavernous steel-shelving interior stands the footprint where the water fountain of my nightmares used to reside.

Not daring to step inside the store, I fight every instinct to run away and approach the new facade. I place both hands, my fingers splayed, on the concrete and shut my eyes. At some point, even my forehead rests against the wall in submission. Tuning out the customers who, no doubt, are wondering what the strange old lady is doing hugging a building, I allow my mind to wander back in time, back to those horrid men.

I never found out their names.

I never forgave them.

I still can't.

They invaded my body again and again.

They held my son hostage and forced him to watch.

They left us broken and scarred in their wake.

They infected my thoughts with fear and hate.

They robbed me of happiness.

They hijacked my life.

Kyle, I made a mistake. All I ever wanted was for the attack to disappear. To forget it ever happened. I'm so sorry. You offered to show me a way out of this hell. I should've listened to you, but I wasn't ready. And now you're dead. Please, forgive me.

As I muttered my apology, a tingle of warmth, some blue pilot light of hope, ignited within me, which I fear could be snuffed. Kyle died, but now I must live for both of us. And I need help to keep this pure but vulnerable flame burning.

For the first time since my world was mashed into a pulpy mess of *Why me* and *What did I do to deserve this*, I opened my heart to the possibility of a new chapter for my life's story. My scars are from my past, but they need not define my future. I reclaim control of fate's pen.

I could never forgive those men for what they took, but I could keep them from stealing my future too. I sense a growing blossom of hope. Hope that begins with the beautiful family God gave me. And Ally. And our future together.

My sobbing leaves a saline stain on the concrete building, but it might as well have been my blood.

◆ ◆ ◆

As I step through my front door, Martin is working at our dining room table. It's Saturday, but he's never been one to relax, or *chillax*, as Kyle used to call it. How I drove home without causing a car accident can only be described as a miracle.

"Where've you been?" He jumps up and rushes to peck me on my cheek. Oh, I've taken that daily kiss for granted all along. Forgetting about it the same moment it was given. I touch my cheek, capturing his kiss. Keeping it safe in the shadow box of my hand. "I expected you home hours ago."

Martin motions for me to turn around so he can help me out of my spring jacket, but I shake my head to stop him. The lump in my throat barely allows me to breathe. I grab his hand and squeeze.

"Margaret? You've been crying. Is everything okay?"

"I heard back from Mr. Davenport again this morning."

"Oh, and does he think we have any case against the hospital?" Given his calm demeanor, Martin must already suspect the answer. These past few weeks, I poked and prodded until Davenport agreed to consult with another lawyer who specializes in medical litigation.

"No. He said after all his follow-up inquiries with the hospital's in-house counsel that . . ." Oh, how do I relinquish answers to my questions? That maybe there had been a malpractice issue that caused his overdose. ". . . Kyle's records are considered privileged information. Any lawyer representing our lawsuit wouldn't be able to gain access to them as evidence. Suing them would be costly, and the odds are stacked against us."

And none of it would bring back Kyle.

"So that's it then?" His words are as gentle as a warm hug, but part of me wishes he would be angry. Then I could pass the baton to him. However, he'd resigned himself once he suspected Kyle had committed suicide.

"I instructed Davenport to accept the hospital's settlement offer." I shake my head, wishing I had another viable option—a way to advocate for my son. Had he not gone to the hospital, he might still be alive. And I called the ambulance and insisted he go there. Was that what led to his death? We'll never know. But one thing was for sure, I kicked Kyle out when he returned home.

"Honey, you did the right thing. I believe the doctors and nurses did everything reasonable to help him. He was fit enough to walk out of there unaided. He was fine. Who could've predicted what would happen twenty-four hours later? And who's to say he didn't intentionally take drugs? The overdose might have been an accident. Or not. We don't know what happened, but we do know that no lawsuit will ever bring him back. We need to let go and move on."

Oh, if I could only believe him. I gave up fighting. I settled. And I have the rest of my life to try to come to terms with my choices. "None of this is fair."

But there is one thing I can control, and I need to do it now, before I lose my nerve. I place my keys in Martin's hand and close his fingers over them. "Would you please drive me to Kyle's grave?"

Not a single word passes between us on the ride over to the cemetery. Martin steers through turns and brakes gently, probably concerned that any extreme motion or comment could restart my weeping, something he'd rather avoid. I don't blame him. I've been a leaky faucet ever since Kyle passed away.

After parking, Martin holds my elbow to help me ascend the few steps to the wrought iron gate; then we let ourselves in. It's empty of mourners, except us. Thank God. Though it's nowhere near sunset, shadows from the maple trees cast purplish light over much of the small brick-enclosed area. We walk single file along the stone slab path to Kyle's and my parents' plots. Then stop.

I can't look into Martin's eyes. He'd see too much of my soul if I did. Instead I kneel on the grass and place my hand on Kyle's memorial stone. As if on cue, the graveyard's resident cardinal lands on his favorite branch and chirps.

"Martin, I need to tell you something. Something I should have told you years and years ago. But I was too scared."

He sinks to his knees next to me. "Scared of me? Margaret, you know you can tell me anything. I'm always here for you. Always have been."

I sneak a look at his face. Those familiar wrinkles. The hazel eyes now contorted with worry. That same Eastern European square jaw that Kyle and Ally inherited, though it's a little fleshier now. He is my home. He always has been. We may have diverged over searching for our surprise granddaughter, but now that I've met her, my heart has softened toward him. Forgiven him. It gives me the strength I need to bare my soul, despite the anguish my words will cause.

A calmness settles over me. I nod, knowing somewhere in the universe I've received Kyle's blessing to break our vow. The vow I should never have demanded from either of us. The priest was right. I owe this to my husband. I'll figure out later how to share it with Kimber.

"I thought if I told somebody—even you—it would've made it a reality. And I desperately didn't want it to be real . . ."

Thirty minutes and a lifetime later, I'd stripped my heart to its core. I exposed my brokenness by revealing my secret to him. I don't know whose tears grace my face, Martin's or mine, but his arms shore me up. His embrace, my penance. Every stroke of his hands against my back applied a balm I didn't know I needed. I've loved this man forever. Why hadn't I let him love me back?

Chapter 26

ALLY

BEFORE

"Wake up, Ally-cat." Mom nudged my shoulder. I was in denial that it was already morning, since I'd stayed up late studying. Truth be told, Lulu had woken me up before sunrise by plopping her furry torso across my face and purring. The best alarm clock ever. Too bad she didn't understand I was on my fall break—a long weekend free from college classes—so there was no need to wake up early.

"Why can't I sleep in?" I rolled over, burying my head under my pillows, whimpering. "No classes. No work. Just a blissful day full of no responsibilities."

"That's the point, sweetheart. I don't have to work today either."

Mom's words took a moment to sink in. When they did, I jack-knifed up, tossing my covers.

"Really?"

It'd been weeks since we exchanged more than a passing *Hey, how are you doing? See you tomorrow* communicated by text. She handed me a steaming mug of coffee.

"Would you be up for a little day trip?" From behind her back, she presented a pair of flip-flops dangling from her fingertips. "Michigan City?"

Nothing like spending an afternoon on a Lake Michigan sandy beach and golden sunshine to chase away the autumn blues and recharge before the long winter.

In less time than you could say *Don't forget sunscreen*, I'd scrounged through my closet for shorts, a towel, and sunglasses. Mom, who'd already packed a little tote bag and gassed up her ancient car, made us some breakfast. Half an hour later, I nuzzled Lulu goodbye, and we hit the road.

My one caveat was that I needed to study during the car ride. With our windows cracked open, coffee mugs in the console, Mom behind the steering wheel, and me riding shotgun with a textbook open in my lap, we headed east.

Midchapter, I sneaked a peek at Mom. Her face was so relaxed. She looked damn near angelic. Not a swipe of makeup. Her blondish hair, which could use a dye touch-up at the ginger roots, was haphazardly thrown into a messy bun at the nape of her neck, wisps flying loose in the wind. On our trip home, she'd have a little rosy glow on her freckled cheeks.

"Thanks, Mom." I didn't say that enough. God, how did we let the entire summer slip away without playing hooky once or twice? But we had. Both of us were so focused on earning money—and me on getting to know Kyle—that we'd overlooked taking any kind of staycation or R & R. We hadn't even painted each other's nails or gone to the movies.

She squeezed my hand but kept her eyes on the road.

Kyle once told me his older sister, Kimber, also used to road-trip with him to Washington Park Beach in Michigan City every year when she was home visiting from college over summer break. They'd spend the day on the sand; then, after a seafood dinner, they'd walk the pier to watch the sunset before heading back home. I forgot to ask him how old he'd been when they stopped. Thirteen?

I'd seen him a few times since that AA evening we'd walked with ice cream, not that I'd been avoiding him. Midterm exams kept me buried in my books and study groups. But I wasn't sure what to say, so I never really brought up his attack after he told me.

Sorry you were forced to watch your mom be brutally victimized. Again and again.

Sorry that you'd blamed yourself, even though all the fault rests entirely with the attackers, not a young boy who wanted to buy a pair of shoes.

Sorry your mom made you promise to keep that trauma to yourself, so instead of reporting the crime and being able to process it with professional help, you numbed yourself with alcohol to bury the pain, the guilt, and the vulnerability.

Sorry your chosen method of self-soothing snowballed into a full-blown, self-abusive addiction.

I already knew he wouldn't listen, then or now. I'd tried to argue these very points that night, with the sunset as my witness. But my insistence that it couldn't have possibly been his fault was met with blank stares and hunched shoulders. God, he'd been five years younger than I am now when that happened.

On the positive side, I'd met my grandfather. Technically he didn't realize we were related when he'd driven me home, but Kyle introduced us. He loved to ski and had been an instructor when he lived in Romania as a teen. I knew nothing about it, so I let him chatter on about chairlifts and black-diamond slopes and the best places to ski in the Midwest. I didn't have the heart to tell him that I was more of a beach girl. But I treasured his words like drops of liquid gold.

Someday Kyle would introduce us properly. Grandfather and granddaughter. He'd promised he would as soon as I was ready. I almost was.

◆ ◆ ◆

Mom and I spread our towels on the sand side by side. The universe had graced us with an unseasonably warm, golden day for early October, but the breezes off Lake Michigan carried hints of the colder temperatures arriving soon.

"Let's hunt for sea glass." Mom was never one to sit still for long. She had too much energy for her own good. So after half an hour of sunbathing, we slipped on our long-sleeve T-shirts and walked along the chilly surf. A smattering of people wandered the beach today. Some fishermen. A few people walked their dogs. An occasional bird searched for lunch. But otherwise the expanse of beach belonged to us as we strolled toward the pier, occasionally stopping to comb the wet sand for unbroken shells and glass.

"Don't get mad, Mom, but can I ask you a question?"

"I hate when you start questions like that. Please tell me you're not failing out of school."

"No. But you'll probably think this is worse."

Mom stopped and turned toward me, her eyes squinting despite her dark sunglasses. "Spill it, Ally. What's going on? Did you get arrested?"

"Arrested? Seriously? Way to be dramatic. I wanted to ask you about Kyle."

"I thought you got him out of your system. Moved on." She made an about-face, and suddenly we were heading back toward our towels at a faster clip. I reached for her hand. She squeezed mine, then pulled me into a hug. "I'm sorry, honey. I wish I hadn't shared his name with you. I never wanted to expose you to someone who would hurt you."

"He didn't hurt me. I was upset. Actually, really pissed off. But we're in a better place now. At least, I think we are."

"So . . ." Mom stared out over the lake's waves. Her loose hair blew back with the winds. "So you're still in touch with him?"

"Yeah. I've seen him a few times since school started. I've gone to a couple AA meetings with him too."

Instead of responding, she wiped under her sunglasses with the edge of her sleeve, her dimple no longer showing. I shouldn't have brought him up. Never once had Kyle been a good topic of conversation for us. But as long as I'd already killed our easy-breezy day off, I pressed forward, though carefully.

"I hoped you would tell me how you guys met." And as if she needed the reminder, I added, "At Spring Mountain University?"

"Oh, sweetheart . . ." Mom shook her head, then exhaled a long, troubled breath. I bit the inside of my cheek to keep from prodding her. Years of living with this woman had taught me that she moved at her own pace, no one else's. So I kept striding with her, letting the water skim my ankles at the edge of the shore. "I was a little older than you—a sophomore. I lived in an off-campus apartment with some friends and stayed around for the summer session. One of my dorm mates heard about a student band playing at a party, and we all decided to crash it."

"You crashed a party?" She might as well have told me she'd parachuted out of a plane. My mom rarely dropped by parties she had been invited to, and when she did, she insisted on leaving early. I guess my tone was incredulous enough that she laughed, so I was glad I'd double-checked.

"I wasn't always working around the clock. I was a little racy back then, in a naive, nothing-can-hurt-me kind of way. It was the turn of the century. They called it Y2K. We were making history. In our minds anyway."

Envisioning her big kinked red hair made me nearly choke on my own laughter. Nope. Mom would always be a no-frills, scrubs-and-ponytail person to me.

"When we got to the party, the band was already playing. Four guys on a stage. Deafening music. So loud you couldn't understand the lyrics. Or maybe they were yelling. I think they enjoyed grinding the guitars, because there wasn't much of a melody. The ironic thing was the band's name—Silence Deconstructed. I think they could have used some."

I tried to visualize Kyle rocking out on the stage, but it was hard to reconcile with the same guy who bought me my iced coffee and valued AA tokens like they were Nobel Peace Prizes.

"The party was packed, but I noticed Kyle the second I walked inside. He was positioned onstage behind the lead singer, playing bass guitar. I didn't know his name, but I recognized him from one of my classes. Tall. Aloof. Black hair hanging long over his eyes. Nice clothes but not too nice. Cigarette burning in the ashtray next to him. A tortured, brooding artist. My kind of guy."

"You hate smokers." Now that I think about it, I haven't seen Kyle smoke a cigarette since the first day I met him. He must've given up smoking at rehab as well.

"Now that I'm in medicine and have seen its destruction, I hate it. I've seen black lungs and people struggling for their last breath because of the tumors. But back then, we were invincible. He was so sexy. I danced by the stage all night and kept making eye contact with him. It worked. He bought me a drink."

Didn't want to hear *all* the grim details. I mean, we knew that I'd been the product of their hooking up, so I cleared my throat, reminding Mom to keep her story on the comfortable side of the parent-child awkwardness continuum.

"Right. So I met Kyle that night. And a bunch of nights after. Until I showed up a month or so later at one of his band's gigs, and he showered his attention on a different band groupie. She went home with him. I know because I followed them back to his apartment."

Yikes. Not sure which personality was worse: my mom the band groupie, or the stalker. Neither of which could I reconcile with the woman I'd lived my whole life with and who was walking barefoot next to me, collecting sea glass.

"When I found out I was pregnant, I tried to call him. He avoided me. What do they call it these days? Ghosting? I left him messages. Notes. Showed up at his shows. He wouldn't give me the time of day. I'd finished my final exam and was packing to return home to Ohio for the rest of summer break when I ran into him at the cafeteria."

My gut twisted for my mom. It was bad enough to get dumped, but to feel completely ostracized and pregnant? I can only guess how angry and scared she'd been. What a terrible hand to get dealt.

"He was sitting with a group of students I didn't recognize. I motioned to him so we could talk privately, but he . . ." Mom kicked at the water, launching a spray against us in the wind. Her voice hitched higher than usual. ". . . he shook his head and wouldn't come over. He stared at me with a challenging smirk on his face, taunting me, as if I were replaceable."

She crossed her arms, picking up her pace, hauling a burden, heavy yet invisible. I jogged to catch up.

"Then what did you do?"

"I marched up to his table. In front of all of his friends and the whole cafeteria full of students, I announced, 'I'm pregnant. It's yours, so don't even ask. Stay the hell away from me.'" Her eyes gazed off toward the horizon, but I suspect she couldn't see it for her vivid memory.

I wanted to hug Mom, but I knew her well enough that I knew now was not the moment. She was fighting against her history, and not only did the enemy father her child, but he was now in my life, for better or for worse. No matter what Kyle had experienced or what demons he was currently battling, that had been a shitty way to treat my mom. And me. Holy crap.

"He put his arm around the girl sitting next to him, then kissed her. When he looked back at me, his face was so passive, so goddamned relaxed, and he told me to get an abortion. At that moment, I . . . imploded. I grabbed a nearby cup of soda and splashed it in his face and yelled 'Fine.'"

"Way to go, Mom. I didn't know you had that in you." A rush of pride flooded my heart for this defiant woman who'd given up everything, including her dignity, to keep and raise me by herself. "Did Kyle say anything back to you?"

"Yep. As I marched out of that damned cafeteria, he said only one thing." A bitter laugh escaped her throat. She squeezed her eyes shut, her shoulders slumping. But she remained silent.

"What did he say?"

"Buh-bye."

Kyle's statement hung between us like a dense fog. Wow, he was really an asshole to her. "No wonder you hate him."

"I don't hate him, Ally. I mean, I did, once upon a time. But I got over that long ago once I realized that without him, I'd never have met the most important person in my life—you." Mom slipped her arm around my shoulders and squeezed. "For that, I will always be grateful. But he hurt me. And I don't want him to hurt you as well."

"Don't worry about me, Mom. I got this."

Chapter 27

MARGARET

AFTER

It's taken me several tries to dial the phone number for my clinic. Each time I get the automated system reminding me to call 911 if this is an emergency. Been there, done that. But I never wait long enough through the end of the recording asking me to leave a message.

I panic each time and hang up. My window of opportunity to return to work within an appropriate amount of time passed about two months ago. Now it's just plain unprofessional. What am I supposed to say? "Hi, remember me? One of your nurses?"

By my fourth try, my hands are shaking so hard that I drop my cell phone. Reentering the land of the living is a bitch.

Martin has no idea I'm trying to go back to work. Not that he won't be relieved, but I don't want him asking me tonight how my conversation went, especially if I end up wimping out. He's been trapped in a living nightmare these past thirty-six hours since I told him about my attack. I didn't want to admit to him that last night was the first full night of sleep I'd had in forever. Progress. I'm on a roll, though I've barely scratched the surface of all the crazy that comprises me.

According to my watch, it's nearing the lunch break for the clinic's staff. Technically we never get to actually eat lunch. It's more of a lull—time to catch up on notes and follow-ups on our morning patients before the afternoon appointments begin in earnest. Maybe we can wolf down a protein bar. If we're lucky.

I slink to my bathroom and rummage through my makeup case for lipstick. I haven't even unzipped the bag since Kyle's funeral. All my tubes and creams must have dried up by now. But ten minutes later, I've crafted a minimakeover that I think would impress Kimber and Judy. At least I've covered the puffy circles under my eyes and the sallow tint that I fear may be permanent.

The drive to the doctor's office takes less time than I'd hoped. As does the walk from the parking lot to the frosted glass door. I can't see through to know who I'll encounter first, but the lights are on inside, and the doorknob is unlocked. For all the butterflies in my stomach, I might as well be hovering at the peak of a massive roller-coaster ride.

The last time I was inside this clinic, I was a full-time nurse, and Kyle was alive. I was a different person then. I had two living, breathing children. My biggest concern was . . . well, wondering if I'd find Kyle passed out from drinking when I got home. Would I have to call for an ambulance?

No one would ever be jealous of my life, either before or after. But it was mine.

In fifteen minutes, patients would begin to arrive for the afternoon appointment schedule. It's now or never.

I can do this. I can do this. I can do this.

"Good afternoon. May I help you?" A middle-aged woman I don't recognize doesn't bother looking up from her computer. Where did Trina, our receptionist of ten years, go?

"I'm Margaret Dobrescu, one of the staff nurses. Is Dr. Lee in?"

"Do you have an appointment?"

"No. But she should be taking her lunch break, and I—"

"She's with a patient. Wait over there. I'll let her know you're here."

Ms. Grumpy sighs as if I interrupted her game of solitaire. I hope she doesn't give our patients this air of irritation. I flip through some magazines, not reading the articles, seething and avoiding looking in her direction.

In all the endless days of working here for almost two decades, no one would dream of asking me to sit in the reception area. Ms. Grumpy could've at least had me wait in Dr. Lee's private office. Hasn't anyone ever mentioned my name to her?

Five minutes tick by. Then ten. A patient I've never seen before exits the office, and all returns to quiet. The receptionist doesn't even say goodbye. Dr. Lee will get an earful when I see her.

"Margaret? I'm so glad you dropped by." As if I conjured her with my thoughts, Dr. Lee rushes into the reception area and embraces me in a hug meant for welcoming the prodigal son—in this case, the prodigal nurse. "What are you doing sitting and waiting out here? Come on back to my office."

Dr. Lee drags me by the hand past examination rooms and our medical supply closet to her charming consulting room. This serene, intimate lounge-type environment is where she meets with patients who are considering elective surgeries or expensive treatments that may not be covered by insurance. She may be my employer and the smartest woman I've ever met, but at this moment, she's my pseudo little sister, and I could hug her five-foot-nothing self.

Before she shuts the door, both nurses and our office manager stop in to welcome me. Dr. Lee speaks with a chorus of smiling nods from the others. "Margaret, please say you are here to announce you are coming back. We've been struggling without you."

God, so this is what I've been missing these few months. Camaraderie. Respect. Why didn't I think I'd be accepted back into the land of the living?

"Yes. If it's okay with you, I'd prefer to work part time, at least initially. Perhaps two or three days per week."

◆ ◆ ◆

Armed with a new pair of scrubs to fit my ever-shrinking frame and assurances that I can work two days per week and substitute as needed, I'm prepared to waltz back into the office as a nurse next week. The icing on the cake is that Ms. Grumpy is a temp, and in a few days Trina will be back in the office from her extended vacation as well.

The old team will be back in business.

On my way home, I drive by the cemetery to share the news with Kyle. Not that he would've cared much about my work even when he was around. I never quite hit his radar, with the exception that I probably knew too much about medicine for his comfort. I hope his view of his life and his loved ones now offers him the perspective that everything I ever did for him—zealous mistake or otherwise—was done out of genuine mother-son love.

Always.

I turn the corner and park by the cemetery gate; then I stop. Another car is parked alongside the retaining wall. I've seen that car before. Here. A little red sedan. My heartbeat picks up a notch. It's the same make and model as the one described on the purchase receipt I found months ago.

Ally?

On creaky knees that can barely handle the workout, I bound up the steps and through the gate, power walking until I glimpse someone standing in front of Kyle's memorial stone. But not one person; two.

One is a young woman wearing a sweatshirt and shorts, and the other, an older woman, is dressed in cream slacks and a pastel cardigan.

Careful to maintain a sense of reverence, I approach the two women but stop several yards away.

"Excuse me for interrupting." When both women turn toward my voice, I recognize her instantly, then extend my hand toward her as I close in on the last few steps between us. "Ally, I'm so glad to see you visiting Kyle's grave again."

She pauses, glancing at the older woman, before smiling and taking my hand. What private message did I intercept? Nervousness? Awkwardness? Certainly not fear.

"I was hoping to find you here. Grandma, this is Kyle's mother, Margaret. This is my grandmother. My mom has been ill, so my grandmother came to stay with us this past week. She'll be leaving to drive back home to Ohio tomorrow."

"It's very nice to meet you . . ." I drag out the word hoping she'll fill in the blank with her name, since Ally didn't.

"Victoria O'Leary. Please call me Vicki. Pleasure meeting you as well, Margaret . . ." I hardly catch the rest of what she's saying, as I sense Ally's reluctance to look into my eyes. Instead Ally tightens her ponytail and steps toward Kyle's grave, leaving her grandmother with me. "I'm so sorry about your son passing away. Ally's told me wonderful things about him. She wanted to visit his grave before I left. I wish I'd met him."

Again, they exchange a glance that lasts a heartbeat longer than necessary. More is going on here than I can interpret.

"Ally told me that she and Kyle would study together. I think it was Intro to Psychology, right?" I steer the conversation back to Kyle, hoping to glean any new scrap of information about him I can.

"Actually, we met before that." Ally's voice is soft and deliberate as if she's worried that I'll judge her. "Last spring."

My mind scrolls back to a time before funerals and death occupied my every waking moment. I hardly recognize that world for its brightness and hope. And what was Kyle doing then? Ah, yes. Rehab. Those were good days—sober days—until he relapsed. But then how did he meet Ally?

"Were you a resident at Carrefour as well?" Even as I ask this, I don't believe it. That would be too much of a coincidence. Plus, Ally seems so healthy. Grounded. Adjusted. After spending so much time with Kyle and those in addiction rehabilitation, I've gotten well versed in the physical signs of a recovering addict.

"No. I met him before he moved in. But I visited him at Carrefour a few times. I even went to a couple AA meetings with him."

My mind swirls. It's not as if I tracked Kyle's GPS signal on his phone, but I had no idea he'd invested so much in his relationship with his daughter. Martin made me assume the news was a surprise to him.

But a more pressing problem hammers at my head. How am I going to break the news that we're related? Ally and Victoria have to know. But they don't necessarily know that I know or that I know they know. Oh, this is making my head hurt.

Another glance lobs between them. I might as well be at Wimbledon for all the silent messages they've volleyed back and forth. Please welcome me into this conversation. Finally Ally raises her eyebrows; then Victoria nods once. They hold hands.

"Margaret? I don't know how to reveal this gently or politely." When Ally's voice trembles, my heart catches in my throat. "Kyle dated my mom many years ago while they were both students at SMU. They broke up after a few weeks, but I'm their daughter."

My heart blossoms into an endless field of tulips in full bloom.

Thank you, Kyle. Thank you, Kyle. Thank you, Kyle.

"Ally, dear, then that makes you my granddaughter." I can't do much more than nod like one of those damned bobblehead toys. Through my tears, I try to smile and clasp my hands to my chest. "I didn't know how all the pieces fit together, but I learned a few days after his death that he'd had a daughter. I've been searching for you ever since."

"He wanted to surprise you." My granddaughter's eyes widen, then begin to well. The blush spreading across her cheeks is as endearing as the dimple showing on her growing smile. Oh, what I wouldn't give to have held this precious child as an infant. "He had this big reveal planned. We were going to tell you on his birthday, Valentine's Day, but . . ."

She doesn't finish her sentence, but she doesn't need to. Kyle passed away two weeks before his birthday. As I'd hoped, she must have been the one who left a piece of birthday cake for him here. And the one-month sobriety chip.

"Was he happy?" My voice is as soft as a breeze rustling the leaves. No hint of the weight within my words betrays all that I hope. That his death was a horrible accident. That my last words to him, *get out*, didn't force him over the edge. That he didn't commit suicide. That he had plans he was looking forward to. "At the end?"

"Yes." Ally bows her head, her ponytail slumped over her shoulder in defeat, her shoulders heaving. I can't see her face, but Victoria's is etched with concern. This woman and I are Ally's grandmothers. "He was excited—hopeful—even with his upcoming court case."

A piece of me yearns to apologize to Victoria for whatever pain my son caused her and her daughter's family. But she's here, supporting Ally. We both cherish this brave little girl who grew up with one parent.

"He gave me this token. I was going to leave it here for him." Ally wipes her eyes with the cuff of her sweatshirt sleeve. She holds a royal-blue chip in front of me. I don't have to read the impression on it to know that it's an Alcoholics Anonymous six-month sobriety chip. One hundred and eighty days. "It's the last one I have."

"You keep it. Kyle gave it to you. I'm sure he also earned it for you."

"Thank you." She slips the chip back into her pocket. "I don't have many things to remind me of Kyle. He gave me the car. His letters. Memories."

"Letters?"

"Yes. We wrote to each other a few times while he was in rehab. I kept them all . . ."

As my granddaughter shares, my mind winds up like a top, ready to spin. I knew there had to be missing evidence. If they exchanged letters, then where were the ones Kyle received from her? And his journals? I make a mental note to call Carrefour as soon as I get home.

"I'd love to meet again, if you don't mind. Share stories about Kyle. I can show you pictures of when he was younger." I'm willing to say or do anything to guarantee another meeting someday soon. "I may even be able to give you some of his belongings—"

"Look, I'm sorry." Ally steals yet another look at Victoria. "My mom never wanted me to meet Kyle, and she'd be crushed if she found out I was getting to know his family."

"Oh!" The breath is sucked from my chest. I belatedly close my mouth and try to dash any sense of disappointment from my voice. "I would never ask you to go against your mother's wishes."

"Thank you. She'd be upset with me if she knew I was even visiting Kyle's grave. I wish she'd be more flexible."

"I can vouch for Ally on this front." A fresh frown creases the skin between Victoria's eyes. "My daughter, Hannah, inherited my husband's obstinance. She cut us out of her life for years because of an argument. I hope time will soften her stance. In the meantime, Margaret, I hope you and I can remain in touch."

"Of course, Vicki. I'd welcome that." How can heaven be pulled from my grip in the very minute I hold it? But then, a flash of inspiration strikes. I turn toward my granddaughter and place my last card faceup on the table.

"Ally, would you consider introducing me to your mom?"

Chapter 28
KYLE

BEFORE

I hopped on the city bus from my community college to head back home. Despite the presunset afternoon, the clouds hovered ominously. We could get our first snowfall tonight. With each stop, the door opened, and a frigid blast of air wafted around the passengers.

My class midterm assessments came and went. Ally rocked her exams at Hemingway U. I didn't do crazy well, but I wasn't the lowest grade in either of my classes. Plus, I aced both my public speaking assignments so far this semester. My impromptu speaking at different AA meetings benefited from my new skills.

Last week after class, my professor had privately asked me to help a fellow student who was struggling with stage fright. I met with this classmate half my age twice to rehearse, and I coached him. Today he'd nailed his speech. Our professor thought I could add value, and I did.

Me.

I couldn't wait to tell Ally. Tomorrow over coffee.

For four months, I'd been sober. In two more, I'd earn my six-month token. It was within reach. I hadn't missed a single AA meeting since the day I opened the door to Ally and she found me at my lowest.

My surprise knack for public speaking made me think about new goals. My graphic design business picked up momentum, and I'd already delivered on three paying assignments. I had two projects underway and bids out on several others. I'd been good at this when I created all the T-shirt and poster designs for my band, and now some local small businesses really liked my edgy take on art.

As the bus plowed farther along its route into the suburbs, inspiration hit. I was going to commit, make it official, and hang my graphic design shingle up. Kyle Dobrescu LLC. Or maybe I should think of a snazzier name. Though I was surprised it had taken me this long to look into the prospect of starting my own business, I'd arrived. A decade or so late, sure. But I was trying to be smart about all this adulting. With my own source of money, I had the potential to live independently. So, as I waited for my bus stop, I was scrolling through apartment listings.

Ouch.

The rental rates were off the charts, even after toning down my expectations from a two-bedroom place to a studio apartment. But I couldn't commit to a lease now anyway. Not until after I figured out my rehab-facility situation. The good news was—assuming anything related to my court-ordered rehab requirement was positive—the delay would buy me time to save money so I could eventually move out of my parents' home.

While my graphic design business was growing and I was building a client list, I'd still need a supplemental source of income to cover rent. Maybe a part-time job. Something dependable, in case my design-project pipeline ebbed more than it flowed. I made a mental note to start working on my résumé. I'd had trouble job hunting in the past, given my track record, but I needed to make a new go of it.

And then I'd need to reinstate my driver's license. Finish my degree.

For a nanosecond, my heart thumped. I shed my jacket to cool down a bit. This was all intimidating as hell. Overwhelming. But at the same time, it felt good. Invigorating. I could do this. Game on.

A thrill ran through me as a scenario played out in my mind. I wasn't sure which news I was more excited to eventually announce to Mom and Dad: that they'd finally be empty nesters or that they had another granddaughter.

Nah. I knew the answer to that. Ally.

It would always be Ally. My parents couldn't help but love her.

We'd figure out how best to spill the beans. Something fun.

◆　◆　◆

Since Mom and Dad were still at work, I arrived home from classes to an empty house. Hoping to keep my juju alive and burning strong, I searched my room for my latest rehab journal. If nothing else, all my therapy sessions had taught me that writing down my goals went a long way to validating them. Success came from baby steps, and I was determined to keep running my marathon.

Damn, now where did I stash my notebook?

Any of them. It didn't matter which one. I peeked under my bed, then rifled through my desk drawers. My bookshelves. Next, my bureau. Within minutes I was hauling all the boxes and shit off my closet shelves and dumping old junk I didn't need to hang on to all over my bed. My room looked like a cyclone had hit it.

Crap, if not in my room, then where in the hell had I stashed them? I could've sworn they were in here. Maybe Mom moved my therapy stuff to the linen closet when I was still at Carrefour?

I left the bedroom mess behind me to tackle the stacks of towels and mismatched sheets in our hallway closet. I searched a little more gently, looking over, under, and behind these stacks, because the last thing I wanted to do was refold the fitted sheets to Mom's *Hospital corners, please* inventory standards. No thanks.

Not here.

The basement with my musical instruments and band equipment? The garage? The pantry?

I ventured downstairs to search the coat closet next to our front door, and I slid all the hangers to one side, exposing a few boxes of forgotten hats, mittens, and scarves. We had so much unused stuff collected here. I'm surprised Mom had never gotten rid of this clutter. I made a mental note to help her sort through the closet and reclaim the space.

As I shuffled my hand blindly around the third or fourth box deep in the closet, I brushed against something hard. Maybe this was it! Excitement drummed through me as I schlepped the whole box into the foyer's light to get a better look.

But the instant my fist gripped what was inside, I knew exactly what it was.

It.

The only it.

My favorite kind of it.

The smooth roundness of it fit in my hand like so many, many others before. And before I could even birth it from the box, I closed my eyes. I knew exactly what it looked like. I could taste it. Smell the antiseptic vapors.

An unexploded land mine—an unopened fifth of vodka.

I must've stashed this bottle in here for an emergency a year or more ago and then forgotten about it. I think at some point I hid bottles in every shadowy nook and corner in every room and behind or under every piece of furniture in this house.

All my nerves shifted to high alert, and my breathing accelerated, becoming shallower as I raised the bottle to eye level. Reading the label. Appreciating the weight of its fullness. The filigree of the red-and-white tape that fastens the cap to the neck. The warning text. The ad copy. The clear liquid that was contained within.

My escape.

My bliss.

My throat muscles mimicked the instinctive contraction of the very first phantom gulp. The sting of the vapors as they hit my palate. The welcome burn as I swallowed deeply and traced its path downward.

At this moment, everything became simple. Just me and the vodka. The vodka and me.

Maybe I could just taste it. A single mouthful. I'd just taste it and then be done with it. I could still go to my AA meeting tonight and add another notch to my tally of sober days. This bottle would be my safety valve. Here if I needed it. Or even if I didn't. Like a seat belt. You didn't even remember it was fastened once you were wearing it, but it was still working for you full time.

Just one—tiny—sip.

Only one.

What harm was there?

I rotated the cap ever so slightly. The taped seal broke on both sides in a satisfying rip. Then the tapered metal cap clicked as it spiraled up the bottle's neck threads until finally it separated. Closing my eyes, I inhaled the liquor, knowing that while it didn't have any identifiable scent, it was also the most enticing aromatherapy I'd ever known.

One sip.

Only one.

As the glass rim touched my lower lip, I froze.

Oh, shit. What the hell was wrong with me? I couldn't do this. Give in?

I pushed the bottle away from my mouth—from me—and stared at it as if it were a viper coiled and ready to strike. It almost had.

Fuck.

I raced down the hallway to the bathroom next to the kitchen, and before I could think another thought, I spilled the vodka into the toilet. All of it. Every last drop. My shoulders slumped as I hovered over the basin. Then I plunged the bottle into the water to ensure I couldn't try to extract any remaining drops later.

God, that was close.

Too close.

I flipped on the bathroom lights over the vanity mirror. As my eyes adjusted to the brightness, I took a close, hard look at my reflection. Trails of tears streaked silver down my face. Yeah. A broken man, but I still had all the pieces of me. Someday I would be whole again. Somewhere in there, all my pieces were mashed together. I had a future. Journal or no journal, I could do this. I *would* do this.

For Ally.

For me.

◆　◆　◆

As I stacked the dinner dishes from the table, Mom pushed my good hand aside and took over the task for me. "Dinner was delicious, honey."

Ever since moving back home from Carrefour, I'd assumed the cooking duties, at least for dinner. Mom and Dad came home from work exhausted. Plus, if they were left to their own devices, we'd be eating frozen pizzas and bagged iceberg lettuce salads most nights. Convenience, not their taste buds, drove their meal choices.

I had both the inclination and the time to cook when I wasn't dialing for dollars—it'd been months, and still no available rehab beds—applying for jobs, or meeting Ally for coffee. My summons could come any day now, but my lawyer, Mr. D., hoped the court's notorious backlog would give me more time to proactively help my case.

Turning on the classic-rock radio station gave me the little boost of energy I needed. While my musical preferences, at least during my

Silence Deconstructed band days, ran toward heavy metal and punk, the soft edges of the familiar tunes from my youth fared better with Mom and Dad.

Tonight's menu was grilled salmon drizzled with a lemon-dill cream sauce, a side of rosemary quinoa, and root vegetable julienne. I found that my digestive system could tolerate more and more these days. I might have even gained back a pound or two.

Once my orthopedic doctor had given me the all clear to start physical therapy exercises on my shoulder, I focused on overriding my pain instincts. And my pain-management options. Upstairs in my backpack was a script for prescription pain meds, ready to fill at the pharmacy. Mom knew it. She also knew she couldn't intervene since I was a legal adult and my doctor had legitimately ordered it. Every night since I started physical therapy, she'd walk in the door after work with her lips pressed together and her jaw flexing. As soon as the scent of dinner wafted in her direction, her grimace melted away, and her shoulders relaxed.

"Kyle, honey. Would you mind helping me with something on my computer?" Mom stood in the kitchen doorway, summoning me. These days, she handled me as if I were a ticking time bomb. Given my past history, I guess she had a good reason. Pavlov and his dogs could have used our family as an experimental data point. But I hoped she and Dad would come to expect the new and improved me.

As if on cue, the intro strumming chords of Rod Stewart's raspy voice crooned through the radio's speakers.

"'Maggie May'! It's your song, Mom." I turned up the volume, then scooped her up with my one good arm to dance her around the kitchen. After objecting that I'd reinjure my shoulder, she finally gave up resisting and let me lead. To make her blush even harder, I started serenading her. With each note, she aged backward, dropping at least a decade of time from her face. Her shoulder-length hair swung back and forth. Her smile beamed as brightly as I'd ever seen it. Dad, initially concerned about all the commotion, stopped in the doorway, laughing. He snapped a photo of us as I waltzed her from sink to fridge to stove and back again. By the time I'd sung the chorus for the third time, I had noticed her eyes had welled. When the last strains of the song tapered off, I twirled then dipped her while drawing out the final ". . . Maggie."

Oh, I really should do this more often. Mom deserved some good times after all the hell I'd put her through. After what we'd survived together.

"Thank you, honey." She snagged the kitchen towel from the stove to wipe her face, then sniffed away any new evidence of emotion. "As I was saying, I had trouble printing an email attachment today. Do you mind taking a look at it? I mean, you don't have to . . ."

"On it."

After tinkering with her computer's driver settings, I resolved her printer problem. Child's play, really. But if being their dedicated in-home tech guy and fixing a meal fit for my discerning palate were all it took to ease my parents' lives, then yes, sign me up.

◆　◆　◆

After the Thanksgiving holidays were over—a holiday I didn't spend with Ally, since she and her mom road-tripped to visit her other grandparents in Ohio—the race was on to the semester's final exams.

Me: When can you meet for coffee?

A. O.: A bit crazy with end-of-term papers and deadlines. Can we meet at the library instead?

Pride flooded my every being. My daughter prioritized studying over social stuff.

Me: Sure.

By the time I found her in her campus's main library, she'd covered a table in a quiet nook with textbooks, library books, a binder, her laptop, and every color of highlighter available. Ally was taking notes on her notes. She'd left a few inches of table space for me to set up camp.

Jeez, if I'd had a fraction of her grit and determination at her age, I'd have stayed on track with my degree and graduated. Shoulda, woulda, coulda.

I nodded toward her scattered resources. "So what are you working on today?"

"Ugh." Her exaggerated groan was loud enough to draw the notice of some nearby students. "I have a chemistry-lab report due tomorrow. When I ran the experiment, my data was all over the place. Inconclusive. I must've done something wrong."

"Wish I could help you." Apparently she didn't buy my sincerity, so we both ended up shushing each other over our giggling. But when I told her about my psychology class and all the famous psychologists with their wacko theories of human development, she'd been jealous of me. I can't remember the last time anyone envied anything about me.

"I have a brilliant idea. I'll register for Psych 101 next semester." She clicked away at her keyboard—chemistry deadline ignored. "Perfect. There's still room in the class, and it fits my schedule. What if you took the next level at your college? Then we can meet to study together next semester."

The lump forming in my throat didn't allow me to answer. So I nodded like a bobblehead toy. Was this what heaven would be like? Because I'm sure I didn't deserve anything or anyone as endearing as my daughter.

Two hours later, as I watched the bus pull away with Ally on it, I vowed to save every cent I made until I could get her a car. It was so much safer than mass transit.

Ally had told her mom we were still in touch. Whether Hannah was happy about it, I couldn't tell, but it hadn't stopped Ally from meeting with me. I'd offered to call Hannah directly—I thought it was important to make sure she knew I wasn't trying to invade her space or compete with her, but Ally begged me to wait. What could I do? Ally lived with her mom. I didn't want to cause any ripples between them or ruin my future with Ally.

Against my better judgment, I resigned myself to honor Ally's request and follow her lead once she was comfortable with me contacting Hannah. At least for the time being.

On the other hand, she wasn't living with Hannah's parents, who, from all Ally's reminiscing, sounded like decent, caring people. Ally never once warned me not to reach out to them. Hopefully they could help me smooth the landscape for Hannah to eventually find some common ground with me. If not Hannah's, I needed—craved—their blessing.

Finding Mr. and Mrs. O'Leary's landline number wasn't hard. Ally had shared with me their names and hometown. Her grandmother—Victoria—had even posted several pictures of Ally on Facebook. As I started my bus ride home, I finally got the nerve to dial them up.

Ally's grandmother picked up on the third ring. It was now or never.

"Hi, Mrs. O'Leary? This is Kyle Dobrescu." The silence on the other end of the line was almost deafening, but it was too late to hang up, since I'd already given her my name. I hoped this wasn't a colossal mistake. "Um, you don't know me, but I'm Ally's biological father. I just wanted to reach out to her close family and introduce myself."

"Kyle! Yes, I'm delighted you called us. Ally has told us all about meeting you this year. Please, call me Vicki."

Chapter 29

ALLY

AFTER

"Allison Marie O'Leary, please tell me you did *not* promise your biological father's mother that I would meet her in person." Mom assumes her sailor stance, with her chin canted up, her arms crossed, and her hospital clogs anchoring her legs. I don't expect her to lunge, but Lulu doesn't take chances and springs away to hide under the living room couch. "I asked you not to contact her."

"I didn't intend to see her, Mom. I took Grandma to visit Kyle's grave before she left town. Margaret showed up while we were there. It was a coincidence. Nothing more." I step back and put my hands up in surrender. I've never seen Mom this upset. Correction. Yes, I have. But it was many years ago when our landlord tried to raise the rent. He changed his mind and gave her a discount instead.

"Then what? You invited her over for tea?" Sarcasm drips from every clipped word she utters. "Aren't we one big happy family?"

"It didn't go down like that. I introduced Margaret to Grandma. It was the polite thing to do. We were visiting her son's grave, after all.

We chatted for a couple minutes in the cemetery. She asked if she could meet you. End of story."

"Yes. That is the end of this story. Cancel it."

"Come on, Mom. Really? You can't find it in you to tolerate the presence of an older woman for fifteen minutes? She's gentle. Kind. And grieving her son. Even Grandma Vicki got along with her. Apparently meeting me has helped Margaret cope with losing Kyle. Plus, she's a nurse, so you both care for sick and injured people. She's going back to work next week." I try to keep the whine out of my voice. At this point, I may have to renege on my tentative acceptance to Margaret. "You care for gang members, criminals, and drug addicts all day long at the hospital. Meeting with Margaret might be a little uncomfortable, but it'll be a cakewalk in comparison."

Mom doesn't reply. God, she's standing her ground on this one. Nothing. Not even a blink. I knew convincing her would be tough, but I thought if I begged and pleaded, she'd cave. A little. She told me how Kyle broke up with her. Yes, he was an asshole, but she said she got over it. But that was him, not his parents. Giving me his contact information was so much more of a hurdle to her than meeting his mother ever could be.

"I don't understand why you're being so stubborn, Mom. I get why you held off giving me Kyle's name. You were worried about me. I love you for that. But I'm also thrilled I got to meet my biological father and spend time with him before he died. I'm grateful you didn't wait until my nineteenth birthday to share his contact information. By then he was already gone. For better or for worse, it also means he is out of my life. Forever. You may not miss him, but I do."

Mom turns on her heel to walk away, so I grab her by the elbow. With lips pressed in a tight line, she faces me, but her shoulders relax a little. A good sign, so I keep pressing my case.

"You moved on from him once. You can do it again now. Forever. Kyle's dead, Mom. Buried-in-the-ground dead. He's gone and will never, ever be able to cause you any more pain."

Mom chases her sigh with a large dose of sarcasm. "If there's a way to hurt me from the grave, Kyle will find it."

Drama much? I roll my eyes but refrain from slamming my hands on my hips and calling her out. "Margaret's been through a lot too. An addict son who died. And Kyle told me about a horrible, violent situation they were both victims in when he was thirteen. Please, Mom, meet with her. Once. It would mean the world to me."

"Fine."

Uh-oh. Whenever Mom says *fine* with that edge in her voice, things are anything but fine.

"I'll meet with Kyle's mother, but here are my conditions." Counting on each finger while holding eye contact, she lists, "You get fifteen minutes, tops. Find someplace neutral to meet, not her home or ours. Nor the cemetery. Not a meal. And if I get too uncomfortable, I'm leaving."

"Thank you." I lunge and tackle her onto the couch. She flops over, laughing and mussing my hair. For that brief moment, it's just the two of us again. We time-warp back to my preteen days, when she was my hero.

She still is my hero.

"Can you promise me one more thing, Ally-cat?"

"Sure, Mom. Anything."

"Please stop hanging out at the cemetery. It's so creepy."

Two weeks later, I'm finally able to drag Mom by her DIY-polished nails to the same café where Kyle and I used to meet. This is the third rescheduling we've done because of Mom. I'm determined not to need a fourth. While the delays frustrated me, they also gave me extra time to prepare for my upcoming final exam week, which was looming over me like a guillotine's blade. Margaret has been totally flexible through this process.

"Mom, can I get you a coffee? Margaret should be here any minute."

"No. I may not stay long enough to drink a coffee." Mom plops into the same upholstered armchair Kyle always used. If I tell her, she'll spring out of here. Despite wringing her hands in her lap, Mom looks gorgeous in her sundress. Her hair, for once not stretched back in a ponytail for work, falls in soft ginger-blonde balayage waves at her shoulders. She really should try to date someone and live a little.

"Seriously, Mom? You can't sit tight for fifteen minutes? Besides, they serve in to-go cups. You can take your drink with you if you hit the ejection button." Mentally kicked myself. I shouldn't be planting ideas in her head. She may decide to leave even before Margaret arrives.

"Small iced coffee. Black." Her eyes dart from me to the café's front door, then back to me. Her face turns an alarming shade of green. Hope her nerves and the pervading scent of roasted coffee beans don't make her puke. "Thanks, honey."

Then it hits me.

Oh, my God. I'm such an idiot. How did I not realize before this second? In a parallel universe, Margaret could've been Mom's mother-in-law. Instead, the potential wedding never happened. Kyle had ditched her. Mom had birthed Margaret's grandchild on the sly, then hid my existence from Kyle and his family. Yikes. My heart twists at the thought of all the awkwardness my mother is subjecting herself to on my behalf.

Crouching so that we're eye to eye, I whisper, "Thank you for doing this. I know how difficult it is for you. I love you."

"Ally-cat, I love you more."

While I'm standing in line to order, the hanging doorbell jingles. Margaret struggles to push the glass door open. After leaving the queue,

I dash over to help hold it open for her. She hesitates, so I hug her first, letting her cling to me, her fingers gripping my arms as if I'm a raft amid the ocean's choppy water. I have no doubt she's hugging Kyle as much as me. When she pulls away, her eyelashes are matted and wet, her nose pink. I guide her to the lounge chairs where Mom is sitting.

"I'd like you to meet my mother, Hannah O'Leary. Mom, this is Kyle's mother, Margaret Dobrescu." Mom stands and extends her hand to Margaret as if this were a business meeting. As if I didn't share blood between the two of them. After they shake for a nanosecond, Mom hides her hands behind her back.

Mom hangs her head and doesn't even open her mouth. I swear I can hear invisible elephants thumping around the café. I swallow back my frustration. Margaret and I wanted this introduction to happen—not Mom—though I expected her to be a bit more socially engaging than this. She's taking *ice queen* to a whole new level of permafrost. My Intro to Psych class this semester did little to prepare me for this moment.

"Hannah." Margaret is the essence of calm, despite Mom's impenetrable shield. You'd think we need a mediator to be in the same room. "I would have contacted you sooner if I'd known Kyle had fathered a child. I found out about her existence after his death and knew no details about her. Or you. I'm grateful to have finally met Ally. And that you agreed—"

"I'm sorry, Margaret. Ally, this was all a mistake." Mom slings her purse over her shoulder, then backs toward the door. I can't believe she's jumping ship. We haven't even ordered our coffee yet. "Margaret, I hold no ill will against you personally, but I'm not ready to play pretend family. I doubt I ever will be. I have few regrets, but one was introducing Ally to Kyle."

"Wait, Hannah." Margaret's call is frantic. At least Mom halts her escape but doesn't return to us. Margaret must be encouraged, so she continues in a slightly calmer voice. "I don't know all that Kyle did to you. It must have been awful, and for that, I can only apologize. But I also want to thank you for raising Ally to be the upstanding, smart, and empathetic young woman she is. I give you all the credit. She is walking proof that you've been an outstanding mother."

"Thank you, Margaret." Mom's shoulders remain tense, but her face relaxes a bit. "I appreciate your recognizing that. Everything I've ever done has been with my daughter's best interest in mind. I'm proud of her and who she's become."

Warmth spreads through my heart, hearing these women speak of me. Both regard each other in a single note of harmony they may never reach again. After hesitating, Mom nods toward me, shrugs, then leaves the café. In her glance, she conveyed her passive blessing that continuing a relationship with Margaret was up to me. I choose yes.

"Your mother is a fierce woman, Ally. She loves you. Very much. I respect her."

◆ ◆ ◆

After Mom escaped from our coffee date, Margaret and I ordered to-go beverages and decided to drive separately over to Kyle's grave site. Part of me is ticked off that Mom can't—won't—accept this slice of my life, but part of me is also relieved. Everything about Kyle and his family flows easier without Mom around.

I pull up behind Margaret's car, then help her carry the box of gardening tools and flowers she brought along to spruce up the grave site for spring.

"Kyle is buried with his grandparents. We were able to get special permission from the parish to place his urn on top of my mother's casket. They always shared a special bond. It meant a lot to me that they will rest in peace together through eternity."

I don't remember him mentioning anything about his grandmother, but I can relate. Grandmas are the best. What's not to love about being spoiled? All the fun; none of the discipline. They love you unconditionally. I wouldn't trade Grandma Vicki, even in the few years we've been able to get to know each other, for anyone or anything. Who else would drive six hours to come to help me out when I panicked? No one.

Weird. I've known for more than a year that Margaret is my biological paternal grandmother. And she seems kind. But will we ever be emotionally close enough for her to truly be my *grandma*? Like Grandma Vicki?

Following Margaret's lead, I pull weeds, clip grass, trade out faded silk flowers for fresh ones, and wipe the caked dirt from the granite headstones. Then Margaret artfully arranges the cluster of sentimental items visitors have left for Kyle: a smooth stone with *Gratitude* etched on the top, a pinwheel, and a small bag of sour candy that the elements have faded, but thus far, the packaging remained intact.

On the sly, I snap a photo of Margaret kneeling and tending to his grave site with my phone, planning to sketch the still-life later. This is the first time I've wanted to draw in months—actually, ever since learning that Kyle died. I'd even stopped carrying my sketchbook in my backpack. Maybe it's time to dig out my charcoal pencils again. The inclination floods my heart with warmth.

"Did you leave this for Kyle?" Margaret sits on her heels and hands me the one-month AA chip. The one I buried here on his birthday. The same day he should've been introducing me to his family.

Every muscle in my face scrunches into a wad of missing Kyle. Reaching for his chip, I clutch it in my hand, remembering the night he gave it to me. Some cell of insanity within me wishes I could use this chip as a portal to reach through to heaven and bring him back. His death was so unfair. I'd finally met my dad. Now he's gone.

Not bothering to wipe my cheeks or my nose, I puddle.

Sobbing.

Shuddering.

Moaning.

Bargaining with God to steal more time with him. Alive.

Awareness of my surroundings creeps back into my psyche, helping me claw out of my hollow darkness. I belatedly sense Margaret rocking me in tandem while rubbing my back. Matching me tear for tear. I don't know how long we've been sitting here, side by side, on the grass next to Kyle's grave. Twenty minutes? An hour? The sun has started descending toward the horizon.

Reality punches me. My to-do list to prepare for final exams is a mile long, but I think I'll tackle that headache tomorrow, when I'll hopefully feel fresh from this Kyle hangover.

I squeeze Margaret's hand to signal my gratitude. Our shared loss. Our missing link.

"Ally, would you please tell me about your time with Kyle? From the beginning?"

Chapter 30

ALLY

College winter break was now officially my favorite time of year. Classes were over. My transcript had arrived, and I got mostly As, even in chemistry. In fact, my scholarship was renewed for next year because of my first semester's GPA. Spring semester wouldn't start for a couple more weeks, so other than binge-watching TV shows with Lulu and a grocery store shift, I had the luxury of free time.

Yesterday Mom and I shared our usual quiet Christmas by exchanging a few homemade gifts under our small lit tree while singing along with the holiday music station on the radio. We even got a dusting of snow, so we bundled up and took an afternoon walk outside. I fixed us fettuccine Alfredo for dinner, while she got ready to work the graveyard shift.

"So sorry I can't spend Christmas evening with you, Ally-cat." The holidays were traditionally a busy time at work—burns, drunk driving accidents, gunshot wounds, overdoses—and with most of the staff vying for vacation time, Mom doubled down on shifts to earn extra money. I saw her so little these days. I was grateful I had decided to commute to college from home and save money this year. That way we maximized our free time together.

"Don't worry about us, Mom. Lulu and I have some big plans to destroy the tree, set the apartment on fire, then devise our strategy for world domination."

"Comforting." I loved seeing her dimple when she laughed. It didn't happen often enough.

Kyle and I were able to visit every week after our final exams ended. We'd planned to meet tomorrow afternoon at the coffee shop, but he'd been a little secretive lately. He asked if I'd be able to spend the whole evening with him. Maybe finish up at an AA meeting.

◆　◆　◆

While waiting at the coffee shop, I texted Jenna my meetup plan. One of these days, I should really introduce Kyle to my best friend, since she knows so much about him. I'd saved our favorite lounge chairs at the café, bought our steaming-hot order—hot chocolate with whipped cream and drizzled with fudge for both of us, because big fluffy snow-flakes were falling outside—and set out my Christmas present wrapped with a red bow.

The doorbells jangled. Kyle walked in with the collar of his black wool peacoat pulled up over his ears, his dark hair dusted with snow-flakes. A small gust of wintry wind chased him inside.

"Merry Christmas, Ally." He hugged me, held up my coat to help me slip into it, then scooped up our to-go cups. "Thanks for treating me. Let's go."

"Wait, what?" We weren't going to sit here for the afternoon? But his grin was quirky and there was a glint in his eyes, so I followed. After pulling on my mittens, I grabbed his gift and chased him out the door. "Where are we going?"

"You'll see." He checked his watch as we walked out to the parking lot. He stopped in front of a compact red car, turned to face me, then dangled a set of keys. Snowflakes clung to his dark eyebrows and hair.

"Nice car. Was your driver's license reinstated?"

"I wish, but not quite yet." He tossed the keys at me. "It's yours."

Catching the keys, I glanced from them to the car to Kyle, who was holding out his arms as if he were some game show host showing the grand prize.

"You're giving me a car? For Christmas? Oh, my God. Thanks, but . . . but . . ." What could I say? Mom would absolutely never let me accept such a gift. It was beyond over-the-top. Too big. Too much. Too expensive. ". . . I can't possibly accept this."

"Yes. You can." He opened the driver's side door. "It's used, with a lot of miles, but in excellent condition. I had a mechanic inspect it— new tires and brakes. There's no loan. It's all paid for. Free and clear. The title is being mailed to you as we speak."

"How did you . . ." Words escape my grasp. I'd seen Kyle dig and scrounge for loose change to pay for our coffee orders. Plus, he wasn't a grand-gesture kind of guy.

"How did I get it here? Well, I could tell you, but then I'd have to kill you." His laughter was contagious.

Since he'd probably have been arrested for driving on a suspended license, I gathered he didn't get caught. "I was gonna say 'pay for it.'"

"I've been saving. Working a bunch of freelance website and design jobs. Believe it or not, I've been planning to buy you a car ever since you first rode the bus to visit me at Carrefour. This is so much safer for you. Especially taking mass transit after dark. I'll feel better, as your father. Believe it or not, I worry about you. I know your mom probably does too."

Yup. She'd blow a gasket. But I reminded myself to close my mouth.

"I've missed celebrating eighteen Christmases and birthdays with you. Had I met you sooner, I'd have given this to you when you turned sixteen." He must be able to tell that I'm not a thousand percent convinced, so he steps to the side. "Look, I'll sell it tomorrow if you don't absolutely love it. Shall we at least take it for a spin?"

Well, what could it hurt to test-drive it? Kyle dashed around to get into the passenger side as I tentatively fastened my seat belt and adjusted the mirrors. I'd had my driver's license for a couple of years, but other than occasionally running errands in Mom's car, I didn't get much practice.

"Thank you, Kyle." The scent of hot chocolate filled the small interior, which was so narrow, Kyle's shoulder almost touched mine. While still parked, I handed him my Christmas present with a shrug. "This is for you. Um, it's not a car."

Ripping the paper, he opened the gift box in seconds flat, much like an excited little boy might do. Pausing, he held up the black hoodie with the Dagger logo I'd purchased off the clearance rack in the back of Hemingway U's school bookstore. He slipped out of his coat and pulled on the sweatshirt. "Perfect gift from my perfect daughter. I love it."

In this single crystallizing moment, all my eighteen years of wanting, begging to find my dad, to have him accept me as his daughter, dissipated into the ether of time. My breath grew ragged, but I reminded myself it wasn't over. We had a whole evening to spend together.

A whole lifetime.

"Here goes nothing." I turned the key in the ignition, and the engine purred to life. "Where should we go?"

"You'll find out soon enough. We have a full tank of gas, and I have a plan. Turn right as you exit the parking lot."

◆ ◆ ◆

It was well after sunset when we crossed the Chicago River into the Loop. I'd never actually driven downtown before. If Kyle noticed my white knuckles, he didn't mention anything. Mercifully the city's notorious traffic was light tonight, and we were using GPS to guide us through the maze of one-way roads. We passed by one lit-up skyscraper after another until we reached Millennium Park.

As soon as we found parking, he took my gloved hand and directed me to the entryway of what seemed to be a winter garden of Christmas trees. A stray flurry or two still fell, but the little that came down this afternoon added a layer of nostalgia even Hollywood couldn't have created. The multicolored twinkle lights glowed in the darkness, with the skyline behind them. We strolled through the crowd admiring the mirrored Bean, then headed over to the massive City of Chicago Christmas Tree. We tried to take a selfie with the big tree behind us, but it sparkled so brightly that only the silhouettes of our heads blocked the light.

"Mind if I ask you a personal question?" I glanced over at Kyle's face, illuminated with an orangish glow from all the twinkle lights around us.

He paused, biting his lip, but then stepped back with an open stance and shoved his hands in his coat pockets. "You've heard and seen me at my worst. Ask away."

"You once mentioned that you proposed to someone, but you're not married. What happened?"

"She's gone."

"Who?"

Kyle turned away so that I couldn't see his face. When he looked back at me, his jaw was clenched and his brow furrowed. "Becca."

I waited for him to continue as we wandered past another few trees. But when he didn't elaborate, I nudged him. "Did she . . . pass away?"

"No, nothing like that. She's doing well, I hope. We met in high school but didn't start dating until after I moved back home after SMU."

Overriding my instinct to blurt out *You mean right after you were such an asshole to my mom?* I deferred that subject to another time. And eventually I hoped to smooth things over so Mom and Kyle could meet and get along. Someday they could attend my college graduation together or sit at the same table in a restaurant. And my wedding. And see their shared grandkids. I blinked away these thoughts, because achieving that plateau of awkward comfort would require long-term diplomacy and finesse. I'd need to create a path wide enough for both of them to share civilly. But a girl could dream, right?

Plus, I didn't want to kill the magic of tonight, though the way his face was contorting, dredging the memory of his relationship with his ex-fiancée, might do that for me.

"I loved her. Still do. I guess I always will." His smile didn't reach his eyes.

"What happened?"

"We dated on and off for fifteen years or so. She had her own issues to deal with—her dad passed away, and she was struggling with medical problems and finances, but she worked her butt off and earned her master's degree. So while she fought hard for her star to ascend, mine tanked. She called my parents and 911 more than a few times when I'd binged so hard I'd be unconscious or convulsing."

I stared at my boots as we walked, not able to face the raw, brutal truth that was Kyle. For the most part, our contact had been positive. He'd always been sober. Except once when I glimpsed him at his low point. I couldn't imagine being there time after time, picking up his broken pieces only to have him fall apart again. Shattering. Hell, if I'd been Becca, I'd have run as fast as I could to get away. Chances were I'd probably see him at his worst again someday.

"But we had good times too. Romantic times. I'll never forget slow dancing with her under the stars on a Jamaican beach."

"Is that when you proposed?"

"No. I should've. Timing is everything, and I bombed it. My proposal came when I was lying in a hospital bed, hooked up to an IV. I couldn't even get on my knee. But I was so in love with her at that moment that I couldn't wait. She'd stayed with me through everything. She was my rock . . ."

A sigh escaped him.

". . . and I'd be the cement block chained to her neck, keeping her from living. Breathing."

He leaned on the barrier fence between us and the ice rink, his shoulders heaving as he sobbed while covering his face. Skaters glided by us, and I tried unsuccessfully to shield him from their notice as he pulled himself together. A stranger offered me a wad of napkins from the nearby hot chocolate stand so Kyle could wipe his tearstained face.

"Did you ever tell Becca about what happened? At the mall?"

"No. No one knows. Except you."

"Why don't you reach out to her? You cared about each other. At least then she'd have a better understanding of your—"

"I let her go, Ally." We exited the Christmas tree park and walked back to the car. The night's chill descended in so many ways. "It's over. She married someone else."

Our drive home was quiet except for Kyle's occasional driving directions. I was mulling over exactly how to break it to Mom that he bought me a car for Christmas and I intended to keep it. I assumed his thoughts involved his star-crossed relationship with Becca or lack thereof. When I drove up to his home to drop him off, I put the car in park.

"Thank you for the car and for tonight. I'm sorry we didn't make it to your AA meeting."

"No problem. I'll go tomorrow."

"Do you think . . ." Pausing, I weighed the risks of my request. If bringing up Becca had sent Kyle into a tailspin, my request could shove him plummeting to earth without a parachute. ". . . someday you could introduce me to your parents? As their granddaughter?"

His head snapped up, looking at the front door to his house. My grandparents' house. When he looked back at me, he'd reclaimed the same Cheshire cat smile he'd worn when he dangled the keys in front of this car a few hours ago.

"Yes! In about a month, I'll be turning thirty-eight years old. I'd love to give my parents a gift on my birthday. If you don't mind waiting . . ."

"Valentine's Day, right?"

"Yep. We'll think of something good. Some way to surprise them."

Because finding out that they have an eighteen-year-old grand-daughter that they'd never known about wouldn't be enough of a surprise? "Okay, but I refuse to jump out of your birthday cake."

"Deal." His laughter filled every nook of the tiny car with energy.

"Awesome. I'm dying to meet them. But I don't want to cause any heart attacks in the process."

"It'll be a shock, but they're going to love you. I know they will. My mom is crazy about her grandkids. She'll be no different with you."

Suddenly butterflies swirled inside my stomach. But what if they didn't love me? What if they felt that their son's surprise daughter was more a scandal, or worse, a burden, than a cause for joy? That I'd bring shame to their family?

Then again, I was their blood relative. Their granddaughter. I already occupied my own branch on the Dobrescu family tree. They just didn't know about me yet.

Chapter 31

MARGARET

AFTER

Kyle didn't take my secret to his grave.

Not even close.

All this time, I thought it was between the two of us. But when I asked Ally to tell me about her relationship with Kyle, she gave me the blow-by-blow, including the night he told her about the attack at the mall. By now she's known for more than six months. I only revealed my news to Martin a couple of weeks ago, so to have someone—even someone as precious to me as Ally—recount my nightmare in a hearsay way, well, I had to swallow back bile.

The silver lining to my hell is that Kyle also told Ally my nickname that same night. To hear *Maggie May* from her lips, for the first time since the night before Kyle passed away, was a gift straight from the great beyond. Somehow, the void as empty as a canyon in my heart began to fill. And my eyes have not stopped leaking since, in a good way.

Lush spring-kissed trees and virgin cornfields zip past us as Martin drives the car along the highway. He holds the steering wheel with one hand and laces his fingers through mine with the other. When did our skin turn splotchy and ropy with veins? We've been together for nearly fifty years. The transition to becoming old happened so slowly that I missed it. In my mind, I'm still in my forties. Fifties tops. Though this year has taken me for a spin.

Martin's been more attentive these past couple of weeks since I shared my secret. Holding my hand more. Bringing me coffee first thing in the morning. Fixing me dinner. Escorting me whenever I go shopping. Back in the day, these attentions would've reinforced my victim status, something I'd have rejected with every fiber of my body. I wanted to live a normal life and not wonder if he was touching me because I needed special care. Or avoiding me because he was repulsed that I'd been some other man's prey. But now, I welcome these gestures in a different light. I hear the subtext that Martin can't acknowledge verbally. That he wishes he'd been there to protect us. That he could have lost us.

Even Ally tried to soothe my memories of the attack. *Kyle told me he wanted to protect you, Margaret. That he'd failed you because he couldn't save you from those men. That if there were one thing he could change in his life, it would've been to not have asked to buy those shoes.*

What a revelation. Every minute of every day since that horrible afternoon twenty-five years ago, I felt I'd let my son down. I was the parent. His guardian. I should've been more careful. Not let us get trapped in that hallway in the first place.

What I could do after the fact was to give him the freedom to forget. Erase the memories. To continue living a normal life. Like every other boy on the planet.

I'd been determined to carry the burden of memory for both of us. I'd never have wanted him to blame himself. But my plan backfired. In some warped, twisted way, we both blamed ourselves. We never even discussed it between us after the attack, though he brought it up to me once—twice, if I count the night before he died. It's taken me all these years to realize we both carried the burden. I should've assured Kyle back then. It was never his fault.

An hour later, we arrived at Kimber's house. Whenever Martin and I have something serious to discuss with her, we swoop into town, treat her to lunch at a nice restaurant, drop our bomb, assure her everything is all right, then scoot out of town. We did it when we listed the childhood home to downsize. When Martin was diagnosed with early-stage cancer. When Kyle was kicked out of Carrefour. And now this.

Since our grandchildren are in school today and her husband is traveling out of town for business, we asked if she would take a personal day off work. Martin and I want to tell Kimber about my attack. In person.

And while I expected Kimber's shock at the revelation and frustration at my not having shared it before now, I was not prepared for her to be upset on her brother's behalf.

"Oh, poor Kyle. Shouldn't you have taken him to a therapist? So he could talk it through with someone?" Kimber buried her face in her hand, rubbing her forehead. "No wonder he hit the bottle to forget that living nightmare."

"Sweetheart, I did the best I could with the situation we were dealt." I reached over to rub her shoulder. When she flinched, I removed my hand. How do you prepare your adult child to hear an ugly truth from your past? After exchanging worried glances with Martin, I lowered my voice to a whisper. "I didn't ask to be a rape victim."

"No, and I don't mean to dismiss it, Mom. I'm horrified for you and beyond sorry that happened." By the time her eyes met mine, tears were streaming down her face. "But Kyle didn't ask to be held hostage and watch you be violated. He was just a kid. Your kid. How could he process a trauma of that magnitude all by himself?"

I choked on my words, not answering for fear of saying the wrong thing and making things worse. She excused herself, then rushed out of the restaurant for some fresh air. I left Martin to sort out the check and followed behind her.

By the time I made it out the main doors, Kimber was pacing the sidewalk out front.

"If my child had witnessed a violent attack, I'd have supported them as they processed the aftershocks. Hired every therapist they needed. Gotten them professional help."

"Kimber, honey, you are right. I wish I had. I also wish times had been different. That I'd been different. Society has evolved since then, and caring for one's mental health is socially acceptable. These days, talk therapy is not only valued; it's encouraged to help process trauma. Times have changed for the better in that respect. Back then, even twenty years ago, if I'd taken him to see a psychiatrist or a therapist, he would've been labeled crazy. It would've added insult to injury. Your brother was in junior high at the time. He would've been teased unmercifully had I booked an appointment and someone found out. I also feared he would've judged himself as broken. Quite a few years had passed by the time I realized I should've been more proactive. By then it was too late."

"Mom, you never even reported it to the police! Or told Dad. You were Kyle's mother. His advocate. No one else even knew, so they couldn't help him." Tears stream down her face. Her arms remain crossed. "He needed you."

Old familiar shame pours over me. The kind I've felt every single day since the moment I realized those men had cornered us in the mall's hallway. Of course I should've reported it. That would've been the rational thing to do. Kimber is judging me through today's #MeToo standards, not yesterday's reality. Back then I would've been blamed. Perhaps not directly. I was the victim, after all. But I would've been quietly dismissed by my friends under the guise of giving me space. Was it fair? Absolutely not. By keeping my secret, I was keeping myself from being labeled. Admitting I was less than whole. No, the reality was that I would never have reported my rape had it just been me.

But it wasn't just me.

My failure was not doing right by Kyle. For his sake, I should've handled it differently. In my defense, I was in shock. I wasn't thinking clearly nor of any consequences of my inaction. I just wanted it to disappear. To create what used to be normal lives. For both of us.

"Sweetheart . . ." I squeeze Kimber's hands until she looks me square in the eyes. "If I could, I'd trade every single minute of my life to be able to go back in time and correct my mistakes."

◆ ◆ ◆

"Good evening. My name is Margaret Dobrescu." I learned that our parish hosted a monthly grief circle for parents. Church basements give me the heebie-jeebies. Even now. Especially now. Clearing my throat, I wring my hands as I glance around at each of the dozen people sitting in a circle of folding chairs. Esoteric yoga music echoes throughout the dank room from a vintage boom box in the corner. It's after dark, but the only light sources are one overhead fluorescent light and a candle burning in the center of our circle. I find comfort in the flame. Permission. "My son passed away four months ago. He was thirty-seven years old and an alcoholic. My last words to him before he died were 'Get out.'"

I share the highlights of Kyle's story with the group, but no one is here to judge. We've gone around the room one by one, each remembering our losses. Car accidents. Suicides. Cancer. Even a murder. Since I'm new to the parent grief support group, I'm the last to share. Martin occupies the chair next to mine, leaning forward with his elbows resting on his knees, his shoulder twitching. Neither contradicting nor adding to my testimony.

Instead of the pervading tone of sadness I expected to encounter at this grief circle, I feel relief. I've been in hiding for so many months because most people have no idea what to say to a grieving mother, so they try to be uplifting. No, time will not heal my pain. No, my life will not move on without him. No, I'm not relieved he's no longer battling his addiction. Nor do I want to change the subject and talk about something lighter, happier. I want—I need—to talk about Kyle.

As his mother, I carried him in my womb for nine months. Nine and a half, if you consider he was born two weeks past his due date in the middle of a blizzard. But motherhood doesn't stop after birthing and raising our children. Every blood cell coursing in my body contains a piece of him. Each atom inside me feels the void he left behind when he died.

Avoiding social engagements and friends' awkward sympathies and pitying glances became an easier alternative to suffering their well-intentioned social gaffes with grace.

But these people here get it. These welcoming strangers are all parents who've lost a son or daughter. They understand that we'd all trade our last years to have a few more moments with our children. And none of us would willingly forgo the pain. Our scars of grief are proof of having loved.

Martin and I didn't ask to join this tribe, but here we are. We belong. These are our people now. In this near-empty church basement with its inadequate lighting, stale cookies, and room-temperature lemonade, I find the last two things on the planet I ever expected.

Peace and acceptance.

◆ ◆ ◆

While ironing my freshly laundered scrubs for work tomorrow, I marvel at how the highway called life has allowed me access to an on-ramp. I'm still not driving at full speed, but at least I'm accelerating.

My cell phone pings with a new text message.

Ally: Do you have a minute?

My heart bursts into a glitter bomb. Not trusting my fingers to type on the screen, I hit the dial button to call her.

"Ally, dear. I'm happy to hear from you. Is everything okay?"

"Yes. No. I mean, I'm fine, but I'm having a problem." Ally's voice trembles over the sketchy phone connection. Her words continue rapid fire. "Mom is at work. Grandma Vicki hasn't replied. I don't know what to do . . ."

"Well, you reached out to the right person. Where are you?"

"I'm on campus. I finished a final exam this morning. I bombed it. Do you think you could meet me at the café?"

"Absolutely. I can be there in fifteen minutes."

A few weeks ago, when I stopped by Carrefour after learning about Kyle's letters to Ally, Miss Genevieve had a box of Kyle's items waiting for me at the front desk. He'd forgotten to pack them last summer when he was expelled. Despite several phone calls begging that the contents of his desk drawer be saved, he never showed up to collect them.

Every scrap of proof of Kyle's daughter I ever wished for was packed in that box, the contents worth more to me than Aladdin's cave of treasures. His letters from Ally. His journals. Speeches he'd prepared about striving to be worthy of being her father. The irony was I found it all after I met Ally. When I no longer needed clues. But what I found packed inside was as much evidence as I'd ever need for Kyle's deep fatherly love for his daughter. He worshipped her.

Now, waiting for my granddaughter to arrive at the café, I purchase her an iced coffee with extra whip and chocolate drizzle. I cordon off the same lounge chairs as before and leave a tissue pack on the side table between us.

By the time Ally strolls through the glass doors, the poor thing looks as if she'd been in a drag-out fight with a raccoon. I temper my enthusiasm for my granddaughter's sake. But the reality isn't lost on me. Of all the friends she could've called, she asked me for help. Me. I know I was third on her list, but I actually made her short list of go-to people in her life. Nothing could've warmed my heart more. She needs me. She trusts me.

Ally walks straight into my open arms and clings. Her shoulders heave. Several patrons turn to stare, so I shut my eyes to block out the distractions. My granddaughter deserves every fiber of my attention. Unconditionally.

"I'm so sorry, Margaret. I didn't mean to hijack your day." With her makeup cried off, the sweet girl looks all of fifteen years old, not nineteen. She's more precious and adorable than she'll ever know or believe to be true.

"Nonsense. You are my granddaughter. I'm here for you any day, at any time. Even on the days I work, I can be available by evening." I hope I've admonished any last shreds of doubt she may have about calling me. She plops into her lounge seat, tucking her feet on the chair, a move that reminds me of all the pajama-clad mornings I missed from her youth. "Tell me, sweetheart. What happened?"

"I bombed my final exam in chemistry this morning. By the time the exam session was over, I wasn't able to finish a third of the questions. I almost didn't bother submitting the test. I didn't come into that exam—or any of my classes—in excellent standing. This semester has been . . . rocky." Her hiccup punctuated her sentence with perfect timing. "I think the deans will place me on academic probation. I could lose one of my scholarships."

I pass her another tissue as she hugs her knees to her chest and hides her eyes. I'm a bit at a loss, because a lot has changed since I went to school way back with the dinosaurs. Personal computers weren't standard until my kids went to college. And then came the whole World Wide Web invention. Pausing, I let her cry for a spell before treading carefully. "Have you thought about talking to your professor?"

"That won't do any good. They have thousands of students enrolled. What would they care if one dropped out?"

I shush her as respectfully as I can manage until she stops going down that path with buried land mines. "Let's not talk about dropping out yet. You were dealt a rough start to your semester, having lost your father. It's always a last resort, but think of how far you've come."

"How special is it to flunk out of college as a freshman?"

"You don't know that yet."

"Well, I'm not going to embarrass myself by taking my last final exam tomorrow."

"Look at me, Ally." I reach for her shoulder, channeling all the love in my heart to her.

Bloodshot eyes that are the mirror image of my son's reluctantly meet my gaze.

"You can do this. You're smart. I met your mother, and she is a force. You inherited that strength of spirit. You gave Kyle the incentive to clean up his act. You've held down a job while going to school full time. Your world collapsed around you earlier this semester, and you've been playing catch-up ever since. Right?"

Ally lets go of her knees, then hugs her stomach. I'm watching to see if her skin turns sallow. As a nurse and a mother, I've cleaned up a lot of vomit over the years, but that doesn't make it any more pleasant.

"Here's what I suggest . . ." My voice shakes. A lot rides on how Ally finds my views. If she can't relate to me, she could move me off her calling list. But at least she hasn't raced out of the café. She's still listening to me. "Study, and take your last final exam. There's no risk in giving it your best shot. Even if you don't pass, you'll have at least completed your semester requirements. Then meet with your academic adviser before your exam grades post."

"How could she help?"

"Perhaps not with your grades, but she can give you sound advice. And she'll let you know your options. Maybe you can retake a class over the summer or even register for a lighter class load in the fall semester to help you regain your footing. Let her know what you've been going through. Let her guide you."

Ally pauses, then nods tentatively at first. She wipes her face dry, then sits taller. "Okay . . . I'll go to her office hours tomorrow after my last exam. Thank you, Margaret."

I extend my hand over the end table between our chairs, and she slips hers in mine and lets me squeeze.

"Good. You're taking a page from your father's playbook. Kyle was the king of reinventing himself."

Chapter 32

KYLE

BEFORE

T-minus two and a half weeks until what Ally and I had dubbed Project Valentine. She'd designed and special-ordered a cake through her grocery store's bakery that we planned to bring over to the house together. She vetoed my suggestion that the icing on the frosting should say *Happy Birthday, Happy Valentine's Day & Congratulations, It's a Girl!* Not sure what she picked instead.

I'd even told Mom and Dad not to make any plans for that night so we could celebrate my birthday together. Mom snorted her coffee when I asked, but as soon as she realized I wasn't joking, she agreed.

Ally was with me at the AA meeting when I'd collected my six-month anniversary token. She walked up to the table with me as I accepted it—the royal-blue aluminum coin that heralded a success. I handed it right over to her.

Sober one hundred and eighty days.

Every bit of those past four thousand hours had been a struggle, but Ally made every temptation-avoiding minute worth it. Right before our semesters started, I'd surprised her with tickets to see the Chicago Symphony Orchestra perform. She'd worn her prom dress, and I, my best suit and tie. We now had a photo of the two of us together, standing under a massive chandelier.

As I came inside from the crisp afternoon air, Mom was waiting at the front door with an envelope in her hand and a deer-in-the-headlights look on her face.

"A certified letter came for you. I signed for it."

My heart sank. Shit. Nothing good ever came from certified mail. Sure enough, when I flipped the envelope over, the return address was the one I'd been dreading—our county clerk's office.

I'd expected the court system would eventually catch up with me. I gambled against time and lost. After peeling off my frigid layers down to the hoodie Ally had given me, which I've worn ever since like a uniform, I braced myself to rip open the envelope.

Please, not before Valentine's Day. Please, not before Valentine's Day . . . I chanted under my breath as a prayer to a God who'd forgotten about me long ago.

Mom stood over me, hovering with her arms crossed.

Shit. February 11. My court date was two fucking weeks from now and a whole lifetime before my birthday.

I handed Mom the paper, then plopped onto the couch, rubbing my eyes, trying to ad hoc our Project Valentine plan on the fly. I drew a breath, then another, gasping for oxygen and feeling slightly faint.

"Kyle, are you okay? You look pale."

"What do you think?" My breath was labored, and my voice weakened as reality crashed in on me. "I got my court date."

"I don't like the way your breathing sounds." She placed her hands on my forehead, then my neck. "You're wheezing, honey. You need to get your lungs checked. And your oxygen levels."

"I'll be fine, Mom. Just stressed." What I didn't add was that my throat had been acting weird again, in a why-did-it-hurt-to-swallow kind of way, but such information would only encourage Mom to keep a closer eye on me. And by weird, I meant really painful.

"Look, you were complaining of being light-headed earlier. Now your breathing sounds labored. Your coloring isn't good. You should go to the ER."

"Seriously, Mom? You're overreacting." But before I could say *Please give me a few minutes to calm the fuck down and process this disaster*, she'd already called for an ambulance. No one had time for this bullshit.

"Let's let the EMTs decide if you should go to the hospital or not."

As if on cue, I started wheezing again in front of Mom. While I was 90 percent sure this was all due to stress, there was that small possibility it could be something I shouldn't ignore. If this had been happening to Ally, I'd probably be making the same phone call. And I'd be really pissed off if she ignored me. I guess I needed to get used to the worrying part of parenting. "All right, Mom. But if they agree I should go to the ER, I'm going to the hospital alone. Nonnegotiable."

◆ ◆ ◆

After spending an endless evening in the emergency room, I'd been discharged with good oxygen levels, a medication patch on my arm, and a bottle of pills to help take the edge off my throat pain until I could see my doctor. So much for my wheezing. I knew I was fine.

Thank God they didn't admit me overnight, because I needed to talk to Ally. As soon as possible. We should move up our little surprise announcement for Mom and Dad. If my court date went south—and it could, since I'd been out of rehab for six months—I wanted her to get to know her grandparents while I was serving time.

Dad had been silent while driving me home from the hospital tonight. Way too late after the Christmas season for any decorations, so the late January darkness was as bleak as my future. "Do you want me to take you to an AA meeting?"

"Not tonight. I need to see a friend." While talking, I pulled out my phone and texted Ally.

Me: Can you meet tonight? It's important.

"Kyle, that's not a good idea. You can't hang out with friends and go drinking with your court date coming up."

"I promise. This is different. I'm not drinking. I've been sober for months. Six, to be exact."

Whether or not Dad believed me, he changed the subject. His shoulder was in constant twitch mode. "Your lawyer wants to meet to prepare for the court date next week."

"Fine. But I have classes and work projects to finish. I hope we can schedule around those."

"He's not optimistic he can sway the judge . . ." Dad didn't have to finish his thought. We both knew my fate. I'd been running from my accountability for too long. It was time to pay. I hoped Ally would wait.

A. O.: Sorry. Not tonight. Mom's working, and I promised her I'd take care of some chores. Coffee tomorrow?

Dammit. The longer I waited, the harder this was going to be. How did you tell your daughter that for the next year, her newfound father would likely be wearing an orange jumpsuit and calling a prison cell home?

Me: Sure. Morning okay?

Dad parked the car as Mom, who'd been keeping watch at the front door, barreled out of the house to meet us. My breathing picked up again. Crap. I was making that same wheezing sound Mom had flagged earlier. Good thing I got the all clear from the ER doctor. If it kept up,

I'd make a follow-up appointment with a specialist. The last thing I wanted other than to go to prison was to serve my time with some sort of respiratory problem.

"Kyle, you're back so soon? What did they say?"

Gee, good to see you, too, Mom. "Nothing you need to worry about. I'll take care of it." As I bulldozed past her to head into the house, I ignored her hovering and questions. I had too many things to process right now. Once I had prison time on my record, how many freelance jobs would slip away from my grasp? But Mom wouldn't leave well enough alone and followed me inside. Every step I took added fuel to my already cagey mood.

"Stop right there, Kyle." She was on my heels and ordered me with that don't-you-dare-disobey-me tone she used to use when I was a kid. Goddammit.

I stopped but refused to turn around. Jesus Christ, when would she treat me like an adult? But the answer came to me instantly. Other than my age, I'd never given her a real reason to accept me as an adult. The onus was on me.

"Your father tells me that you are skipping your AA meeting to meet with your friends tonight. Why would you go out drinking?"

"He misunderstood. It wasn't a party, and my plans have been canceled." Shit, she always assumed I'd be drinking. I'd trained her too well.

"After everything we have gone through to help you, your priority is still vodka? You need to grow up. Get yourself clean, and stay that way. What's the judge going to say next week?"

"I just said—"

"You're already at risk of serving prison time because you couldn't stay sober long enough at Carrefour. And now you're not doing anything to help your case. I can't sit back and watch as you ruin your life."

"I told you already. There was never a party." Crap, a whine crept back into my voice.

"That's what you said every time for years." The frown on her face is inscrutable. Anger? Frustration? Both? One thing was for sure—she wasn't happy. "I can't tell you the number of times I've found you passed out drunk."

"Okay, you're right. I screwed up. That was then." I stepped toward her, hoping to reason with her. Wishing for half a second that I could show Mom my six-month sobriety chip to prove it until I remembered that Ally had it. "But it's not like that now. I've been sober for six months and plan to stay that way. Look, Maggie M—"

"Don't you dare 'Maggie May' me. You can't sweet-talk your way out of this one, Kyle. I'm done watching you fall on your face and ignore the problem. I am your mom."

"Look, it's different this time. I promise. It'll all make sense soon." Despite me trying to take the edge off my tone, every word I uttered was sending her spiraling into a tailspin. Couldn't blame her. Not with our history. "You need to trust me."

"Trust you?" She stopped pacing in front of me, her voice jumping an octave higher.

Shit. I should've avoided the *T* word. Too late now.

"How dare you bring whether or not I trust you into the equation? I've wanted to trust you every minute of every day these last twenty years, but I've witnessed you fail over and over. The distractions. The lame justifications. Your web of lies . . ."

"Lies. Like living our lives like the past didn't happen? It's time we stop keeping secrets, Mom." My stomach flip-flopped as I glanced at Dad. Poor guy had no idea what we were even talking about. It'd been over a decade since the last time I'd even alluded to the attack in a conversation with Mom. We'd have to cut to the chase. Soon. For his sake, if not for ours. Plus, Ally already knew. "We both need to heal. To accept it and move on with our lives."

"No." Her face turned ashen. She jerked her head back as if I'd punched her. She knew exactly what I was referring to. Her wide-eyed stare imparted some warning I couldn't quite interpret. Terror? Hatred? Retribution? "Never."

Shit. I should've read the room and not plowed forward quite so fast. Dad is standing nearby, and I have to backpedal hard. I hadn't intended to bring this up tonight. "Please, Mom, give me a minute and hear me out—"

"You can't betray me now. You promised." She shook her head frantically. Her voice rang hollow. With every step I took toward her, she moved one back. Her fingers were splayed apart, holding up some invisible barrier between us. Our tango dance from hell. "Get out, Kyle."

God, what a mess. I eyeballed Dad, who shrugged back at me. So I made an about-face and walked to the front door but then stopped. Behind me, I heard Dad bitching at her. "It's below freezing outside, Margaret. Where will he sleep tonight?"

We'd all been through this drill before. Typically whenever Mom got this worked up, she needed time to cool down. Dad would cut me some slack and check me into a motel for the night.

But tonight was worse. Much worse. I'd forced her to face the enemy. I recognized the wild fear and panic in her eyes. I'd seen it once before in real life and in every nightmare since.

"I'm sorry, Mom." My shoulders slumped. Once she calmed down, I'd bring it up again—more gently next time. I hoped she'd forgive me. Eventually. Plus, once Mom met Ally, she'd understand. It might even buy me some goodwill points.

She stopped halfway up the stairs, her voice dripping with acid. "I said get out."

◆　◆　◆

"You're going to jail?" Ally's eyes were as wide as bull's-eyes in the harsh sunlight on this winter morning. This was a term she'd probably only heard on the news and in TV cop shows. Dropping this bomb wasn't exactly the high point of our father-daughter relationship. Jeez, it's not like I'd had a great night's sleep at the motel last night, so I was groggier than I should be while delivering this news.

"Not definitely, but since it's a strong possibility, I want to introduce you to my parents before my court date instead of waiting for my birthday." Dammit, all our fun plans were going down the drain. "If the worst case happens, you'll at least get to know them while I'm . . . away."

"Um, okay. I think. Sure." She scanned the café with wild eyes. I couldn't even imagine what chaos was swirling inside that sharp brain of hers, what bubbles of innocence I'd popped. But we no longer had the luxury of time. If the judge gave me a reprieve, we could laugh about this crunch. If not, well, then hopefully Ally would be willing to pick up our relationship where we left off once I was paroled. Maybe she'd write to me once in a while. "I have class and work. My shift at the grocery store ends at seven. I'm free after."

"Perfect. Meet me at my parents' house tonight at seven thirty. We'll have dinner. I'll introduce you to them. You may be the bright light in their nightmare. How about salmon for dinner?"

That gave me a few hours to smooth things over with Mom, so at least she'd be in a better mood this evening. But something made me stop gathering my things.

"Thank you for being flexible, Ally. I know this is all coming at you really fast."

"That's okay. They're my grandparents, right?" She twisted her ring.

"Don't worry. My mom and dad are going to love you."

She tightened her ponytail, then twisted her ring again. But a few minutes later, and after sipping at her coffee, she reached into her backpack and asked, "May I?"

"Actually, do you mind if I take a look at your sketchbook?" It was a risk. She'd never opened up and offered me a glimpse. Her extended pause and glance away made me fear I'd stepped too far over the line.

I'd already asked so much of her today. But just when I was about to backpedal, she handed me the spiral-bound book.

Electricity crackled through my fingertips as I turned the pages, careful not to smudge any of the unstable charcoal finishes. Page by page, her images sprang to life with three-dimensional energy. A tabby cat. Several of Hannah. A few young people, who I assumed were her school friends. A grandmother-age woman. Way too many different versions of me. Sunlight streams through a bedroom. My one-month AA token. A self-portrait of her.

Who did she inherit such genuine talent from? Hannah? Not from me. Words escape me.

"I . . . you . . . you blow my mind. You and your art are amazing." My heart had thawed the day I met her—my daughter. I reached for her hand and squeezed it until she looked at me.

"No matter what happens tonight, Ally, I will not abandon you. I love you."

◆ ◆ ◆

After I arrived back home, Mom and Dad weren't there, so I got right to work whipping the place into shape. It took a while to find where Mom had hidden her bucket of cleaning supplies, but once I'd commandeered it, I sprang into action.

My wheezing picked up again, as did the pain in my throat. My pain meds were helping, but not much. Attacking some stray dust bunnies caused me to cough up a storm, complete with new throat pain, the likes of which I hadn't felt since strep throat. I may add visiting the urgent care clinic to my to-do list tomorrow.

Vacuuming, dusting, and scrubbing the bathroom—cleaning any of the common areas that Ally might venture into tonight, since it'd be her first time inside here.

Two hours later, our home looked spruced up. I'd found a scented candle or two to light tonight. Then I wandered into the kitchen to prep our dinner. My efforts were for Ally's benefit. And Mom's and Dad's. I owed them and needed to start pulling my own weight. It was time, and God knew it was long past due.

Swallowing away the metallic taste that'd taken over my mouth, I dashed upstairs to my room to decide what to wear tonight, though I stopped midway up to catch my breath and wait until a wave of dizziness passed. What did you wear to introduce your daughter to your parents? Something casual but nice. Smart.

Soon Ally would arrive.

I paused to recall what the nurse had told me about the patch on the back of my arm. Was she even a nurse? Who knows? Everyone wears scrubs and masks in the ER. But I don't remember her warning me against showering with it on. So I grab a towel, undress, then head to the now sparkling bathroom. The scent of lemon detergent spray still lingered. My heartbeat was thumping so hard I might as well have sprinted up a mountain. Cleaning must be more of a workout than I'd anticipated.

God, why was I feeling so light-headed? Twice I paused while shaving, worried that I'd slice my chin if I lost my balance. Maybe I should eat something. I lean against the sink to steady myself, struggling for breath and dizzy. My fingertips were tingling.

Holy shit. My wooziness wouldn't dissipate. I couldn't catch my breath. Last night, the ER doctor gave me a clean bill of health. Good oxygen levels. My lungs sounded fine. Breathing was fine. Now I guess my wheezing sounded a little louder, but this dizziness shit was creeping me out. The last thing I want to do is reschedule our dinner, but I might need to go see a doctor again tonight. I nixed the shower plan and opted instead to get dressed.

But as I attempted to step into my boxers, the floor swayed as if I were on a boat in choppy waters. My breathing turned fast and shallow.

My lungs couldn't inhale enough air. Another wave of light-headedness overtook me, so I sat down on the side of the tub. I leaned over to hang my head between my knees. But I kept rolling forward and whacked my forehead against the side of the sink while crashing down. The next thing I knew, I was on the floor staring at the ceiling.

Jesus, that hurt. A flash of white-hot pain ripped through my head and my bad shoulder. Did I crack my skull? Rebreak my clavicle in the fall?

My pulse sounded too loud in my skull. While collapsed on the bathroom's tiled floor, I gritted my teeth, drawing rapid breaths to stave off the pain. I reached up and touched the bonk above my eyebrow, but my fingers came back covered in blood. Shit. I must've really gashed my forehead in my fall. Did I need stitches? My body wouldn't obey my command to turn over so I could crawl to my phone. Why wouldn't my limbs cooperate? Wooziness made me gag, then retch. I could barely eke a breath.

Oh, my God. I needed to get to the hospital. Or at least call for an ambulance. But my phone was downstairs. What the hell was going on?

Fear ripped through my senses like a hot blade through butter. I yelled for help, but the only thing escaping my mouth was some kind of gurgle. It didn't matter anyway. No one was home. Mom had always joked that I was a cat with nine lives. I'd been this close to death before. I had to have at least one more life that I hadn't used up.

This couldn't be it—the end.

My vision blurred until darkness settled over me, my lungs refusing to inflate.

Please, no! Just one more chance, God. I promise I'll do better.

I needed to see Ally again.

Chapter 33

MARGARET

AFTER

Martin took the day off from work and is mowing the lawn. I've already scoured the bathrooms, changed the sheets on all the beds, and vacuumed the carpets. Next up is tidying the kitchen. All this after a late day working at the clinic yesterday and less than five hours of sleep. Kimber, her husband, and the grandkids will arrive this afternoon to spend the Memorial Day weekend with us.

My birthday is this weekend as well, but I've already warned Martin and Kimber that I'm not ready for any sort of festivities, my passive-aggressive code for "No surprise parties, under pain of disinheritance." A family barbecue with a store-bought cake and candles is about as much celebration as I can handle. No gifts either.

This will be the family's first gathering since Kyle's funeral. All these milestones make for predictable crying jags. I haven't advertised to anyone else that my birthday will be exactly four months, to the day, since the day he died. Not exactly something to celebrate, yet here we are. I'm no longer counting the years since my birth. From this birthday on, I'll be commemorating the number of years without Kyle. Better yet, the number of years with Ally.

But I don't have the luxury of time to dwell on my new normal. I'm running on stores of energy I didn't even know existed. In the next few hours, five people will be coming for a three-night stay, and I have yet to go grocery shopping. At least I'm checking off my spring cleaning while the calendar still calls it spring. It might as well be the dog days of summer outside, for the heat and sticky humidity. Thank God for air-conditioning and a neighborhood pool for the grandkids to enjoy.

While midway down the stairs to the basement carrying a laundry basket, I hear my cell phone ping in the distance. Now where did I leave it?

Five minutes later, I finally hunt down my cell phone and find a text message waiting for me.

Ally: Do you mind if I bring Grandma Vicki along?

Me: Of course not, sweetheart. She's always welcome. See you both tomorrow.

I may have stipulated no birthday gifts, but that doesn't mean I can't give one to my family.

◆ ◆ ◆

"Mom? I thought I heard someone tinkering around here. What are you doing up so early?" Kimber patters into the kitchen, barefoot in her pajamas, to find me sipping my coffee. I've been up for hours, enjoying the quiet before the family chaos ensues—all good but also draining. When I stand, she wraps me in a great big hug. "Happy birthday, Mom."

"Oh, sweetheart, I'm so glad you brought everyone here for the weekend. I love that we're making . . . happy . . . family memories." I pour her a cup of coffee, then motion for her to follow me to our back deck. Sliding open the glass door takes some finessing, but after a few stealth moves, we're relaxing in lounge chairs, ready for the view. Everyone else is sleeping in, but I cherish the few moments of peace. My daughter and I enjoy birthday coffee at sunrise.

"How are you coping, sweetheart? I've been so wrapped up in my own feelings I'm afraid I didn't support you as much as I should have."

"Don't worry about me. I miss Kyle. Every day. But before he died, I used to go months without hearing from him or knowing anything about what he was up to unless you gave us updates—usually nothing good. I'm glad I visited him in the hospital last summer, though. Knowing my last words to him while he was living were 'I love you' has helped me cope."

I love you is infinitely more tolerable than *Get out*, but I'm grateful she doesn't have to live with my regret. As the first hint of light tinges the dark sky, a bird swoops in and perches on my bird feeder. Its red wings appear a burnt shade of gray in this dawn light, but his call is unmistakable.

A cardinal.

I've long since subscribed to the belief that our loved ones visit us from heaven in the form of cardinals. This one has made weekly and sometimes daily visits to my feeder all spring. But to show up on my birthday morning at sunrise, well . . . how can I not take that as a birthday greeting from Kyle?

Thank you, my dearest son. I love you. Forever. Please watch over your daughter.

The whole family will visit his grave later today. Though I may never know how or what happened that caused his death, I firmly believe he is with me, guiding us. He's happy. At peace. That knowledge calms me and my questions—pennies from heaven.

Besides, he led me to Ally.

"Mom, I've been thinking a lot about what you and Dad told me. About your attack. I really wish you'd told me sooner. Even back then. I was an adult. As horrific as it was, I could've handled the news. Helped you. Supported you. And Kyle."

"I'm sorry, sweetheart." I reach over and squeeze her hand. "Your grandmother always said 'The road to hell is paved with good intentions.' She was right. I thought keeping it a secret would help Kyle, you, and your dad. You were starting a career in New York at the time. I didn't want to derail you. Learn from my mistakes. Don't keep secrets from your loved ones. Besides, they'll eventually find their way to the surface."

"We can't change the past, and neither can you, Mom. I get it, and I love you for it. Life is messy." She slips her arm around my shoulders, snuggling her head into my neck. "Not talking about your attack may have festered, but Kyle had other demons. You can't take the blame for his alcoholism."

Kimber makes it sound so simple. Too simple. I'm surprised she doesn't understand, being a helicopter mom herself to her three precious darlings. Like mother, like daughter. But today is my birthday. I'll dwell on my shoulda-woulda-coulda tomorrow. Morning sunlight pours over our faces. I shut my eyes and accept the warmth flooding over me.

"I was worried about losing you to your grief over Kyle. But you've picked up the pieces. Gone back to work part time. Dad told me you're both attending a support group. I'm proud of you."

"Proud of me?" The guffaw escapes before I can stop it. "Who's the parent here?"

"I'm glad you gave up trying to find Kyle's daughter. No. *Glad* isn't the right word. Relieved, maybe? You were a bit too obsessed with searching for her. But it's hard not to wish she really existed. I'd have loved to have met my niece."

Give up? I almost choke on my coffee. My daughter should know me better than that. I'll never give up on my family. Not knowing Ally's name, age, or even where she lived were obstacles. But time wasn't one of them. Eventually I'd have found her, even if we hadn't bumped into each other at Kyle's grave.

Smiling into the sun, I squeeze Kimber in a fierce mama-bear hug, then smooth out her hair like I used to when she was little.

I still have one card to play.

The tantalizing scent of grilled shish kebabs wafts around the park's gazebo. Two picnic tables are pulled together under a canopy of leaves, complete with a tapestry table runner and artfully arranged plates of cheeses, berries, and salads. The tin bucket stuffed with a prism of flowers stands at the end, enticing me to snap a photo of my Tuscan tablescape.

The best part of a late-May birthday is dining alfresco.

As I pour glasses of lemonade for each place setting, I keep a look-out for my final guests to arrive. I set an extra space for Kyle. On his plate, I displayed my favorite photo of the two of us, an action shot of him twirling me while we danced to "Maggie May" that night in the kitchen. Neither of our faces are clear, but we're both laughing. The photo never fails to give me shivers of happiness. Thank God Martin captured the moment. Me and my son.

My birthday tableau is perfect.

Almost.

Rechecking my watch, I contemplate texting Ally to make sure she has directions to the park. I'll give her five more minutes.

Classic-rock notes float overhead from speakers as my son-in-law operates the charcoal grill and my youngest two grandchildren scamper about, chasing each other in a game of tag. Their laughter is my favorite sound in the world. Sunshine highlights the golden tresses of my oldest granddaughter, who is either editing her phone's playlist or plotting world domination. Judy and my brother-in-law, who drove into town for the occasion, join Martin and Kimber, tossing cornhole beanbags and teasing each other.

At long last, the sounds of gravel under tires reach my ears, so I check my lipstick, pinch my cheeks, and smooth out my sundress. This could go one of two ways, heaven or hell.

Please be heaven.

Ally's silhouette is barely identifiable as she walks from the parking lot through the small trail. Finally she enters the clearing holding hands with Victoria. I slip away to greet them.

"I'm so glad you're both here." After kissing their cheeks, I hold Ally's precious face in my hands. "Are you ready to meet the Dobrescus, honey?"

"No." Her eyes flit back and forth from meeting mine to seeing all the activity in the distance behind me. She swallows hard. This must be intimidating for an only child of a single mom. I can't help but be proud of her.

"Don't worry, sweetheart. They're going to love you as much as I do."

Ally shuts her eyes and slips her hand into mine. With her honor guard—me on one side and Victoria on the other—we march toward my family. Strength in numbers.

Kimber notices our approach first and halts midtoss. One by one, everyone stops what they're doing and zombie-shuffles toward us, each with quizzical looks on their faces.

Once we've arrived, I turn toward Ally.

"Everyone, let me introduce you to someone very special. This is Allison O'Leary. She goes by Ally. And this is her grandmother, Victoria. Ally's . . ." My words choke my throat, so I take controlled breaths while searching Kimber's face. Then I turn to Martin. But my voice cracks. "Ally is Kyle's daughter."

The gasp I hear is followed by silence.

Nothing.

Dead silence.

Please, someone, say something. Don't leave this poor child hanging here.

Ally's hand squeezes mine in a vise grip.

Victoria's breath hitches.

Oh, dear.

I'd hoped they'd be ecstatic. As happy as I was—am.

Please?

"Kyle's daughter?" Martin walks up to her and grasps her shoulders. He pauses as wonder overtakes his face. His chin trembles, his eyes well, before he crushes her to his chest. "That makes you my granddaughter, Ally."

Instantly the spell is broken, and everyone rushes at us in a flurry of hugs, shrieks, and laughter.

And acceptance.

"Mom, how did you find her?"

"Ally, did you ever meet Kyle?"

"How long have you known?"

"So we're cousins?"

Ally—my phantom Boo—answers each question, her smile growing wider and more excited as each moment blends with the next. She is one of us. I always knew it.

I wish I'd thought to hire a photographer or a videographer to capture Ally's introduction, because I'll never remember all the beautiful sentiments shared and the way my family absorbed her into the Dobrescus as if we'd known her all her life. But I also know I'll never forget any part of tonight.

If only Kyle were here.

But then again, he probably is.

We did it, Kyle. Thank you for giving us your daughter.

After we burned the shish kebabs and traded Kyle memories for hours and I blew out a single birthday candle, our classic-rock music was replaced by the chirping of crickets. We lingered in the park until well after sunset, then cleaned up our space with the help of the twinkle lights hanging in the park's gazebo.

Ally motions me away from the activity to chat privately.

"Thank you for today, Margaret. I grew up always wondering if I had cousins, and now I've even met them. Meeting Kyle's family was a dream come true."

"I couldn't be happier, sweetheart." If I grin any harder, my cheeks will cramp. "I wish your mom were here too."

"She . . . uh . . . had to work tonight. Maybe someday." Her face drops for half a second before brightening again. "Oh, and I know you said no birthday gifts, but I have something small for you."

Ally hands me a silver frame. Behind the glass is a black-and-white sketch. I'd recognize his eyes anywhere. And the angle of his jaw. The planes of his face. Kyle. On the bottom right are scrawled initials: *A. O.*

"Ally, sweetheart, did you draw this?" Chills raced down my spine and then spread to my limbs. Speaking turns impossible. There was something so lifelike captured in the image. If I didn't know better, I swear I could see him breathing. Smirking. Calling me Maggie May. With something glinting in his eyes. Pride? Love? Drive?

"Yeah. It's just a copy. I kept the original sketch. It's my favorite of all of the ones I drew." She toed her sandal into the grass. "I hope you don't mind . . ."

"Not at all! I love it. Thank you, honey." I know exactly where I'm going to display Ally's portrait of him at home so that I can see it every day. "I'd love to see your others too."

Kyle, you're nearby, witnessing this moment with your daughter, right?

She slips me another package, this one a thick envelope with a small bulge in the middle.

"I meant to give you this a few weeks ago, but it took a while for me to figure out how to digitize a cassette tape. My mom once recorded a band concert for Silence Deconstructed. Here. It's Kyle's music. And a photo we took together over Christmas."

My heart does a triple backflip as I clutch the envelope to my chest.

"I also made copies of the letters Kyle wrote to me while he was in rehab. I thought you'd appreciate reading his words."

Goose bumps cover my arms. I thought I'd exhausted every little nostalgic memento from Kyle's life, but I was wrong. His child—this precious young woman—embodies everything good and wholesome about my son. She personifies him. Miracles do happen.

The lump in my throat doesn't allow me to speak. Instead, I clutch my granddaughter to my heart, letting her pull away first.

"Thanks for helping me out last week. I did what you suggested and met with my adviser. You were right. She helped me figure it out. I have a plan now."

"Anytime, Ally." I wipe my wet cheeks with the back of my hand. "Any day. Any hour. I'm here for you. And I will always love you."

The smile that covers my granddaughter's face melts any last trace of insecurity I ever had about today.

"Happy birthday, Marg—" A twinkling light reflects off her bright eyes. "Would you mind if I call you Grandma Maggie?"

Epilogue

HANNAH

Clocking in on my twelve-hour hospital shift—the third day in a row—and whoa, these middle-aged bones weren't meant for this level of winter weariness. At least it's not the overnight shift.

Not sure if it's a full moon today, but the ER has been crazy lately. The packed waiting room promises to keep us busy all night long. I could use a few more minutes of peace and quiet before jumping into the trenches.

I glance at my watch, which sits right next to the small name I had tattooed on my wrist eighteen years and ten months ago—Allison Marie. It's been a lifetime, and yet it seems like only yesterday that she was born. Now she's starting her second semester of college.

God, I love that child. What would I have done without my Allycat? She's my heart. My everything. My pulse falters whenever I recall that I almost lost her when she was born. Back then, it was just the two of us—a single mom and a baby—against the world. But we made it through everything together.

"Hannah?" I look up to the door of our glorified coat closet that doubles as a break room to see my nurse manager with a clipboard in hand. "I know your shift doesn't start for another fifteen minutes, but a new patient is in Bed C. Adult male. Arrived by ambulance. Respiratory concerns. Susan is intaking him, but she needs to leave early. Family emergency. Can you please take over for her?"

"Sure. No problem." I hop up and tighten my ponytail, rushing out into the controlled chaos that is the emergency room nerve center. Doctors, nurses, med techs, and assistants swirl around me in choreography that only we can understand.

I love working in the ER. Together, the medical professionals on our team are the frontline soldiers fighting against the physical hell that nature and man can throw at us. Most of the time we win. The heartbreaks from our losses keep us humble.

After jogging down the hallway, I reach the glassed-in room with Bed C. Several ER staff are already inside, making assessments. Energy zings around the patient as Susan confirms his symptoms, applies a blood pressure cuff to his arm, and clamps an oxygen monitor to his finger.

"I don't even know why I'm here. Probably to placate my mother. She called the paramedics because she heard me wheezing, but my breathing seems fine now." A hollow laugh punctuates the patient's statement. It sounds vaguely familiar.

"Mr. Dobrescu, let's go over your medical history."

Dobrescu?

My blood freezes in my veins. No. It couldn't be. Not him.

Anyone but him.

People and machines obstruct my view, so I can't sight-confirm my fears. My dread. Just in case it's him, I step behind the computer cart's monitor so he can't see any part of me. Then I flip my lanyard hospital ID backward for good measure.

After I hand Susan the scanner, she zaps the barcode from his hospital bracelet, and I squeeze my eyes as his information loads on the monitor. Then I open them.

Kyle Dobrescu.

In the flesh.

While Susan finishes inserting his IV, I get my first unobstructed look at him. He appears sickly thin, like a cancer patient whose hair has grown back. His square jaw and deep-set brown eyes are as prominent as ever. He's sitting up in the bed, alert and chatting with Susan. He's even charming, asking if she has any kids and how old they are.

Bile stings the back of my throat, threatening to spew all over the monitor, so I take a few deep breaths to settle my stomach. It's been nineteen years since we breathed air in the same room. Nineteen self-recriminating years of wondering what my life would've been like had I never crashed that damned band party. The only good thing that came from meeting Kyle Dobrescu was Ally.

As Susan exits to clock out, she winks at me, passing over his care. But in her rush to leave for her family emergency, she forgot to swipe her ID card on the computer to log herself out. As far as the computer is concerned, she is still his med tech. Not me. There won't be any digital footprint of me on his records. I console my conscience that I can always log in later.

Turning myself on autopilot, I rattle off the standard medical history questions. Forcing my fingers, which have turned to jelly, to type his stats, I update the medical records system. Kyle's patient file is pages and pages long. Good Lord, how many times has he been in the hospital?

If only Ally could see the information revealed in this computer program, the endless stream of hospital admissions, detox, and substance abuse interventions. She'd see the real Kyle Dobrescu. Not *Mr. Good Time Help Me Be a Better Person* guy.

All those years, I tried to blot him out of our lives. I was so close to success. Once Ally started college, she would've launched. She'd be surrounded by smart, accomplished people who were driven by academic goals and professional aspirations. Those were the kinds of influences I'd always dreamed of exposing my daughter to.

Oh, why did I give in and pass along his name to Ally? If I could take back any day in my life as a do-over, it would've been that single moment of parental weakness on her eighteenth birthday. I derailed her.

As Kyle recounts his recent shoulder surgery and subsequent ICU stint, I realize it wasn't at this hospital. Since none of the records are in our system, I manually input the details into his patient file. Pancreatitis flare-up. Which, based on his medical history, meant he'd been drinking again.

Little bits and pieces of his medical history register in my consciousness. He'd ripped the intubating tube out of his throat? Too bad it didn't rip a hole right through his esophagus. He would've bled to death before an ICU nurse or doctor could've intervened.

Why hadn't the universe cut me a break six months ago? That would've solved all my problems. Silently. Quickly. Cleanly.

My gut clenches.

Wait. What am I thinking? This isn't me—who I am. I don't wish anyone harm. Ever. I dedicated my adult life to saving people. That's the real me. I've never judged any patient, even the ones arriving at the ER handcuffed to their ambulance gurney and with police escorts.

Then again, none of them ever charmed my naive, unjaded daughter into believing in second chances. None of them ever tried to convince my Ally that a sobriety stint justified a close relationship—

No. What if his intentions truly are pure? What if all he really wants from her is a father-daughter relationship?

But how can he? He's a broken man who is a slave to his addiction. It's only a matter of time before he shatters her heart, as he did mine.

When the novelty of fatherhood wears off, will he ghost her? Will he drag her down into addiction right along with him? Or worse, drive while intoxicated and kill her?

Oh, my God.

A sixth sense begins to unsettle me.

His phone call.

Just after Thanksgiving, my mom let me know that Kyle had reached out to her. He introduced himself and convinced her that he was invested in his relationship with Ally. At the time, the news had seemed innocent enough, if not bizarre, though I'd been irritated that he'd had the gall to ingratiate himself in my family without my permission.

Now I'm seeing it through a new lens. A heart-stopping lens. Every nerve in my body switches on high alert. I try to still my hands, but they won't stop shaking.

My mama-bear alarm trips within me. How could I have been so naive that I interpreted his phone call to my parents as anything but predatory?

Holy crap.

Kyle's been silently casting his web right under my nose this whole time. He somehow got Ally to share our home address. He bought her a freaking car for Christmas. Who does that? He convinced her to attend AA meetings with him. And then took her to see the holiday lights. And the symphony. They meet for coffee and to study together all the time. This past year, he reached his claws into the minutia of her life and grabbed hold.

She's trapped.

This epic failure lying on the ER gurney in Bed C has been grooming my daughter. For what? I don't know. But she's bought into his schtick hook, line, and sinker. She's his biggest fan.

How on earth had I missed the signs?

My throat runs so dry, I can hardly articulate my next set of prescribed questions. Suddenly, my mind is hyperaware of my immediate surroundings. The metallic taste of antiseptic pervading the filtered air. Every ping from the machines. Each intonation of Kyle's voice as he answers me.

My vision tunnels toward the blank computer screen awaiting my input. My breath hitches.

The hint of light.

A single cursor blinks white like a beacon on the dark-mode background.

This is my sign from the universe—my cue. As I type in the prescription meds he's currently taking, my mind spins wildly. I have one job in this world that supersedes even my commitment to helping my patients—to protect my daughter from harm. She may be an adult, but I am still her mother.

One of our doctors brushes by me to enter Kyle's room, joins him at his bedside, and listens to his breathing through the stethoscope.

"Mr. Dobrescu, your oxygen levels are normal. Your lungs sound clear. Your vitals are fine." The doctor stands by the patient's bed, his voice cautiously optimistic and conversational. In the ER, our job isn't to solve chronic problems. It's to triage and stabilize them, then either admit the severe cases or send the patient home to follow up with their doctors at their earliest convenience. Had the diagnosis been more serious, the doctor would've adopted a grave, super-professional tone.

"I think your wheezing sound is likely due to inflammation in your esophagus. It's probably viral, but if it continues for more than seventy-two hours, you should make an appointment with your ear, nose, and throat specialist for further evaluation. Your discharge papers will include a referral to a specialist if you don't already have one."

"So I'm being discharged? I'm free to go?"

"Soon. It'll take a few minutes."

"Jeez, I swore my mom was overreacting when she called for an ambulance. I felt fine. She wouldn't believe me."

"Oh, I know! Mothers are like that. Can you say 'Overreact much?'" The doctor chuckles as he signs off on different forms for our legal department stacked on his clipboard. "Should I send a note home with you that your doctor gave you the all clear?"

"Hey, I could use one. She's a nurse. She probably wouldn't believe me otherwise." Kyle joins in, and they bond within their private little mom-bashing club right in front of me.

Hot breaths escape my mask. I'm certain my neck and cheeks have turned ruddy. How dare they criticize mothers? But I don't have the luxury of time to be insulted. They'll never get it anyway.

Once the doctor signs his discharge papers, it's all over. The second Kyle steps out of this room, I'll have lost my chance.

My shot.

The universe offered me this single opportunity to correct my colossal mistake. Ally may believe in second chances, but I know better. I've seen the worst of the worst here in the ER. Try as they might, they return again and again. He's already leeched onto my Ally-cat. He'll just drag her under with him.

Not on my watch.

As I scroll through Kyle's digitized medical history, my fingers turn to ice, and the laptop's touchpad barely responds to my swipes. What I'm about to do will crush Ally. Her spirit. Her optimism. How can I snuff the very flame that burns so brightly within my daughter? How will I live with myself—my guilt—if I knowingly harm someone, even Kyle? I can't . . .

For a nanosecond, I almost give up and let the fiery moment pass me by.

But then the universe prods me forward. Of all the pages and pages of Kyle's medical notes, the cursor lands on the very information that matters. The medications he's currently taking, plus those that have been administered since he arrived this evening. The field is populated with one particular opioid analgesic that is known to cause severe complications when combined with this doctor's go-to pain-management med, fentanyl.

The blinking cursor taunts me, reminding me that I have one job above all else. To protect my daughter.

I do it.

I hit the backspace key until Kyle's contraindicated medication disappeared from his records.

Gone.

In its place, I stealth-type the generic name of a milder drug, one without as many complications as other medications, then roll the computer cart toward the doctor after he motions to me for it.

"What is your pain level right now, Kyle?" The doctor scans my recently modified notes as I concentrate on keeping a neutral face and blending into the scenery. But my pulse is jackhammering so hard I can barely hear their exchange.

"Mostly I feel a sharp pain in my throat, especially when I laugh or cough. Midrange. Maybe a five-plus on a scale of one to ten." Yes, Kyle is well versed in emergency room speak.

I squeeze my lips together to keep from screaming.

"I'm going to prescribe a steroid for your throat swelling and a fentanyl transdermal patch to help manage your pain. It should last for about seventy-two hours. Since it could make you drowsy, don't drive or operate machinery while you have it on. It'll take twelve to twenty-four hours for the medicine to kick in. We'll apply it here before you leave. Our med tech will fill a small script for oral pain meds in case your wheezing gets worse before you can be evaluated by an ENT."

"Sounds good. Thank you." Kyle and the doctor shake hands. The doctor shoves the computer cart back over to me, then exits to move on to the next patient.

Just me and Kyle in the same room. Thank God I'm wearing a surgical mask so he can't see my face. I work quickly and efficiently on muscle memory, slipping the IV tube out of his arm and removing all the probes and monitors attached to him. I refuse to make eye contact, but he doesn't ask any questions, nor does he seem to realize we know each other, let alone share a daughter. After handing him his clothes to change into, I force a raspy voice. "Leave the hospital gown on the bed. I'll be right back with your medication and discharge papers."

Five minutes later, I returned armed with papers, a pack of pills, and the opioid patch the doctor would never have prescribed had he known the daily medication I'd deleted from Kyle's history. An overdose is inevitable.

"Please roll up your sleeve."

After wiping and drying the back of his arm, I rip open the packaging, then peel the sticker backing. I pause, holding the patch, knowing that I am about to violate the very core of everything I've ever learned and promised as a medical professional.

Then I think of my Ally-cat.

I will never, ever be given another chance to intervene. To protect her from her father. Legally I can't interfere because she's an adult. It's now or never—a gift from divine providence. A calmness overtakes my soul, warming it with thoughts of my daughter's future without the potential pain and conflict all caused by the disaster of a human in front of me.

I pause.

Yes. I can live with the guilt because it will rescue her. From him.

Then, with steady hands, I stick the patch onto the back of Kyle's arm and firmly rub it in place, sealing both of our fates in the process.

I hand him a cup of water along with his first dose of medication. "Here are your discharge papers. You are free to go."

When Kyle finally looks into my eyes, he kinks his head to the side, his brows furrowing slightly. A hint of confused recognition flashes across his eyes. "Have we met before?"

Yes, Kyle Dobrescu. Yes, we have.

"Once. Many years ago." I blink back the tears that are welling in my eyes as I leave. But when I reach the doorway, I turn back to face him. "Buh-bye."

The End

ACKNOWLEDGMENTS

A twist on an old proverb is "It takes a village to publish a novel." My tribe is chock full of gifted, supportive people who not only believe in my passion project but have been committed to helping this novel reach readers around the world.

I'd like to thank Marlene Stringer—literary agent extraordinaire—whose vision for and confidence in my writing has buoyed me in countless ways.

To Melissa Valentine, who first championed my novel; Charlotte Herscher; Gabe Dumpit; Kyra Wojdyla; Sanjita E.; Jenna Justice; Iris Winslow; Elyse Lyon; and the entire team at Lake Union Publishing, I'm humbled by the warm welcome to the Amazon Publishing family. Thank you for your expertise and for turning my dream into a reality.

I'll be forever indebted to my critique partners, Amy McKinley and Emily Albright, and my beta readers: Gina Heron, Jessica Riley Miller, Marian Cotromanes, and Carolyn Wendler. These talented women have helped me mold and polish this novel and every work of fiction I've ever penned.

While writing a novel is mostly a solo journey, the path to publishing is not, and I'm grateful for that. So many authors I admire have helped me along the way by sharing their time, wisdom, and mentoring support. I am humbled by the generosity of Adriana Trigiani, Hank Phillippi Ryan, Mary Kubica, Mary Burton, Samantha M.

Bailey, Tessa Wegert, Michelle Gable, Maggie Giles, Heather Webb, LynDee Walker, Heather Bell Adams, Art Taylor, Alan Orloff, Barb Goffman, Aimee Hix, Josh Pachter, K. L. Murphy, Karen Chase, Fiona Quinn, Heather Weidner, Teresa Inge, Lauren Parvizi, Kris Spisak, Elle Blair, Jill Witty, and Susan Klobuchar. Thank you for inspiring me and paying it forward.

Book people are the best people. I'm blessed to have found so many writers and book professionals online who've cheered me on in the trenches, especially the members of #5amWritersClub, #NaNoWriMo, International Thriller Writers, the Central Virginia chapter of Sisters in Crime, Women's Fiction Writers Association, SleuthSayers, and the James River Writers. I'm winking especially at Janet Reid and Kate Rock.

Sending a shout-out to my besties who encouraged me over the years, offered a shoulder to cry on, and shared a laugh (and a toast) to commiserate and/or celebrate. Here's to Kathie S., Anne-Marie M., Cindy C., Terri S., Beth C., Olivia R., Ginger G., Suzi R., Missy M., Christina J., Cathy B., Drew R., Karen C., Sheri K., Ali G., Nancy M., Betty R., Katherine N., Johana G., Julie D., Terry S., Kim A., Lyle D., Carrie T. (a.k.a. Louise to my Thelma), Frances B., Dave W., Ivy Z., Tracy H., Lynn H., Kristen P., Cheri P., plus all the ladies of the Hunton Book Club and the epic turn-of-the-millennium San Francisco Book Club. Cheers, y'all!

To Bobbi, my in-laws, and the extra-fabulous out-laws, I appreciate all the encouragement you've given me. I adore our big fat Irish family.

To my mom, dad, and siblings, thank you for the touching, heartbreaking, hilarious, and even awkward memories that inspired the fictional Dobrescu family. I love each of you, as well as the magnificent people who have joined our family since.

And to D. J., Elyse, Maya, and Bryce, you are my everything. Love to infinity and beyond.

AUTHOR'S NOTE

Kyle and his struggle with alcohol addiction were inspired by someone near and dear to me. The details within this novel were based on my observations of my loved one, which is just one portrayal of many addiction and rehabilitation journeys other alcoholics experience.

Many online resources are available to readers who would like to learn more about managing addiction, alcoholism, and suicide prevention. The global organization mentioned in this novel is Alcoholics Anonymous (visit www.AA.org). Below are a few mental health resources publicly available to those in critical need in the United States:

- RAINN National Sexual Assault Telephone Hotline: 1-800-656-HOPE (4673)
- National Suicide Prevention Lifeline: 1-800-273-8255 or 988
- National Alliance on Mental Illness HelpLine: 1-800-950-6264
- Crisis Text Line: Text HOME to 741741
- Substance Abuse and Mental Health Services Administration National Helpline: 1-800-662-HELP (4357)

DISCUSSION QUESTIONS

1. *The Hint of Light* is narrated by three characters: Margaret, Kyle, and Ally. How does each of these characters bring a unique perspective to the novel?

2. "Motherhood is not for the weak." Several forms of parenting relationships are featured in the novel: mother-son, mother-daughter, father-daughter, and grandmother-granddaughter. How did the characters each approach their parental relationship? What did they do well, and what could they have improved upon?

3. Kyle suggested that battling his addiction is not just a day-to-day struggle but hour by hour. Given the unlimited availability of a legal drug such as alcohol, what are some ways a recovering addict might adjust their life and lifestyle to function within society?

4. After meeting Ally, Kyle was determined to overcome his addiction in order to be worthy of a relationship with his daughter. Do you believe in second chances?

5. After the loss of her son, Margaret obsessed over finding his secret daughter. How did searching for her granddaughter help her overcome her grief?

6. Do you think Hannah was justified in keeping Kyle out of Ally's childhood?

7.   Kimber's last words to her brother were "I love you. Unconditionally." How can family members support those with addiction while avoiding enabling them?

8.   Margaret and Martin have a long-lasting but complicated relationship, fraught with secrets and conflicts. How would you characterize their marriage?

9.   The priest told Margaret, "The secrets we bury deepest can hurt us the most." Do you find this an accurate statement? How might Margaret's and Kyle's lives have differed had she not insisted they keep the attack secret?

10. Margaret realized "Kimber is judging me through today's #MeToo standards, not yesterday's reality. Back then I would've been blamed." How fair is it to judge decisions made decades ago using the socially accepted standards of today?

11. Kyle was waiting for his birthday to introduce Ally to his parents. How might his fate have changed had they been introduced sooner?

12. "Our scars of grief are proof of having loved." Each of the characters processed their grief differently. How else could they have supported each other to heal more completely?

13. As protective mothers, Margaret's and Hannah's parenting narratives paralleled each other. How did their choices—both good and bad—affect their respective children's lives?

14. The novel's title—*The Hint of Light*—alludes to an inflection point or an aha moment. For Margaret, the break in the clouds suggests newfound hope for a brighter future. In Hannah's case, the interpretation was more ominous. How might someone's unconditional love of another skew their perception of events?

ABOUT THE AUTHOR

Photo © 2021 Lindsey Pantele Photography

Kristin Kisska is a native of Virginia, where she currently resides with her family and their moody tabby, Boom. She holds a BS in commerce from the University of Virginia and an MBA from Northwestern University. She is the author of a dozen short stories published in anthologies. *The Hint of Light* is her debut novel.

Kristin loves hearing from friends and readers at www.KristinKisska.com.